PLAIN FEAR

FORBIDDEN

A NOVEL

LEANNA ELLIS

sourcebooks
landmark

Published by Sourcebooks Landmark, an imprint of Sourcebooks, Inc.
P.O. Box 4410, Naperville, Illinois 60567-4410
(630) 961-3900
Fax: (630) 961-2168
www.sourcebooks.com

Library of Congress Cataloging-in-Publication Data

Ellis, Leanna.
  Plain fear : forbidden : a novel / Leanna Ellis.
      p. cm.
   1. Amish—Fiction. 2. Widows—Fiction. 3. Pregnant women—Fiction. 4. Life change events—Fiction. I. Title.
  PS3605.L4677P565 2012
  813'.6—dc23
                          2012016292

Printed and bound in the United States of America.
             VP 10 9 8 7 6 5 4 3 2 1

ALSO BY LEANNA ELLIS

Plain Fear: Forsaken

To those who feel lost and need to be found,
I hope you find hope within the pages of this book.

He has sent me to bind up the brokenhearted,
to proclaim freedom for the captives
and release from darkness for the prisoners,
to proclaim the year of the LORD's favor
and the day of vengeance of our God,
to comfort all who mourn,
and provide for those who grieve in Zion—
to bestow on them a crown of beauty instead of ashes,
the oil of joy instead of mourning,
and a garment of praise instead of a spirit of despair.
They will be called oaks of righteousness,
a planting of the LORD for the display of his splendor.

ISAIAH 61:1–3

PROLOGUE

A KIVA RAN TOWARD THE light.

Its glow in the moonless night blazed a path before him, beckoning him, drawing him toward it with the force of gravity. Icy rain stabbed his face, melting under a torrent of scorching tears.

Save him. Save him. Save him! Her words chased after Akiva like vile hounds ready to rip apart his flesh.

He focused on the beam and ran straight toward it as hard as he could, until his world glowed an angry red. The pain pulsed and throbbed, consuming him. Arms pumping, legs stretching, muscles straining, he prayed it would sear him, burning up every thought, every emotion, every memory, until he was no more. Then he wouldn't have to remember her. *Hannah.* Nor her plea to save *him*—Levi.

Once Hannah had given Akiva hope, promise, love. Now he spat her name out like a bitter root.

But he could not banish the memory of the lie smoldering in the depths of her eyes. He could have accepted her hatred, even her anger. He'd expected it, even planned for it. But her deceit? Her disdain? Her disgust? It corroded his thoughts and distorted his love for her into a boiling, fuming explosion.

What did *she* know of love? Her beliefs, emotions, desires were simplistic. *Levi!* Of all people, his own brother. Akiva had offered her eternity, and she wanted to live an insipid life in Promise with Levi. Her betrayal scalded him.

He pushed himself, running full out, as fast as he had that day when he was eight years old. He'd hidden in a copse of trees beyond the woodworking shop, gasping for air, fear grinding into him. Rules were fixtures in their household, and if he broke one, then Pop made sure not to "spare the rod." Pop had been searching for him, and he'd brought along a switch. The running and hiding had done no good though—after buckling beneath the shiver of cold and gnawing of hunger, both switch and boy were eventually broken.

Now, Akiva felt the same bite of winter but a growling hunger of a different sort.

The light before him intensified until it separated into two distinct orbs racing toward him. A screeching sound ripped through the night, and suddenly he barreled into a metal object.

The impact rattled his bones, but he stood straight as a concrete pillar, unwavering, fortified with his anger. Bracing his hands on the warm, wet metal, he glared through the windshield. He could see two sets of wide, startled eyes staring back at him.

He slammed his hands again on the car's hood. The metal trembled, and the concussion of vibrations shot up his arms. Inside the car, the woman cried out. Akiva thought it more of a surprised sound than fear. But the fear would come.

For two years, Akiva had hoped a piece of himself—Jacob's humanity—still existed inside him. He had believed once it was a positive thing, a trait to which he could cling, and nurture. A piece that separated him from the others like him.

But he was wrong. The ragged shred of compassion was a weakness. A weakness that left him vulnerable. The tiny slivers of emotion sliced through him. All hope and purpose poured out of him, pooling around him, until there was nothing left. Words, once a comfort, scattered in his mind, and he grasped at them as if they could save him.

"'Farewell!'"

His voice shattered like broken shards of glass. He shook his head and stared up at the gray clouds and tried again: "'A long farewell—.'"

He collapsed forward over the hood of the car. Squeezing his eyes shut, he tried to remember the words, the poet, even the sentiment. But he was empty—empty of words, empty of feelings. Empty of everything he ever was or ever wanted to be.

Sleet turned to snow and spattered his face and back, slowly reviving him. Were the snowflakes his prayers falling back to earth, unheard, unanswered? Ancient words chilled his soul and sputtered out of him: "'And when he falls, he falls like Lucifer, Never to hope again.'"

"Hey!" the man inside the car called. "You okay? What's wrong with you?"

The coldness inside Akiva solidified, and he looked up, stared ahead of him at the dirt and sludge on the windshield, at the bits of snow and sleet, the tiny flakes glistening. The woman fumbled with a cell phone, the pale glow reflecting fear and uncertainty in her eyes. The man peered at him over the rim of the steering wheel.

Akiva pounded the hood again. "Get out!"

The woman screamed. This time, fear saturated the shrill cry.

The horn blared, and the man waved his arm over the steering wheel. "Get out of the way, or I'll run you over."

Akiva tapped his forefinger on the hood—*tap, tap, tap*—then he gave a caustic laugh. "'Once upon a midnight dreary…'" His forehead pinched as he fumbled the words. "'Dreary…forgotten lore…'"

Snowflakes speckled his face, and he laughed again, felt a spark, a flame deep within. "'I muttered, "tapping at my chamber door; Only this, and nothing more…bleak December…dying ember…ghost upon the floor…"'"

His gaze penetrated the windshield again, and the fear trapped inside the car renewed his strength, charged him like a bolt of electricity. Once more he tapped the hood as if he was tapping on a windowpane. "Tap, tap, tapping…"

The car jerked as the driver shifted into drive. The wheels inched forward then lurched to a stop again. Akiva grabbed the door and ripped the metal section off its hinges. He tossed it aside as if it weighed nothing, the door clattering and clanging against the asphalt.

"What are you doing?" the driver yelled, pulling back away from the opening, cowering and blocking the woman at the same time. His hands were shaking, his mouth opening and closing. "You want money? That it?"

But Akiva simply smiled.

He paid no attention to the cries, screams, or wails. He tore into flesh, ripping and severing. His interest wasn't in gorging himself. He didn't bother tasting or savoring but simply destroyed, until he was covered in the sticky warmth of their blood.

Heaving and gasping, he glared down at the bodies. No satisfaction, which usually followed a kill, came, no fulfillment.

Silence hummed about him. He lifted his chin, staring out at the bleak night with its heavy clouds and softly falling snow. The fire inside hardened the last bits of emotion into glassy shards, and he felt shame and disgust at the memory of Hannah's eyes. The awareness. The understanding. The shock and horror of who he was, what he had become. Despair collapsed upon him, suffocating him with the inescapable and unchangeable truth.

Then the words of the illusive poem finally came to him, and he spoke:

> *"'And his eyes have all the seeming of a demon's that is dreaming;*
> *And the lamplight o'er him streaming throws the shadow on the floor;*
> *And my soul from out that shadow that lies floating on the floor*
> *Shall be lifted—nevermore!'"*

CHAPTER ONE

Six Months Later

I T WAS BLOOD RED. Rachel held the ripe strawberry just above the stem, and with a slight twist, broke it off. The plump fruit plopped into her hand and rolled over, the leaf tickling her palm. Such a delicacy, heart shaped and so easily bruised—the fragile strawberry needed protection, just as her baby nestled deep inside of her did.

She touched her rounded belly, where Josef's baby squirmed inside her. A sudden bulge of its elbow or knee pushed outward, and she gently rubbed it back into place. She gave a wistful smile. "Easy, little one."

Rachel.

The whisper of her name sent a chill through her. She turned and looked behind her. Only Mae was in the field with her, and she knelt two rows away. "Yes?"

Mae glanced up from tending Timothy, her one-year-old son. "What is it?"

Rachel tilted her head. "Didn't you call me?"

"No." Mae plopped a strawberry in her own basket. "No, I—"

"Bah!" Timothy called out, his voice tilting upward at the end in that timeless way of a baby playing with language. He pointed his chubby finger at the dirt.

"Bug," his mother corrected. As he reached for the crawling insect, Mae scrambled up from her sitting position and batted her son's hand away. "No, no. No eat the bug, Timothy."

The toddler sputtered a cry, and Mae scooped him up, snuggling him against her hip, and distracted him by pointing out a butterfly that flitted from a green stem to land on a tiny white flower.

Rachel's heart faltered, and her smile vanished beneath a sudden cloud of despair. Josef would never know moments like this with their baby. Her dear husband was buried in the nearby cemetery, six feet underground, six months gone. He would never teach his son how to plow a field or harvest corn or smile at his daughter's first attempts at sewing or making blueberry muffins. He'd never sit their baby upon his knee or hold it close or pray over its soft, downy head.

During their six weeks of marital bliss, Rachel had lain by his side at night, feeling his breath at her temple and his heart near her own. They had whispered their hopes and dreams of a large family, of the seasons pieced together into a quilt of years. But none of it would unfold. And it was her fault.

Guilt seared her heart. Closing her eyes, squeezing them tight, she tried to push the feelings back inside, even while a tear rolled down her cheek. She whispered the same prayer she did each day, "Oh, Lord, forgive me...forgive me. And may Josef forgive me too. Help me guide and guard his baby."

Her hand smoothed over her distended belly. If her mother and father had their way, Rachel would marry again, and another man would raise Josef's child as his own. But to Rachel, their baby was Josef's only legacy. No matter who came into their lives, her heart and baby would belong to Josef.

Carefully, she placed another strawberry in the basket with the growing mound of others. As a child, she'd always loved harvest season, especially June, when berries ripened and she could taste the sweet burst of flavor on her tongue. Now, the warm dirt cushioned her knees, and the sweet, tender fragrance of sweet peas, daisies, and roses growing nearby scented the morning air. Hope bloomed around her, and yet she couldn't quite believe she'd ever pull out all the weeds from her past.

"Rachel," Mae called, "I'm going to take Timothy back to the house. He needs an awful good nap." The little boy rubbed at his eyes.

Rachel nodded and plucked another strawberry.

Mae took a step toward the house then hesitated. "You will be all right?"

Again, Rachel nodded, keeping her gaze downward and avoiding Mae's puckered brow. In moments like this, Rachel wondered if everyone was whispering behind her back, expressing their concern, and plotting to keep someone near her…just in case.

Then Timothy cried out again, and Mae turned back to him. They headed toward the small house, which was attached to the back of the larger one, where her husband Ernest's parents still lived with their brood of boys: Ezra, Eliam, Ezekiel, Ethan, and Eli, who was the youngest at age fourteen.

Rachel had only recently begun working for the Troyer family. They had a fruit-and-vegetable stand on Slow Gait Road, where they sold buckets of strawberries, sugar snap peas, sweet corn, cherry tomatoes, and new potatoes to locals, neighbors, and the tourists who came each summer to stare wide-eyed at their plain ways. After Josef's death, Rachel had moved back home to live with Mamm and Dat again, and soon began to seek work. Her parents had advised against working so soon after Josef's death and before the baby's birth, but she needed to feel as if she was accomplishing something, contributing to the family, and avoiding the concerned gazes that followed her everywhere.

The simple task of picking the strawberries, though, was too simple, for it gave Rachel far too much time to ponder her loss and her baby's future. Thankfully, the Troyer family was large enough that someone was always nearby plowing fields, plucking weeds, hoeing the garden, hammering a fence post, or simply feeding livestock and providing plenty of distractions. Mae often brought Timothy out to the fields, and the energetic and fearless toddler kept both Mae and Rachel busy chasing after him.

But now, Rachel was alone. She glanced around at the empty fields of their Pennsylvania Amish countryside, around to the deserted barnyard. A bedsheet snapped on the clothesline. A bee buzzed near her ear. It was too quiet, too still.

She should have appreciated the peaceful tranquility, since she was so rarely left alone these days. At home, her little sister, Katie, chattered away, as if filling the silence with words might plug the aching hole in Rachel's heart. Or Mamm kept her busy with chores and quilting bees and bake sales. At night, Dat gave detailed descriptions of his day and all the chores accomplished, and avoided what Rachel did or how she felt or if she wrestled in the night with dark dreams or cried herself to sleep. Always someone stayed by her side. Katie slept in the same room. Conversations revolved around the day-to-day, minute-to-minute details, and not the past, not the pain, not the giant hole Josef's death had left.

Her middle sister, Hannah, often came to visit, as well. But ever since Hannah had married Levi and moved into their little house next to the Huffstetlers', a tension had developed between sisters like static electricity, invisible, yet even a glance or word could rub Rachel the wrong way and jolt her with its existence. Was it because Hannah had found love when Rachel had lost hers? Was she so shallow as to wallow in jealousy?

When Hannah and Levi had married, Rachel felt relief. Hannah had finally let go of Jacob and clasped a new and real love and life with Levi. Yet a part of her had remained numb from Josef's sudden death.

Maybe Rachel simply resented everyone hovering around her, handling her like fragile glass. Maybe she begrudged the way they'd moved on with their lives. Maybe she wasn't as strong in her faith as she'd hoped.

Six months ago, when Hannah and Levi had delivered the news as gently as possible, a glass box had descended on her. All the voices speaking to her, words of comfort and concern, were muffled and distorted. She'd focused on her baby, keeping her baby within her womb, and pushed all questions aside.

From time to time, she allowed her thoughts to wander. She fretted and dreamed about Josef—of his being thrown from his buggy, of a car slamming into the buggy. Of blood.

Steadily, she withdrew into herself more and more. She didn't want to know the details of Josef's death. *What would it matter anyway? Would knowing the details, blaming someone or something change anything?* She would still have to forgive. She would still have to move on. She would still face having a baby on her own. The sad fact was that Josef was gone. Forever.

Maybe his death was the cause of the tension. Hannah knew the details but wouldn't speak of it to Rachel. If pressed, she spoke in vague terms: "It was an accident. Josef is in a better place."

A better place? Of course, heaven was better than here on earth, which was what they'd been taught. But Josef had been too young to die. He was needed here to be a husband and father. Didn't Hannah understand? But her sister had simply remained stoic and unapproachable on the subject.

Still, Rachel feared her past had finally caught up to her and the words of Moses would come to pass on her and her baby: *And the LORD passed by before him, and proclaimed, The LORD, The LORD God, merciful and gracious, longsuffering, and abundant in goodness and truth, keeping mercy for thousands, forgiving iniquity and transgression and sin, and that will by no means clear the guilty; visiting the iniquity of the fathers upon the children, and upon the children's children, unto the third and to the fourth generation.*

Rachel tapped down her tumultuous emotions and searing questions and attempted to soothe her soul with God's word: *For we know that if our earthly house of this tabernacle were dissolved, we have a building of God, an house not made with hands, eternal in the heavens. For in this we groan, earnestly desiring to be clothed upon with our house which is from heaven…Therefore we are always confident, knowing that, whilst we are at home in the body, we are absent from the Lord.*

And now, in this rare moment when she was totally alone in the fields, she should have felt reassured. Life was finally getting back to normal, and she should feel peace settling around her, hedging her in. But instead, a sense of foreboding descended on her like a sudden lightning storm.

The sky, however, was clear, and the sun made its slow, reliable rise into the bright June day. Rachel dabbed at the perspiration on her forehead with the hem of her apron. *There's nothing to worry yourself over.* Even though she'd had a slight scare at the beginning of her pregnancy, all was well with the baby now. Her back ached though, and she kneaded the muscles at the lower juncture near her hip, thinking how nice it would be to have Josef offer his dependable arm or solidness to curl up next to at night and make her feel safe.

A ruffling breeze stirred the loose strands of hair at her nape, and a chill rippled down her spine.

Rachel.

She lifted her chin. Had she heard her name on the wind?

It was a silly thought, and she brushed it aside as she waved her hand to shoo a bumblebee. Her gaze strayed away from the strawberries and across the field. As far as she could see—the fields of corn and hay, the whitewashed house with laundry hanging on the line, and the weathered barn where goats and chickens meandered—she was alone. Still, despite the warmth of the sun slanting downward out of the bright blue sky, goose pimples speckled her arms.

Pushing up from the ground, she stood, arched her back to stretch out the kinks, and picked up the two full baskets of strawberries. The wind stirred the heart-shaped leaves of a mulberry tree, and her footsteps faltered. There it was again—her name.

Rachel.

She stopped, turned, but there was no one around, no one at the barn or on the porch, no one calling to her. *Was it her imagination? Or too many sleepless nights?*

When she reached the house, she placed the baskets of berries on the back porch, so Mae's husband could drive them over to the fruit stand when he returned with the buggy. She glanced toward the green-shaded windows and wondered if Timothy was napping already. Not wanting to disturb Mae, she tiptoed down the steps and walked along the path toward the barn where more baskets were stored.

It felt good to stretch her legs and move instead of crouching down in the field. She passed a tiller and plow, then the fenced-in yard containing the family's chickens and irascible rooster. Several goats were penned nearby; one of the kids had climbed a stack of hay bales, while an expectant mother goat lay in the shade, chewing her cud.

The barn door was wide open when she entered, and a whiff of smoke wrinkled her nose. She glanced around for its source. "Hello?"

No one answered. As she moved farther into the barn, the haze of smoke vanished. *Could Eli Troyer have been smoking again?* But she didn't spot the fourteen-year-old or anyone else for that matter. A harness clinked against a metal pole, and Rachel flinched. Then she noticed the open window and soft breeze, and laughed at her nerves.

The snuffling of a horse reassured her all was as it should be, and the smell of dust and manure filled her nostrils with familiarity. Toward the tack area, stacks of half-bushel and full-bushel baskets, which were used for collecting the vegetables and fruit and sold at the stand, were nested in a tall pile. She gathered several in her arms, resting the bottom one on the top of her belly.

When she heard her name again, she jumped. The baskets tumbled and scattered on the floor. This time, the sound of her name wasn't floating on the wind or a puff of cloud. This time, it was distinct and solid, as if she could grab hold of it.

"Rachel."

Her breath snagged on her windpipe as she turned. She fell back a step. A dark-haired man stood between her and the open door, his face in shadows. But his silhouette, his stance, the tilt of his head and timbre of his voice reminded her of Jacob Fisher. A shiver shot through her. "Jacob?"

Deep laughter rang out, and the rumble of it vibrated through the barn, unsettling her even more. Out of the corner of her eye she saw the sudden movement of a leg sticking out of the hay in the loft above and suddenly disappearing. *So Eli was up there smoking, after all.* A minute ago Eli's sneakiness would have irritated her, but she was now too stunned by the man in front of her to feel anything but fear.

She blinked, focusing on the one who looked so familiar and yet not. Those dark eyes mesmerized her, made her feel as if she was falling with nothing to grab onto. "Who are you?" She took an instinctive step backward. "W—what do you want?"

"*You.*"

CHAPTER TWO

I T WAS TIME. ROC had been planning this for weeks, careful to gauge the time and location, careful to give himself every advantage, careful no innocent bystanders were in the way.

When Father Roberto Hellman had helped him destroy the vampire Camille in the quiet, unassuming Amish cemetery of Promise, Pennsylvania, Roc had learned that the smell of blood—any blood, human or vampire—drew bloodsuckers from miles around, circling like sharks.

Even Roberto had been startled by how many vampires existed in his own neck of the woods. He had always claimed to know the bloodsuckers' strongholds, one of which was New Orleans, but maybe he didn't know as much as he thought. Or maybe age was catching up to him.

Six months ago, the priest had been quick enough to snag a hungry vampire on the prowl, which had then led them to another and another. Roc had lost count of how many vampires they'd disposed of in the following weeks and months, each time destroying the bodies (and evidence) in bonfires.

"Is that how to make sure they don't come back from the dead?" Roc had asked, still learning what he could about this new, disturbing world. He'd never wanted to explore the supernatural, or super-unnatural, and had shunned it at first, until forced to confront it after the death of his wife, Emma.

Roberto shook his head, his blue eyes blazing, his gaunt face flushed from the recent fight. Firelight flickered across his features and deepened the shadows along his cheekbones. "Just keeps the authorities from knowing anything."

Having been a cop, Roc was keen on this aspect, yet suspicious—forensics had ways of knowing. "But what about the remains? Bones and teeth?"

Kicking at the ashes, Roberto tapped down on a persistent ember before it caught the surrounding grass afire. "Nothing remains. Look for yourself."

When Roc tried to find any pieces of the vampire—bone, flesh, or hair—among the charred logs, ashes, and embers, he'd found nothing.

Through it all, Roc had learned: preparation was everything. Over the last few months, he'd worked hard to get his body in shape; chasing vampires wasn't for couch potatoes or alcoholics. He'd used weights Roberto stored under his cot and taken to running every morning. He was back to the shape he'd been when he first entered the police academy. And this morning, Roc was as prepared as any vampire hunter could be.

But he and Roberto wouldn't be a team tonight. Not this time.

The last few months of staking out vampires and the challenge of destroying them one by one had taken a toll on Roberto, deepening the creases in his face, darkening circles beneath his eyes, and making him seem even more frail than usual. Of course, he wasn't frail, not by any stretch. But Roc didn't want to risk the old man's life. At some point, Roc would have to go solo or find a new partner. So, he'd planned this attack without Roberto's knowledge.

But he wouldn't be totally alone. Not that he couldn't

handle it...*them*...alone. But he wasn't keen on dying either. And backup could be useful. He wasn't a rogue force all by himself, and he certainly wasn't on some suicidal mission. He respected the power of his enemy and would not take it for granted. So, he'd brought along an apprentice, whom Roberto had introduced him to a month earlier.

Ferris Papadopoulos looked as if he'd stepped off Mt. Olympus and was ready to battle the netherworld, which was a good thing, because in actuality he was. Young and bronzed by the Grecian sun, this affable youth had come to Roberto months earlier from the recommendation of a fellow priest in Mexico City. Celibacy had apparently been a problem for Ferris, and so his mentor had suggested he serve the Lord in a different capacity.

Ferris began learning right along with Roc, challenging him in his workouts and strategizing self-defense moves. The kid was ready. Or as ready as he'd ever be—no one was ever fully prepared for the first battle: the whispering assault, the black eyes that made the world tilt, the first thrust of a weapon, all the blood, and the hard, unrelenting stare into the face of death.

This morning, which looked more like night than day, heavy gray clouds hovered over the University of Pennsylvania campus. Through research, Roc had learned of its Philomathean Society. One of its heralded archives stated: "Philomathean fierce blood suckers, foulest of the vampire brood." So Roc had dug into the society, its members and sponsors, which had led him to a certain Professor Victor Beaumont.

His credentials appeared solid until Roc looked beneath the surface, where his origins were dubious at best. With a background in literature and his last teaching position at Tulane University, the professor had a loose connection to

Akiva, who had once gone to New Orleans for a literary tour of his favorite authors. But Roc needed more to go on.

Checking with U of Penn students had brought to light a few of the professor's idiosyncrasies and his penchant for dark stories. It was rumored he'd had an affair with a student a couple of years ago, and when he dumped her, the coed had left school. In reality, she had disappeared, and her parents had been searching for her ever since without success.

Then there were the initiation rites of the Philomathean Society. All involved blood.

It warranted Roc's following the professor. For the first week, all had seemed normal, even dull. But then the professor had disappeared for more than twenty-four hours, even missing one of his classes. According to his students, Professor Beaumont often vanished on a full moon. So Roc broke in to investigate the professor's house, and found a freezer full of plastic containers, labeled and dated—blood.

The next day, Roc had been waiting for the professor after his class on nineteenth-century American literature. Surrounded by his students like he was some sort of rock star, Victor Beaumont walked out of his classroom. He had spiky silver hair and matching goatee. He wore a tweed jacket, and beneath it a plain brown T-shirt, and faded jeans. As the tall, smiling man left the building, backing his way through the doorway, he'd tilted his shades downward and winked at Roc. Roc's hackles rose at the sight of those black, sin-filled eyes.

Now, even in the cloying humidity and the feeble light, the stately College Hall, with its gothic style, looked as if Lurch might answer the door, if a doorbell had been available to ring. Beyond the tops of the leafy trees speckling the campus, a light glowed in a fourth-floor window. It was where the society held its secret meetings, had its library and archives, and even housed an art gallery. It was where Roc fully expected to find the professor.

With summer and the weekend in full swing, the building was empty. At a side entrance, to access the building, Roc used a "borrowed" student ID Ferris had procured. Ferris followed him inside. They were both dressed for the warm weather—T-shirts and jeans—and utilized the stairwell rather than any elevator, moving parallel to each other along the wide expanse of steps. The younger man was already gripping a wooden stake, a replica of Roc's, in anticipation of the bloodbath to come. Ferris's brown eyes were wide as he peered into the dim corridors and passageways. A flickering light overhead made a buzzing sound.

Nerves gripped Roc as they always did in the moments before battle, and he suspected the kid must feel the same on his first kill. Nothing Roberto could teach or Roc could say would prepare Ferris for the point of impact, the final thrust, the rush of blood. To take a life, even the life of a vampire, was never easy. Maybe even worse. For eternal hell, if one existed, awaited these monsters. Looking into their dark eyes, the glint of life fading, the strength waning, the fight dying, was not for the weak of heart or purpose.

The kid was strong, though, determined and full of what Roberto called divine providence. Ferris believed God had sent him on this mission, to learn from Roberto and purge the world of this pestilence known as vampires—it was a noble cause. But Roc's motive was simpler in nature—pure revenge. *Still, how would Ferris actually perform in the fury of battle? Would he falter? Hesitate? Run?* The unknown set Roc's nerves on edge.

The vampire they hunted today had done nothing

personally to them. Personal vengeance wasn't necessary. The simple fact was that this creature was a bloodsucker, requiring food, and that ultimately meant human pain and death. But Roc also suspected this one might lead to Akiva. And Roc wouldn't quit hunting till he found Akiva and destroyed him.

The stir of air-conditioning ruffled Roc's hair, which had grown longer and thicker over the past months. A clicking sound alerted him, and he paused, his hand clenching not only his Glock but also wielding the wickedly useful wooden stake Father Anthony had given him back in New Orleans. His gaze snagged and narrowed on a yellow Post-it note stuck beneath the edge of a door as it flapped like a wounded bird's wing. Roc leaned against the wooden railing, glanced right, then left, and held a hand up for Ferris to wait.

A quick shift in focus revealed Ferris had moved ahead without waiting. He had already reached the next shadowy landing of the fourth floor, and his gaze seemed fixated on a hallway ahead of him. Without a backward glance in Roc's direction, Ferris crept forward as if being summoned.

Roc gave a whispered call, "Hey!"

But Ferris rushed forward. From his stance, Roc suspected Ferris saw something up ahead. But then the kid's arm went slack, his weapon pointing toward the ground instead of being raised in battle-ready position. *Did he hear the whispers?* Those whispers had the ability to confuse and confound, to turn someone's thinking into a twisted spire of indecision.

Roc raced up the stairs, taking two at a time, pausing at the top. His Glock couldn't save Ferris or him but it could buy them precious seconds. He took a shallow breath, his back to the wall, and then launched himself around the corner, bracing himself, ready for anything, pointing the 9mm. At nothing. An empty hallway met him. His gaze bounced around the walls and ceiling and doorways. Ferris must have shot forward out of Roc's range. Roc cursed and pushed on. He glanced sideways as he passed closed doors, trying to spot any signs, warnings, or traps.

When he reached the end of the hallway, Roc crouched low and turned, glancing to each side, peering into the darkness of an open doorway. How many times had Roc told Ferris "We have to work as a team"?

But then again, Roberto had always added his own mantra: "Don't trust anyone." Roc had challenged him on that once. "Why work together then? Why trust this kid? Or even me?" With his sharp blue gaze, Roberto had pierced him. "I don't."

"Ferris?" Roc whispered, his gaze searching past the shadowy lines of chairs, tables, and bookshelves.

Then he heard the scream. It came from behind him, down the hallway in the opposite direction Roc had already searched. The scream went on and on, reverberating through the hallway and through Roc's chest. He ran back toward the stairs, down another hallway, crashing through a door, bruising his shoulder. A series of closed doors awaited him. Roc sprinted past each, chasing the scream, and slammed his knee against a table, racing toward the cry of desperation.

And still the screaming went on and on.

CHAPTER THREE

I have a rendezvous with Death
At some disputed barricade
When Spring comes round with rustling shade
And apple blossoms fill the air.
I have a rendezvous with Death
When Spring brings back blue days and fair.

AKIVA HAD BEEN WATCHING Rachel for days, weeks, months, waiting for her belly to ripen, waiting for the right moment, waiting for her to finally be alone. At home she didn't venture far, not like Hannah had, and someone always accompanied her. But now...now his opportunity had arrived.

It amused him that she could recognize him, where the one who had betrayed him had not. Of course, Hannah had opened her mind and heart readily then, and so Akiva was able to veil himself from her, out of love and in order to protect her until she understood. But Rachel saw him for who he was, who he wanted to be: Jacob. Maybe those days in New Orleans had meant more to her than he had ever suspected. Maybe his plan would be easier than he had thought.

He stayed in the barn's doorway, his gaze penetrating the shadows. The sun warmed his back. But he didn't approach Rachel. Not yet.

She trembled all over, from the top of her prayer *kapp* to her plain, dirt-smudged sneakers. Her eyelids fluttered nervously, her gaze shifting to and fro, searching above as if heaven would offer help. "W—why me?"

"Don't you know?" he asked in his most alluring voice, the same voice he'd used to cajole many of his victims.

She shook her head, as if dismayed. "You loved m—my sister."

A rustling above alerted Akiva. It was the boy, who could do nothing to stop this. If Akiva had to, he would kill him.

"Didn't you love Hannah?" she asked.

Akiva's gaze narrowed. *What had that lying, conniving traitor told Rachel? Had Hannah told Rachel how she'd deceived him into believing she cared? Had she confessed her dark thoughts and longings? Or owned up to her dishonesty?* No, he doubted her ability to be truthful about anything. She had probably only spread lies about him. Or maybe…maybe she had remained silent, mortified by her failings, shamed by her own sins.

He took one step toward Rachel, clouding her mind with whispers. "I remember the good times we had, Rachel, do you?"

"I don't know you."

"Yes, you do. You called me by my name."

"Jacob?" This time when she said his name he had to read it on her lips, for no sound emerged. She shook her head. "It cannot be. You died."

"What if I didn't? All things are possible, are they not?"

Her head tilted to study him, as if intrigued.

Then he took another step in her direction. "So you remember then…the times we shared?"

She looked aside. "Foolishness."

"But fun." He smiled as her skin flushed. Her heartbeat

was strong, calling to him. He reached her side, turning his head and keeping her gaze locked with his. "You didn't seem to think it was foolishness then. In fact, you liked the way I made you feel." His tone soothed and lured. "You liked the things I showed you."

Her blue eyes filled with fear. But she didn't move away. He had her.

"You liked me, didn't you?" He dared to touch her earlobe with the tip of his finger and drew an invisible line along her jaw and neckline. Her pulse leapt beneath his touch. "You cared for me."

"How could I not? But…" Her voice faltered. "I love Josef. I am married—"

"He is gone." Akiva dismissed the notion immediately. There would be no lies between them.

Her eyes widened, as if surprised he would know, and then narrowed as if questioning his knowledge.

Did she not know? Had Hannah truly lied?

"I keep track of all that goes on here," he said. "After all, this is where I grew up. It was my home. I know the pain you have suffered, Rachel, over the past few months."

She glanced downward toward her heart, then her gaze sprang back to meet his. "Then you know that Hannah married."

His body tensed, and he grew cold. He forced his voice to remain calm and unaffected. "She made her choice."

"What is it you want, Jacob?"

"I told you."

"Are you coming back to stay? To live here?"

He laughed, and all in the barn went silent. Not even the boy above in the hayloft made a sound. "Rachel, Hannah has not been honest with you either, has she?"

"What do you mean?" The fluttering of her lashes told him so much—she suspected the lies.

"Did she tell you what happened to Josef?"

Her breath froze in her chest. Her gaze shifted sideways, and her fingers plucked at her apron. "It was an accident," she said in a rush. "An accident on the road…in the buggy."

He leaned closer. "What if it wasn't?"

She recoiled as if he'd struck her. "W…what are you saying?"

This time, he remained silent, letting his question linger and sink deep into her soul. "Come with me, Rachel. I will explain everything to you, things Hannah would not tell you. I will tell you how Josef died."

Her gaze flicked above his head. *Was she praying? Or seeing something? Oh, the boy. Of course. Did Rachel worry he had overheard their conversation? Maybe he would tell someone. There would be questions when Rachel disappeared. But nothing would be done. The Amish would do nothing. They didn't like to call in the English authorities. Not that they could do anything either. What would it matter anyway, what this boy might say? They would not find Rachel. Ever.*

A slow smile tugged at Akiva's lips. He could take care of the boy without much effort, but then…if he did, Rachel might not go quite so easily. And he wanted her cooperation. At least for now.

Rachel's fear pounded and pulsed around her and consequently through him. Her hesitation, insecurities, and doubts twined about her. "B-but," she managed, "why do you want me to go with you? How is it possible? You were dead. They…Levi…Hannah…your family…everyone said you were dead."

"Do I look dead?"

She remained silent as if any answer had died within her.

"Touch me."

She hesitated.

"Go ahead." He smiled. "I won't bite."

Slowly, her hand moved upward toward his chest. Before she touched the place over his heart, she lifted her hand higher until she cupped the edge of his jaw.

The warmth of her skin shocked him, and a raw hunger pulsed inside him. He used his restraints not to snag her around the wrist and burrow his face into her neck. Instead, he drew a slow, steadying breath. "They lied to you, Rachel. They deceived you too. For I am not dead. You do not need to fear me. I will not hurt you." His gaze shifted down toward her belly. He could hear the blood pulsing through the womb and the tiny heartbeat fluttering. "I need your help."

She pulled her hand away. "My help?"

"You were right all along, Rachel. You told me to forget about New Orleans. You told me to go home to Hannah. You told me what I was doing was dangerous. And it was. Now I need your help."

"But what happened to you?" She took a step back, yet her body angled toward him. "Where have you been?"

"I will explain it all to you." His gaze sharpened on her as he penetrated her mind, whispered thoughts of hope and longing into her. She was thirsty for attention, for companionship. She was alone, so alone, and her emotions drifted like an unmoored boat. He would be her anchor.

She gave a slight shake of her head as if to ward him off, but she couldn't. "I tried to forget everything I'd seen. Everything you and I—No." She took another step back. One hand rose like a barrier between them and the other touched the rounded side of her belly. "I don't want to remember. Please…I…" Her fingers splayed wide as if they could protect her baby as she backed farther away from him. "I can't—"

Her voice cracked, opening the crevice in her heart, giving him a glimpse of her greatest need.

"Rachel," his voice coaxed, "you have to fix things."

"Fix what?" she pleaded.

He lifted one shoulder awkwardly, then it settled back into the straight, powerful line. "Josef. Me. Only you can do it, Rachel. Only you."

"But how? What can I—?"

"Come with me." He held a hand out to her, palm up and beckoning as if he didn't have the sheer power to force her. "I will show you. And I will tell you about Josef."

She whispered her husband's name as if it was a prayer and met his gaze straight on. "But Jacob—"

"I go by Akiva now. Didn't Hannah tell you?"

She shook her head and swallowed hard. "Why?"

"It's a long journey we have ahead of us. I'll tell you on the way."

"But—"

"Don't you want to help Josef?"

The toe of her black tennis shoe turned inward. "My family is here." She glanced downward toward her belly. "And the baby is coming."

"Yes, of course. That is why it's important you come now, before your baby's time. You will be home in plenty of time to give birth."

"I just want to forget—"

"But you can't, can you?" he interrupted. "Only God can forget the sins of the past. Has He forgotten yours? You haven't. You can deny things happened, Rachel, but that doesn't change anything. And now *you* must pay the price. Only you. All sin requires a sacrifice, does it not?"

She nodded and took a step toward him, as if a string attached to her heart pulled her forward...then another step and another.

His hand stretched outward toward her, and she dipped her fingertips into the cup of his palm. Before she could regret her action, his fingers closed over her hand, his grip tightening.

And she walked out the barn door with him into the sunlight.

CHAPTER FOUR

DEATH WAS A RELATIVE term.

In most cases it brought to mind someone who had gone to sleep permanently, suffered through the Big C, been struck by a car or lightning, shot or even stabbed, and eventually tidied up by some mortician and laid to rest in a casket, hair combed, hands folded, eyes closed. But no matter the cause, benign or otherwise, it didn't usually involve this much blood. Not even the bodies Roc had seen with chewed necks compared to this.

He stared down at Ferris's body. Or what was left of it. No point in trying to take a pulse. The vampire hadn't killed Ferris to feed on his blood. He'd killed for revenge or to prove he could or simply to frighten those who were still living. Whatever the reason, it had worked.

The cold fear pulsing through Roc's veins was quickly smothered by a deep, searing anger. Crouching low, Roc kept a hand firmly not only on his Glock but also the sturdy, thick stake. Where there was blood, there was usually a vampire close at hand. The hairs at the back of Roc's neck stood at attention, making him alert and aware someone…some *thing*…was watching…waiting…stalking him.

His first glance around the room searched windows and doors—escape passages and hiding places. But the room had only one window, which was closed, one door, the one Roc had come through and which was directly behind him, and one air-conditioning or heating vent near the baseboards. No cracks marred the walls. No fireplace. No cupboard large enough to hide a man. The red painted walls were brighter than the blood now staining the wooden floor.

Furniture crowded the room. Along the walls, dark walnut-stained bookshelves were polished to a high sheen. Glass shielded the rows and rows of books, which looked like soldiers on parade, the faded brown, black, red, and blue covers as worn as uniforms, but trimmed with gold lettering and flourishes. Splatters of blood dotted the glass. As always, Roc took in his surroundings in a flash, focusing on the details: a silver candlestick, an old-fashioned pipe, a quill and ink jar. An imposing cabinet stood adjacent to the oblong table in the middle of the room. He imagined college students sitting in the wooden chairs, discussing books and classes, the women arguing their point, the young men just hoping to get laid. *Did they know what their professor was? Did they suspect? Had he killed here before? Or was the professor only one of many hiding out in this academic sanctuary?*

There were no other signs of life in the room, only the sound of Roc's breathing. *Where could Professor Beaumont have gone?*

Roc suspected he was still there. Somewhere. Maybe not in this exact room but here…in the building. Hiding. Preparing. Maybe even bringing in reinforcements for a feeding frenzy. Vampires, he'd learned, didn't run. They feared nothing. Their egos were like those of politicians. They believed they were bigger, stronger, beyond the laws of nature even. A chill stole over him. His fist tightened on the stake, and the grooves and grainy texture beneath his palm pinched his skin. Beaumont would become intimately acquainted with the wicked point.

In a rush of swirling sounds, whispered words filled his ears and head. The room began to spin about him. Roc couldn't understand what was being said, as the words were spoken just below his auditory range or in some foreign language or maybe it was simply gibberish. But he recognized the blatant warning sign that a vampire was near. Very near.

In a lightning fast move, Roc jumped away from the corpse and turned to face a tall, scarecrow-thin vampire. Beaumont stood in the doorway, blocking Roc's one escape route. He had a long, angular face and thin, wiry gray hair, which stood up on his head like tiny porcupine quills. He looked professorial in a tweed jacket and khaki slacks, like he could easily give a lecture on the history of vampirism or the best way to dismember your enemy.

"Good morning," the professor said, his tone mild. "Welcome to our little club here on campus."

"You know what this means." Roc edged around the room, careful to step over a piece of Ferris and managing to keep his gaze trained on the vampire. His heart pounded against his rib cage, each beat full of anger and revulsion.

"Of course." The professor sat in a chair and straightened the starched edge of his slacks. "Two for the price of one."

"It means your gig here is up."

The professor gave a hearty chuckle, and the sound reverberated around the room and built in intensity, roaring against Roc's eardrums. "Would you care to make a bet? Not that I'm much on doing so, mind you, although I have occasionally been to the racetrack. It can be rather exhilarating. But"—he gave a slight shrug, appearing rather bored with the whole conversation—"this outcome is easy to foretell and holds no suspense. At least not for me."

"I wouldn't be so sure."

Victor dipped his chin toward his chest and slanted a look in Roc's direction, his dark eyes intense, and erased all pretense of humor. "You think because you've managed to destroy a few careless vampires that you can follow me around then show up here where I live and breathe and work, and destroy me as easily." He indicated the floor where most of Ferris lay. "Look around, my friend." He raised his head in a defiant, haughty manner. "You have been misled. If you had any intelligence, you'd remove yourself from my presence before you meet the same fate." He hooked his hands around one knee and leaned back in a casual pose, but the detestation in his half-lidded black eyes grew in intensity. "But I suppose the time for that has now passed."

Despite the way those eyes made him feel—as if he was tumbling down a dark hole—Roc took another step toward the vampire, keeping his feet firmly planted. "Yeah, I'd say so."

"Well, then, let me explain what will happen, shall I?" Slowly, Beaumont stood and walked along the opposite side of the table from Roc. He trailed a finger along the high backs of the chairs, following the federalist curve and slant of the polished wood. "I can make it quick, as I did for your friend there, although I would imagine it didn't seem too quick by the way he was screaming." A wicked smile spread his pale lips and gave a glimpse of shiny teeth. "So I suppose it's all in one's perspective. But rest assured, it will end for you. Even when you think you can't take the pain anymore, take comfort in the fact that it will eventually stop." He halted at the end of the table and faced Roc fully. "And you will die. So go ahead and say your little prayers or confessions or whatever it is you feel you need to do to ready yourself for the hereafter."

Roc gritted his teeth, forced himself to restrain the anger surging through him. "I'd rather die than become one of you."

Again, the professor laughed and shook his head. "Well, of course, you'd say that. But don't worry. I would never choose someone like you to change. You would not handle the power well. And believe me when I tell you this. There is power to have. So those who are changed must be chosen carefully."

Roc's gaze shifted above to the ceiling, to the shelves with stacks of books, to the table in the middle of the room with a deep mahogany finish. "You have some criteria for deciding that?"

"I would tell you, but then I'd have to kill you." Beaumont laughed, this time louder and longer, obviously amused with his pathetic joke. "Oh, yes, I almost forgot…that's my plan." The twinkle vanished from his dark eyes, and they turned a flat black, a sliver of white parenthesizing the blackness. "We never disclose our secrets, even to those about to die."

"In case they get the upper hand?"

"As the college kids like to say, dream on."

"And did you change Akiva?"

Beaumont tilted his head sideways and blinked slowly. "Is that why you are here? You're looking for Akiva?"

"It's one reason."

"So you're multi-tasking." Beaumont laughed. "Well, you're way off track."

"We're about to find out." Roc jerked the Glock upward, aiming and pulling the trigger all in one motion. In a fraction of a second, Beaumont vanished.

Laughter surrounded Roc, embraced and confused him. He took a step back, tripped on something, then another step, looking behind and around and finally up. The curved edge of a wing stretched out along one outstretched limb of the chandelier. It wasn't a fancy light fixture with crystals dangling or bulbs flickering like a flame. The solid black iron looked sturdy, as if forged by the resolute ideals during the Revolution. Eight arms branched outward off the main stem, arcing downward and ending with a cap of stained glass.

He didn't wait for the laughter to die down or for the wing to move again. He aimed and fired six bullets right into the light fixture. Roc immediately covered his eyes with his forearm, as a wild array of pops and sparks ignited above him. Glass rained down, striking the table and floor and shooting outward. Tiny shards of glass pierced Roc's skin. Then the wing transformed into an arm, and the rest of the body took shape as it fell from above, pulling the chandelier out of the ceiling and crashing onto the table. One leg split, tilted the tabletop, which slanted downward, pouring glass and iron to the floor.

Roc raced toward the body, which had three wounds: one each in the neck, shoulder, and leg. Wielding the stake, Roc opened a new one in the middle of the chest, driving the tip into the now scarred table. Before the professor could do anything other than flinch and convulse, Roc gripped Beaumont's ankle and looped a leather strap around it and the table leg. By the time Roc rounded the table's end, the vampire was sitting up and struggling with the stake centered in his chest. But Roc didn't pause. He hooked another strap, which he'd pulled from his pocket, around Beaumont's neck, jerked him back, looped the strap's free end around another of the table's legs, and knotted it tight.

Just as Roberto had taught him, the bound vampire was now powerless. So began the waiting game. Waiting for the vampire to bleed out. At first, Beaumont thrashed about on the table, snarling and growling, but the wound in his throat made a gurgling sound as air bubbled up into the hole the bullet had made.

"Saying your prayers?" Roc asked.

With the knife Roc now always carried strapped to his calf, he slit the arteries as Roberto had shown him, which would speed the process of dying. As the blood drained, so did the life of the vampire. His movements slowed until he lay completely still. Only then did Roc lean back against the wall, sweat pouring from him, as he stared at the demolished room, too exhausted to consider what to do.

Chapter Five

Rachel did not come home yesterday from the Troyers'." Dumbfounded, Hannah Schmidt Fisher stared at her grandfather in the weak morning light. With his beard long and the lines in his face deep, Ephraim Hershberger stood tall and straight beside his daughter, Hannah's mamm, who looked as if she was clinging to the porch railing for support.

Each morning since she had married Levi last December, Hannah and Levi left the little cottage on the Huffstetlers' farm and drove their gray-topped buggy to her parent's farm, where Levi worked with her father and Hannah helped her mother. Arriving this morning to the news that her pregnant sister was missing sent a chill down her spine. "B-but where could Rachel be? Did you talk with Mae and Ernest?"

"Your dat did last evening." Mamm looked pale, as well, as if she hadn't slept. "It is mighty strange for Rachel to behave so. Your dat...Daniel is beside himself. He's thinking he should drive to town and check at the hospital in case she had more problems with the baby. But I can't imagine her not telling nobody, *ja*? Just going off for help that way. Without her mamm knowing."

Ephraim patted his daughter's arm. "The good Lord is watching over her."

Hannah trembled all over, shaken by the news, frightened by what it could mean. "Does Levi know?"

"I expect your dat is telling him now," her grandfather said, his voice somber and calm, the direct opposite of how Hannah now felt.

She glanced over her shoulder at the path she had taken from the barn. The fields beyond were green, the corn stalks rippling in the breeze, and her gaze slid toward the springhouse. It held so many memories from the past year, when she had housed Akiva until she'd realized his deception. The memory burrowed deep inside her now and made her heart pulse with uncertainty.

Could Akiva have returned? Could he have taken Rachel? Or…could he have done something similar to what he'd done to Josef? Those eyes had looked on her with vile hatred and burned in her memory. Her heart stopped as she imagined her sister…her dear sister. She'd hoped and prayed Akiva had gone away for good, but the truth was she'd always worried he'd return. *But if so, why now? Why Rachel?*

It didn't make any sense, and so she pushed the disconcerting thoughts aside. Most likely Rachel was having some difficulty with her pregnancy. She'd probably taken the buggy to town to see the doctor, who those in her district often sought when something besides home remedies were needed. Because of the problems Rachel had experienced early on the night her husband had died, she probably hadn't taken any chances. She wouldn't have wanted to worry Mamm either. But maybe the doctor had seen fit to place Rachel in the hospital. Maybe there hadn't been time to drive all the way out to the farm and tell the family.

Hannah took a deep breath and walked up the porch steps, clinging to the railing to steady herself, and offered her mother a comforting hug. Levi would know what to do. His calm demeanor would soothe all of them. "It will be all right,

I reckon, Mamm. We should pray Rachel is feeling better and not experiencing…"

But her voice trailed off at the *thunk* of the barn door. Levi rushed through the doorway, Toby trotting alongside him, barking and leaping. Levi pointed toward the barn and ordered the yellow lab back inside, his tone stern. Then his gaze sought hers, and an electrical spark shot through Hannah. She often experienced a similar feeling at her husband's glance, but this time it was different. Her breath caught in her chest. Something was wrong. Very wrong.

Levi, his movements strong and sure, his head bent with determination, rushed through the chore of hitching the horse, and Pete seemed to sense the urgency and stamped his hoof. Then Levi climbed onto the bench and grabbed the reins, turning the buggy around and driving straight toward the house.

He pulled back on the reins as he approached the porch. Morning sunlight glinted on his burnished blond hair, but his blue eyes pierced her. She'd seen the many different shades of his eyes, the pale tenderness when he held her, the darkening of passion as he leaned in to kiss her, the light of humor as his mouth curved with a smile. Now, the flat planes of his cheeks compressed, and his lips thinned with tension. "I'm heading over to the Troyers'. Will you join me, Hannah?"

She glanced at her mother, not wanting her to be alone. But then, her youngest sister, Katie, came through the back door and stood on the other side of Mamm. Answering her husband, Hannah said, "Of course, Levi." She gave her mother another hug then motioned for Katie to stay near their mother's side. "I'll be back soon, Mamm. Levi will know what to do."

Levi walked toward her, Eli Troyer at his side. Levi's manly shape only emphasized Eli's teenage gawkiness. The boy's long, gangly legs and arms had outgrown his pants and coat by a couple of inches. He had a thatch of blond hair cut in the traditional bowl style, but his hair was a shade or two darker than Levi's. He was almost as tall, but his shoulders weren't yet as broad. In the Amish way, Eli, at age fourteen, had finished the last year of his schooling and would be helping out on the farm from now on or finding his own trade for when he married and had a family of his own. Of course, the teen's face was smooth where Levi already had a beard, indicating he was married, which caused her heart to swell.

The last six months had been filled with a peace and contentment Hannah had never known. Levi's heart was deep and full of a selfless love. The joy she had felt in the safety and comfort of his arms at night faded when she had spent time with Rachel. For her sister had been in mourning for her husband, and Josef's death was most probably Hannah's fault. If she hadn't invited Akiva into her mind and heart and welcomed him into her home, then none of those events would have happened. Guilt, at first a heavy stone in her heart, had accumulated into a wall between her and Rachel. But she couldn't confess what she knew and had done to Rachel. How could she tell her sister how horribly Josef had died? It would have been too painful and disturbing and might have risked the life of the child Rachel carried. *But now, was Rachel's disappearance another stone of guilt?*

The seriousness of the situation kept her feet firmly planted in the summer grass as she waited impatiently for her husband and Eli to approach the buggy. She stood beside Pete as the horse dipped his head and nibbled the grass. She couldn't read Levi's or Eli's expressions shaded beneath the flat bills of their straw hats.

When they had arrived, Levi had first spoken to Ernest Troyer, Eli's older brother, the one now considered the head of the family and farm. He had not been here when Rachel was working in the strawberry field yesterday morning, but his wife, Mae, had been. She last saw Rachel when she'd taken their toddler inside for a nap, leaving Rachel alone. When Mae returned a couple of hours later, Rachel had been gone. Mae had assumed she'd gone home as usual.

It was one of the other Troyer brothers, Ezekiel, who had suggested the youngest, Eli, might have seen something. He was the only one left on the farm that morning. So, Levi had walked out to the field where Eli was plowing, bringing him back to Hannah now. But did the teenager know anything?

"Eli was in the barn yesterday," Levi said as they reached her.

She pinched her hands together in an effort to quiet her galloping heart and looked at the younger man's face. "Did you see Rachel then?"

Eli shook his head, and his gaze shifted sideways, avoiding hers.

"Are you sure, Eli? You didn't see Rachel?"

"I told you." He gave a nod to Levi and left them alone.

Hannah stared at her husband. Her throat tightened on a sob. *What would they do now? Where would they go? How could they find help?*

Levi stepped toward the buggy and held out a hand for Hannah.

"Levi, she couldn't just disappear."

"Maybe she is at the hospital."

"You know as well as I do that is not the case." She covered her heart with a hand. "I can feel it. I know."

He didn't deny or refute it. His lips flattened, pinching the corners of his mouth in a grim line. Glancing back at Eli's retreating back, he shook his head.

"You think he's not telling the truth?"

"I didn't say that."

But he didn't have to. She sensed it too. "But what if he knows something? What if he saw something?"

"I cannot make him talk. And I don't know, maybe he doesn't know anything."

Her throat convulsed, desperation rising up inside of her. "What are we going to do? We have to help Rachel. What if—?"

Levi wrapped an arm around her shoulders and tucked her close to his side. "There's only one thing for us to do."

CHAPTER SIX

Dark clouds leached the light out of the morning sky, which spilled over the church, casting it in a ghostly luminescence. The gray and mist made it feel as if time had stopped, hovered between night and day, hope and despair. Nothing stirred, not even in the shadows.

Roc watched from the confines of his Mustang for long minutes, making sure no one had followed him. He knew the real reason he delayed, but time was ticking away, and precious minutes were escaping.

He yanked the rubber band out of his hair, pulling strands out with it, and tossed the rubbery circle on the dash beside the attached GPS system. He shook his head in an effort to clear away the images, which jumbled his thoughts together. In an attempt to rid himself of the memory, he wrenched the keys from the ignition and jerked open the door, surprised at his own sudden action. It was time to fully face his mistake, his guilt. It would never be clearer or more painful than when he looked into Roberto Hellman's crystal-blue eyes and confessed he'd killed Ferris. It was his fault he'd believed the young man was ready and put him in harm's way, and he'd wear the stain of Ferris's blood forever.

Sweat poured out of Roc as he walked the lonely path he'd taken so many times over the past six months. It was too early for the pink-dressed nuns or even the most determined and dedicated churchgoers. The grounds remained deserted and quiet. Even the surrounding neighborhood, which housed the occasional bar, was hushed as if in reverence for the loss of Ferris. He reached the stone cathedral, its domes and arches pointing heavenward, its spires indicating *the way*. He passed stained-glass windows with fierce angels soaring through the air or standing as if on guard to protect the sanctity of the church.

He remembered then to make the call. Using his cell phone, he dialed the number once then disconnected after one ring. By the time he'd walked the length of the building and rounded the corner, he dialed again, allowing it to ring three full times; then again he severed the call. Twenty more paces to the rectory. He passed the main entrance and went around to its side door, which was set in deep shadows. He couldn't actually see the wooden door and its ancient lock until he stepped onto the landing and his knuckle met wood with four succinct raps.

He waited, his breathing harsh in his own ears. He turned away to stare at the solitary path he had come, a path also leading to the garden the priest tended as faithfully as he tended his flock. Of their own accord, his feet took to the path, as if he no longer had a will, and he walked in the silence past the rectory and school to the alcove. The burbling of the fountain in its center had a calming effect and washed over Roc. He walked to the round stone edifice and placed a booted foot on it, just inches from the water line. He'd never really paid attention to the statue before, never cared. The rain clouds gave the white marble a soft glow, as if it was lit from its very soul. The Virgin Mary bathed the baby Jesus upon her lap, and just beyond her right shoulder stood a powerful angel, its face stern, its wings massive, its sword pointing downward as it stood guard over the young mother and her child.

For Roc, the Virgin Mother had always seemed full of accusation, but this rendition of Mary's face was soft and delicate as she tended her baby, and he wondered if his own soul could ever be cleansed of his sins.

Then a hand pressed against his shoulder. Roc dodged sideways and swung around while pulling his Glock free of its shoulder holster.

"It is all right, Roc." Father Hellman spoke calmly, saying Roc's name with the guttural articulation at the end, the way St. Roch was often pronounced. "If I wanted to hurt you, you'd already be a goner."

Roc had let down his guard. One lapse of judgment was all it had taken. In a way, Roc wished for that sort of release. Yet, he drew a steadying breath and replaced the Glock in the leather holster again. "That's comforting."

The priest wore a button-down blue chambray shirt with his priestly collar beneath, as well as a pair of worn jeans. He didn't appear to have been awakened by Roc's phone calls or knock. "You seemed far away just now. Are you all right?" His gaze dropped to Roc's chest and Roc glanced downward. Even though his T-shirt was black, it was stained, some places wet, others dry. The coppery scent made it clear it was blood. "You were in a fight?"

Roc nodded.

"Are you hurt?"

"It's not my blood."

Roberto motioned for him to follow. "Come. You can clean up and tell me about your adventure. And—"

"Do you have a drink?" A tremor rippled through Roc's hand.

Roberto eyed him carefully. "We will see."

They walked the few steps back to the rectory in silence. Roc waited, glancing over his shoulder, while Roberto unlocked the wooden side door and led the way down the steep, narrow stairwell to the tiny room he occupied. It held only a small wooden desk, rickety chair, and cot where Roberto slept and studied. A musty smell filled the space, but Roc wasn't sure if it was from the man, the room, or the many books filling the bookshelves. Even more books were piled on the desk.

Roc sat on the rickety chair, a place he'd occupied many times in the past months. From underneath the cot peeked a forty-pound barbell Roc had used in his effort to get battle ready. Effort he now considered wasted. Often this tiny room had been a place where he had learned about a world he'd never wanted to discover, but tonight it was his confessional.

Usually, Roberto sat on the cot or paced along its long side as he taught and educated both Roc and Ferris. But tonight, he knelt at the end and pulled a wooden crate from beneath. The hinges of the lid creaked as he lifted it and pulled out a dusty bottle. The dark container had no label. The liquid inside sloshed about invitingly as Roberto uncorked the top. He poured the whiskey-colored liquid into two glasses and handed one to Roc.

With a slight shrug, Roberto said, "Sometimes one needs to numb oneself. This is not an easy task, what we have been given."

Roc's hands shook as he stared into the amber liquor, which could bring temporary peace. He sniffed its aroma. Scotch. Aged at least twenty years if Roc had to guess. The good stuff. Or at least better than the rotgut he'd grown accustomed to. He almost wished for the harsher drink to punish himself. His soul longed for oblivion, where he could forget all he knew, all he'd done, his mistakes, guilt, and foolhardiness. His eyes filled, and the Scotch wavered before him like a golden sea of serenity. But there was no peace for Roc, no comfort, no redemption.

"What happened, Roc?" The priest's kind voice seemed to come from far away.

It took every ounce of control not to toss back the Scotch and let it slide through his veins. Instead, Roc set the glass on the desk with an awkward thump and stood. He walked around the room wanting to avoid why he'd come here. But he couldn't. With growing heaviness, he slumped onto the cot, hunching his shoulders forward. "Ferris is dead."

Shock eclipsed Roberto's features. His eyes filled with tears, but they did not spill over. He leaned back as if all the air had been sucked from his body, his limbs sagging. Roc had expected dismay or even anger, but this reaction drove the dagger of guilt further into his heart.

After a moment, the old priest sputtered, "H-how?"

Roc rubbed the sweat off his palms along his jeans-clad thighs, back and forth along the tense-as-rope muscles as if he could punish himself or somehow infuse his system with courage. "It was my fault."

"Your fault? I do not understand."

"I took him with me to confront a professor at UPenn."

Roberto's eyes and mouth rounded, and his skin turned pasty white. "The Philomathean…"

Roc went cold inside. "How did you know?"

"I've known for years…for years. But it has been too powerful to penetrate, the vampire—"

"Victor Beaumont."

Roberto nodded, his mouth pinching at the corners.

"You knew? But why didn't you tell me?" asked Roc, shocked into anger. "Why—?"

"Tell you what? That the group existed? When we were strong enough, I thought maybe we might"—Roberto shook his head—"but alone? Never. It was impossible." He turned his back on Roc, stepped away, before turning back to face him, his features stricken with raw grief. "And you are too rash yet. If I had told you about the professor, then I would not have been able to hold you back for long."

"And while we waited"—Roc tasted the vehemence like vinegar on his tongue—"more innocents died."

Roberto glared down at Roc. "We can't save everyone, Roc. You should know that. And you should know that Ferris was—"

Roc swiped the Scotch out of the priest's hand and sent it flying across the room. It smashed into the wall. Rivulets ran down the whitewashed plaster. Splinters of glass slid across the floor.

Strong hands gripped Roc's shoulders, and the older man gave him a stern, fatherly look. "Ferris knew what he was getting into. He knew the risks, just like you and I know. It is not your fault. Ferris is dead. But it is not your fault."

"But—"

"No!" Roberto's voice exploded in the room, the sound reverberating and pulsing against Roc's eardrums. "It's not your fault. Accept it. Repeat it."

But Roc's mouth couldn't form the words. His throat closed, jerked, and convulsed. He shrugged aside Roberto's firm hands and turned away, unable to look into the priest's probing gaze.

"Where is he now?" Roberto asked, his voice quiet in the stillness of the dank room. "Where is my—?" He swallowed hard. "Where is Ferris?"

"His body is still at the university. Along with the professor's."

"You killed him too?" Astonishment saturated Roberto's voice, but there was really nothing astonishing about it. Fury had fueled Roc, and it was all a red haze now. There was no satisfaction in murder, not when they had suffered a devastating loss such as Ferris's.

"I have to go back and take care of things. Before they are discovered." Roc sank back onto the cot, his limbs weighted, his soul depleted. "It's worse than—" He stopped himself from speaking of the gore. "You can't go. I will—"

Roberto clapped him on the back. "They will take care of it."

The hair on Roc's neck prickled. "They?"

"Oh, yes, Professor Beaumont was not alone. But they will not want to be discovered, and so they will clean things up. They will not want investigators snooping around their sacred site."

"But Ferris—"

"Is gone."

A silence throbbed inside the room. Roberto sat beside Roc, folding his hands together. Was the priest praying, simply grief stricken, or planning their next attack?

"Roc," he finally said, his eyes still closed. "I was not always a priest."

The simple statement surprised Roc. He thought of Anthony back in New Orleans, his childhood friend who had become a priest and first suggested to Roc his wife had been killed by vampires, although Roc refused to believe him back then. "Of course not. No priest ever is *always* a priest. You're not born with that collar."

Roberto's eyes fluttered open. "I was much like you at one time, bent on revenge. And I studied with a priest named

Alejandro. A brilliant man. Scholarly. Gracious. Full of compassion and great humility. He cared for me after my sister, Maria, was killed. That is when my tutorials began about this life. And it was much later…after—" His lips tightened and then relaxed before he continued. "I had begun to travel and didn't see Alejandro much in those days. Once when I returned, I discovered he was missing and hadn't been seen in weeks."

Slowly, Roberto leaned forward, resting his forearms on his knees. He stared at the floor. "I tracked him down." Then he met Roc's gaze. "And I killed him. Alejandro. It was the hardest thing I ever had to do. But he had been changed. And he was waiting for me. He expected me to do it."

Roc drew a shaky breath. "There is no end to all of this, is there?"

The corners of Roberto's mouth tensed with what appeared to be regret. "Not that I can see. And yet, we have a holy occupation."

"Nothing holy about it," Roc protested. "I'd prefer to go back to living like I didn't know any of this." Roc stood, paced the floor, crunching glass beneath his shoes. "What good does it do anyway? So we kill one vampire? Big deal! There are plenty to take the professor's place. There are just more killings, more murders, more blood."

He felt spent, depleted of everything. He had nothing else to say, no more arguments, no more questions. He stared at the wall and the spilled Scotch, which was wasted now. So much blood spilled. All of it a waste.

"Is that how you felt about being a cop, Roc?"

The priest's question jarred him. "What?"

"When you were a cop, did you think: what's the point? There's always another robbery, another murder, rape, whatever. Crime never ends."

Roc buried his fingers in his hair, sliding the pads along his scalp. That life seemed so distant. "I don't know."

"Yes, you do. You knew then, just as you know now, that your job is important, even vital. That other lives are depending on you."

"But it does no good."

"You will never know how much good it is doing. Only God knows the lives you have saved by killing Professor Beaumont. If he were to be allowed to continue…" Roberto shook his head as if that would be the end. "Only God can see the future and what would have been had you not acted."

"But Ferris—"

"Enough! Do not speak his name again." Roberto's voice turned to stone. "He is gone. He had a mission as well as you do. Despite the hazards. He wasn't seeking fame or a long life. He was trying to make a difference. He sought purpose. And he accomplished that. His death helped bring about the destruction of a powerful vampire. And purpose is what you have too, Roc. You have a destiny only you can fulfill. Just as I do. Then one day, I will die, probably the way Ferris did. But lying in a bed and waiting for the end is not our way or our destiny. We live boldly. And we will die the same way. But without regrets."

"But—" The buzz of Roc's cell phone interrupted him. He pulled it from his hip pocket but dumped it on the bed.

"Answer it," Roberto said, and he began picking up shards of broken glass off the floor. "That is the only way to find out the answers you seek."

It was a local number, Pennsylvania area code. "Yeah? This is Roc."

The clearing of a throat made Roc's muscles tense. "Roc Girouard, this is Levi Fisher calling."

"Levi?" He cupped his hand over his forehead. "I'm surprised to hear from—"

"I need your help."

With one simple statement, all Roc's questions and doubts slid into perspective. He would go and confront whatever evil Levi was now facing. Not because he thought it would help end the vampire curse, or because he believed God wanted him to, but because it was all he could do. If he didn't, it would haunt him for the rest of his life. For not only did he seek vengeance, but absolution from all of this guilt.

CHAPTER SEVEN

Levi and Hannah sat side by side at the wooden table, their dour expressions making it seem as if they had never smiled in their lives. They didn't hold hands or even glance at each other, but they were clearly of one mind.

"Thank you for coming, Roc." Levi spoke first in a somber tone. "Hannah's sister, Rachel, was taken by Akiva."

Roc sat back and folded his arms over his chest. "How do you know?"

"Where else would she be?"

Roc laughed but caught himself. The worried slant of their brows and tension around their mouths forced Roc to curb his sarcasm. "Look, Levi, people go missing all the time. It doesn't mean it's vampire related. It doesn't even mean foul play. The person could have gotten lost, decided to start a new life, ended up in the hospital."

"You know what happened, Roc."

"How would I know that? And neither do you, Levi." Roc leaned forward, bracing his arm on the table next to the iced tea Hannah had prepared for him. "Look, I know you're worried, but there could be a million reasons why Rachel didn't come home yesterday."

"Her husband died at the hands of a…of…Akiva." Hannah spoke this time, her voice slow and calm. But there was an underlying layer of fear poisoning her words and the peaceful atmosphere in the small Amish home.

"You can't even say it!" Roc's voice detonated in the room, and with it his temper and frustration over his own denials. "Vampire. Vam—pire. Let's say it all togeth—"

"Roc." Levi's voice dipped lower in a fatherly intonation.

But something inside Roc had come unhinged. He clung to the edge of sanity by his fingertips, fighting, struggling, clawing his way back. He had come here expecting the worst, expecting it to be about Akiva. But now that he was here, the grief of Ferris's death wouldn't leave. He couldn't...wouldn't believe everything bad, everything he would have to deal with for the rest of his life, was because of vampires. Maybe if he didn't believe, then it would erase the last few hours and six months...or even the past few years.

Why, he'd lived almost thirty years without any knowledge of vampires, and by God, maybe he could go back to some sort of solid ground of common sense. Good grief, with all the years of police work in his hip pocket, he'd never run into vampires or anything supernatural. Evil existed, sure, because evil ruled in the hearts of men and women. All manner of debauchery and treachery went on in the night and broad daylight, things normal people didn't want to know existed. And it happened often. But was it all because of some great conspiracy with vampires at the helm?

The deep end of craziness repelled him, and he made a quick decision. "I can't help you, Levi." He pushed back from the table. "Hannah, I'm sorry, but I can't."

Her brown eyes widened, but it was her husband, Levi, who spoke. "Why not?"

What could Roc say? He hadn't been able to help Ferris. Or Josef. Or Emma. He might as well admit this particular mission was useless. But how could he explain that to this desperate couple, who were looking to him for answers? When the sad fact was Rachel was probably already dead.

He remembered the pictures of Ruby Yoder, the young Amish woman killed a few months back: fearful frozen gaze, chewed neck, and drops of blood on her apron. Details. Sometimes he really hated the details he couldn't expunge. He didn't need all of this again. No more details. No more blood. No more death. Maybe he'd just go live on a beach, stare at the ocean blue, the waves slurping onto the sand, receding and surging forth again, and simply forget.

But he couldn't. It was impossible. Because he remembered Rachel's blue eyes, her slim neck, her slight blush at forgetting her married name. He didn't want to see her like Ruby Yoder or Emma. But could he stop it from happening again?

The expectation in both Levi's and Hannah's gazes poked at him. "Look"—he glanced downward, ran his hands along his thighs in an attempt to wipe away his own blame—"I can hook you up with the right law enforcement, if she's truly missing, but that's all."

"If that's the best—"

"No." Hannah interrupted her husband. She didn't glance at Levi for permission or apology but stared straight at Roc with a solid intensity. "No law enforcement will understand what we're up against. But you know, Roc. You understand." Her eyes welled up with tears. "You're Rachel's only hope."

She opened her mouth but then closed it, her lips tightening. The tears disappeared, and a fire sparked in those brown depths, a fire born of understanding and desperation. "I don't want my sister to end up like Ruby or Josef. It's my fault this happened. But I'm helpless without your help. Please, Roc."

Roc swallowed, cutting off the angry, defensive retort

rising in his throat. He didn't want to be anyone's last hope. Because then they didn't stand a chance in hell.

"It's not just one life we're asking you to save." Levi hooked an arm around his wife's shoulders. They were a concrete force together, as if fortified by each other's presence. "Rachel is pregnant."

The simple statement made Roc's decision for him. Not because he thought he could do anything to stop Akiva, if that was who in fact had taken Rachel, but because it wasn't one life at risk but two. So if he was going to do this, he wouldn't make assumptions He would approach this disappearance like any other, like any sane cop oblivious of supernatural phenomenon.

He drew a calming breath, a pathetic effort to slow his racing heartbeat. "Look, Levi, Hannah, I'm not unsympathetic to Rachel's disappearance. But really? We're gonna jump to the conclusion that some vampire grabbed her? That's reason number one million, seven hundred fifty-nine thousand, two hundred and eleven. Before we jump to that most bizarre conclusion, let's examine a few other possibilities."

Levi and Hannah sat perfectly still and waited for him to continue.

"She lost her husband." A flash of memory came to mind, Josef lying in the cemetery. "So she's a widow." Roc tapped his leg with his thumb as he thought of all the possibilities, all the reasons, all the explanations, which filed logically and rationally through his mind. "Maybe she's seeing someone else."

Hannah shook her head.

"She could have done so without telling you."

Levi shook his head this time.

"She could have been seeing someone outside the district." Roc kept on with the possibilities, trying to jar loose their tightly held belief that this involved a vampire. "Maybe she started seeing an *Englisher*."

"Roc," Hannah said with firm conviction, "our parents had suggested other single men who might take up the mantle of fatherhood for Josef's baby, but she wouldn't—"

"If it was someone they might not approve of, then they might not know either. You probably wouldn't even know."

"She would not risk being shunned."

Roc blinked but kept on. "She might."

"She was never alone," Hannah said in crisp tones.

Roc frowned. "What do you mean?"

"We kept an eye on her. Others kept watch too," Levi explained, glancing at Hannah. "Because we feared something like this might happen."

"Okay, then maybe she went to the doctor. She was pregnant, right? So maybe the hospital—"

"And how would she have gone?" Levi questioned.

Roc opened his mouth then closed it. Back in New Orleans, there would have been a dozen ways for someone to get to an ER. But here in Promise, Pennsylvania, where buggies outnumbered cars, or at least seemed to, where telephones were rare commodities, in the Amish community at least, where hospitals weren't even the first choice, the possibilities were more limited. Would a pregnant woman have hitched a horse to a buggy by herself? Maybe. But then wouldn't they be missing a horse and buggy? One of those red scooters so many of the youngsters used going to and from school was out of the question for a pregnant woman. If she'd asked for a ride from a neighbor, then the neighbor would have told the family, and the whole community would already be in the know. The natural grapevine wove through the community, tying them all together and keeping them better informed than any telephones, newspaper, or twenty-four-hour news station could.

Levi shifted in his chair. "I admit, Roc, we jumped first and foremost to a difficult conception. But I went over to our Mennonite neighbors and used their telephone. I called the doctor in town. He's the one in our district who looks after some of the women, especially those expecting. He hadn't seen Rachel for over a month."

"Since she had problems before," Hannah explained, "we thought maybe she was having trouble and went straight to the hospital."

"The simplest explanation is usually the most likely," Roc agreed.

"Usually." Levi nodded his agreement. His stony gaze revealed no doubts as to what he believed had happened to Rachel. But still the Amish man let Roc think it through without interrupting, without arguing his case. He simply waited. It was Hannah who reached over and touched her husband's sleeve, but Levi cupped her hand, patted it once, twice, and they both watched Roc with solemn gazes.

Frustrated with them, with himself, with the whole situation, Roc pushed away from the table and walked toward the back door of their kitchen. He stared out the window at the yellow daisies planted around the base of a stout oak. Life had certainly been simpler before he'd ever come to Pennsylvania. If he'd been on a drinking binge for the last six months, then he could easily doubt all he'd seen, doubt his sanity, doubt the blood and bodies. But he hadn't been drinking. His eyes had been opened to an even more frightening world than he'd ever known existed. And he couldn't close his eyes just because he wished it away.

"But why?" he asked, without facing the Amish couple.

"Why would he...Akiva...this *vampire*"—he emphasized the word they seemed reluctant to use—"want Rachel? It doesn't make sense." Roc remembered meeting the woman, Rachel, several months ago in his desperate search for a killer, before he really understood what evil he was trying to expose. She'd been newly married, and neither had known her husband would soon be dead. It wasn't because the woman wasn't desirable, but he wondered what suddenly made her attractive to a vampire. His gaze shifted from the peaceful scenery of farmland toward Hannah.

"I think..." She spoke softly as she stared down at her lap, the ties of her headpiece trailing downward. She wore the simple clothes he'd learned were required by the Amish. The white *kapp*, the plain dress of some earthy tone, this one being green, the apron pinned in place with straight pins, and the solid black tennis shoes.

"It's all right, Hannah," Levi said in a soothing voice.

She gave a bob of her head. "I think he wants to hurt me." She glanced up then, her brown eyes seeking understanding from Roc. "Because of what happened."

Roc remembered how Hannah had agreed to go with Akiva. It had been her sacrificial attempt to save Levi. But the vampire had pushed her away, not wanting her without love, if her heart had belonged to Levi. None of it frankly made sense to Roc at the time and made even less now. But if anyone knew Akiva, Hannah did. Still, the voice of reason intruded. "It's been six months. Why now?"

"Why not now?" she asked in return.

"But why wait so long?" Roc persisted.

"Maybe," Levi suggested, "Akiva was waiting for the right opportunity. As I said, we had been keeping a close eye on Rachel."

Roc quirked an eyebrow. "So you thought Akiva would return?"

Levi rubbed his jaw where it was covered by a thick growth of beard. "We worried about Rachel, wanted to help her if she needed it. But I also had concerns, not only for Rachel, but also for Hannah. Revenge is a powerful tool."

"Akiva…Jacob"—Hannah used the vampire's human name, the boy she had known and loved—"he knew Rachel. She went with him to New Orleans during their *rumschpringa* years."

Both of Roc's eyebrows lifted. "Were they *together* back then?" He wasn't sure Hannah and Levi understood what he meant by that particular English word. "Were they dating? Or whatever you call it?"

Hannah plucked at the ties of her headpiece. "I don't think so…but…"

"But" told him more than anything else. He read the hesitation in her eyes. She wasn't sure. "But what? The more I know the easier it will be for me to find them, to help her."

Hannah rolled her lips inward before speaking. "Rachel wanted Josef even then, but I'm not sure what went on between her and Jacob. She said nothing about that time, but…"

When she didn't continue, he voiced her doubts: "You're not so sure."

Her slim shoulder lifted in a shrug. "I wasn't there. It is not for me to say anyway. Gossip is—"

"Gossip is about all we have to go on, apparently." Roc walked over to the table and took a long drink of the sweetened tea, the ice clanking in the glass. Rattled, he focused on the details. Details mattered. "Do you have a recent picture of Rachel?"

Hannah shook her head. "We don't hold with—"

"Yeah, yeah, I know." He frowned. Searching for a missing

person was never easy. The list of those missing in each state was astronomical and sobering. But the Amish rules for not allowing photographs complicated things. "No photographs. The *Ordnung* should reconsider just for safety purposes."

"The Lord is in control," Levi stated.

"If you were so convinced of that, then why did you call me?" Roc challenged.

"The good Lord can use you too, Roc. And I believe He will help us to find Rachel."

Roc could never understand this quiet young man's rock-solid, unshakable faith. Was it faith or rationalization? Levi had no idea what they were up against, much less the odds of ever finding Rachel. Alive or dead. And without a photograph, the odds of identifying her went down too. "Did she ever go to a dentist, have x rays taken?"

Hannah nodded. "Of course."

"Well, that's a start." He saw a piece of paper on the counter, grabbed it along with a pencil, then thrust it in front of Hannah. "I need you to write out a description of your sister: hair, eye color, height, weight, moles, scars, tattoos, any identifying marks, birth date. Anything else you can add that might be helpful."

His statement was met with silence. For a long moment, they simply stared at each other, waiting...*Waiting for what?* Roc wasn't even sure what to do, where to go. *Would going to the police help Rachel?* Maybe he'd let Levi handle that aspect, so he could begin searching. *But where?*

"Where was she last seen?"

"At the Troyers'," Levi said while Hannah wrote out a description of Rachel on the paper. "She was working there each morning, picking strawberries and vegetables for their stand."

"The Troyers on Slow Gait Road?"

Levi nodded.

"And who was the last to see Rachel alive?"

Hannah flinched, and he immediately regretted phrasing it that way. But at the same time, she had to understand what they were up against. Or maybe she already knew—as long as she knew there were worse things than death.

Levi reached over and took hold of Hannah's hand. "Eli Troyer. He's but a boy."

"Can I talk to him?"

"He doesn't know anything."

"Levi—" Hannah stopped herself.

The corners of Levi's mouth compressed. "I spoke to him earlier. He knew nothing."

Hannah twisted her hands together. "That's what he said."

Roc raised an eyebrow of doubt. Obviously Hannah hadn't believed the boy. "Won't hurt for me to try."

"Then I will take you to him."

"Can you go after them…Akiva and Rachel?" Hannah laid the pen across the paper. "Bring my sister home?"

Roc rubbed the back of his neck. Where would he begin? Where would Akiva have gone? And if the vampire wanted revenge, why hadn't he killed Rachel here? Why hadn't he left her body for Hannah to find? There were too many questions, too many unknowns. "Yes to the first, but I don't know on the second. No promises."

"We aren't asking for any guarantees. The matter is in the Lord's hands." Levi stood and walked to the door where he retrieved his hat off a peg in the wall. "We don't have much, Roc, but we will pay you."

"I don't want your money, Levi."

"What do you want?" Hannah asked.

Roc released a pent-up breath. "For this to be over."

Chapter Eight

THE AUTOMOBILE GLIDED ALONG the highway, passing vegetable stands, suburbs, and eventually the state line. Blinking only rarely, Rachel stared at the streaks of colors, unfazed by the speed of departure. Her mind fixated on nothing. She wasn't nervous about riding in the car like some Amish were. She wasn't worried about the future. She wasn't afraid of the man sitting next to her. She simply felt numb.

Greens and blues and yellows mingled and shifted from one color to the next until it became a rainbow of hues, distorting any distinctive lines and blurring all landmarks into a kaleidoscope of hazy objects that meant nothing and couldn't hold her attention.

Even though bright sunlight streamed through the windows, the air-conditioning kept her cool and comfortable. Eventually the constant blowing against her face irritated her, and she angled the vent away from her. A light cascade of music trickled out of the speakers behind her. Mostly instrumental, it did not hold her attention either but cocooned her in a sheltered world all her own.

She rested her hands in her shrinking lap, her arms tucked around the mound of her belly. A sudden kick of her baby nudged her arm and jarred her out of the cobwebs of her thoughts. A glimpse of a billboard, advertising a restaurant in Baltimore, caught her attention. *Baltimore? As in Maryland?*

She sat up straighter and gripped a leather strap along the door. *What was she doing here? Why had she agreed to come? For Josef, but what could she do for her husband now? Where were they going?*

"I need to stop." She spoke before thinking, meaning the car, the trip, this madness.

Akiva glanced over at her, his brows slanting into a frown. "What for?"

The baby kicked again, and she pressed her hand against her belly. "Because…I have to stop."

Akiva's gaze shifted downward toward her belly. "I'll look for a gas station."

She nodded and kept her gaze trained on the windshield, searching for an exit, but all the while trying to think of what to do, where to go, how to get back home. "Where are we going?"

"Tonight?"

"*Ja*, tonight." She could think no farther.

"Knoxville or thereabouts. We'll see how far we can make it. But I wasn't planning on making stops."

"Knoxville?" She swallowed a sudden lump in her throat. *Knoxville, Tennessee?* Her shoulders tensed with indecision. "How far are we going in all?"

He tapped his index finger against the top of the steering wheel. "I'll let you know."

"Is there a hurry?" she asked.

"Aren't you in one?"

She lifted a shoulder and settled it back into place. "*Ja*, I suppose." She smoothed a hand over her belly, straightening the blue fabric of her dress and the overlaying apron. He'd said if she helped she could return home to have her baby. The sooner the better. "I reckon I didn't think we'd go this far…or for so long." A weight of worry pressed into her chest. "My family will be worried. I should have told them—"

"I left them a note for you, so they wouldn't worry."

A flurry of whispers invaded her thoughts. She glanced at him then, studied his profile: the straight edge of his nose, the firm jutting of his jaw and chin. He didn't seem the type to leave a note, to reveal his inner thoughts, to broadcast his intentions, and yet she had no reason to doubt him. "You left a note?"

"Of course. I didn't want to cause any problems. Your sister will understand and keep your folks from worrying overmuch."

Rachel drew a steadier breath as a swirling cloud swept over her, but the questions, excuses, and reasons she should turn back pushed her clear. "But I need to get home. The baby is coming soon."

"Not that soon." He nudged the wheel gently to the right, and the car veered off the highway and onto a side road. Up ahead, a gas-station sign tilted at an odd angle, and the lower right corner was broken. "Want me to get you something to drink while you visit the ladies' room?"

She hadn't realized she was thirsty or hungry. She hadn't realized a lot of things. It was as if a cloud bank crept over the edges of her mind and turned her around. "That would be nice, *danke*."

He pulled to the side of the brick building. One lone, dilapidated car was parked toward the back, and she figured it belonged to whoever was working inside. *Could she speak to that person? Would he…or she help her call home? Or at least a neighbor?* Akiva parked, and Rachel stared straight ahead. On the side of the building were two doors, both with oval signs, one with a male figure, the other with a lady's shape.

"I'll meet you here," he said.

Disappointment congealed inside her. She wouldn't have to go inside the actual building, and she wouldn't have a chance to speak to the attendant. After a moment, Akiva whispered, "Come on."

Rachel pushed open the car door. It took a moment for her to unfold her legs and get to a standing position, as the baby was in the way and sitting on her bladder. Her joints ached, and the muscles along her lower back cramped. She arched her back and leaned against the car for a second before heading toward the restroom.

"Right here." Akiva's voice trailed after her.

She turned, shading her eyes against the blood-red setting sun, and nodded. "Where else would I go?"

"Exactly." His point poked through the hazy cloud and chilled her.

When she reached the marked door, it was locked. She stepped away, waiting for whoever might be inside. But maybe there wasn't anyone in there. No other cars were in the parking area, just the rundown one. Maybe she needed a key, and she could speak to the person inside the building after all.

She turned and almost bumped straight into Akiva. He glared down at her.

Licking her dry lips, she explained, "It's locked."

He didn't move out of her way.

"I'll go ask for a key," she suggested.

He reached past her and folded his hand around the metal knob. "Sometimes these doors are tricky." He gave the knob a shake then turned it, his hand squeezing hard, and pushed the door open. "No one is in here. No key needed."

She gave him a nod, ducked her head, and entered the dark room. Behind her, Akiva flipped the light switch, and the overhead bulb fluttered and caught, giving off an eerie glow. Then he left her alone.

For a full minute, she stood in the quiet of the small room, and the haziness disappeared. The gray floor sported stains she didn't want to analyze. The white enamel sink contained a pool of pink liquid soap along one side. Graffiti had been scribbled on the walls in black marker, red lipstick, and blue pen. The flickering fluorescent bulb gave her skin a slightly green hue, and she stared at her reflection in the mirror. Her eyes were wide, her lips pale. She touched her cool cheek.

What should she do? What could she do?

But the answer came as soon as she thought the question. There was really no question, no other answer. She would go with Akiva. And she would pray to the good Lord she would return home soon.

Resigned to continue the journey, she washed her hands before opening the door again. Of course, Akiva was waiting for her, leaning a hip against the side of his car, his gaze hard and impenetrable.

———

The plastic lemonade bottle tilted precariously, and Rachel jerked awake at the cold touch of someone's hand on hers. "You're about to spill your drink."

"*Danke.*" She cupped the bottle with both hands. The remaining pink liquid was warm, but she drank down a tart gulp. Her neck ached from her head bobbing and swaying while she slept as Akiva drove. Darkness stared back at her through the windshield, fog filled her head, and nothing looked familiar. She blinked, trying to clear her thoughts from sleep. The sun had long since set, and now headlights glared at her as cars passed on the other side of the highway, going where she wanted to go.

She shifted in her seat, straightening out her legs, feeling her calf muscles contract. "Where are we?"

"Tennessee."

His answer stunned her. "Already?"

"You tired?"

"A little." She shifted in the seat, her backside not quite numb. "You must be too. You've been driving a long time."

"We're almost there."

Why did his pronouncement stir a froth of distress inside her? "And what will we do there?"

"You can sleep if you want."

Sleep would be good. Normal. *But what was the purpose of coming to Tennessee? What was the purpose of all of this?* Her stomach gurgled, either rejecting the lemonade or begging for more. "Maybe we could get a bite to eat."

His gaze slanted toward her, and his mouth curved in a half smile. "Of course. I am hungry too."

His deep tone and dark look made her stomach clench.

A few minutes later, he pulled into a motel parking lot and left her in the car alone, making the locks click into place as a squawk and beep sounded. She waited as he walked into the motel's lobby. It took only a few minutes before he returned with a key. *One key.*

Stunned, she blurted out, "We're staying in the same room?"

"Seriously, Rachel, you're worried about *that*?" He chuckled as he slid back into the driver's seat and started the engine. Driving around the corner of the yellow-painted building, he parked near the back. "I got a downstairs room so you don't have to climb any stairs."

She followed him to Room 142, waited while he unlocked

the door, and then entered behind him. It was a narrow room, with one double bed, a desk, and a wall-mounted television. She walked only as far as the corner of the bed then stopped. "I can't stay in here. Not with you."

He closed the door with a hard thunk, jerking the chain in place, and her skin flinched. Chuckling, he cupped her shoulder with his chilled hand. "Rachel, get over your high-and-mighty morality." He leaned close, his breath brushing her neckline and sending a shiver through her. "You and I both know what you've done in the past. You're not so pure you can't stay in a room with a man who isn't your husband, can you?"

It felt as if he'd tossed a cold bucket of her sins in her face. Her body began to tremble. *What did he expect? What did he want?* "But I'm married and—"

"You think Josef is gonna come bang down that door in a torrent of male pride and ownership? Think again, Rach."

"Jacob." She hesitated, realizing she spoke the wrong name, the name he no longer wanted to be called. But he'd called her "Rach," said it in the way Jacob once had. "Jacob," she said again, hoping to reach some part of him that had been connected to her, "I'm pregnant."

This time when he laughed, the sound swelled inside the room as if it would bust the window. His gaze slipped down-ward, past her breasts to her swollen belly as if he was caressing her, and she shivered. "No kidding. Really? And you think I want a piece of this?" He grabbed her bottom through the back of her dress and gave her a squeeze. "Think again."

Her skin crawled at his touch, and her face caught fire with embarrassment.

He released her and plopped down on the bed, lying flat and taking up a good portion of the mattress. He crossed his ankles and clasped his hands over his belly. "Get ready for bed."

Get ready? How? She couldn't move. Not purposefully. But she trembled from her prayer *kapp* all the way down to her tennis shoes. Finally, she noticed a doorway at the end of the room, which she figured was the bathroom. She started toward it. At least privacy would give her a moment to recover.

"Can I touch it?" His voice sounded soft and stopped her.

"It?"

"In your belly."

"The baby?" She glanced downward, and soft whispers descended upon her, wrapped around her. "I reckon it would be all right."

She took an awkward step toward him and waited. He swung his legs off the bed and approached, reaching out, his hand hovering inches away from her belly. His breath fanned the top of her head. She finally reached out and took his hand, his skin cool and smooth, and settled it against the side of her stomach, where the baby had last kicked. "Sometimes it takes a moment before the baby moves."

"Does it kick often?"

"To me, it seems that way. But I don't know about other babies." She looked just past Akiva, not into his eyes, but she could feel him breathing, feel his anticipation, his keen interest. She remembered how at ease she had felt with Jacob so many years ago. His hand on her shoulder, waist, knee had never seemed to touch who she was deep down inside. He had fondled and touched her intimately in ways that made her burn with embarrassment and regret thinking about it now, but she had felt separated from herself then, as if someone else lived and breathed inside her.

But now, she felt keenly aware of the breadth of his shoulders, his shallow breathing, his hand pressed against the tautness of her belly.

Then the baby shifted.

Akiva sucked in a breath and jerked his hand away. "That was it! I felt it."

She nodded and stepped away, turned her back on him and faced a pale blue curtain covering the wide window facing the parking lot. Near the bottom of the curtain was a brown stain. *Was she to stay with this man in a room, in the same bed even? What would Josef say? Her Mamm and Dat?* Shame washed over her. *What had she done?*

Akiva cleared his throat. "You'll want to change for bed."

"I don't have any clothes. I didn't bring anything."

A long pause filled the space between them before he spoke again. "I'll get you some."

She faced him again. "Jacob…Akiva…how long will I be gone from my home, my family?"

He blinked slowly as if he hadn't considered that question. "As long as it takes."

"But—"

"This is how it must be, Rachel."

Her lips pressed together. Her legs turned to boiled spaghetti. Her thoughts seemed all twisted around.

"Go to bed."

And so she did. She sat down on the edge of the double bed, trying to forget the similar motel rooms she'd shared with Jacob as they'd crossed half the country together, the rumpled sheets, their shared sweat and heat. Worse, she refused to think about Josef. She toed off her tennis shoes, left her socks on her feet, and lay down on the bed, turning on her side, bending her knees to brace the underside of her belly, and closing her eyes. Akiva moved about the room, but she never experienced a dip in the mattress of him lying down beside her. She remained quiet and still, her heart fluttering in her chest, as her thoughts drifted and swayed and finally melted into nothingness.

But dark dreams emerged. Shadows reached out to her with long, spindly fingers, clawing at her. A drumbeat resounded in her head; cries split her skull.

She bolted upright, blinking against the darkness. Red pierced the blackness, and she stared at the threadlike numbers glowing beside the bed: *12:06*. She listened, straining to hear Akiva or movement. *Something*. But only her ragged breathing filled the room. She wasn't sure how much time passed as she sat in bed, her heart thumping, her skin damp with sweat, her mind turning from the images that had played across her sleep.

Then the lock shifted. The knob turned. The door opened. An outside light illuminated Akiva's pale features.

"What's wrong?" he asked, his gaze settling on her.

"I had a dream."

"Haven't we all?" His remark had a caustic bite. He tossed a plastic bag onto the bed. "It's the best I could do."

Tilting her head, she watched him close the door, lock it, then slide a hand between curtain and window, staring out at the parking lot for a moment, as if watching for something.

"Go ahead," he said without looking in her direction. "Open it."

She reached for the plastic bag and pulled out a peach-colored nightgown. It was made of a flimsy material, something synthetic and slinky, and it slipped through her fingers like water. It wasn't anything like her white cotton gown at home. Longing welled up inside her.

"You hate it."

"No, it's just…different."

"Different than what you wore when we drove to New Orleans?"

Her face flared at the memory.

"Go on and change. It's late. And we're leaving early." He nodded toward the tiny bathroom. She'd discovered earlier it had only a toilet and shower. No bathtub. Two towels had been folded and perched on a metal rack. Outside the bathroom was a sink with barely enough room to place a toothbrush.

"*Danke.*"

"Yeah, sure." He stripped off his leather jacket and flung it over a chair.

She noticed a stain on the front of his shirt, and his gaze followed hers. He tugged at his shirt then yanked it over his head, wadded it up and tossed it in the trash. His chest was pale with a smattering of dark hair.

"Hurry up." His tone brooked no argument. "You need help taking off your dress?"

Galvanized, she stood up from the bed, wobbled for a second before righting herself. "I can manage."

Changing in the small bathroom was not easy. Her hip bumped the doorknob, and her elbow knocked into the shower's plastic curtain as she took off her *kapp*. With shaking hands, she began removing the pins securing her apron in place. Finally, she slipped off her dress and folded it. She wished there was a mirror to check her appearance before she walked back into the motel room. The nightgown wasn't as revealing as she had feared, but her full breasts jutted forward, and her round belly pushed against the supple fabric. She unwound her hair and let the long strands cover her shoulders and chest.

She flipped the switch in the bathroom, dousing herself with blackness, and then stepped out into the now-darkened room. The curtains over the window blocked any lights from the parking lot. A soft glow from the blinking red numbers on the bedside clock helped her navigate her way back to the bed, slowly and carefully, until she bumped her leg against the mattress. Using it as a guide, she maneuvered around to the side she'd occupied earlier and settled on the edge, grateful for the darkness.

She could see Akiva's shadowy form on the other side of the mattress, only a foot away, but he was quiet and still, hopefully asleep. She began to breathe easier and deeper. Cautiously, so as not to dip the mattress too much to draw his attention or disturb him, she stretched out on the bed on top of the covers, cushioning her head with the thick pillow, which smelled of Clorox. She wiggled her bare toes and stared up at the blackened ceiling. A breath of air-conditioning blew across her body, and her skin puckered in response.

The moments ticked away, and she felt the baby inside her shift and turn. Often at night, she felt the baby move, and she figured it was because she was finally still herself. Her eyelids grew heavy, and she blinked slowly, breathed deeply, and began to finally relax.

"You're still beautiful, Rachel." Akiva's voice came out of the dark and startled her. "'It was a little budding rose, Round like a fairy globe, And shyly did its leaves unclose Hid in their mossy robe, But sweet was the slight and spicy smell It breathed from its heart invisible.'"

His words floated over her like cool water. She remembered how he used to quote poetry. "Is that a poem?"

"Emily Brönte."

"Who?"

He shook his head. "Doesn't matter."

"I'm sorry if I woke you."

"You didn't. Are you cold? Do you want under the covers?"

"I'm fine."

Quiet once again trembled between them. Akiva rolled to his side, and his gaze settled on her as solidly as his hand. Her eyes stayed wide and searched only the ceiling, which had a crack running from the door to the middle. Her pulse pounded in her ears, and her heart thumped beneath her breastbone. When he reached out and wrapped a lock of her hair around his index finger, her scalp tingled at the gentle touch. She held her breath, waiting, wondering, worrying: *What did he want? What would he demand?*

"You haven't changed so much, you know, Rachel?"

She stiffened. "You're wrong. You don't know me."

He straightened a long lock of her hair then released it. His hand hovered near her shoulder then slowly lowered along the length of her body, grazing the side of her breast, which caused her a sharp intake of breath. But he kept moving as if he didn't notice or care.

Once Jacob had been insatiable about sex. But maybe he no longer wanted sex with her. *But what did he want?* His hand finally came to rest, his fingers splaying outward over the tautness of her belly. His hand was overly warm, his touch like a brand. The baby kicked in what seemed like a direct response.

"He's strong."

She remained silent, afraid to speak or move. When his hand didn't shift, she finally said, "I don't know that it's a boy. It could be—"

"It's a boy." His voice was firm.

"What are you doing here?" Tears from a hidden place shot to the surface and burned her eyelids. "What do you want with me?"

"It's for your baby's sake."

Her hand touched the other side of her rounded stomach. "My baby? Please, Jacob...let me go home."

"When your baby is born. Then you can go."

Her heartbeat sputtered. "But you said...I could be home in time for the baby's birth. Why so long?"

"Less than three months, I would guess."

"Yes, but why?"

"For your safety."

It felt as if a cold hand cupped her throat and squeezed. "W-what do you mean?"

"Trust me, Rachel. That's all I ask. After your baby is born, then you can go."

Puzzled by his words, she remained on the bed, not moving as his hand stayed firmly against her belly as if he owned her and her baby. The seconds stretched out into minutes and hours.

Eventually, seeking a more comfortable position, she turned onto her side toward Akiva, bent her knees to relieve the low ache in her back, and slept.

———

She dreamed of Josef. He was standing before her, watching her; then he reached his hand out as if to touch her stomach, their baby, in an effort to protect the small life and guard her. But his hand hit a thick glass barrier, which thumped at the contact. He splayed his hand against the glass, unable to reach her. His eyes filled with so many words he couldn't seem to say but she seemed to know, because those words were in her heart. She placed her hand against the cold glass, desperate to reach him, to reconnect.

For a long time, he simply stood there, separated and yet not. Then the glass trembled beneath the pressure of their love, their needs, their hopes, and a crack shot through it, starting at the place of contact between their palms and splintering outward.

She awoke, blinking against the early morning light and shivering beneath the blanket. The space beside her was empty. Akiva was gone.

CHAPTER NINE

Eli Troyer stuck to his story. But by the way he slanted his gaze away from Levi and Hannah, Roc read between the lines.

They were gathered in the Troyer barn, and slivers of light slanted through the slats of wood. Roc sat on an old wooden crate. Beside him, Levi and Hannah spoke quietly to the teenager, hoping the truth would pour forth.

Again, he shook his head. "I told you all I know."

Roc fiddled with the miniature notebook he carried, twisting the metal spiral until it had unwound from half the paper holes. Finally, he'd had enough, smacked the pad of paper on the crate, and stood. "It's all right, Levi. No sense in pressuring the boy. We'll do the best we can with the information we've got."

"But—" Hannah said then stopped. Her eyes filled with desperate tears, and she twisted her hands together.

Roc gave a nod to the youngster. "If anything comes to you, anything at all, let Levi know. He knows how to get in touch with me."

"I will, but I don't know anything."

"So you said." Roc walked out of the barn, followed by a reluctant Levi and Hannah.

"I'm sorry that was a waste of time," Levi said, heading back toward his buggy.

"No worries, Levi. I'll let you know if I learn anything."

Roc opened the door of his Mustang then stopped and patted his jeans pockets. "I forgot my notebook." He gave a wave to the couple. "You two go ahead. No need to wait on me. I'll just be a minute."

Hannah and Levi climbed into their buggy and were off down the dirt driveway, heading back toward their home, the horse's hooves making a crunching sound in the gravel.

Roc eyed the barn. For being squeamish about electricity, the Amish sure had a lot of power lines and cords running this way and that. Things weren't always as they seemed.

He ducked back inside the barn and saw Eli puffing away on a cigarette. The teen snuffed it out and coughed, a cloud of smoke billowing around him.

"Didn't mean to intrude. Just forgot my notebook."

Eli jumped up from the hay bale where he'd been relaxing. Roc thought about warning the kid about smoking in a place that could go "poof!" with one spark but decided against it. He had bigger issues at the moment.

Roc scooped up the notebook, flipped through it, then stuffed it in his hip pocket. "You know, it's a shame. I don't wanna tell Levi and Hannah, but the likelihood of finding Rachel is slim to none."

Eli looked as if he'd just swallowed his cigarette.

"These things rarely end well. You remember Ruby Yoder, don't you?"

Eli nodded, a tight movement.

Roc shrugged. "That's how it goes. I'll do my best. But without much to go on…well, there just ain't much to go on." He lifted his hand in a wave. "All right, I best get on out of here. Thanks for talking to us today."

He walked toward the opening. One step. Two. Three. He'd seen the look—Eli was caving. But he didn't have many more steps till he'd be out of the barn once again. Four. Five. The shadow of the doorway slanted across him. A few more steps and the sunlight would smack him.

Maybe Roc had read him wrong. He'd believed Eli was holding back, not wanting to say anything in front of Levi and Hannah. These tight-knit communities could often be difficult to infiltrate. Everyone knew everyone else's business, but still everyone was careful what dirty laundry they aired. And here in the district of Promise, smoking a cigarette would be looked down upon.

Or maybe Roc should have played bad cop. Maybe he should have shoved Eli Troyer up against the side of the barn and shaken whatever information the kid had out of him.

Sunlight now seemed harsher in light of his failed bluff, and he squinted against the sun's rays as he stalked toward his Mustang, defeated. And now, where would he go? How would he find Rachel?

He was halfway in the car when he heard, "Hey."

Eli stood in the shadow of the barn. He'd placed his straw hat on his head and fisted one of his suspenders.

"Yeah?"

"I saw her."

Roc slammed the door closed. He walked back toward Eli, not breaking eye contact. "You saw Rachel?"

The boy swallowed hard and gave a quick nod. He had shed his coat, and his suspenders pinched the fabric of his white shirt over the sharp slant of his shoulders.

"Where?"

His gaze darted toward the house and field.

"I won't say anything to anyone," Roc assured him. "But if you have important information that could help me locate Rachel, then I need to know."

Eli licked his dry lips. "In the barn here. I saw her here. She was talking to a stranger."

Roc took a slow breath. *Were Levi and Hannah right then?* "A stranger? Who? What did he look like?"

"Can't rightly say. I was up above."

"In the loft?"

"I heard him…this stranger…an *Englisher*, I reckon, asking Rachel to go with him."

"Go where?"

Eli shrugged.

"What *did* he say?"

The boy stood completely still, his face passive.

"Look," Roc pressed, "time is ticking here. Every minute could put Rachel in more jeopardy."

Rubbing his jaw, Eli thought carefully before he spoke. "The stranger said something about how she could help Josef."

"As in her husband? How could she help him?" Roc pushed back the hair off his forehead. "How do you help a dead man?"

"I don't know. That's just what the man said." Eli glanced toward the house. "I don't know no more."

"Did Rachel seem to know this stranger?"

Eli shrugged. "I thought he was a boyfriend or something. Weren't my business. But she went with him, of that I'm sure. You gonna write all this down in that notebook?"

"I'll remember it. Did he say his name?"

Scratching his head and tilting his hat precariously, Eli kept his gaze slanted away from Roc. "She acted like she knowed him at first, then didn't. K…Keev…Kevin maybe? Nah, that weren't it. I don't recall."

But it was close enough to chill Roc's blood. He now knew for sure what he was up against. He clapped the boy on his shoulder. "You did right by telling me."

"You think you can find Rachel? Bring her home?"

"I sure hope so," Roc said. Because the alternative wasn't good.

CHAPTER TEN

In the greenest of our valleys
By good angels tenanted,
Once a fair and stately palace—
Radiant palace—reared its head.
In the monarch Thought's dominion—
It stood there!
Never seraph spread a pinion
Over fabric half so fair!
Banners yellow…
But evil things, in robes of sorrow,
Assailed the monarch's high estate;
(Ah, let us mourn!—for never morrow
Shall dawn upon him, desolate!)
And, round about his home, the glory
That blushed and bloomed,
Is but a dim-remembered story
Of the old time entombed.
And travelers now within that valley,
Through the red-litten windows, see
Vast forms that move fantastically
To a discordant melody;
While, like a ghastly rapid river,
Through the pale door,
A hideous throng rush out forever,
And laugh—but smile no more.

A KIVA IMAGINED EDGAR ALLAN Poe wrote this poem with the apartment building where Akiva had lived in New Orleans in mind. Hoping at one time to bring Hannah back here temporarily, as he'd imagined them finding a place more suited for their future lives, he was now without Hannah, without hope, and without any place else to go.

"Akiva!" a throaty voice called to him. The deep tone defied the woman's voluptuous form spilling over the boundaries of her extra-large clothes. "What you be doing here now?"

His footstep didn't falter as he approached the building. Wrought-iron gates painted black surrounded its courtyard, and on the top step sat the old woman he'd known for almost two years. Her name was Orphelia, which wasn't her original name, just the one she had adopted since her changing.

He squeezed Rachel's hand and whispered, "Stick close to me."

She kept pace with him but didn't answer. He'd bought her English clothes in Tennessee: maternity pants and top. Amish attire stood out and became memorable. This way, she looked ordinary, uninteresting, and could easily be overlooked—except, in this place. She was alive, which made her intriguing to those who lived here.

The sun glowed an orangey-red along the horizon and made the elderly buildings appear gilded, like blood pouring out from a wounded heart, spilling down along the straight sides and over awnings.

"Where you been all this time?" Orphelia spoke in a tone that would have been suitable if they'd been three streets away, but Akiva whisked Rachel past the older woman without acknowledgement, reaching the heavy door at the top of the steps.

The reddish hues of sunlight glinted on the brass handle,

making it burn as if it opened the gates of hell. He braced himself for demons to pour outward at his appearance, but the darkened entryway looked deserted.

Akiva grabbed Rachel's arm and jerked her against him. "Stick close. You hear me? We're going straight to the top of the stairs. Don't stop for anything."

"*Ja*, okay." Her footsteps sounded heavy on the stoop, and she stumbled over the threshold. He righted her and ushered her inside.

Orphelia snagged his other arm. She had some strength in those old hands and some swift moves. She'd risen up from the step and now stood next to him, holding him fast at the threshold as Rachel slipped through his fingers and went obediently up the stairs. Akiva met Orphelia's black eyes. She had a wide, dark face and thick, wiry hair, salt-and-pepper in color, which stuck out in all directions. Exotic scarves covered her round, lumpy body in a jambalaya of colors and textures that didn't seem to go together and yet complemented her perfectly.

"Where you been, Akiva?" she asked him again.

"Up north."

"Long time you gone." Her Creole accent rolled across her tongue in a smooth, thick sound like molasses pouring over pancakes. Orphelia's big black eyes shifted toward Rachel. "You bring a souvenir back with you?"

Maybe this wasn't a good idea. But where could he take Rachel?

Orphelia's smile flashed, a gold eyetooth winking. "You gonna share with us?"

But as he always did with the bloods, he ignored her comments, shrugged out of her grasp, and walked right past Orphelia to the wooden staircase. He couldn't see any of the other dwellers, but he sensed them, heard their whispers. *This was a very bad idea.*

Rachel was already reaching the second landing when a door opened in front of her. A deathly chill settled on Akiva.

Stephanos stepped into the hallway and leaned against the doorjamb. He had a sinewy body and looked much younger than he was. He had been the first blood Akiva had met living in the building. His shoulder-length hair had an unkempt look in its loose brown waves, with two blond streaks framing his face. He wore outlandish clothes—a velveteen jacket, silk shirt, faded skinny jeans, along with scarves and necklaces, bracelets and rings—all of which Akiva figured were a compilation of things the vampire had picked up throughout the two hundred years he'd lived in New Orleans.

Stephanos had once told Akiva, "I was a sailor on the *Mohongo*, come ashore to enjoy a doxie or two, when I met the wrong one." The wide Mick Jagger mouth grinned. "Or maybe I should say the right one, eh?"

Akiva had laughed with him but wondered if he could believe what he said. "Where'd you come from?"

"Galway, Ireland. The famine hit us hard, and I got work with the McCorkells. Never looked back."

"You don't sound Irish."

Stephanos had elbowed Akiva in the ribs. "Been here longer now. Right around…" He paused then shrugged. "Never was much good with my arithmetic. Came over to stay for good in fifty-three. That's eighteen fifty-three. So it's been a while."

"Ever think of goin' back?"

Those black eyes stared at him. "Why would I do that?"

With Stephanos's eccentric looks, Akiva originally thought this was a building for dead rock stars and had looked around to see if Elvis, Kurt Cobain, Jim Morrison, or Jerry Garcia had apartments here. But these dwellers of the night brought a whole new meaning to the Grateful Dead. It had proven to be a good place to live after Akiva had been changed. Nobody bothered nobody. Nobody cared if they heard strange sounds coming from apartments in the middle of the night or even screams.

Stephanos was one of the most dangerous. Akiva had seen him bring young girls and women into the building. They'd disappeared into Stephanos's apartment, clinging to his hand, curving their bodies around his as they sought a good time. But Stephanos was merciless. Akiva had heard the unending screams.

Now Stephanos's black gaze traveled over Rachel, noting each swell and curve with keen interest. "Well, hello. And who are you?"

Rachel kept her hand on the railing and glanced back toward Akiva as if he would save her. He might have to try. He leapt up the last few stairs in one bound and put an arm around her shoulders. With a brief nod, he said, "Stephanos."

"Akiva." The vampire smiled, but his gaze remained on Rachel. "This your rent?"

"I sent payment while I was away."

"You were gone a long while." Stephanos shrugged a shoulder then ran a ringed finger along Rachel's bare arm. "This could be payment for my watching after your stuff."

Akiva stepped between Stephanos and Rachel, blocking her with his body. "What do you mean?"

"You weren't here. Others wanted such a choice apartment."

"So? I paid—"

"So, others were interested. Others needed a place. Some wanted to know more about you, where you came from, what interested you."

A growl emanated from Akiva's throat.

Stephanos's smile widened, then he chuckled. "Don't worry." He placed a congenial hand on Akiva's shoulder. Still he continued to watch Rachel with great interest. "I watched out for you. And you—"

"Look what Akiva brought home with him!" Orphelia's voice trailed up the stairs after them. "Do you see? Can you smell her?" She drew a great breath, expanding her broad chest like an opera singer.

Stephanos breathed deeply, luxuriating in the delicious scent emanating from Rachel. "I do indeed."

"She expecting," Orphelia said, coming up the stairs. "He cannot—"

"Enough!" Stephanos shoved a hand out toward Orphelia, and she immediately stilled. "Akiva knows what he is doing, right?"

Akiva gave Rachel a nudge to the next set of stairs, and she stumbled again but righted herself this time. Akiva moved behind her, his hand still on her arm, but his gaze remained on Stephanos, who gave a slight wave of his fingers. "See you later." He leaned to one side in order to gain one more look at Rachel. "You too, beautiful."

When he reached the top floor, Akiva opened the door to his apartment without a key. *What would a lock accomplish here?* It wasn't necessary or helpful. He couldn't keep the bloods out, and no halfway intelligent criminal would dare cross the threshold below. At least not and live to tell about it.

But one quick glance told him others had been in here. His keyboard's cover was on the floor, the keys and controls exposed to dust, and the power turned on. His state-of-the-art stereo hummed, and CDs, which consisted of an eclectic pairing of greats from Bach to Beethoven and Meatloaf to Ozzy Osbourne, were scattered on the floor.

Something fluttered above him, but he ignored the fact they weren't alone. Here, they would never be alone. He should not have brought her here. Rachel leaned in the direction of the lumpy sofa he'd inherited, but he pushed her through the apartment. He couldn't leave her alone for a moment, because another blood might swoop down and end his plan. "Come on. We're not staying."

"We're not?" she asked, looking dazed and confused.

He shook his head. "It's too dangerous."

She tripped on a cord stretching from the wall socket to his stereo. "Dangerous?"

"Come on." He pulled her past the never-used kitchen toward the bedroom, which was where he kept pieces of his old life: his books about the authors he loved and their writing in novel and poetic forms, the Amish clothes he'd been wearing when Camille had changed him, and pictures he'd taken with a camera utilizing a telephoto lens. He'd returned to Promise after he'd been changed, simply to take photographs of Hannah: while she hung out the laundry on the line, rode in the buggy, carried eggs, and chased her little sister in the yard. He'd framed them around his bedroom, and he would lie on the bed, not needing sleep but aching for her and staring at those photos. This was where he had birthed the notion he would change her. The hope she would live with him throughout eternity. But it would not happen now. And he would not live without her.

He slammed shut the door to the bedroom, closing off the rest of the apartment, and stalked across the room toward the dusty bookshelves. The books were there, although he could tell many had been moved or riffled through. Some reposed on their sides. Some lay open, their spines cracked, their pages ruffling in the breeze of the air conditioner.

Akiva swerved toward the narrow closet and slid open the mirrored door. His black broadcloth coat, white shirt with dried bloodstains, suspenders, and straw hat were still inside. A fine layer of dust speckled the shoulders of the coat. Even his old, worn work boots remained on the floor.

Turning back toward Rachel, who now sat on the edge of the bed, he noticed something…something missing. The photographs of Hannah were gone, the frames blank vistas of cardboard backing.

He circled the room, staring at the tilted frames, stepping on broken glass under his feet. A growl rumbled in his throat and erupted as he knocked over a lamp.

"What's wrong?" Rachel asked.

"Everything!" He whirled toward her, and she cringed. But he stalked toward her. How could he explain? How could she understand what had been taken? Stolen! He kicked a foot at the bed and swore. Rachel only blinked at him. "Get up. We have to get out of here before—"

"Before what?" a high-pitched feminine voice asked.

Both Akiva and Rachel turned. A waif of a girl stood in the partially opened doorway. She had a pixie haircut like Peter Pan and skinny arms and legs sticking out of blue-jean shorts, and a pale pink shirt. She looked to be about ten or twelve.

"Who the hell are you?" Akiva asked.

"Jacob!" Rachel reached out to the child as if to protect her, when it was Rachel who needed protection from the black-eyed, pint-sized vampire.

"Did you do this?" Akiva ripped an empty frame off the wall and hurled it straight at the girl, who shifted sideways a couple of inches and avoided the launched missile, which smashed into the wall. The broken frame and glass crashed to the floor. "Did you steal my pictures?"

The young girl tipped her chin downward and shook her head. Innocence exuded from her, but those black eyes told Akiva she was anything but.

He narrowed his gaze on her, unsure if he should believe her or not. If she'd tampered with his stuff and stolen the pictures of Hannah, he'd rip her head right off her swanlike neck. "You tell whoever did, they have twenty-four hours to bring my stuff back."

Then he grabbed Rachel's hand, flung open the bedroom door, and whisked her out of the apartment and the building, well aware that several pairs of black eyes trailed them.

CHAPTER ELEVEN

THE GOOD NEWS: ROC knew what they were up against. The bad news: it was Akiva.

Chasing vampires wasn't like chasing a criminal. They didn't leave fingerprints or credit-card trails. They left only blood.

Roc had squeezed as much information as he could from his old cop friend, Mike. Which amounted to nothing much. The Philadelphia cops knew nothing about this latest disappearance of an Amish woman, and they cared less. Roc had driven all over Lancaster County, from Promise to Intercourse, asking folks if they'd seen Rachel Nussbaum. He couldn't get any useful information though.

No one had seen her for days or weeks. It was as if she'd simply disappeared. No one had seen a man with dark hair and darker eyes, either. The Lancaster sheriff's office acted a bit more interested, in light of the Yoder girl's death, but they were like a fly swatter batting at Goliath. Roc had been to the train station, bus depot, and airport, and he'd come up empty.

What a fool he was for agreeing to chase after a hungry vampire and his next victim—an innocent, pregnant widow. *Did it get more pathetic?* Heck, he should go straight to CNN where this would be a great story. Or maybe *The National Enquirer* would be interested. Yes, definitely, add a vampire or alien and any sleazy rag would print the story on its first page with a big headliner: "Vampire Kidnaps Amish Widow." Papers would definitely sell. Maybe they'd theorize it was a vampire from outer space. And then Roc would be locked up in the loony bin.

He could hear the boys back in NOPD. "Knew Roc was losin' it."

"The alcohol pickled his brain."

"Nah, losing his wife put him over the edge."

His last-ditch effort was Mike again. Even though out of uniform at the moment, he still had cop eyes, which narrowed suspiciously on Roc. "You're drunk, aren't you?"

"No. I'm telling you, this woman is missing—"

Mike tossed a thick manila folder onto his cluttered desk. "So are all of these folks. From kids to old folks. Teens who ran away. Kids who disappeared in the night. Some pedophile neighbor took a hankerin' to 'em. Or their dad picked 'em up one day after school before Mom got there. And *bam*— they disappeared. For good. No trace. Nothing. Grandfathers who wandered out of the nursing home. Aunts who went to the grocery store and never returned home, their car found on some deserted road. Wives, husbands, daughters, sons, grandkids all searching and desperate to find these missing folks. Some have been missing thirty years. This Amish widow ain't the only one, my friend. So good luck."

Good luck was right. It was like finding the right straw hat in a pile of Amish ones. Rachel wasn't the only one missing though. But the likelihood of finding Rachel seemed more hopeless than all these other folks combined. All these missing folks had recent pictures, stats listing their weight and height. A few who had been missing for a while had drawings of what the person might look like after all these years. But for Rachel, there wasn't even a starting photograph, just

Hannah's description: "blond, blue eyes, a smidgen shorter than me."

Knowing what Akiva was and his modus operandi, Roc figured Rachel was already dead. Negativity had nothing to do with his prediction. It was a simple probability. And it was Roc's fault, the way Ferris's death was his fault too…and Josef's…and Emma's. The list was long and growing.

Driving back, he thought about his own wife, the lost years, the empty hours. A raw ache of grief surged upward and hopelessness stole over him. Levi and Hannah had made a bad mistake asking him to search for Rachel. *What use was he anyway? What was the point?* He'd search and eventually some kid would head out to a creek to do some fishing and find an abandoned sneaker, then a hand…It always ended the same.

A flash of a neon sign caught his attention, and he steered his Mustang toward a liquor store to buy a bottle of rotgut. The brand or year didn't matter.

He returned to the bed-and-breakfast where he'd been staying on and off for the past six months. When he first arrived in Pennsylvania, the NOPD had been footing his bill, but after they cut him off, Roc had bunked sometimes with Roberto, sometimes with Mike, and occasionally in his car. But tonight, he needed a soft bed, and his usual room was available.

"Need help with your luggage?" the redheaded teen, Suzy, asked.

He shook his head and took the key. She wore black nail polish. "You still into vampires?"

She grinned. "Werewolves."

He tilted his head. God help him if the next battle he had to face was against giant wolves.

"And angels," she added. "They're cool."

"The chubby kind with harps?"

"No, the kind with gigantic wings and big, honkin' swords."

"Swords, huh? Now that's something I could use." He retreated toward the door, ready to get in his room, eager to drown his depression.

"I think you're really a vampire fan," she said.

He shook his head. "If I ever saw one, I'd kill it."

She laughed. "Just don't let one bite you."

He turned, backing his way through the screen door. "Why's that?"

"Then you'd be a vampire."

"Is that what it takes?" he teased.

"Has some sort of venom or something...I don't know what...gets in the blood." The girl kept telling him about vampires like she was an expert. Maybe she was. Maybe she should be the vampire hunter. He stepped out into the cool night air.

A sidewalk led around the two-story house to his rented room. His foot caught on the edge of the concrete, and he stumbled. A hand stuck out and righted him, and Roc gazed up into the face of a tall man. Fear took hold of Roc in a split second, until the man's eyes—golden, not black—registered on him.

The stranger had a smile like a star. "You all right there?"

"Sure, yeah."

Roc rushed on, irritated for not seeing the stranger before. He didn't like surprises. He should be more alert. Pay closer attention. But once again he was a failure. A failure at saving Emma. At finding Rachel. He fumbled with the key, shoved it into the slot, and the door finally gave way. He pulled the bottle from inside his jacket and took a long pull, then let the door close behind him. Clunking the bottle on the nightstand, he chucked off his jacket, gun, and stake. He tried to yank off his boots, finally having to sit down on the bed and tug hard to release his foot. Then he flopped back onto the sun-dried pillowcase and breathed in the summery scents, which he promptly drowned with more whiskey.

His thoughts swirled downward into dark places, drifting past understanding and consciousness. He glided in and out of sleep, sometimes not even aware of which world he entertained. Emma floated along beside him for a while until turbulence separated them. He lunged for her, tried to grab her hand, but he woke himself instead.

He sat up in bed, blinked at the darkness enfolding him. Sweat stuck his clothes to his skin, and he tugged off his shirt and hurled it across the room. Then once more, he turned back to the bottle for comfort. Each swallow carried a wave of guilt and remorse, and the grief pulled him under the surface.

When he awoke again, spluttering and coughing, the room undulated around him like a giant wave rippling across the bed and dresser and television. A light at the end of the bed made him squint, and he struggled to sit upright, bracing a hand against the mattress to keep from toppling over. He blinked against the light, which slowly solidified into a form…a form of a man.

Roc tried to remember what he'd done with his Glock. "Who the hell are you?"

"Pay attention, Roc," the man said in a gruff voice, a voice that sounded too familiar to be dismissed.

Roc's throat closed as if a fist gripped it. "Dad?"

Remy Girouard glared at him from the end of the bed. He had a wiry frame and pale, watery eyes. Years of drinking and hard living lined his face. "You're not finished yet, son."

"What would you know about that?"

"Get up, Roc. There's a life depending on you."

Then the image flashed brighter and disappeared. Roc blinked against the sudden darkness. His elbow collapsed, and he fell back against the bed, breathing and sweating heavily. A sob welled up in his chest, and he choked and coughed. He rolled sideways and grabbed the bottle off the bedside table. After gulping the rest of the whiskey, he fell back against the pillows, feeling the bed jounce and time ripple around him in concentric circles of dreams and visions.

Eyes blinked at him, and he jerked open his own, but he could still see them: black eyes staring, leering, glaring. Among the dark orbs were Emma's, her gaze solemn and calm. And there was another pair: blue and pleading. *Rachel*.

A pounding woke him next. The cacophony crashed against his skull. Then the door swung open. The heat of the night poured inside, and Roc stared at the shape of the man in the doorway, blinking and trying to register where he was, what he was doing, what was happening. His limbs felt weighted, as if he couldn't lift even his little finger. Nor did he care to fight or struggle anymore. Resigned, he tilted his head back, exposing the vulnerable place along his neck as his heart pummeled his rib cage.

The man stepped quietly into the room and closed the door behind him. Roc had seen many expressions, from joy to frustration and from fear to anger, in those particular eyes, but he'd never seen this particular look before. The eyes tilted downward at the corners. The mouth stretched wide in neither grin nor grimace. "Feeling sorry for yourself?"

Roc grabbed for the bottle, missed, and grabbed again. "Toasting Ferris." And Emma. And Rachel. And maybe even his dad, for it had to be his father's ghost who had visited him earlier. "And all the dead on my account."

"How selfish can you be?"

Roc blinked slowly, trying to sort through what the priest had said. Finally, he took a long, slow drink of whiskey. "There's a glass in the bathroom. If you want some, you better hurry."

"You're selfish, Roc. Wallowing here in self-pity." Roberto lifted a giant-sized chip bag off the table and dropped it.

Roc didn't even remember eating chips or buying them. Had he driven to the store? Or were those from his car? Maybe the redheaded teen—what was her name?—had gotten him food. He didn't know what day it was or how long he'd been drinking. He wasn't sure which scared him more: not knowing or knowing too much.

The priest didn't give him time to answer or defend himself. "Trying to kill yourself with all this drinking, I suppose. And stoking your ego, which is bigger than I would have imagined. To think you have some ability to cause someone else's death when you didn't even lift a finger."

"That's right. I didn't lift a finger." His words slurred, and he drained the rest of the bottle. "So why bother?"

"Why bother?" Roberto snatched the bottle from him. "Because lives are at stake! Are you going to let Ferris die in vain?"

"Is that v-e-i-n?" Roc laughed and saluted the priest with the bottle. Roberto's image wavered before him, and the starkness of his black-and-white collar blurred into gray.

"Did Levi call you?"

"Levi?"

Roc nodded, which made the room tilt and do a slow roll.

"Are you talking about Levi Fisher? Akiva's brother?"

"Yeah." Roc forced himself up off the bed, tripped over a boot, and stumbled forward. The room kept moving even when he remained still…or almost still. He couldn't steady himself. He sat on the edge of the bed and bent forward in case all he'd poured into his body came right back out. He braced his head with his hands as if he could make the spinning stop. "She's missing."

"Who's missing?" Roberto demanded. "Hannah?"

Roc shook his head then decided against the maneuver. He slumped back against the headboard. "Her sister. Rachel."

"This the one that lost her husband?"

"Yeah." His head throbbed, like when his dad had taken a baseball bat to it.

Suddenly Roberto was moving around the room in fast-forward motion. He plopped a wet rag at the back of Roc's neck and stuck a warm Diet Coke in his hand. "Drink up. Sober up."

"What for? It's a lost cause."

"Yeah, yeah, yeah. And you're a lost cause too. If I were feeling nice, I'd let you wallow in self-pity, but right now you have to go find this woman. She's pregnant, right?"

Roc took a sip of the warm Coke and bubbles worked their way back up his esophagus.

"I know what Akiva wants with her," Roberto said.

"Yeah, a snack."

"No. She's not dead."

"And you know this how?"

"She's in danger. And her baby is in more so."

Roc tried to follow not only what the priest was saying but his movements around the room. His eyeballs ached and pulsed. "I've done all I know to do. I don't know where to go, where to look."

"Maybe you're looking in the wrong place."

Roc sat straight up, tilted, then straightened. *Wait, was that why his father had come here? Did Remy know something? Was he trying to lure him back to New Orleans?*

It seemed the only place Roc knew to go.

CHAPTER TWELVE

I T WAS LIKE A graveyard for Mardi Gras floats.

Rachel followed Akiva through a maze of pathways around the float carcasses and buildings, which looked like oversized caskets. Moonlight slanted onto the abandoned or forgotten floats, gleaming off the skeletal frames, the pieces looking like jagged teeth and splintered bones. As they rounded the corner of a warehouse, each of her steps felt as if they could be her last. They'd been on the move for days, drifting, running, hiding. Today had seemed as long as a year, the minutes and hours piling up inside her, weighting her limbs and eyelids.

After they had left Akiva's New Orleans apartment, they'd toured the city streets until the sun disappeared beyond the horizon and night settled in. At times, Akiva had raced through yellow and red lights, and at other times puttered through green ones. His fancy car wove in and out between cars and trucks. He'd press the gas pedal, and the car would shoot forward; then he'd slam on his brakes, and Rachel would jolt forward and back until her stomach knotted and shoulders tensed.

They'd found tiny motels and stayed only briefly, long enough for Rachel to wash and doze, stretched out on a lumpy mattress. Then they repeated each day the drive through and around the city. Akiva's intensity had frightened her.

She dared to ask: "Are we lost?"

"No!"

"Are we looking for something…for—?"

He'd slammed his hand against the steering wheel. "Just let me think! All right?"

And so she'd remained quiet and still, not wanting to attract his attention or fury.

This city's night was different than Promise's, where quiet tucked the farms and businesses in around the edges, and the stars shone brightly in the night sky. New Orleans was noisy and intense with neon lights, honking cars, and blaring sirens. The warehouse district now absorbed the city lights and sounds like the scientific oddity she'd heard about back in school—a black hole. She felt alone, helpless, and at the mercy of Akiva, who was not her friend as Jacob once had been.

When she'd first come to New Orleans with Jacob, Rachel had experienced the raucous celebration of Mardi Gras. Jacob had been enthralled with the booze and drugs so easily bought and consumed right on the streets, but she had been stunned by the freedom the partiers had shown: dancing in the street to the suggestive music, shouting and calling obscenities, unbuttoning shirts, flashing body parts, couples kissing and groping right out in the open.

Jacob's eyes had glittered with excitement, and he'd bought her piña coladas until her world tilted, and she'd clung to his arm as she teetered on high heels she'd bought on their journey into the South. He'd pulled her into a darkened alley, where they bumped into another couple, the woman's bare legs locked around the man's pale hips. The darkness hid Rachel's red-hot embarrassment, but Jacob had made some remark, more apology than anything, and pulled her farther into the shadows.

With her senses whirling from the alcohol and pounding music, she'd tasted the bourbon on Jacob's tongue. His hands probed and pressed against her as his pelvis ground urgently against hers. Arguments had surfaced in her mind, only to be swept away by the waves of alcohol drowning her questions and hesitations and the stirrings of pleasure his fingers erupted inside her as he'd unzipped her tight-fitting jeans and slid them down her thighs. The warm night air had caressed her bare flesh, and she'd given herself over to the moment and Jacob.

There, right there in the alley with the smells radiating from the garbage bins, was the first time they'd "done the deed," which was how Jacob had referred to it. She ignored the way his careless remark nettled her. The fact was she hadn't been a virgin when he'd taken her in the alleyway, nor had she been his first. Later at the motel, she'd teased him. "You can't think of a better phrase, Mr. Poet?"

He scrutinized her for a moment, his gaze sliding over her as if he was unbuttoning her blouse one button at a time. He moved her back toward the bed, until her knees bumped the mattress, and she sat. Formally, he knelt before her. When he'd spoken, he'd used a deeper, reverent tone he utilized when quoting a poem—"'A sweet disorder in the dress...'"

He lifted her foot and braced the sole of her high heel against his thigh. "'Kindles in clothes a wantonness: A lawn about the shoulders thrown into a fine distraction—'"

His finger slipped beneath the strap at her heel and slipped the shoe off her foot. As he quoted more, he drew a line along her calf, making the skin along her arms pucker. "'An erring lace, which here and there enthrals the crimson stomacher—'"

He massaged her muscles, cupped her foot in his hands, and bathed her skin with his gentle, tender touch until flutters

tickled her lower belly. "'A cuff neglectful, and thereby rib-
bands to flow confusedly: A winning wave, deserving note,
In the tempestuous petticoat—'" Slowly, his hands skimmed
upward along her legs, behind her knees, along her. "'A careless shoe-string, in whose tie I see a wild civility: Do more
bewitch me than when art is too precise in every part.'"

A few minutes later, breathless and languid, she lay beneath him, stretched out on the bed, and whispered in his
ear, "That's a mighty long way to say I want…"

"To get it on? Or off?" He laughed and rested his head
against the curve of her shoulder, his weight blanketing her.
"The poem's called 'Delight in Disorder.'"

Her hand slid down his back and rested along his narrow
hip. "I like that. It fits."

He nudged her with his groin. "It sure does."

He had been full of questions. *Do you like this? What does
this feel like?* And boldly, he'd told her what he wanted. But
the sex had meant nothing more than two teenagers explor-
ing and experimenting. She hadn't loved Jacob any more
than he had loved her. His heart remained with Hannah,
just as hers had no other name etched on it than Josef. While
she'd been in a strange place, doing things Josef would not
approve of, she hadn't been the same plain girl from Promise,
Pennsylvania. How could she ever have garnered Josef's
attention anyway?

The truth was, she hadn't wanted to leave home or Josef.
She'd hoped telling him she was going to New Orleans with
Jacob Fisher would push him into some sort of a declaration.
But it hadn't. He hadn't said anything to her at all, and a part
of her heart crumpled. She'd already told Jacob she'd go, so
she went.

But a couple of years later, after she'd returned home and

settled back into a plain lifestyle, a miracle had occurred: she had finally married Josef, and they never discussed any previous experiences. He treated her as a virgin bride, and she followed his lead, wanted to feel the way he saw her. Their time together had been sweet and fervent. He had come to bed each night eager, and her body had readily responded, but he hadn't talked about what they did together in the dark, beneath the quilts of deep purple and forest green. He had whispered of his love, his adoration, but they had not laughed together in bed, and they had not spoken of their wants and needs.

She wanted to forget the deep, encompassing emotions that had been such a part of making love with Josef. Her husband was gone. And she was here now. Tired of being frightened. Exhausted from travel. And ready for whatever awaited her to be over.

Akiva unlocked a metal door and pushed it open. When she hesitated before stepping into the gloomy darkness, he clasped her hand. The door clanged shut behind her, and she flinched. The safety and security of home and faith seemed very far away. She attempted a prayer, but it felt as if that door had been shut and locked, as well. Whatever was about to happen, whatever Akiva had planned, she deserved.

But her baby did not. She wanted this nightmare over, so she could take her baby home to safety.

"Not much farther." Akiva's voice resonated through what seemed like a spacious, barnlike area and rebounded off a metal ceiling.

He led her into the womb of the building, and her eyes began to adjust. Shadows and silhouettes took shape and grew into solid objects and forms. Crazy jester heads loomed out of the darkness. Their colorful collars and curved hats reminded her of those long-ago days in New Orleans when she and Jacob had laughed at the silly, bizarre decorations. Carnival masks lined shelves, some in stacks and others haphazardly, as if they'd toppled over. At the end of one row, a leviathan blocked their path. It gave her a jolt, and she sucked in a breath. Her belly contracted, and the baby kicked. Akiva hesitated but said nothing. Even his angry presence was better than being alone, even if she didn't trust him or understand what he wanted.

Something scuttled along the wall, and she caught a glimpse of a long, thin tail. Mice and rats didn't bother her. Only the unknown of what she was doing here gnawed through her defenses.

At a metal spiral staircase, he began the upward climb, and she followed, keeping a hand on the railing. The baby kept her off balance, and she moved in an ungainly and awkward fashion. The higher they went, the darker it became, until he helped her onto a narrow walkway that swayed slightly with each step.

It was hot and muggy, and perspiration prickled her forehead. They eventually reached a doorway, which he unlocked and pushed open to reveal a small room set high aloft the shelves and vast space of the warehouse. His hand at the small of her back encouraged her to enter first. The flooring had a more solid feel, and a tiny amount of relief sifted through her. He flipped a switch, and a light above her head flickered on, twitching until it caught and glared. She blinked, tilting her chin downward and recoiling at the sudden brightness. The room held a bed, chair, and table. Cool air poured out from a box in the corner, and she was able to breathe easier.

She moved around the small space. The bed was narrow

and plain, the desk scarred, and the chair had a rung missing. It might require more faith than she had at the moment if she sat upon it. "Where are we?"

"Your new home."

"New home? But you told me if I came here I could help Josef." She turned to face him…but she was alone.

Akiva had left, shutting the door between them. The key in the lock twisted and clicked, the sound loud and defiant in the quiet of the room. As he walked away, his footsteps faded into nothing, only to be drowned by her restrained sobs.

CHAPTER THIRTEEN

RACHEL RESTED ON THE bed, curled on her side, the baby nestled between her palms as she rubbed circles across her belly. Sometimes her stomach contracted, the skin growing taut, and after a moment or two, it relaxed. It wasn't painful necessarily, but it made her anxious.

The room was dark but cool, the fan in the corner working overtime, and the sporadic hum her only companion. At least she didn't have to share a bed with Akiva, but being alone with her thoughts seemed equally dangerous.

Time had lost its meaning. Before they'd arrived at the warehouse, she'd lost track of the days. But now, even day and night eluded her. No window allowed her to track the sun or moon. Akiva came and went, bringing her food: an apple, crackers, water.

"What do you want with me?" she'd asked. "How can I help Josef?"

But he'd quietly shut the door, giving no answers, no reasons.

Had it been minutes? Hours? Days? She had no idea. She slept some of the time, dreaming of Josef. Once she woke, speaking his name, tasting it on her tongue and savoring the sweetness of his memory. Then she'd cried herself to sleep again.

This time, when she woke, she listened for sounds outside her door but heard nothing. She usually didn't hear Akiva coming up the steps, and his arrival always startled her. But, at least for now, it sounded as if she was truly alone.

It felt like she'd been locked away and forgotten. *What if she went into labor and had no one to help her? What was her family thinking…doing? How could she get away from Akiva and find help?*

Only one answer came to her. Slowly, she rose from the bed, reached for her prayer *kapp*, and covered her head. She knelt beside the bed, even though her lower back ached and the grains in the unfinished wood floor bit into her knees. Bowing her head, closing her eyes, she prayed, and after a while, her prayer gave way to song, a hymn.

> *"When I survey the wondrous cross*
> *On which the Prince of glory died,*
> *My richest gain I count but loss,*
> *And pour contempt on all my pride.*

> *"Forbid it, Lord, that I should boast,*
> *Save in the death of Christ my God!*
> *All the vain things that charm me most,*
> *I sacrifice them to His blood."*

When the door opened this time, she didn't move. She didn't look up. She didn't even stop singing.

> *"See from His head, His hands, His feet,*
> *Sorrow and love flow mingled down!*
> *Did e'er such love and sorrow meet,*
> *Or thorns compose so rich a crown?*

> *"Were the whole realm of nature mine,*
> *That were a present far too small;*

Love so amazing, so divine,
Demands my soul, my life, my all."

She finished the refrain, and whispered "Amen," as if the song had been her prayer.

"What are you doing?" Akiva's tone sharpened.

She met his dark gaze. A steady stream of light poured through the opening behind him, creating a silhouette of light and dark, and the tension in the room silenced her. She kept her head lowered.

"Prayers will do you no good."

She leaned against the mattress and pushed to her feet. "You don't believe in God, Jacob?"

"Many believe in God, but not that He answers prayer."

She eased herself onto the edge of the bed and looked at him with a calm she had not experienced in a long while. "But what do *you* believe?"

He remained silent for a moment, and his gaze shifted downward, as if examining his own heart. "I don't believe God would help me." He looked at her again, those eyes so dark, so void of emotion, so captivating. "Or you, either. You are more like me than you want to believe, Rachel. Out for your own good. Seeking what will benefit you. Nothing or no one else."

Her heart jolted, his words hitting their mark. She drew a steadying breath, but it snagged on the guilt lodged deep inside her. "I am not like *you*."

He shrugged a shoulder dismissively. "Jacob, then."

She shook her head, and the ties of her *kapp* rippled.

"You think God just wipes all of your sins away?"

"God forgives," she said, her voice stronger than she felt. "Even after all I have done. Even all you have done, Jacob."

He laughed, but no humor entered the bitter sound. "You are more naïve than I imagined."

"It is not what I believe or you believe about God that matters." She clasped her hands together, resting her forearms against the sides of her belly. "It is what the Bible says that matters. That is the truth. 'For this is my blood of the new testament, which is shed for many for the remission of sins.'"

"For 'many,' huh?" He blew a breath between his lips, puffing them out. "I do like the sound of that though— *blood*." He tasted the word like it was a ripe, summer peach. "Believe whatever foolishness you want. Maybe God will help you, Rachel. But not me."

She tilted her head sideways, studying this man, whose heart must be aching. "Are you truly unrepentant?"

The skin around his eyes tightened. "You don't know what I've done. Or how I feel."

"I don't have to know."

He took a step toward her, his hands fisted, his features fierce and tense, as if he might launch an attack of some kind. "If I told you, you'd faint dead away."

"You cannot threaten me. God will allow what He will to happen. To me. And to you."

His features hardened into a mask.

But she did not shrink back from his intensity. Her prayers had fortified her with a calm, supernatural strength. "I told you I'm not as naïve as you believe. But it doesn't matter if I know what you have done. Or what you *will* do. God knows. And He forgives those who are repentant."

"What about those who are not?"

"Jacob, you knew the truth. Have you so quickly forgotten what you were taught?"

"I knew enough to look for my own truth."

"Is your truth the same as God's? Where has your truth gotten you, Akiva?" She used his new name deliberately and let her question sink into him before adding, "I will pray for you."

She bowed her head, but he interrupted her good intentions. "Job prayed, and look what good it did him."

Drawing a slow breath, she did not wish for an argument, and yet something prompted her to say, "Job was a righteous man. He did not lose his soul. So I will pray for you." Again, she bowed her head.

"It's a waste of time." He whirled away from her. "I didn't come here for a biblical discourse. Come on."

She kept her head bowed and formed a prayer in her heart.

"Now!" His voice filled the room, her head, vibrating through her. He stood just outside the door. Beyond him, bright lights illuminated metal beams and empty spaces, and yet at the same time, darkened his features.

"Where are we going?"

"If you don't need the facilities"—he grabbed the door handle—"then I won't bother."

Blinking against the bright light, unable to see Akiva's face, just his shape, Rachel stood as quickly as she could manage, but the sudden movement made the room waver. She braced a hand against the bed and slowly, she straightened, not daring to take a step until she knew she wouldn't crumple like an empty potato sack. Akiva had already left her, the door open, and was halfway down the spiraling stairs.

"You coming?" he called.

"Yes." She followed after him, hurrying out of the room, waddling more than walking, and she supported the base of her belly with a hand. Refusing to look down below the swaying walkway, she feared she would lose her balance and fall to the concrete-slab floor far below. The narrow, curving stairs slowed her pace even more.

When she reached the bottom step, Akiva took off again, his posture rigid. He was still wearing what looked like the same jeans and jacket, just like she was still wearing the slacks and maternity top he'd given her back in Tennessee. But he didn't appear grimy the way she felt.

He led her through a maze of corners and bends, down long aisles of row upon row of Mardi Gras hats and faces, twisting and turning until she had lost her way and could not have found the stairs again if she'd wanted to. It was the same each time he came for her and took her to the facilities. The warehouse felt warm and damp. Sweat dotted her forehead. A pressure built against her bladder, an urgency she had tried to ignore when she'd been waiting up in the room alone and forgotten.

"In there." He pointed toward a particle-wood door.

The handle jiggled in its socket when she turned it, and she thought it might come right out of the door. She was met with darkness and ran her fingers along the wall for the light switch.

Akiva brushed against her and reached past. "It's a chain."

The single bulb above her head glowered down at her, and the chain swayed back and forth. Akiva backed out, shutting the door, which didn't lock, and leaving her in a tiny room that boasted a cracked enamel sink and filthy toilet that probably had not had a good scrubbing in years.

When she washed her hands, she cupped her hands and splashed her face. The cold water refreshed her, and she yearned to take a bath and scrub herself from head to toe. But Akiva was waiting.

Finally, she twisted the precarious handle and looked out

into the hallway. But Akiva seemed to have disappeared temporarily. She hesitated. *What should she do? Find the stairs? Find a door and bolt? But where would she go?* She had no money, no way to contact anyone who could help get her back to Pennsylvania. She was stuck here at the mercy of Akiva.

After a moment of indecision, she decided the best course of action was to return to the "facilities" and utilize the sink as much as she could. Locating a nail stuck in the wall, she removed her shirt and underclothing and hung them so they wouldn't touch the toilet or floor, which was spotted with dead crickets and cockroaches. She used a damp paper towel and dotted it with pink liquid soap, then rubbed it over her torso and under her arms.

"Akiva!" A woman's loud voice came through the cracks around the door.

Rachel panicked, covering herself with her hands, but the door beside her remained closed. Despite the warmth in the warehouse, a chill stole over her, puckering her skin in its wake. Hurriedly, she grabbed her clothing without bothering to dry her skin. The hooks and eyes at the back didn't catch at first, but then she finally pulled on the blue maternity top. Water spots dotted the material where her skin had not yet dried. Still, she stood in the tiny room, her breathing rapid and constricted.

"Come out, come out, wherever you are!" The woman's deep, throaty voice sounded familiar.

A smidgen of hope shot through her. It was the black woman they'd seen on the steps of Akiva's apartment building. Akiva hadn't liked the woman, hadn't trusted her. *Was that good or bad?* Since she didn't trust Akiva, she figured the woman had to be good. And maybe her only chance.

She fumbled with the handle and opened the door a crack.

She didn't see Akiva in the hallway. Venturing farther, she pushed the door open another inch. "Hello?"

"Well, well, lookie what I done found." The heavyset woman lumbered around the corner. The vivid colors she wore clashed like Amish and English cultures often did. "Where is your guardian, eh?"

"Can you help me?"

"Oh," the woman trilled, her dark eyes glittering, "I can indeed." The woman continued walking toward Rachel with slow, steady, careful footsteps, head tipped downward, and large black eyes glared with an intensity that took Rachel's breath. A tittering of sounds, murmurings soft and low, filled her mind, distorted her thoughts. Rachel twisted her head, trying to break away from them, but the tentacles of whispers wrapped tighter around her.

The woman drew in a breath through her wide nostrils as if sampling and savoring the air. Slowly, she grinned. "Akiva should not have left you alone."

CHAPTER FOURTEEN

TRANSYLVANIA, LOUISIANA

THE SIGN GRABBED ROC'S attention. *Transylvania, huh?*
Of course, the real Transylvania was in Europe
some place. But he also knew the vampires he'd met and
killed loved irony. They might enjoy living in such a place.
It wouldn't hurt to take a look around.

Raw gut instinct guided him off the highway. Or maybe
his instinct had flipped out like a GPS system gone berserk.
The journey he'd been on the last few months had certainly
made him feel like he'd lost his compass reading. Or his mind.

Still, he took Highway 65 toward the remote town of
Transylvania. Maybe it was simply a diversion for vampire
freaks. Or a trap set by vampires to lure in gullible idiots
who'd read too much King, Rice, or Koontz. Or maybe
this little detour would give him some kind of a lead.
Because once he reached New Orleans, he wasn't sure what
he was going to do or how he was going to find a pregnant
Amish widow.

He remembered Rachel's blue eyes staring at him un-
blinking in his dreams...or nightmares. Was she already
dead? Laying in some field, half-covered by the new growth
of summer, her flesh rotting in the heat?

Or had she been changed? Had Akiva changed her out of spite toward Hannah? Was her skin cold to the touch, those eyes darkened to the color of midnight, the real life-light snuffed out of her? Would Roc then be forced to kill her too?

There were many possibilities. But Roberto's belief kept Roc pressing the gas pedal toward the floorboard. If Akiva held her captive, alive and not yet changed, frightened, alone, and desperate, Roc had to rescue her. *Did she know what Akiva was? Did she know death would be better than what the monster might have in mind for her? Or her baby?*

From an easy distance, he spotted Transylvania's water tower, where a bat had been painted on the round vessel's side. *So it wasn't some imagined place out of the convoluted spaces of his mind.* This town had a warped sense of humor and obviously invited curious tourists…or trapped them. Maybe they even had a connection to the underworld of the bloods. Roc reached over and placed a hand on the hilt of the stake, which lay across the passenger seat, the wicked point stained with layers of blood.

As he came into town, if you could use that word accurately, he slowed his Mustang and looked around the flat plains with few trees to break up the monotony. It looked deserted, as if the citizens had moved on down the road, and their houses had gone after them. He passed a post office and general store, which boasted "See our bat and Dracula tee shirts."

He figured he should move on too, but he pulled up next to the general store, a red-bricked building, flat and boring. It looked like it had been built on a tight budget back in the 1970s. A blue post-office box sat out front.

Roc strolled inside the general store. A musty odor greeted him, and he walked among the dusty, tasteless items of rubbery bats and plastic teeth. It didn't look as if they were doing a booming business here in Transylvania. Maybe they hadn't heard of the latest vampire crazes, with glittery vampires more friend than foe, or the TV variety with sexy, Southern accents.

"What can I do for ya?" The male voice came from the back, and the thick accent reminded Roc he was definitely back in Louisiana.

Roc's arm flexed, bumping up against his Glock in a reflexive move that gave him comfort as he turned. "Get much traffic this way?"

"Not too much." An older man lumbered toward him. He wore faded blue overalls no longer capable of buttoning along his wide sides. Beneath the straps, his T-shirt might once have been white but hadn't seen Clorox in ages. His tennis shoes had lost their laces. But Roc focused on the eyes. Hazel. Not black. The man's teeth had gone the way of the citizens and obviously weren't about to take a bite out of him. "You into vampires, son?"

"Into them?" Roc had a definite déjà vu feeling about this particular conversation. But he thought of the stake stuck in the back of his jeans and hidden under his jacket. "Sometimes. You ever have paranormal stuff happen around here?"

"Whatcha mean?" The man's Louisiana accent was as thick as the dust lining the shelves. "Aliens? Ghosts?"

Roc nodded. "Or the like."

"Here tell there was a ghost 'round these parts." His thick tongue slapped at his dry lips. "Now I ain't ne'er seen it or nothin' just heard the stories. You a ghost hunter?" He arched his back, and his belly jutted forward. "You from that ghost-hunter TV show or something?"

"I prefer vampires."

"That's what we get here most often, but not too often."
He scratched his rounded belly.

"You get vampires, or folks that like 'em?"

The man grinned, showing his pink gums. "That's a good
one." And he kept chuckling like he hadn't heard a good
joke in a month of Sundays.

"I'm actually looking for a fella." Roc adopted the man's
accent in the way he'd learned to make people feel comfortable around him and confide in him. "He's got a pregnant
woman with him. You seen somebody like that 'round here?"

"Not any time soon. Fact is, I ain't had no visitors this
entire month."

Hope deflated inside Roc. So this had been a wasted stop.
"Well, nice talkin' to you, then."

"Sure I can't sell ya a bat or something?"

"Not today. Thanks." Then he saw a black T-shirt. Across
the front in white letters shaped like teeth, it said "Got bite?"
with a trail of blood dripping down to the hem.

"You have this in a large?" Roc asked.

Chapter Fifteen

F ROM HIGH ABOVE IN the rafters of the warehouse, Akiva
watched Orphelia approach Rachel. He recognized the
look, knew its deadly intent, saw in the depths of her eyes
the burning hunger.

He swooped downward, arcing and swerving over the
shelves and boxes, swooshing over Rachel's head, his body
unfolding, shifting, and changing, joints popping back into
place, muscles and sinews stretching, until he landed on his
two solid feet in front of Orphelia. "Get out!"

The older woman stopped her advance on Rachel midstride
and drew up, lifting her bosom with her forearms and challenging
Akiva with her own solid stare. "I came to give you a message."

Panic shot into his veins and charged through him. A
message meant purpose. This was no coincidence. "How did
you find me?"

She gave a deep-throated chuckle. "I followed you. It was
not so difficult." She slid her hands along her wide frame.
"You think old Orphelia can't get around so good, cause I
look old. But you don't know old. And I still have lots of
ways to get around." She glanced upward at the rafters from
where he'd flown. "As you do."

"Seems like a lot of trouble to go to for a message."

She leaned forward, her unusual odor filling his nostrils
with lilies and citrus and blood. "It is an important one."

Akiva crossed his arms over his chest and waited. Behind him, Rachel's shallow breathing, her heart fluttering in her chest, and her blood coursing through her veins distracted him. Thankfully, his appetite was sated. But what about Orphelia?

She tugged at the flowing material covering her arms and readjusted the scarf around her neck, taking her time as if she had all the time in the world. "*He* sent for you."

"Oooh! Let's hurry, then," Akiva said, his words mocking. But his stance remained firm, unmoving.

"You are a fool, Akiva."

"For not knowing who 'he' is? Or for not caring?"

"Of course you don't know. You are ignorant of so much."

Her words rankled him.

"You never bothered to learn about us, and you have missed out on so much. So much knowledge. Even now you are wondering how I followed you, how I could know where you are hiding. Still, I will tell you of your ignorance.

"Giovanni." She whispered the name reverently. "He is our leader. It is a great honor to be summoned by him. Either that or"—her features crumpled, her brow folding downward—"the most terrible."

"Giovanni, huh? Why doesn't he just come here if he wants to speak to me?"

Her chin jutted backward, and she stared at him for a long moment, as if he'd started babbling nonsense. "Giovanni goes nowhere. Especially not to a place like"—her gaze darted around the shabby hallway—"this."

"Well, I can't go see him. So take a message back to his highness and—"

"You cannot refuse him." Her dark face went slack. "To refuse is…no one refuses Giovanni."

"Sure I can." He turned and faced Rachel, bracketed her shoulders with his hands.

But Orphelia spoke again. "I will not give him that message."

He shrugged and nudged Rachel to move back away from Orphelia. He would take her on a different route through another part of the warehouse and back to her room, then he'd have to figure out another hideout. At least one vampire now knew where they were, so Rachel would not be safe. He had to move her, keep her safe. At least until her baby was born. Then, her welfare mattered not at all.

"You cannot anger Giovanni," Orphelia warned. "It is not allowed."

Her words acted like a spike clean through Akiva's heart. *Who cared about angering Giovanni? Who showed so much as a cat's hair concern about angering Akiva?* Resentful at once again being on the outskirts and not mattering, he swung around, his hands fisted. "I don't care if this Giovanni blows a gasket! No one cared about pissing me off. No one cared to ask if *I* wanted this life. Whoever-the-hell-he-is matters nothing to me. Tell *him* that!"

Her eyes widened with horror. "That is a death sentence."

"Good. Bring him on. Let's have it out. Right here." He took a threatening step toward her. "Now."

"So it is truc, then? This is what you want with the pregnant woman?"

"It's none of your business what I want or do."

Her eyes narrowed. "Oh, but it is. It truly is. Or at least Giovanni's business. He is in charge of this region. You must see him. You must speak to him." Her gaze shifted toward Rachel, who stood slightly behind him still. "Before…you do anything reckless."

"I am not afraid of him."

"You should be." She flicked her wrist. "It is not my concern if you want to die. Maybe you do. And maybe Giovanni will be the one to kill you. But believe you me, he can make you suffer first. He can make you beg to die."

But Akiva had already pleaded more ways than Sunday for death. And he would, one way or another, die.

Orphelia glanced toward Rachel. "You are afraid to leave her alone. Yes, of course. I understand. You do not trust even yourself with her. Why then me? Or another? But if I promise to bring someone to watch her…someone who will not harm her…will you go and see Giovanni with me?"

"Whom would I trust? You?" His nostrils flared with defiance.

"Acacia. She is young. She will do what she is told. She will not harm the pregnant woman."

Akiva wrestled for a moment with his thoughts and reasons. If he refused, then he'd be back on the run for at least another six weeks. If he took the chance, then he could confront Giovanni and maybe end his nightmare for good. Or buy himself enough freedom to end it himself in a few weeks.

What continuously stabbed at him were Orphelia's words: "'You are ignorant.'" He'd fought ignorance his entire life. He'd tried to educate himself beyond the picket fences and green shades of his Amish upbringing. But had he been as she said? A fool?

"All right," he finally said. "Bring Acacia here. But if anything happens to Rachel, it will be you who will suffer."

"Acacia will not harm the woman," Orphelia's solemn nod made her jowls tremble. "Of this I know for certain."

CHAPTER SIXTEEN

ROC DROVE PAST ST. Joe's three times but could not bring himself to visit his childhood friend and the church the priest served. *What would he say to Anthony now?* "You were right about creatures that go bite in the night?" No way. He wouldn't give him the satisfaction.

Deciding he could more readily tuck tail and go to his ex-partner for help, Roc crossed New Orleans, snaking through traffic from the Garden District to Lake Pontchartrain. He hadn't been in contact with Brody since the NOPD had cut Roc loose six months ago from the investigation of the murdered trick-or-treater. Roc had taken the investigation to Pennsylvania as a favor to Brody, because the murder resembled not only Emma's but also disappearances up North. When Roc had tried to explain over the phone what was going on, Brody had accused him of drinking and cut off the money supply.

Now, he caught his ex-partner in the parking lot of his apartment complex, and Brody glared through his mirrorlike aviator sunglasses. "You still drinking?"

"No," Roc said.

"You need money, then?"

"Can we talk?"

"How much?" Brody reached for his hip pocket.

"I need a favor, not money."

Brody's arms were crossed over his thickly muscled chest. "So what is it this time?"

Roc glanced over at a couple getting out of their car. "This isn't the place."

Brody rolled his lips inward and finally gave a nod toward his apartment, leading Roc out of the Louisiana heat. "You've got five minutes."

Once inside the apartment, Roc explained in sparse terms about Rachel's disappearance.

"You got nothing more than that to go on?"

Roc shook his head at the beer Brody offered, obviously a test, and leaned back in Brody's recliner, gripping the armrests.

Brody still carried his car keys in his hand, as if eager to be on the road and off to wherever he was headed. But first, Roc had to discuss Akiva and Rachel. He needed direction. He needed help. "That's the straight and narrow."

"It's like finding a needle in—"

"Yeah. Something like that." Roc stared at his own reflection in Brody's shades, which the cop hadn't bothered to remove. He imagined what this looked like to Brody. An ex-cop, drunk, hanging onto the bottom rung. Brody jangled his keys, a sign this conversation wouldn't be long. "You in a hurry?" Roc asked.

"As a matter of fact." Brody pointed toward the door the jagged edge of a key.

Maybe Roc should have taken the beer. At least it would have bought him a few extra minutes. Reluctantly, he pushed up from the chair where he'd given Brody a scant overview of Rachel's situation, minus blood-sucking vampires. Not every detail was worth mentioning. Disappointment weighed on him. He needed Brody's thoughts on where to go, what to do. He should know himself, but he felt confused and stymied with fear that he'd already cost Rachel her life. Maybe he should have stayed in Pennsylvania instead of heading to New Orleans, following what he'd decided was his father's advice from the great beyond. He'd kept that embarrassing detail from Brody too.

A whiff of cologne caught Roc's attention as he walked toward his ex-partner. Brody was dressed in starched jeans, nice boots, and wore a loose jacket, as any detective would in order to hide what he was carrying in a shoulder holster. "You got a hot date?"

"Something like that."

"What's her name?"

"Focus, Roc." Brody opened the door and stepped out into the bright sunlight. "Why would this Akiva take a pregnant Amish widow? Were they lovers?"

"Maybe. He grew up Amish. Loved Rachel's sister, but Hannah rejected him. The motive may be revenge. This Akiva is dangerous." Roc descended the steps, the metal banister warm against his palm. Sunlight sparkled off the blue pool water in the middle of a courtyard. He turned and waited for Brody, who had locked the door. His ex-partner was shorter and stockier than Roc. "Look, I didn't want this case. Hannah and her husband, Levi, came to me. Desperate for help."

"Obviously." Brody headed back toward the parking lot. "With a name like Akiva, how hard could it be to find him?"

A splash and girlish squeal behind him made Roc turn toward the pool. "No listings for Akiva, phone, address, anything. It's as if he doesn't exist."

"Maybe he doesn't. Or doesn't want to. What made you think he brought Rachel to New Orleans?"

How could he explain his own father...or ghost...or

phantom of his imagination had set him on this course? His gaze slid over the bronzed bodies lying around the pool and the couple frolicking in the water, splashing and kissing. "He's been living here for a couple of years. Likes the dark side, if you know what I mean."

"Dark side? You mean dealers, gangs, what?"

"Voodoo."

Brody grunted and walked around the edge of the pool and out the side gate. "And it gets more interesting. You think she's to be a sacrifice or something?"

A chill ran through him at the memory of Roberto's suspicion of what Akiva had in mind for Rachel and her baby. "Something like that."

"Didn't know those voodoo hoodies still did that. I mean, I've heard rumors about the old days, but nothing to make me think they do much beyond dance around in the moonlight, high on weed."

"Might be worth a look-see. You know where the lowdown is?"

"Haven't had any cases in that area lately." He stopped beside his black decked-out Chevy truck. With his hands stuck in his front pockets, Brody offered a slight shrug. "But I'll ask around for you. Other than that, Roc, that's all I can do. You're on your own."

CHAPTER SEVENTEEN

RACHEL SAT ON THE one chair in the tiny room, her hands folded over the maternity T-shirt covering her rounded belly, her ankles crossed and feet bare. On the scarred desk sat a greasy bag filled with fried chicken. The warm, tasty scent made her stomach rumble with the need for home. She made a plate out of a napkin and opened the container of mashed potatoes. "You're sure you don't want any?"

Acacia sprawled across the bed, belly to the mattress, as she danced two dolls belly-against-belly over the coverlet. Gripped in a tiny fist, the girl doll with thick, matted hair bobbed and swayed in a jerky fashion. The boy doll looked as if he didn't know what to do then flopped over face-first into the blanket.

When Acacia didn't answer, Rachel asked again. "Would you like some chicken?"

The young girl shook her head. The short mop of blond hair partially hid her dark, magnetic eyes. Slight of build, she looked even more so in the black leggings beneath a summery dress, which had daisies and bumblebees all over it. If she'd been soaking wet, she wouldn't have weighed a hundred pounds.

Rachel hesitated before plunging the plastic spoon into the creamy white mound. Maybe she should wait till Akiva returned, but the scent of gravy and fried chicken demolished all her good manners. She scooped up mashed potatoes and tasted the salt immediately. They were good, not as good as Mamm's, but still good. Her gaze slid toward the young girl. "You're not hungry?"

"I'm always hungry. Orphelia says I'm a piglet." She made snorting sounds, which turned into giggles.

Rachel tilted her head toward the bucket. "You're welcome to some chicken."

The girl made a face. "Not for that."

Rachel had learned not to look directly into Akiva's eyes or into this girl's, otherwise she felt off-kilter, like she was falling in slow motion.

Acacia released the girl doll, which toppled over the male, stiff limbs clicking against one another, and then Acacia swung her legs around and scooted off the bed, abandoning the dolls in a tangled mess.

Rachel wondered what this little waif of a girl was doing with such a strange person like Orphelia. *Why was she here in the middle of the day? Was school out for the summer, as it was back home in Promise?*

"Where is your home?" Rachel asked.

"Here. New Orleans." She extended the name into more syllables than necessary.

"Were you born here?"

Acacia released a light sigh as if she hadn't thought of her birthplace in a long while. She walked along the length of the twin bed, straightening the blanket and sheet. "South Carolina. That's where I'm from."

"And your folks moved here?"

"My folks?" She shook her head then shrugged a shoulder. "I came on my own."

"But you're so young. Where are your parents? Your family?"

"Dead."

Her flat tone knocked the breath out of Rachel. Instantly, her heart ached for this little orphan. "I'm so sorry."

"It's not a big deal."

So much pain and loss in this world. "I lost my husband only six months ago, and I know how difficult…" Her voice trailed off.

Acacia swayed in front of the boxed air conditioner while the motor whirred, the air blowing her hair back from her face. She closed her eyes, her smile widening, like she was on a carnival ride and didn't have a care in the world.

Her odd response raised Rachel's eyebrows. *But who was she to judge anyone else on their grieving?* She certainly hadn't handled everything the right way in the last few months since Josef had died. In fact, she'd probably been too harsh with Hannah on her sister's long, drawn-out grief over Jacob Fisher. Now she understood better.

"So who do you live with?" Rachel asked.

The young girl twirled and flitted about the cramped space in the locked room as if a bigger kid were manipulating her arms and legs and she was simply a puppet. "Orphelia," she answered. "I stay with her some. Or not. Don't matter much. But she's the only one who'll put up with me."

Rachel's heart constricted at the thought of no one taking care of this little girl, no one making sure she ate properly, tending her clothes, tucking her into bed at night, worrying when she got sick, or checking her schoolwork. She wanted to mother Acacia, or at the very least, care for her like she often did Katie. Tears stung her eyes thinking about her little sister.

The girl stopped, her arms frozen at odd angles, and stared at Rachel. "You gonna cry or something?"

Rachel offered the little girl a gentle, understanding smile. "No. I'm—"

"Why are *you* here?" Those alluring black eyes blinked slowly. "I mean, what does Akiva want with you anyway?"

"I don't really know." Feelings of missing home welled up inside her, rising and surging toward the surface. Rachel dabbed at the corner of her eye with a napkin. "I would really like to go home though."

"Me too, sometimes. But I've gotten used to New Orleans."

Rachel remembered the conversation between Akiva and Orphelia, and the way the older woman had questioned him. "What does Orphelia think?"

Acacia waved her hand through the air as if her fingers were trailing a particle of dust twirling about her. "'Bout what?"

"About why Akiva brought me here."

"Oh." She twirled again and collapsed onto the bed, letting her limbs go limp like a rag doll's. She laughed, her chest expanding, but she stopped suddenly, her gaze darting toward Rachel and then away.

"Acacia?" Rachel said carefully. "Do you know what Orphelia thinks?"

"Sure. Don't everybody?" She nibbled on a fingernail.

"Acacia?" Rachel prompted.

"She ain't exactly quiet on the subject. Orphelia told me not to say nothing though."

"Why not?"

The girl picked at a nail, and a bit of pale pink polish flecked off. "Orphelia's funny that way."

"You can tell me. I won't say anything."

Acacia blew out a breath, and her chest contracted. She pursed her lips as if considering for a moment what to say. She stretched her arms out wide on the bed, and her hand rolled over to pluck at a thread on the blanket. "Akiva's gonna do the forbidden."

Rachel's heart lurched. She swallowed a sudden lump and forced herself to say, "The forbidden?"

"Ya know, killing hisself." The girl spoke as if suicide and death were the same as pancakes, bike riding, and sunshine.

Rachel's brow scrunched downward. *How could someone think of such a forbidden act? Taking away the Lord's will. And why?* But if it was Akiva's plan, then why was she here?

"Why would he need me then?" Rachel asked.

"He doesn't need *you*." The girl straightened her shirt. "Just your baby."

Rachel's hand automatically went to her belly. Her lungs constricted, as if she couldn't draw a full breath. "My ba—" She choked on the word. "But why?"

Acacia sat up and swung her legs against the bottom of the bed, making a clicking sound with her heels against the frame. "'Cause that's how it's done."

She spoke in a tone as if it were the most obvious answer in the world, but what the girl said didn't make any sense to Rachel. "W…what do you mean?"

"He can't do it—kill hisself—like you would." She made motions with her hands to indicate a hanging, slitting wrists, or a gun to the temple. Her innocent, placid face gave the motions an even more gruesome bent.

Rachel's stomach lurched, and the blood drained from her face.

"Blood gives life," Acacia stated. "Right?"

Rachel nodded, remembering what she'd learned in school so long ago about the heart pumping blood to all the organs and extremities.

"But," Acacia explained like she was old enough to teach

a class on the subject, "blood from an infant, it's bad." She squinched up her face. "Like poison to us."

The edges of Rachel's vision wavered and quivered. "Blood?"

"What else?" A hint of a smile played at the corner of Acacia's pink bowed mouth. She leaned forward, her gaze intensifying. "From everybody else, blood is"—her eyes slanted upward as she smiled, and then the tip of her tongue touched her upper lip—"delicious."

At Rachel's intake of breath, Acacia tilted her head to one side and studied Rachel as if she were a ladybug crawling along a windowsill. "I could change you. I know how."

Rachel's heart pounded, the sound thumping and pulsing in her ears, and she attempted to quiet the noise throbbing through her entire body by covering her heart with a hand. She wasn't sure she understood what the girl was saying, but instinctively, fear chilled her. "What do you mean?"

"Ya know, *change*. It's not so bad. I don't hardly remember it anymore."

"I don't…" Rachel shook her head, but her whole body was shaking and trembling. "What are you talking about?"

"Becoming a blood…a vampire. Then you can't die. Well, not as easily as you can now. You can live forever. Unless you try to kill yourself. Then I guess you'd be dead."

Rachel leaned back, fear making her hands tremble, and she gripped them together. "And you live forever by…drinking…" She couldn't bring herself to say it.

"Well, it's not that easy. But as Orphelia says, it ain't rocket science neither."

"I…is that what happened to Jacob…Akiva?"

"Yeah. Of course. Me too." Her hands settled in her lap as she twisted her fingers together. "Most of us change our names afterward. 'Cause we feel different. We don't feel like our old self no more. I guess we ain't the same. I used to be Ann Marie Marshall from Spartanburg, South Carolina." She grinned. "Now I'm just Acacia. I like that name, don't you? Acacia. Acacia." She tested it out with different inflections and dialects. "Acacia."

Rachel felt as if her brain were compressing and her heart leaping out of her chest. She couldn't speak, couldn't manage a single word in answer to the girl.

"Ah, now I've done it. You're upset. Don't you worry none. I won't change you…" She grimaced. "Giovanni hates that word—*change*. He calls it awakening. Sounds fancy, don't it? So I won't awaken you. Orphelia would be mad as a wet hornet if I did anyways. Giovanni too."

The girl flopped back onto the bed. "Why, the last time I changed somebody, Orphelia threw one giant hissy fit and Giovanni threatened to make me his slave. 'Course I know why he wants that." She patted her chest and traced the lines of her shoulders and upper arms with her hands until her arms were splayed wide upon the mattress. "He likes all the pretty girls, boys too, and offers to educate them." She blinked her black eyes solemnly, as if she were talking about playing hopscotch. "But Orphelia won't allow him to touch me. And 'cause she protected me, then I promised I wouldn't do that awakening thing no more. So's when I eat, I make sure I kill the person good. It's best that way, I guess."

Staring at the young girl, Rachel could no longer see the sweet, innocent face. Now all she could see was a monster.

CHAPTER EIGHTEEN

GLIDING OVER THE MAGNOLIAS and moss-draped oaks, two and three stories tall, to the shaded sanctuary below, Akiva transitioned back into his usual form and planted his feet solidly on the smooth, grassy plain.

Orphelia had already landed and was walking ahead of Akiva, her footsteps determined across the clipped green grass. Up ahead, surrounded by a fortress of stalwart oaks, the antebellum mansion gleamed white with its giant pillars and wide front porch. Someone darted out of a side door, skirted the yard, and disappeared into an outbuilding.

A gleaming statue peered around a tree's trunk. Akiva noticed other more implike statues, white and smooth, hidden among the oaks, and his mind ventured toward a poem he'd read and pondered:

Chisel in hand stood a sculptor boy
With his marble block before him,
And his eyes lit up with a smile of joy,
As an angel-dream passed o'er him.

He carved the dream on that shapeless stone,
With many a sharp incision;
With heaven's own light the sculpture shone,
He'd caught that angel-vision.

Children of life are we, as we stand
With our lives uncarved before us,
Waiting the hour when, at God's command,
Our life-dream shall pass o'er us.

If we carve it then on the yielding stone,
With many a sharp incision,
Its heavenly beauty shall be our own,
Our lives, that angel-vison.

Was this then the hour he'd been waiting for, yearning for, when the final chink in his statue would be complete? Would his dreams be shattered and pulverized by the decisions and mistakes of the past? He imagined the carver's chisel, slicing through flesh and bone and removing his heart, only to discover it no longer beat but had hardened into stone.

"Are you coming?" Orphelia called. She had paused and turned toward him, shading her eyes with a hand. A slight breeze rippled the vibrant, flowing material wrapped around her body in loose waves. "You can't keep Giovanni waiting."

He took a more leisurely pace, spying the chiseled forest pixies, sprites, and fairies, but soon he reached her. "How did Giovanni acquire all of this?"

She started again toward the mansion. "You really are ignorant of our ways, aren't you?"

Akiva glowered at her back, but he put his emotions on a short leash. "Maybe because no one bothered to share."

She motioned for him to catch up with her. "Camille should have handled all of that, I'll admit."

"Why Camille?"

"She the one changed you, ain't she? It's the duty of the one who changes another to educate and train. But maybe you not make it so easy on her, eh?" She shook her head slowly. "I would guess not. You a challenge always.

"So you want to know: how does Giovanni get anything? He takes. He takes whatever he wants. It is not so difficult." She sounded breathless as she lugged her large frame across the expansive yard. "He has been around a long time. Some say longer than those trees there." She pronounced her "th's" as "d." "No one really knows. But he's owned this place long as I've known him, that's right."

Akiva smiled to himself. "'He who plants a tree plants a hope.'"

"What you say there?"

"'He who plants a tree plants a joy...plants peace.'" Akiva's footsteps slowed. "This Giovanni must be..." *What? Powerful? Hopeful? How could a vampire be hopeful?* Yes, they believed they had acquired eternity, and yet they were not a happy, joyous lot. Or at least not the ones he had met. Maybe this one would be different. Or maybe Akiva simply wished it were the case. He longed for a simple peace. A plain joy. But those things were now impossible.

"We have many of us in powerful positions," Orphelia explained as she walked. "We help our own, yeah? And those in power overlook certain things, things that give money and secrecy. Do you understand? Giovanni is most secretive about his past. It would not surprise me if he is three hundred years old. He knows much. And it is not easy to reach his level of authority. Of course, you know the rent you pay for your apartment goes to him."

"He owns the building?"

"He owns many things here and in the big cities of New Orleans and all the way up to Jackson. His region is extensive. You would be wise to acknowledge how powerful he is."

He nodded his understanding of her not-so-subtle warn-ing as they climbed the wide steps to the veranda.

"And if he did not own that building where you live, then you would have more trouble from the authorities. Things get overlooked, yeah?"

As if their approach had been scrutinized, the door im-mediately opened without a knock. A thin, pale person of diminutive size greeted them with a slight bow and inquisi-tive gaze. Akiva could not tell if the creature was male or female. A thatch of gray hair capped smoldering black eyes, eyes holding ancient secrets. "Orphelia," the butler said in an anemic voice. "And who do we have here?"

"Lynn," Orphelia acknowledged the person dismissively, "we're here to see—"

"You're late"—Lynn's slight smile vanished—"and he's not too pleased." Those black eyes seemed to take in every detail of Akiva. "Not pleased at all."

"It couldn't be helped." She whisked her bulk through the open doorway, the hem of her dress sliding over polished marble floors.

Akiva stepped into a world seemingly centuries past. Flowered, flocked wallpaper and antique furnishings had been preserved with the upmost care. What looked to be servants, wearing the same black slacks and white shirt as Lynn, hurried and scurried through the vast mansion like ants on secret missions. They seemed to pay no attention to the newly arrived vampires and kept at their tasks, yet Akiva sensed they were all paying very close attention, as if every word was logged and registered, analyzed and retained.

Lynn shuffled past Akiva in an attempt to lead Orphelia, but she ignored the slight creature and trounced through the grand entryway, which boasted marble flooring, polished, intricately carved wooden showpieces, and gilded-framed artwork. Seeming to know her way around without need of a guide, Orphelia stormed through the fortress, rounded the edge of the wide staircase and its gleaming mahogany banister. Like a ribbon of blood running along the center strip of the stairwell, the carpet was plush and bright red.

Akiva paused, staring up at the crystal chandelier and the lights sparking off the beveled-glass teardrops, which dangled from each golden limb. The glittering life of a vampire maybe wasn't as dark and painful as he'd imagined.

"He's not in the library this morning, Orphelia." Lynn finally caught up to her at a set of double doors.

With a hand on the brass knob, Orphelia turned, her features disgruntled. "Well, where's he at, then?"

Lynn gave a stiff bow. "If you will follow me, I will present you."

Orphelia gave a vexed wave of her hand and swiped the sweat off her beaded brow. "Hurry up, then. I haven't got all day. And this chore has taken up way more time than it should have."

She grumbled and complained as they retraced their footsteps and entered a magnificent room with a thirty-foot ceiling, a broad, ornate fireplace, and dark wood paneling. Many of the lavish frames showcased glorious landscape paintings with lush, bucolic settings. Others were of battles, blood spilled, swords gleaming, bodies lying spent, limbs at awkward angles. Furniture was sparse but elegant, and Akiva suspected the room's purpose at one time was for dancing. He wondered what it would be like to see a room full of vampires all doing the minuet or jamming to Eminem. In one corner was a spiraling staircase. It led to an overhanging balcony, which was either for a small orchestra or simply a place for Giovanni to look down upon his subjects.

At the far end of the room, French doors led to a veranda. Sunlight poured through the beveled windows in lush spotlights, which illuminated the gleaming hardwood floors. Lynn stopped at the second door, turned, and held a hand up to Orphelia. "Allow me to see if this is a good moment. If you know what I mean." Lynn gave a chilling smile. "I will be right back."

Lynn slipped through the door before Orphelia could protest and closed the door decisively. With a huff, Orphelia turned to Akiva. "The little snit. Thinks he's so almighty important."

"He works for Giovanni?"

"He's a servant."

"As in slavery?"

"Of course. It simply means he did something against the rules—"

"Bloods have rules?" *Did they try to impose order and decorum on chaos and death? How many rules had he broken over the past three years? And did he really care?*

She gave him a sharp look. "And now Lynn must pay for his crimes with allegiance and servitude toward Giovanni."

"Is that always the sentence? To answer the door for Giovanni?"

She snorted. "He got off light, if you ask me."

"What did he do?"

"It don't matter. Just keep in that thick head of yours that the punishment is often much worse. You'll find no grace here." Shrugging, she continued, "When his sentence is up, Lynn will be free once again. But I'm telling you—"

Her tirade ended abruptly when the French door opened again.

"This way!" Lynn chirped and pushed the door wider.

They stepped out onto a veranda. Instantly, Akiva thought of cool, shady days and tall glasses of mint juleps. A wide assortment of empty rockers and wicker chairs was scattered about the covered porch. One chair, though, appeared to hold some importance, as it had a high, arching back like a great fan. In it sat a man of medium build with a dark swath of hair and equally dark mustache, all matching his black eyes. He wore a faded Hawaiian shirt, which hung loose, and a pair of khaki pants. At ease and in control, he looked like a contemporary plantation owner overseeing his property and affairs.

In one hand, he held a tall, narrow glass filled with what looked like tomato juice, but Akiva could smell the tangy scent of blood. Sticking out of the glass was a celery stalk. He lifted the glass toward Akiva and Orphelia, and the ice rattled against the glass. "Good morning."

Orphelia's features froze, as if she could hide her thoughts and reactions behind a mask. "Thank you for seeing us so quickly, Giovanni. We are sorry it took us so—"

"So this is Akiva, huh?" Giovanni asked, his dark gaze pointed, gliding over Akiva like a flat blade against a throbbing vein.

Akiva stepped forward, head lifted, shoulders squared. "I am."

"Well, it's about time you came to see me. It's been much too long, actually. You've been awakened…What? Five years already?"

"Two years and nine months."

"Detail oriented, eh? I've been remiss in not welcoming you into the fold." Giovanni stood and stretched out a hand to Akiva. "But I will say in my own defense that you were a might reticent."

Akiva said nothing but stayed where he was, not moving, not shaking hands, not trusting.

"Please, have a seat. Would you care for something?" Giovanni snapped his fingers, and a servant instantly stepped forward out of the shadows to await his command. "I can highly recommend this little concoction. A very good year." He sniffed the drink like he would a brandy. "1988." He chuckled.

But Akiva shook his head. "Nothing. Thank you."

"Very tasty." He sipped the drink and smacked his lips. "A Bloody Mary." He tilted his head and studied the drink for a moment. "Was her name Mary, I wonder?" He shrugged and laughed. "I can't remember. But mixed with vodka, it's an exhilarating combination. Of course the secret is not in the Tabasco sauce but in the Worcestershire. And of course, the specimen must be quality. And she was. Oh, indeed, she was."

Orphelia was leaning forward, her hungry gaze intent on the glass. "I'll take—"

"You can wait inside." Giovanni waved her away and backed toward his own chair. "This shouldn't take long." He never even looked in Orphelia's direction but kept his gaze trained on Akiva. "I'd like a few minutes alone with our new friend."

Orphelia's features melted, her jowls sagging, before her thick lips twisted. But she kept whatever comment to herself and backed toward the door. With a sharp glance, even though seemingly affable, Giovanni seemed to see everything that went on. His household ran like clockwork wound up by fear. Akiva could sense it like the deep darkness just before dawn.

Now alone with this vampire, Akiva stepped forward. Giovanni offered his hand once again like a gentleman. *Or was it a challenge?* Akiva hesitated then finally clasped the vampire's hand. A mistake. The instant palm met palm, a jolt shot through Akiva's body, and his gaze locked with Giovanni's. Everything around them tilted and whirled. Akiva struggled to release his hand, his thoughts, his emotions from Giovanni's grasp, and finally pulled free. Or maybe he was simply released.

The older, more experienced vampire smiled pleasantly, as if unaffected by their connection, and sipped his drink again. "You are one of us now."

"What do you mean?" Akiva rubbed his tingling palm against his other one as the sensation spread to his other hand. "What is this?"

With a wry smile, Giovanni leaned backed into his chair, obviously comfortable with his position. "You have the mark now."

"The mark?" Akiva stared as this palm, but he saw nothing different. Slowly, the prickling sensation subsided.

"Let's just say you're in the fold. It makes it easier for us to find you…if you're ever in trouble. We take care of our own."

A cold hard weight hit Akiva's stomach. Now he could never escape them. Not on this earth. Not on this side of hell.

Giovanni sipped again from his glass, oblivious to Akiva's discomfort, and smacked his lips. He lifted his glass as if in a salute. "She would have made a good vampire, don't you think?"

Akiva cleared his throat and sat on a vacant rocking chair. "Who's that?"

"Bloody Mary, Queen of England. She had a taste for blood, don't you think? And no qualms about ending a life. You can't be squeamish and be a vampire. I've seen those awakened who struggled and faltered, guilt ridden by antiquated morality, and they wasted away. Doesn't happen often, though. The will to survive is as strong as the instinct to breathe. You have learned that, haven't you?"

Akiva refused to play whatever game Giovanni was enjoying. He sensed the conversation could so easily swirl into a vortex and take him under. Giovanni eyed Akiva levelly. If his time was short, and maybe it was, then he would meet his end calmly and boldly. He remembered the engraving on a monument he once saw, the statue of a young woman lying in repose.

> *When the knell rung for the dying*
> *soundeth for me*
> *and my corpse coldly is lying*
> *neath the green tree.*

Akiva could almost hear the slow gonging of a bell in the far distance, calling to him, warning him, and he paid no heed. He cared nothing for this life. "Why did you send for me? And why is Orphelia so scared of you?"

"Orphelia scared?" Giovanni's eyes widened with feigned shock then creased at the corners as he laughed, clearly ignoring the first question. "She's not afraid of anything. Least of all me. She is one tough blood in her own right. I wouldn't want to cross her. Not that there isn't one who should be feared. But *me*?" He laughed again then stopped abruptly. "Are you asking if *you* should be afraid?"

Fear fled Akiva. *What could this vampire do to him, really? Kill him?* Death would be a welcome relief. But then he remembered Orphelia's words: "He can make you beg."

> *When the turf strangers are heaping*
> *covers my breast,*
> *Come not to gaze on me weeping*
> *I am at rest.*

Akiva lifted his chin defiantly. "I'm not afraid. So why did you want me here?"

Giovanni's expression remained on the surface affable, and yet something hot smoldered in those black eyes. "Well, of course, you'd be curious about that, wouldn't you? I certainly would. Curiosity is a gift. And you always had an abundance, didn't you?" He leaned back, relaxing into the wicker chair, his personal throne. "I admire your forthrightness. So let's get right to it. You're in a hurry, from what I understand."

"Yes, I am."

"You want to get back to that pretty young woman you brought to New Orleans with you."

"Maybe."

Giovanni tapped a finger against his lips. "She is pretty. Is she your servant?"

"Excuse me?"

"It is okay if she is. I have many servants myself. Some are paying off debts they owe me. Some needed closer watching." He waved a hand. "But is she yours?"

"No."

"What is she to you then?"

"A friend…or used to be."

"And what do you intend to do with her?" He raised his drink again, allowed the light to spark against the nuances and cuts in the glass. "Toy with her? Awaken her? Kill her?"

Why was it Giovanni's business? Anger sliced through the tether he'd placed around his emotions.

Giovanni spoke before Akiva could. "It's all right, if that's your plan. Some of us like to play with our food occasionally before dining. Keeps things interesting when we grow bored. And it's so easy to grow bored with so much time."

He watched the sunlight through his glass, tilting his head to study the array of colored lights, and then his gaze hardened. "But if you intend to awaken her...or as some say 'change' her into one of us..."

His lip curled as he used the word, and he allowed the notion to linger between them. His index finger jerked upward and settled back against the armrest of the wicker chair as if ticking off the seconds. "I actually prefer the word *awaken*. Isn't that what it is? You live all your life thinking life is simply a march toward death, and then someone awakens you to the truth, to how the world really is, how it can be, how it will be for you." He smiled as if reveling in his own awareness and difference.

"Then what?" Akiva shifted the conversation back. "You said if I intended to change her..."

Giovanni shifted in his seat. "Then we would have to discuss your reasons. I am not unreasonable about these things. I will say awakening someone is exhilarating. Quite sensual. But it can be rather tricky if you don't know what you're doing. Still, I do insist those of us operating and living in my district adhere to the rules. And you must get permission before turning someone...anyone...into a vamp." He laid a hand against his chest. "It's not my rule, you understand."

"Then whose?"

One of Giovanni's eyebrows arched upward. "The one you *should* fear."

"Who's that?"

Giovanni waved his hand, dismissing the question as if it wasn't Akiva's business to know. "So is that your plan, then?"

"Why all the fuss, all the rules?" The question was automatic. Akiva didn't bother hiding his disdain for useless rules that only made the one who conjured them up feel self-important.

"That's a good question. Seems like a logical thing to do: start changing…awakening everyone. Then we'd certainly outnumber any of those crazy fools who think they can defeat us. But if we all went around awakening our dinners into diners, then we'd soon have nothing to eat now, would we?" He took a long pull on his drink and sucked the drops out of his mustache. "So, is that your plan for the woman you are keeping?"

"No."

"Then what?"

"She's an old friend."

"Missing your old life, are you?" Giovanni leaned against the tall wicker back of his chair. "It's understandable. You have not mingled with our kind much since your awakening. We try to give a little space, especially when we sense such intense anger in a newly awakened vamp, but at some point you need to embrace your life and your new family."

"Family?" Akiva's lip curled with disgust.

"Yes, indeed."

Akiva stood abruptly, and the chair rocked back and forth, knocking against the back of his legs. His hands fisted as he attempted to restrain the surge of anger pulsing through him. "I never asked for this."

"No one usually does." Giovanni's tone remained calm and soothing. "Most people don't know this magnificent possibility even exists. If they did, they'd be lined up down the lane."

"Camille was the one—"

Giovanni shot forward, cutting off Akiva's complaint. "Were you there when she was killed?"

The intensity in Giovanni's gaze and the tension in his body put Akiva on full alert.

The mood had shifted abruptly. Giovanni looked into his glass as he stirred the red mixture. "Camille was something, wasn't she? She wielded her powers well." Then his features calcified. "Were you there when she died?"

Akiva shook his head more to loosen the bonds Camille had wrapped around him. "No. Not really. We were surrounded and tried to escape, but she was caught."

"And you could do *nothing*"—Giovanni's tone sharpened—"nothing to help her?"

"If I could have, then she would be here now."

"Did you allow her death as revenge for awakening you?"

Akiva shuttered his emotions, veiled his thoughts in case Giovanni attempted to read them. But he had sensed no more probing into his mind. Still, he ventured forward cautiously. "If I had wanted to take revenge on Camille, I would have done so myself."

With a satisfied nod, Giovanni leaned back slowly again, examining the fingernail on his index finger. "Were you two lovers, then?"

The question surprised Akiva, and he sensed Giovanni's flippant question was simply a cover for a greater desire…his desire to know the truth, the root of which Akiva suspected came from jealousy. "No," he lied. "Never."

"She wanted you." Giovanni's gaze slanted toward Akiva. "You had to know that."

"It would not have mattered if she'd been the last woman or blood or—"

"You loved the girl from your past…was that it?"

Akiva's muscles tightened. He couldn't answer. The cold hardness of that long ago monument seeped into him again.

All my life coldly and sadly
The days have gone by
I who dreamed wildly and madly
am happy to die

"Is this one, the woman you brought here," Giovanni asked, "the one you loved?"

"I told you," Akiva said, through gritted teeth, "she's a friend." And yet she wasn't. She was an old lover. A playmate. Yet he had none of those feelings for Rachel any more. His reasons, his purpose, his pain was buried inside the red haze surrounding her sister.

"She's pregnant," Giovanni said as if revealing a big secret, even though it didn't take much of a glance to know the truth about Rachel.

"So?"

"Well, that is *the* problem, you see?"

Akiva shook his head. "No, I don't."

"It is forbidden, not just by me"—Giovanni placed a hand against his chest once more, as if denying his own power and embracing it at the same time—"but by the Great One."

"The Great—"

"The Great One forbids it. Not just for the protection of humans but for our own. You see, killing an infant is the supreme act of defiance. Some have done so accidentally and lived to…well, died to regret it." He chuckled at his own pathetic joke, but then his expression hardened. "An infant is toxic to us. Some say it is because of their innocence. But that's an old vampire's tale. It does not matter why; it matters only what is. And toxic it is. A few vampires have ended their lives in such a way. Those foolish ones who could not understand, who could not adjust. Not many, mind you, but a few." His gaze leveled on Akiva. "You wouldn't have something like that in mind, would you?"

Akiva met the probing stare with his own defiant one. But his mind was reeling, churning, scattering into a thousand shards. He clung once more to his one last hope.

> *Long since my heart has been breaking*
> *Its pain is past*
> *A time has been set to its aching*
> *Peace comes at last.*

Would Giovanni attempt to stop him? He could admit the truth and allow Giovanni to punish him. But he didn't want to die at the hands of a vampire. Or anyone else. He wanted to die on his own terms, when and where he chose. Then it would be too late for Giovanni...or the "Great One" to do anything about it. In a calm, reasonable tone, Akiva answered with a question. "Why would I want to do that?"

"No one knows a man's or vamp's heart, now does he? Not even I. Not even the Great One."

"God knows." Akiva spoke the words so softly he wasn't sure if he'd actually said them aloud, and his voice carried the timbre of his father's, a simple statement his father would have uttered many times, conviction ringing loudly in each syllable. But Akiva wasn't sure he believed that anymore...or maybe ever. It certainly didn't seem true now that he had been awakened. And yet, even in his awareness, some things happened that did not make sense.

"God?" Giovanni's laughter spread outward and engulfed them. "We are our own god."

"Then why do you have to adhere to someone else's rules? Gods make their own rules."

Giovanni's gaze narrowed. "This is why I told Camille that someone with your background was troublesome."

"Because of my belief in God?"

"Because you cannot think outside the box you were raised in. You cannot truly understand."

But he understood far more than Giovanni gave him credit for.

For a moment, he considered asking Giovanni to explain the otherworldly creatures he had seen while in Pennsylvania. Especially the old woman guarding Hannah's little sister. It was like some sort of costume: the ancient sagging skin, gray hair, weakened bones. But the fire in the old woman's gaze not only held heat but power and authority. At first, Akiva had believed the creature was Hannah's grandmother. But then he'd learned the old woman was already dead and buried near his own grave. *Had she been a ghost?* No. The form was solid. Steel girded the voice. When the old woman had stood, she'd had strength beyond measure in her stance.

Maybe Giovanni had never experienced such a creature. Akiva certainly had never seen anything like it in New Orleans. Maybe this place was too dark for such a light.

"Akiva." Giovanni interrupted his thoughts. "You are known for attempting to do things that are forbidden, such as wanting to change your friend, Hannah, without permission."

His mention of her name stoked a fire inside Akiva. So Giovanni knew. Knew more than he was letting on.

"It is why Camille went after you, tried to stop you."

"You sent her?"

Giovanni's mouth pulled downward to one side, making Akiva believe Giovanni regretted his decision.

"Why her?" Akiva demanded.

"I trusted her." The muscles in Giovanni's face sagged

for only a second, until he gave himself a stern shake and straightened in his chair, leaning heavily on one of the armrests, as if his momentary lapse into regret was now over. "There was a time when I would have given her anything. Anything. But I suppose she was wrong to trust me, to do my bidding."

Thrusting what he hoped was a stake into Giovanni's heart, Akiva spoke. "Then it is you who are responsible for her death."

Giovanni didn't flinch or grimace. He took the verbal assault as if he deserved it.

Finally he looked up. "You may go now, Akiva." His lips tightened over the words. "But know that even death won't protect you from such a vile act. You have been duly warned."

Chapter Nineteen

Discarded limbs lay askew among the cricket and cockroach remains, and prosthetics and crutches hung from the walls, which might be appropriate for an old hospital or museum of medicine, but this interior room resided in the bowels of the chapel at the St. Roch Cemetery, in the heart of New Orleans.

Roberto had told Roc of his namesake, Saint Roch, months earlier. But Roc paid as little attention then as he did when his own mother had told him she'd named him for the beloved saint. It all seemed foolish and sentimental and had about as much to do with him as a pair of tap shoes.

"This is what you wanted me to see?" Roc asked Brody, who'd called him earlier in the day and simply said, "Meet me at St. Roch Cemetery. You'll want to see this." Roc had prepared himself to see yellow tape for a murder scene and a body covered by a plastic sheet. He'd imagined peering underneath and seeing blue eyes staring blankly back at him. But there was no body here. No remains. Just these plastic body parts apparently left in honor of the saint attributed with healing and miracles.

Inside the chapel, the light was dim as a tomb, creating more shadows than light. Brody stood beside Roc, looking over the testaments to the miracles St. Roch had performed. "Just something I thought you'd find interesting. Over the

years, folks have brought tokens to honor St. Roch for the
miracles of healing. You've heard of St. Roch, right?"

"Yeah."

"His divine intervention saved lives during a yellow fever
epidemic back in the 1800s." Brody clapped a hand on Roc's
shoulder. "Think you can live up to that?"

An odd question, which Roc decided his former partner
on the police force was simply teasing him with, but the jab
came too close to his doubts about his abilities to destroy
vampires and help anyone, including Rachel. "Next time
yellow fever hits the city," Roc said, "give me a call, and
we'll see."

"Deal." Brody's grin broadened.

Roc remained silent and headed back toward the door.
Eager to leave the stifling heat inside the chapel, he stepped
onto the marble step, momentarily blinded by the sunshine
pouring over the monuments.

A long driveway led out to the wrought-iron gate, each
side crowded with tombs and monuments with angels and
crucifixes guarding the dearly departed. Sunlight reflected off
the stonework, and Roc slipped on his sunglasses to block
the sharp glare. Brody snapped his in place too, and led Roc
around to the back of St. Roch's to a mausoleum. Many
of the vaults had marble vases filled with red, yellow, and
pink flowers, the plastic ones remaining vibrant in spite of the
heat, while others wilted or turned brown under the relent-
less summer assault.

"So what did you want me to see?" Roc asked.

"A little gris-gris."

"What's that?"

"Voodoo crap. Somebody putting a spell on a lover or
husband or neighbor." He veered right, crossing slabs of

marble, where some names of the deceased had faded while other carvings remained clear and bold through the years. He stopped next to a statue of a mourning woman bending to place flowers on the grave of a loved one. Nestled in the juncture of hip and thigh was a bundle of mismatched items that would have better belonged in a junkyard.

"Looks like trash."

"Good thing you've got me here to interpret." Brody knelt and fingered a bunch of feathers. "Black candle. Rooster feathers. See those pins jabbed in that doll? This is for sure a spell." He picked up the candle, and Roc protested. "Ain't no fingerprints. And ain't no law against this stuff anyways. But this is what I thought you'd wanna see."

Under the candle was a photograph. Before Roc could get a good look, he recognized the white *kapp* and somber clothes. Then he studied the face—Hannah.

"You know her?" Brody asked.

Roc nodded. "Her sister is the one missing."

"Then you might be right. The one you're looking for might already be dead."

A sick sensation gripped Roc's stomach. "Are you saying this Akiva is into voodoo?"

"I don't know. But maybe we can find the answers tonight."

Roc quirked an eyebrow at Brody. "Tonight?"

"Yeah. What's the date?" Brody asked.

"June twenty—"

"It's St. John's Eve. Biggest night on the voodoo calendar. And I have us a party to go to."

CHAPTER TWENTY

S HE WAS YOUNG, NO more than fifteen or sixteen. Skinny jeans hugged her narrow hips and twiglike legs. A flimsy top showed off the soft curve of her breasts, and its shortness flashed glimpses of her pierced belly button when she moved. She walked with a confident stride at a feisty pace, swinging her backside in a look-but-don't-touch fashion. Scooping up a penny off the sidewalk, she revealed a peace-sign tattoo low on her back. But it was when she reached the corner of the street that Akiva read her hesitation. A group of construction workers whistled at her, and she shot the finger toward them, which only made them laugh and call out obscenities. And behind her kiss-my-ass demeanor, fear lurked in her eyes.

Akiva walked straight toward her, his head bent as he fumbled with his wallet, and then his shoulder knocked into her. It was a hard enough blow to gain her attention but not enough to bruise or send her sprawling. She elbowed him back, a spunky gesture, and he bent double, grimaced, held his breath. His wallet fell from his fingers to the sidewalk. He left it there long enough for her to glimpse the hundreds spilling out.

"Whoa there, sugar. I surrender." He grabbed for his wallet and placed a hand over his gut. "That's some punch you got." He raised one hand as if he were in a holdup and offered her his wallet, which she took.

She flipped it open and pulled out his license, which was one he'd had made for times like this. "Jacob Riley, huh?" She glanced at him, but the pull of the cash was too much. She yanked out a few hundred dollar bills, and he watched her jaw drop before she recovered her shock.

"You hard up, sugar? Take what you need."

She slanted her eyes at him, studied him for a moment, then shoved the bills back into his wallet and pushed it toward him. "You're crazy for carrying that much around here. Someone with more weapons than I got will kill ya sure as lookin' at ya and take that wad you got in your pants."

"I'm not too worried."

She gave him a once-over. "How come?"

"'Cause I got you for protection." He patted his stomach. "You pack a wallop."

She grinned.

He hooked his arm through hers and walked her in the opposite direction she had been heading. "Come on, I'll buy you dinner."

"I guess you can afford it," she said, smiling. But then she yanked her arm free—he'd made too quick of a move to touch her—and she stopped in the middle of the sidewalk. Folks streamed around them on either side. "But I ain't going anywhere with you."

"A smart move." He shrugged as if it didn't matter to him. "Well, then I'll bid you *adieu*." He turned and strode two full steps before she called to him.

"Jacob Riley."

He looked back at her. "I go by Jake. What do you want now? The keys to my Jag?"

"Maybe." She laughed as if delighted with the idea. "So where you gonna eat?"

He nodded toward an Italian restaurant where he'd taken a few of his meals. "Dario knows what he's doing."

Her gaze traveled across the street to the restaurant with a chalkboard out front listing the day's special. "Well...maybe it wouldn't be so horrible..."

"Eating with me?"

She nodded, still somewhat hesitant.

"It's up to you. What'd you say your name is?"

"Julia."

He gave a slight bow and clicked his heels together. "Well, Julia, if you'd care to dine with *moi*..."

She grinned and stepped toward him, hooking her arm through his proffered one. "You aren't from around here, are you?"

"I am not. And yet, New Orleans is now part of me. But you aren't from here, either. Just two vagabonds searching for some place to belong."

"How'd you know?" she asked. "I mean, that I'm not from here."

He twisted his features with an isn't-it-obvious look. "You're too sophisticated for these yahoos on the bayou."

Her chest puffed out slightly. "I'm from Big D."

"You're a long way from home, young lady."

"I got my reasons."

"Don't you have a hot date tonight?"

"Later. I always keep 'em waiting."

Chuckling, he strolled her across the street and into the dimly lit restaurant with flickering candles on the tables. He plied her with calamari, fettuccini alfredo, and cannoli. She ate like she hadn't eaten in a month. He sipped a glass of wine and let the red liquid flow through his veins, both lulling his appetite and stoking it.

He learned Julia had had enough of a boyfriend in Texas…a guy named Bruce…and her folks ragging on her…always wanting to know where she was and who she was with and getting in her business…and teachers who didn't know nothing from nothing. His focus lifted as he watched her swallow and the muscles in her long neck contract and release.

"You sure you don't want some?" she asked, holding out the cream-filled pastry toward him. A glob of the cream clung to her upper lip.

He shook his head. "Not now. You go ahead and enjoy."

Finally, she shoved her plate away and leaned her elbow on the table with a sigh. "So, now what?"

He watched the candlelight play over her features as she smiled uncertainly. "'Smiles form the channels of a future tear.'"

Her smile faded. "What?"

"Nothing. Your smile is disarming. But I bet you know that."

Her gaze shifted as if she didn't understand what he was saying. "It's one of your best weapons."

"Oh!" She grinned broad enough for a dimple to wink at him. "Sometimes I don't know what you're talking about."

"You're not the first to say that." He reached forward as if to take her hand but instead took hold of her wrist, felt her pulse strong and vibrant, and twisted her arm slightly to gaze at the hot-pink watch she wore. "Is this time correct?"

"Nah. It quit."

He smiled. "Why do you wear it, then?"

She shrugged and pulled her hand back. "I like it."

He nodded. "It's late. Come. I will walk you home."

She remained sitting when he half rose. "I don't have a…I don't have a place."

He seated himself again. "Where do you live, then?"

"On the streets. I thought you knew." Her gaze dropped

to the red-and-white checked tablecloth. "And I figured you wanted another kind of payment."

He gave a lengthy study of her. She looked so vulnerable, so young. Then he stood. "Come on. I know of a safe place you can stay. You'll have no worries." At least not anymore.

Her eyes rounded, full of unshed tears. "Okay...I guess you seem safe."

Safe. He wanted to laugh. If only she knew. If only he'd known. But he hadn't been looking for safety when he'd met Camille. He'd been looking for adventure.

Jacob had met Camille at a secret meeting nearly three years before, after a whispered invitation came to Jacob via a guy who provided him with weed. Jacob had taken Rachel, and together they'd watched the regular worshipers strip naked and dance around to the beat of drums, their bodies glistening with sweat and firelight. It had been a turn on.

The most exotic woman he'd ever seen walked up to them, smiling seductively. "You are new here?" she asked in a throaty voice, making Jacob's tight.

Instantly, he'd wanted her. And if Rachel hadn't been with him, he would have made a move. "Yeah," he'd managed. "I am."

She flung her long curtain of black hair off her shoulder. "You should join in." Her gaze raked down his chest to his groin, and he felt his own reaction to her invitation. "It's much more fun that way."

"We're just visiting." Rachel had tugged on his hand. "Maybe we should...uh..."

Reluctantly, Jacob had allowed himself to be pulled along by Rachel, even though the woman's black eyes made him feel like he was slowly falling head first into oblivion.

"Come back," she had said, a whisper of a smile curling her lips. *Or had it only been a whisper in his head?*

After that, Rachel decided she'd had enough of New Orleans. Jacob figured she was scared off by the crazy rituals those folks had, like boiling a live chicken and dancing with snakes. She took a bus home to Pennsylvania. But Jacob had stayed. The woman with the black hair and blacker eyes had beckoned to him in his dreams and turned his daydreams to torture.

So he'd gone back, waiting for another secret meeting. But the warehouse had been vacant. He'd tried again and again, waiting and watching impatiently, his body tight with need and longing, remembering those black eyes summoning him in his sleep.

Finally he had arrived on the correct night, when the parking lot was a jumble of cars and the steady, rhythmic beat of the drums echoed through the warehouse. Jacob pushed impatiently through the crowd in search of her.

Just when he thought she wasn't there, that he would never see her again, she appeared almost out of nowhere. Suddenly, she was standing before him, as if she had been the one waiting for him. Her sensuous mouth glistened red and vibrant, curling upward on one side. "You came back," she walked toward him, her hips swaying, her breasts jiggling beneath a flimsy dress. And those eyes looked deep into his soul.

He couldn't speak or move but just stood there watching her.

"Would you like a drink?" she'd asked.

He took the one she offered and downed it. He had never tasted anything as sweet and potent, and his thoughts and visions wavered, the drumbeat resonating through him.

"You feel it, no?"

He nodded.

Slowly, she slipped the straps of her dress off her shoulders and wiggled her body until the silky material pooled at her feet. Her body was a smorgasbord of delights, and he responded eagerly and readily in hopes of sampling.

Then she turned her back on him and walked toward the group of worshippers who danced in some ancient rhythm. But he heard her call over the drumbeat and chanting, "Come, Jacob."

Now, he looked at this young girl…a girl searching for a place to belong, a place to be safe. He could change her. She looked at him with trusting eyes.

It was what he wanted her to think: that she could believe him, trust him. She just didn't know she was placing herself in the hands of someone who no longer had feelings of hope or regret. He'd watched her gorge herself on food, and now it was his turn. He smiled and held out his hand toward her. "Come."

CHAPTER TWENTY-ONE

THE MUSIC WAS SO loud it could have awakened the dead. The syncopated drumbeat, which sounded as if it was rumbling across the African plains, rocketed through the cavernous warehouse and thrummed through Roc.

Brody had brought him to the St. John's Eve voodoo ritual, a festivity Roc had learned went back to the Druids when they celebrated summer solstice; then the Christians overtook it with St. John the Baptist's birthday. Voodooienne Marie Laveau married a few Catholic beliefs to Dominican voodoo, and voila, new traditions were born, resulting in this party.

Roc wasn't sure what to believe at this point, nor was he sure where Brody had gone since he'd brought him to this remote warehouse district. He'd suspected there was a connection between voodoo rituals and what Jacob Fisher had gotten himself mixed up in during his time in New Orleans, and the gris-gris found in St. Roch Cemetery solidified his suspicion. Now he just had to figure out a way to connect the dots and create a path to Akiva.

"They once celebrated St. John's Eve out on the shore of Lake Pontchartrain," Brody had explained earlier. "Back in the 1800s, the high-and-mighty wealthy citizens of New Orleans would go and watch the festivities. Some would even take part. But during the last few decades, voodoo worshippers went underground, so to speak, and kept their rituals secret. Which is how so many rumors get started about them, and which makes it doubly hard to find out the truth."

"How'd you find this place?" Roc asked.

"I have my own secrets."

The time when they'd known and anticipated each other's thoughts, uncertainties, and decisions was long past.

Roc stood on the outskirts of this gathering, surprised at all the people—different races and ethnicities formed in a loose circle in a wide space on the warehouse floor. They were already well into the ceremony, swaying to the beat as if they were in some sort of trance. In the center stood a woman with a red drape of a dress, which touched the floor, and a yellow turban wrapped about her head. She held a wooden box with bells attached all over it, which tinkled and clamored enticingly as she set it on a table and opened the lid. Immediately, a snake reared its head through the opening, and those gathered gasped. Some shook as if they'd received an electrical shock.

"You with him?" A black man stepped beside Roc and nodded toward Brody, who was across the room in a small group, observing the participants. Brody seemed to know these folks and vice versa. It gave Roc an unsettled feeling. Hadn't Brody said it had been a while since he'd heard anything about voodoo rituals? But then again, a cop had to rub elbows with all kinds.

A sheen of sweat made the black man's shaved head glisten in the candlelight. He wore a loose-fitting shirt and shorts. His feet were bare on the concrete floor.

"Yeah," Roc answered and stuck out a hand in greeting. "Roc."

"Luis." The man clasped Roc's hand. His palm was callused

and as thick as his Cajun accent. With a quick squeeze, he released Roc's hand. "Brody says you okay."

"As okay as I know to be."

The man grinned. "That's good. I like." He clapped Roc on the shoulder. "You seen this before?"

"No. I'm a virgin, I guess."

Luis laughed. "That's our priestess there. She loves virgins."

Roc stared at the woman with the turban, who was allowing a snake to lick her cheek. Obviously, she loved a lot of things Roc had no inclination to learn about, but he was here to watch, to learn, to know. He'd given up the right to turn away from the bizarre, the macabre, or even pure evil when he'd become a cop, much less a vampire hunter. Both in and outside the police department he'd witnessed unprecedented greed, corruption, and treachery. This was the land of lawlessness. Staring into it with wide-open eyes had destroyed any hope he'd ever had of making a difference.

He remembered something his friend Anthony had read to him. Not a bedtime story by any means, the ancient text had said something about "the lawless ones." Were these, the participants in this strange ritual, the ones Anthony had spoken of? Had the priest known?

"Brody," Luis said, interrupting his thoughts, "says you have the gift of sight."

"Sight, huh?" Roc glanced across the way at his expartner. Brody's head was bent as he spoke to a woman dressed in colors rivaling the priestess's. Had Brody told some story about Roc to get him in the door and accepted? "I've seen more than I ever cared to."

"Ain't that the truth?" A vein pulsed along Luis's scalp. "You'll see some things tonight. You just waits."

Roc watched the priestess dance around, gyrating her body

like a snake slithering through the grass, reaching toward a half-naked man. When their hands connected, the man jerked and trembled, shook and shivered all over, then danced like a whirlwind, spinning and leaping around the circle.

"That's sure nothing I ever saw in Pennsylvania."

"Oh, sure," the man said, "don't know of nothin' like that up there."

"It's Amish country," Roc explained, "and they're a bit on the conservative side."

"That so? If you ran into these folks on the street, you'd never believe they could be involved in this. They's from all walks of life. We gots doctors and lawyers. Heck, if you was to say they was here, they'd sue your ass. I reckon you never knows about folks though."

"I reckon."

"You from Pennsylvania then?"

"Nah, I'm a Louisiana boy, born and raised in St. Tammany Parish. But I've been up North for a few months."

"That right? I knows someone from Pennsylvania, nows that I thinks on it."

"Oh, yeah? He Amish?" Roc half joked, but he kept his gaze flitting back and forth between the man and the action in the center of the warehouse, where the worshippers were trembling from their heads to their bare feet. Many moaned and groaned as their bodies rocked and gyrated to the drum's rhythm.

"Yeah, yeah, I think maybe he was Amish at that. Or had been. Or knew of 'em anyways. I can't recall just what now."

"He still around?" Roc indicated the group of folks dancing to the dark rhythm. "We might have something to chat about."

"Might at that. Seems to me he still around. Far as I know.

Ain't seen him in a while, but he used to come here. I sees him out there hoodooing with the best of 'em." He snapped his fingers twice, trying to jog his memory. "Now what *was* that fella's name?"

Roc waited, his muscles tightening with anticipation, but he tried to restrain his eagerness.

"Hmm…it was one of those common Bible names."

"John?" Roc suggested.

"Maybe. Don't know." Luis's interest in the topic faded, shifting into acute avoidance.

"Maybe it was—"

"No, don't know. I probably get it wrong anyways. I do that." Luis's body swayed with the beat, the muscles in his arms flexing and veins popping to the surface of his dark skin. "It's getting heated out there."

Roc watched as those dancing began to shed their clothes as a snake might shed its skin, rubbing against one another and leaving their clothes on the warehouse floor. When he glanced back at Luis, the man was gone. He'd joined the dancers and was sandwiched between two women; one straddled his thigh, rocking in an ancient sexual rhythm, and the other cupped his backside, her arms snaking around his torso. Feeling voyeuristic, Roc backed away from the circle and leaned against the wall.

He'd pushed the man too hard, too fast. For some reason, Luis hadn't wanted to remember the man from Pennsylvania. *Was it possibly Jacob? Akiva? Or someone else?*

The rhythm of the drum and dancers became more frenzied, the tempo picking up and commanding the dancers to follow. Some drifted off into the shadows and others stayed in the circle, going from partner to partner. Roc's own body began to respond. He glanced down at his hand and rubbed a bruise on his thumb. *What was he doing here? And how would being here help him find Rachel?*

"You looking for the Amish girl?" A voice came from his left. A woman bent over and unstrapped her sandals in an unhurried pace, her hands sliding along her calf and foot. She couldn't have been much more than the legal age, but he'd learned a long time ago it was often hard to tell women's ages. She had skin the color of melted caramels. Her foot was braced on the seat of a metal folding chair, and her skirt draped downward toward the floor.

"Don't look at me," she hissed, never glancing in his direction. Her movements didn't quicken or slow. She kept her focus on first one sandal then the other.

Roc glanced back at the dancers, but his full attention was on the woman only a few feet away from him. Through tight lips, he said, "I am looking for—"

"She not far. From what I hear."

"And what's that?"

She bent down and placed her sandals carefully under the chair. "She in danger, this Rachel."

His gaze darted sideways again—the woman straightened and began unbuttoning her dress, working her way down a long row traveling from neckline to hem—then he jerked his gaze away. "How so?"

"Akiva have her."

Roc's heart thrummed, jerking and pulsing in the frenzied swell of the drumbeat. "Where?"

"You figure that out, mister. She close. Just so you know, you didn't hear nothin' from me. But take her and run for your life."

He looked back at the woman, who let her dress slide off her shoulders to land in a soft pool at her feet. But he wasn't looking at her shapely form. He stared straight into coal-black eyes, and the darkness told him more than he'd expected. Then she strode forward with long, determined strides to join the dancers, leaving him with a shiver of heat.

CHAPTER TWENTY-TWO

*H*AD ACACIA JUST CONFESSED *she had killed? And drank blood? And did all sorts of abominations?*

Rachel's vision wavered. Blood pooled in her legs. She braced a hand against the desk to keep from passing out.

"Orphelia says I'm bad." Acacia shrugged a narrow shoulder. "I guess she's right. I do bad things sometimes."

Rachel sat very still, feeling as if her heart had frozen. A portion of her brain began to pray fervently, frantically— "Oh, Lord…help me." Over and over again she thought the same prayer without any elaboration.

The girl was looking at her like she wanted forgiveness, which was something Rachel didn't have authority to give. But it did give her a place to start. "Everybody makes mistakes."

"I s'pose. But I keep making the same ones over and over. Just can't help myself."

"You mean k…killing people?"

Acacia tilted her head as if contemplating the sin of murder. "Nah. I gotta do that. How else would I live? I mean, really. Do you worry about killing cows and pigs and fish and stuff so's you can eat?"

Could this child do something worse than murder? Or was her whole right and wrong so skewed she had no idea what right and wrong truly was? Were people now simply animals to her? When Rachel spoke, her voice trembled. "So…what do you do that's so bad?"

Acacia giggled then pressed the tips of her fingers against her pink lips. "I play tricks. Usually on the other vamps. I rearranged a couple of apartments, moving Stephanos's stuff to Erika's, and hers to his." Another giggle bubbled up in Acacia. "Boy were they mad. Orphelia just laughed and said, 'You is bad, Acacia. Real bad.'"

Suddenly an idea sparked in Rachel, and she took it as divine revelation or intervention.

Attempting a smile, Rachel feared it might be a look of revulsion instead. "You know"—she leaned toward the little girl and tried for a conspiratorial camaraderie—"we could play a trick on Orphelia and Akiva right now. Wouldn't that be fun?"

"Oh, no. Akiva don't never laugh."

Rachel leaned back, tapped her chin. "You're right." She remained quiet for a moment and let the seed she'd planted in Acacia start to grow. "It's a bad idea. I shouldn't have even suggested it."

Feigning interest in the fried chicken, Rachel picked at the bones but couldn't manage to swallow any of the meat. Her stomach was churning and heaving with images: rituals she'd witnessed while in New Orleans with Jacob, now mixed with pure imaginings of what this girl did, and what Jacob…now Akiva…did, and what he wanted to do. She tried to block the pictures from her mind, but they assaulted her. The prayer she'd been praying was silenced by her fear.

Another giggle from Acacia shifted Rachel's focus. The young girl's dark eyes glinted with mischief, and Rachel's heart began to beat more steadily with hope. "What was it you had in mind?"

Rachel shook her head and shoved the scraps of chicken into the paper sack. "It was just a silly idea."

"It's okay. You can tell me," the girl insisted. "We don't have to do it. We could just laugh about it ourselves."

Rachel managed a smile. "That's a good idea. Well, I was thinking we could hide…you know out in the big area, among the shelves somewhere, and then when Akiva came back, he'd have to search for us. And then we'd pop out of our hiding place and surprise him."

Acacia laughed, the sound so innocent and yet full of something darker. "I got a better idea." She jumped up off the bed and rushed to the door. "We could…come on, and I'll show ya."

Rachel's heart pounded. Carefully, so as not to spoil the mood, she stood, her joints stiff from sitting for so long, slipped her bare feet into her tennis shoes and followed after the young girl, who didn't just walk but frolicked out the door and out onto the landing, like she was chasing butterflies in a meadow.

"Isn't this fun?" Acacia turned to look at Rachel, her face split in a big grin, like they were playmates.

Rachel nodded and held tight to the side rail.

"So where should we hide?" The girl looked down into the warehouse from the landing outside Rachel's room. "I know! We could go up to those beams."

"I think I'm too big to do any climbing like that."

"Oh, yeah, I forgot. I can change, but you can't. Well, we could—"

"Is it day or night?" Rachel asked.

"Night."

"Then that's perfect."

"Why?"

"We could go outside, and Akiva wouldn't see us. *We* could see him approaching. And when he goes inside, we can laugh, and he won't hear us."

"You're right! If we laugh inside, he'd know for sure."

Rachel's heart skipped ahead of itself. "Then when he comes back outside, we'll surprise him."

Acacia giggled, bending slightly at the waist as if she couldn't contain the laughter. "I like it! He'll be mad, but Orphelia will be with him. She'll get a good laugh out of it. And she won't let him hurt us."

The girl zipped down the stairs, her footsteps light. Rachel descended more slowly, yet her heart pumped like she had run the entire way. When they reached the bottom of the warehouse floor, they walked together through the dark. Occasionally, Rachel saw red eyes glaring at them—mice or rats, she suspected.

Acacia skipped ahead and turned back toward Rachel. "What's it like to carry a baby inside you like that?"

The girl's question surprised Rachel. It was a typical question from a child. And this was a child. Although she wasn't a child. Or was she? Confused, Rachel focused on what the girl had asked. "It's nice. And sometimes it's a bit uncomfortable."

"Does the baby move around in there?"

"Sure."

The girl stared at her tummy for a long while. "That must be weird, huh?"

Acacia's eyes looked moist, and Rachel wondered if she was thinking of her own mother. The hardened young killer still had such innocence about her. But no more questions were asked; Acacia simply turned and led the way toward the door.

"I better peek outside and make sure Akiva isn't coming."

"Okay." Rachel tried to act casual and completely unconcerned, as if she wasn't about to bolt for freedom. She offered up a prayer of desperation, not for herself, but for her baby.

What would she do? Make a run for it? Wait for another opportunity? But if she waited too long and Akiva came back, then her one chance would be lost.

The door creaked open, and Acacia stepped outside boldly, confidently, and disappeared into the darkness. What would it be like to be this little girl and have no fears? As it was, Rachel trembled all over, scared to move forward, scared to stay where she was. She glanced behind her then stared at the door. Her heart pounded heavily and awkwardly. Her limbs wobbled, as if her legs would collapse under her and she'd crumple to the floor. *For ye have not received the spirit of bondage again to fear; but ye have received the spirit of adoption, whereby we cry, Abba, Father.* She bowed her head, fingered the tie of her prayer *kapp*, and simply whispered, "Abba, Father."

A calm settled over her and strengthened her from the inside out. Rachel laid her palm against the warm metal door and waited, counting to herself and wondering if she should follow Acacia. But she sensed she should wait. *Was it fear guiding her? Or was it God's steady hand?* One minute passed. Then another. With each second ticking away, Rachel's heart sped up until the blood pounded against her eardrums and her head felt as swollen as her belly.

Then the door pushed toward her, and Acacia's face appeared. "Rachel!"

"I'm right here."

"Come on! Let's—"

Acacia was suddenly jerked backward, her eyes widening. Her mouth opened, but her words were cut off.

Rachel caught the door with her hand. An outside light shone down on a face she had seen before, a face like an avenging angel. The man had dark coloring, dark hair, dark eyes, dark expression, yet his eyes were only brown, more coffee-stained than the solid black ones of Akiva, Orphelia, and Acacia. She'd met him somewhere…*New Orleans?* No, back home at Josef's family farm.

She had time only to open her mouth, no solid thought even forming, before she, too, was yanked outside into the wet-blanket heat.

What was happening? How was he here? Why was he here? She sensed maybe he was an answer to her prayer.

"Rachel," he said, urgency in his tone, the fierceness in his gaze alarming her more than Acacia's black one. "Who is this?"

He held Acacia in some kind of a viselike grip, her arm wrenched behind her back. But Acacia's expression was not pained or fearful, more tolerant. The calm look frightened Rachel even more, for the girl had boasted of doing things Rachel never could have imagined. Which put this man's life and her own at stake now.

"H…her name is Acacia."

"Is she a vampire?" he asked.

"A vam—?"

"One of *them*," he added. "Like Akiva."

Before Rachel could answer, Acacia moved with amazing speed, spinning away from the man. But he had tethered a leather strap to her wrist. When she lunged at him, he produced a wicked wooden stake and pointed it at the girl's chest.

"Wait! Please," Rachel cried. No matter what Acacia had done in the past, Rachel wanted to help and protect the young girl.

Acacia tipped her head sideways, her face looking so young and innocent, and she blinked those big black eyes. The silly game was now over; the playmates were now on opposite teams. With strength coiled in her petite muscles, she pounced, knocking the stake out of the way. The almost three-foot piece of carved wood arced through the air before crashing to the ground. Rachel's gaze had followed it, and when she looked back, Acacia and the man were grappling and struggling and rolling on the ground.

The girl snapped and snarled like a rabid dog. The man pushed his arm straight, trying to keep the girl from biting him. But she lunged again, and her teeth sank into his shoulder. His face compressed in pain, and his mouth opened with a silent scream. He kicked the girl off him, but she was back in an instant, and they were locked once again in a deadly battle.

Rachel didn't know what to do. *Stay? Help? Run?* Her heart raced as if she were making a run for it, but her feet were planted, unable to move.

His gaze locked with Rachel's. "The stake," he gasped. "Get it."

The piece of wood looked like a stalagmite. Or was it stalactite? She'd learned the difference in school, but she couldn't remember now.

"Rachel!" The man grunted and bit out her name.

Stumbling sideways, she retrieved the stake. She tried to hand it to him, but he tumbled and rolled over the ground with Acacia. He pushed with both hands against the girl's shoulders, trying to get her off of him. But the tiny orphan had incredible strength.

"Stab her!" he hollered. "Now!"

Rachel hesitated. *Who was he? Who was the girl, really?* She didn't believe in violence or killing, and yet…she couldn't let the girl hurt this man. She couldn't let Akiva hurt her baby. And if she didn't escape now, while Akiva was gone, all might be lost completely.

She didn't want this man to hurt Acacia either. She was but a child. But somehow the girl was winning against a full-grown man. Blood ran in rivulets down his arm. His elbow kept buckling, unable to push the girl away. Blood smeared Acacia's smooth chin and cheek. She snapped and snarled, trying to get at him. If she succeeded, would she come for Rachel next?

When only inches separated the man and girl, Rachel thrust the stake between their bodies.

It jerked out of her hands. The man grunted and thrust forward. Acacia's eyes widened. Then she fell back but could go only so far with the tether about her wrist. She stumbled and then collapsed onto the ground, the stake pierced through her chest.

Bent in pain, and yet determination powering him, the man staggered forward and yanked the stake out of the girl's chest. Blood rushed out, pooling around the girl's abdomen, soaking her dress.

Rachel couldn't move, couldn't think, couldn't manage to do anything. In horror, she stared as the man bound Acacia with the leather strap to a metal pipe sticking out of the ground. Then with a knife he yanked from inside his boot, he slit the girl's throat.

A gasp sounded as if it came from far away, but when the man turned to stare at Rachel, she realized she had made the sound.

"She'll die quicker that way. And we don't have time to waste." He held his hand against his wounded shoulder and stepped toward Rachel. "Hannah and Levi sent me to find you. Do you have anything inside that you need?"

It took what seemed like several minutes for the man's words to process through her brain. *Hannah. Levi.* She clung to the names, her heart pounding, filling her ears with a thumping sound. Then her gaze fell again on the man waiting on her. *What had he asked her?*

The girl was making gurgling and gagging sounds, and her black gaze sought Rachel's. But the man stepped between Rachel and the girl.

"Rachel"—his voice was firm and full of authority, like her father's—"we can't stay here. Do you need anything from inside?"

No. There was nothing here for her. Nothing she wanted or cared to remember. She shook her head and realized she was shaking all over.

"Okay, then, we have to go. Now!"

CHAPTER TWENTY-THREE

Is it for fear to wet a widow's eye
That thou consum'st thyself in single life?
Ah! If thou issueless shalt hap to die,
The world will wail thee, like a makeless wife;
The world will be thy widow, and still weep
That thou no form of thee hast left behind,
When every private widow well may keep
By children's eyes her husband's shape in mind.

WITH SHAKESPEARE'S SONNET LINING his thoughts, Akiva returned to the macabre warehouse with all of its carcasses of parade vessels picked over by vandals. He had taken a detour on the way back, pausing long enough to pick up a bite and finished her off in the alley, and his senses were sharp. The wooden structures and metal bits gleamed in the moonlight. The night was deathly quiet: not a sound in his footsteps, not a flutter of a bird's wing, not even a breeze to stir the heat.

He moved fearlessly through the wreckage and debris and rounded the corner of the building. A scent in the air slowed his pace. He sniffed again. It wasn't the ripe odor of fresh blood. It was a tainted smell he'd smelled only once before—when Camille had—

And he was already running before he finished the thought.

He stopped at the sight of the body splayed out in front of the side door. The short, skinny limbs had a lifeless tilt. The head tipped back at an abnormal angle, revealing a gaping slash along the throat. Dark blood coated the neck, chest, and abdomen, pooling on the concrete around the body. The eyes, vacant and void, stared up toward the night sky.

His pace slowed as he stepped over the body, not even looking down at the girl, and flung open the warehouse door. He wrenched it from its hinges and sent it cartwheeling across the yard, crashing into a float's base.

A low hum greeted him inside. He stalked toward the back, his body shrinking, changing, and morphing as he tore through the building and flew up past the stairs to the second level.

The door was open. Rachel was gone.

Akiva emitted a low growl as he changed shape again, his joints popping into place, his limbs lengthening. He lobbed the bed against one wall, smashed the chair, and pounded the desk until it shattered and collapsed under the force of his clenched fists.

Heaving with each breath, Akiva whirled back around toward the broken pieces in the room. His insides jumbled together and broke apart. *Where was she? Where did she go?*

It didn't matter, because he would find her. No matter what. Once more, his thoughts returned to Shakespeare.

> *Look, what an unthrift in the world doth spend*
> *Shifts but his place, for still the world enjoys it;*
> *But beauty's waste hath in the world an end,*
> *And kept unus'd, the user so destroys it.*
> *No love toward others in that bosom sits*
> *That on himself such murderous shame commits.*

Anger pulsing through him, he took off into the night. As he ran, his body morphed once more, folding, transforming, and emerging into a compact form with expansive wings. He beat the air, and wind rushed against his face. Gliding, feeling the drifts and currents pushing and pulling him, he soared over bridges and roadways, houses and cars. When he'd first been changed, this was the only place he'd found solace— the wind in his face, the air lifting and buoying him on a fast current that was better than any rush or surge of adrenaline. It was where he found peace. If only temporarily.

But now where should he go? What could he do? He swooped and swerved, snapping his wings with a firmness that be- trayed his anger. *Would Rachel simply head for home, back to Pennsylvania? Or would she hide?* Someone must have helped her escape. He couldn't imagine she had killed Acacia all by herself. *So who was with her? Who could be in New Orleans?*

Not Hannah. Not Levi. It had to be that blasted hunter, whom he'd met in Pennsylvania. Akiva had wanted to clap him on the back for killing Camille. But this time, Roc Girouard would have to die. And he would make Rachel suffer too.

I have a rendezvous with Death
At some disputed barricade,
When Spring comes back with rustling shade
And apple-blossoms fill the air—
I have a rendezvous with Death
When Spring brings back blue days and fair.

Seeger's poem sharpened his senses, and he honed in on the apartment building where he had a room and plunged downward. Orphelia wasn't in her usual spot on the stoop, so he swept through the doorway and up the stairs, shifting and changing, his limbs expanding. His movements were smooth, and he swept up the stairs to the first landing, not going all the way to the top to his own room. He stopped on the landing and faced a closed door. He knocked once, then twice, and had to wait a long time until the door opened.

"Ye-e-e-s?" Stephanos peered through the narrow space, a smile curling his wide, garish mouth. His hand slid down the opening of his gold satin shirt. He wore a red velveteen jacket that ended with a sweeping sleeve, and the tail touched the floor at his heels. "What can I do for you?"

"I need something."

Stephanos flicked his collar outward. "I'm entertaining."

Akiva heard a high-pitched squeal and jouncing of what sounded like bed springs. He doubted Stephanos's companion viewed the situation as entertainment. "Who could help me find someone?"

"Human or vamp?"

"Human."

"You want a cop, then." He rubbed his chest. "And that would be a new blood we recently acquired. That brat Acacia actually did it without Giovanni's permission." He shrugged. "But it's been useful, I suppose. His name is—" He stopped abruptly, and one corner of his mouth curled upward. "And what are you gonna do for me?"

Akiva was in no mood to play games. "What do you want?"

Stephanos's smile broadened.

Akiva braced himself, hands clenching in defiance. "Not that."

Stephanos laughed. "I'm not like Giovanni. No boys for me."

"You want a girl, then?"

"I want the one you brought here."

"Done."

With a flourish of his wrist, Stephanos gave a slight bow. "Then you're looking for a vamp named Brydon."

Akiva flushed with the excitement of the chase. He would take pleasure in killing Roc Girouard, such great pleasure.

———

It may be he shall take my hand
And lead me into his dark land
And close my eyes and quench my breath—
It may be I shall pass him still.
I have a rendezvous with Death
On some scarred slope of battered hill,
When Spring comes round again this year
And the first meadow-flowers appear.

As the stanza rang in his head and drove his excitement higher, Akiva stepped toward Stephanos. "Where do I find this Brydon?"

Amusement glinted in the flamboyant vampire's black eyes. "And, what," he said slowly, as if leading a reluctant horse, "will you do for me?"

Akiva banged his fist against the door, which swung wide. Behind Stephanos, he saw the edge of a bed and a bare foot with red toenail polish secured around the ankle by a silk scarf. The foot strained against the binding. "What else do you want?"

"I'm tired of that brat sneaking into my room. Last week, I had company…and there she was."

"What do you want me to do? Read her a bedtime story?"

"Take care of her. Destroy Acacia." Stephanos hissed the words.

Akiva hid a smile welling up inside him. This was too easy. But he didn't want Stephanos to think he was too eager or that the deed already had come to its grisly end. "Isn't killing another vamp against the rules?"

Stephanos laughed. "Since when did you ever worry about the rules?"

"She's just a kid."

"A kid who kills. Not so innocent, is she?"

Akiva dropped his gaze to the floor, as if he was considering the proposal. "Why don't you kill her, then?"

"Because Orphelia would kill me."

He blinked. "You scared of that old bat?"

Stephanos laughed again. But he didn't make another argument. He simply waited on Akiva's response.

Pretending to dislike the request, Akiva whirled away from Stephanos, took a few steps out onto the landing, then ever so slowly turned back. "Well, don't worry then. Consider Acacia dead."

"I will." Stephanos closed the door partway then stopped. "Oh yes, the fella you want works for the NOPD." Then he reached out and grabbed Akiva's arm when he would have turned away. "Take care of Acacia first. You hear?"

"Absolutely."

Again, from Seeger's poem, he focused on what he must do.

> *God knows 'twere better to be deep*
> *Pillowed in silk and scented down,*
> *Where love throbs out in blissful sleep,*
> *Pulse nigh to pulse, and breath to breath,*
> *Where hushed awakenings are dear…*

But I've a rendezvous with Death
At midnight in some flaming town,
When Spring trips north again this year,
And I to my pledged word am true,
I shall not fail that rendezvous.

CHAPTER TWENTY-FOUR

HIS SHOULDER WAS ON fire.

Roc swerved the Mustang around a corner, his GPS system attached to the dash guiding him through the streets of New Orleans. He leaned forward, pressing his weight against the steering wheel, gritting his teeth against the pain. Darkness beat down on him. He blinked, trying to clear his vision, but the red, yellow, and green traffic lights blurred into the streetlamps' glare and store windows' glow. It became a warped psychedelic swirl of colors, sliding and swerving as he tried to focus on the white lines, which wavered and shifted down the paved road. He couldn't hold the Mustang steady, and it veered to one side then the other. A horn blared, and he jerked the wheel left.

"Are you okay?" Rachel gripped the strap along the door.

"Fine," he bit out. He overcompensated with the steering wheel and swerved the car back the other way. Sweat poured down his face. His shirt was damp with a mixture of sweat and blood.

"You don't look fine to me." Rachel placed a gentle hand on his arm. "Pull over, and let me look at your shoulder."

"I've gotta make a call." Colors slid past him like some sort of hallucination, the same way his thoughts skidded out of reach.

"I can do it for you," Rachel offered. "Whom do you want to call?"

He dared not take his gaze off the road, except to glance occasionally at the GPS map. Red lights flashed in front of him. *Brake!* He stomped on the brake, and the car jolted to a stop, slamming both Rachel and him forward then back. He swept his good shoulder against his face to mop up the sweat.

"I could drive," Rachel suggested. "Jacob taught me. It's been a while, but—"

"I'm okay." But he wasn't, and he knew it. Still, he repeated it as if saying it made it so. "I'm okay."

He stared straight through the bug-matted windshield. The car stopped in front of him now advanced through the green light. Behind them, a horn blasted, the sound elongating as an irritated truck driver whipped around him.

Roc managed to get the Mustang going forward again, but he was having trouble concentrating, reading the street signs, following the GPS map. He should know where he was, but he was confused, disoriented. His shoulder throbbed, feeling like an oversized football shoulder pad, which he'd worn playing football in high school.

"Maybe we could just stop for a minute." Rachel's calm voice broke into his thoughts. "I'll stop the bleeding, and then we can go on."

The bleeding. *The blood!* His heart gave jerky, haphazard beats. "Are you crazy? *He's* after us by now. And he won't stop—"

"I know that." Again, her voice was soothing, like a pool of bath water he could float in. "But if we don't stop"—her voice took an edge—"then we won't get very far if you crash the car or bleed to death."

"*He* will smell it—the blood." Roc took a risk and glanced at her. She had one hand on the door strap and another on her rounded belly. "They can smell blood like a shark."

"Okay. Okay." Rachel's breathing was shallow. "Then all the more reason to stop the bleeding."

At least that made sense. Sort of. Bleeding like this, he was a danger not only to her and her baby but also to anyone else on the road. He studied the buildings and roads ahead and wrenched the steering wheel, making the car swerve and the tires squeal. The car hit a bump of uneven pavement and jolted them as they drove into an alleyway.

It was dark back here between decrepit brick buildings. So dark he couldn't see much of anything when he turned off the headlights. Only the GPS map glowed on the dash, and he jerked the cord out of the cigarette lighter. He didn't want anything to give away their location. Total blackout was their only hope.

When he'd driven as far as he dared into the darkness, he brought the Mustang to a jerking stop. He leaned his head back, closing his eyes, breathing hard through his mouth, and allowed his body to relax for the first time in more than an hour. Rachel reached for the door handle.

"Don't get out of the car. It isn't safe. Not here." He swung his gaze in her direction, tried to sharpen his words for emphasis. "If he finds us—" He breathed heavily, unable to finish. She was watching him closely, as if absorbing all he was saying. *But did she believe him? Did she understand what a danger Akiva was? What danger she'd been in?*

"Roc," she said, her voice featherlike, "can you twist toward me so I can bandage your shoulder?"

He looked into her blue eyes, which he could barely focus on, and leaned close. He clung to the dazzling blue lifeline. He had to make her understand. "Don't leave me."

She shook her head. "Of course not. You're okay. You'll be okay."

Roc groaned and closed his eyes. She didn't understand. But it took too much effort to explain what he meant. If she decided to take off on her own, then he wouldn't be able to protect her. And he was going to protect her, even if it killed him. Which it was beginning to feel like it might.

He pressed his good shoulder toward the passenger seat and his wounded shoulder as far as he could toward the steering wheel and her. Pain throbbed down his arm and into his chest cavity, the pulsing ache seemed to go on and on. He sucked in a breath, and it whistled as he released it.

"I'm sorry," Rachel whispered and pressed against the wound.

He couldn't lift his arm, so he maneuvered it with his other hand, lifting his forearm and dropping his hand into his lap.

"Do you have a flashlight?" she asked.

"No. No light."

"How can I see what I'm doing then?"

"Just put pressure on it." He leaned his head against the headrest and watched her shadowy figure. Blood loss was making his head swim. "That's all we can do for now."

She lifted a hand and hesitated before touching him. Finally, she unbuttoned his shirt, her fingers nimble and quick, as if she'd made up her mind what to do and realized she had no choice.

He tried to lighten the moment. "Don't worry. I won't get the wrong idea here."

Her fingers paused briefly. He tried to smile but feared it was more of a grimace. Finally, she went back to her task, fumbling with the button near his waistband.

His shirt scraped against the wound. A long string of curse words hurled through his mind, but he clenched his teeth to keep from saying something that might shock this Amish woman. Rachel jerked the material loose and tugged the tails out of his jeans.

"Are you always in this much of a hurry?" It fell as flat a vulgar joke in front of the Pope, but he needed something to distract him from the red-hot pain.

Rachel paid no attention to him as she slipped the fabric off his good shoulder. Compressing it into a thick wad, she pushed it against the wound, leaning against him, placing as much of her weight into it as she could. He bit down hard on the words jamming into his throat. Her breath brushed his cheek and fanned the feverish heat spreading over his body.

His vision swayed, the edges forming a gray circle. Pain, Roc learned, had a variety of colors. He squeezed his eyes closed, and across the insides of his eyelids a palette of reds drifted, arced, and exploded. The throbbing went flat, and the vibrancy faded to black. He leaned his shoulder hard against Rachel's hand, and pain shot through him like a searing brand, which scorched his flesh and turned his vision to a blinding white.

And then like a shade pulling downward over him, he saw nothing.

He was floating on a bobbing, swaying current. This wide river rumbled him along at a frenzied pace with a swoosh and rush. Maybe he was finally approaching the delta of afterlives he'd been longing for. A burbling and rumbling brought him close to the surface, and he wrapped his arm around something soft and warm, a buoy in the vast expanse of dark waters.

"Roc!"

He heard his name like it was a pinball bouncing around the stars, a pinball with strings wrapped around him, and it somehow slowed the dark river's progress. Something tugged on his arm, as if a tree limb or rock snagged him.

"Roc!" The voice calling to him arced into a note of panic.

His eyelids fluttered against a heaviness weighting them. With much effort and struggle, he forced his eyes open. A solid blue gaze met his befuddled one.

"Are you okay? I thought I'd lost...that you'd..." Her voice broke.

He realized he'd slumped sideways against the passenger seat, and he was nearly in Rachel's lap. He pushed with his good arm and fell back into his own seat. "Where are we?"

"I don't know."

He jerked upright, and pain jabbed him in the shoulder. The Mustang was stopped, the engine humming, but the lights were off. "Why'd we stop?"

"We had to stop the bleeding. Your shoulder, remember?"

The bleeding. The girl vampire had bitten him. *What did that mean? Was he doomed? Was this the beginning of his being changed? Had anyone ever been bitten and lived to tell the tale without wanting to take a bite of their audience? Did a vampire bite carry some sort of venom that infected the person? Would it kill him slowly? Or would it change him forever?*

A thick wall of panic rose up inside him, its hard edge pressing against his windpipe, and he gasped for air. His soul darkened in those few seconds. If he let it, fear would cut him off from hope completely. But he wouldn't give in. Not yet. Not now.

Because first he had a job to do: he had to get Rachel somewhere safe. He had to get her to someone who would protect her from Akiva...and possibly even himself.

CHAPTER TWENTY-FIVE

AKIVA WATCHED THE SLOW rise of the three-quarter moon. Its yellowish hue, like a guarded cat's eye, slanted its gaze on unsuspecting prey.

> When I do count the clock that tells the time
> And see the brave day sunk in hideous night…
> That thou among the wastes of time must go,
> Since sweets and beauties do themselves forsake
> And die as fast as they see others grow;
> And nothing 'gainst Time's scythe can make defence
> Save breed, to brave him when he takes thee hence.

Shakespeare must have had a dark side. Maybe he'd seen the bite taken out of the moon during bloody sunsets, smearing its stain over the horizon. Or maybe he'd witnessed the wickedness of the full moon, bloated with incantations and causing seas to rise and men to lose common sense. If there was a time of day Akiva liked best, this was it, the teetering on the brink of one night and another morning. There was a hushed expectancy in the air of what might have been and what would be, and it hovered along the breeze and weighted the clouds.

Anticipation surged through his veins as he waited outside the cemetery, leaning against the side of his Jaguar. There didn't seem to be much activity here, but the area's reputation was bad. Robberies, disappearances, voodoo hexes were abundant. But Akiva had nothing to worry about. Others should be frightened of him. Which might explain why the street was empty. Like forest creatures hiding and crouching low when a predator stalked past, maybe the locals sensed danger and retreated inside.

A predator needed patience, and his was stretching in an inhuman way. Waiting had never been his strength. He restrained himself from pacing, from checking the clock on the dash, from leaving. Other vamps didn't adhere to clocks. They moved at their own pace and arrived when they pleased. They never worried about being late or missing out—time was on their side.

A beam of headlights flashed as a truck turned toward Akiva. He remained in his slouched position, in the shadowy depths, and watched the truck drive past. A dark figure Akiva did not recognize leaned over the steering wheel. The vehicle moved at a quick clip past him, but he could hear a Chopin classic: Nocturne No. 2 in E-Flat Major, as the speakers vibrated with each note. He decided this one wasn't the one he was waiting for, but then the red taillights flared, and the truck came to a stop.

A minute, then two, passed before the driver's door opened. Slowly, a man emerged, stood on the pavement, and turned his back on Akiva. He didn't seem to be in a hurry or worried about this dangerous part of town. He fiddled with a cell phone, tossed it into the empty seat, and closed the door with a bang. Finally, he turned and walked toward Akiva, his pace casual, his stance relaxed. But even from this distance, Akiva could see his gaze was as black as a sinful soul and as intense as a panther on the prowl.

When he stood ten paces away from Akiva, the man said, "You wanted to see me?"

Akiva straightened. "You know Stephanos?"

"I do."

"He said your name is B—"

"I go by Brydon now."

"Interesting name."

"So is Akiva."

Akiva nodded his agreement. "I went with a derivative of my former name."

The man said nothing, not sharing his reasons or seeming to care about engaging in any sort of conversation. His foot scraped against the pavement. He had those now-familiar black eyes and a bulky frame of solid muscles. This man was strong in his former life, but now changed, he was like a Goliath or Samson. Not impossible to beat, but damn tough.

"How long have you been changed?" Akiva asked.

"Not long."

"Bet you know the number of days."

"Forty-seven."

"And nights. The nights were the longest for me." Akiva's mouth pinched at the memory of those lonely moments when he'd fought against the raw need of hunger...and lost. "Don't worry, you'll stop counting eventually."

Brydon's face remained dark and serious. "What do you want?"

Akiva didn't want to reveal his need too soon. If he seemed too eager, then payment would be extravagant. But this new blood wanted to hurry up and get on with it, so he opted for a casual tone. "I'm looking for a guy...Roc Girouard. You know him?"

"Maybe." He crossed his arms over his chest. "Why?"

"Looking for him is all."

"Oh, yeah? Why's that?"

"It's not him specifically that I want. It's what he has."

"And what's that?" Brydon had a bored tone, and yet there was an edge to it, as if he could slice through Akiva with his next sentence.

"A woman."

Brydon laughed, a razor-sharp sound, which revealed not even a hint of a smile. "You can get one of those anywhere. What's so special about this one?"

Akiva shook his head. "Not special at all. Rachel took something from me, and she has to pay for it."

Brydon grunted his understanding. "What do you want me to do? I don't know this woman. I don't even know where Roc is at the moment."

"He might contact you. If he does, I'd like you to tell me."

"Why would I do that?"

Akiva quirked an eyebrow. Brydon's answer could be revealed to Giovanni, who would not like it. *Oh no, he wouldn't like it at all. Loyalty to a human was not tolerated. Did this newly changed vamp know Giovanni, know of his power, his influence over the others?* He asked: "You have loyalty to this Roc Girouard?"

"I have loyalty to no one. Not unless I owe them something."

"And do you owe Roc Girouard?"

"If I did, I don't anymore." His voice had a biting chill. "So what you gonna give me in exchange?"

"You're new. There's much you don't know. Much you don't understand yet. Information is power. Especially in this new world of ours. But I can help you. In fact, I want to help you. I can introduce you to those with power."

"Oh, yeah? And who's that?"

"Giovanni. I can introduce you. Can't manage in this new life without knowing *the man*."

"We've already met. What else you got to offer?"

A coldness settled over Akiva. He tried not to reveal surprise over this ingénue already meeting the most important vampire in the area. Now his collateral wasn't worth much, and he had little else to offer. So he asked, "Instead of wasting time, going back and forth, let's just get down to it. What do you want?"

Brydon smiled then, but there was an arctic fierceness in the look.

CHAPTER TWENTY-SIX

"Yea, though I walk through the valley of the shadow of death, I will fear no evil."

HER RESCUER WAS DYING. Rachel was lost, alone, helpless. But she feared for her baby more than for herself.

While whispering the twenty-third Psalm as a prayer, she kept an eye on both the roadway and Roc. He was pale and sweating, not to mention still bleeding. His eyelids lowered slowly then jerked open again, and the car swerved in and out of its lane. The last time she'd felt this helpless in a car, Jacob had been behind the wheel and under the influence. But Roc hadn't been drinking. He was seriously injured, and he leaned forward against the steering wheel as if it held him upright. When his car veered into the next lane, Rachel gently touched the wheel and straightened out the car's trajectory.

First a right turn, then left. Roc seemed to know where he was headed, but he was also dazed, almost unconscious. *Did he know where he was going? Were they both helplessly lost? If he died, what would she do, how would she find help, how would she ever get home?* She prayed the good Lord would keep Roc alive. The prayer seemed selfish, so she added another for the man's wound to be healed and for God to keep her baby safe.

Then he turned the car once more, into a parking lot of what appeared to be a church. She missed the full name, as they passed it too quickly and hit a bump, which made the car jounce and sway. A stark white steeple rose into the night sky like a beacon of hope. When the car came to a jarring halt, she drew a calming breath and whispered a prayer of thanksgiving. At least they were someplace. Maybe someone here could help them.

As if in slow motion, Roc leaned forward and rested his head against the steering wheel. His right hand slumped against the gearshift, palm upright and defenseless. *Had he passed out again? Died? What should she do?*

"Roc?" She leaned forward, thought she heard him breathing through his mouth. Carefully, she touched his arm. "Can you hear me?"

She glanced over her shoulder and peered out the back window. No one appeared in the deserted parking lot. There weren't any other cars in sight. All seemed quiet. Peaceful. The windows of the church remained dark. *What if no one was here? What if Roc simply stopped because he couldn't go any farther?* Maybe she should try to find someone to help him.

Fumbling with the lock, she yanked on the handle, and the heavy door swung open. But Roc grabbed her arm, his grip, fierce with urgency, pinching her flesh. His eyes were wild.

"I'm not leaving you," she reassured him. "I'll be back. I promise. I'm going to find someone to help you."

"Anthony." His voice sounded raspy.

"What?"

His eyes burned with fever. "Get Anthony."

"Anthony who?"

His grip slackened, and his head lolled against the steering wheel again.

"Okay. Anthony. I'll find him."

"He's the priest. And he…" Roc's eyelids fluttered, and

his gaze fought to focus on her. He mumbled something else, but she couldn't understand him. A lock of hair fell across his forehead, and he looked vulnerable, like a lost little boy.

She reached out then stopped herself, her fingers curling into her palm. "I'll be back, Roc."

More than six months ago, she had lain in her marriage bed, so afraid she was losing her baby. Josef had gone for help and she'd prayed for her baby. But not for her husband. Once again, guilt tightened its grip. She hadn't known he needed prayers. *But would prayers have saved his life?* Now, she simply prayed for them all.

Easing out of the car, she felt the small of her back pinch, and she rubbed the spot but kept moving toward the first building. She knocked politely at first and then louder, but no one came. She waited and glanced over her shoulder toward the fancy car. She could see Roc's shadowy frame slumped in the seat and feared waiting much longer. He needed help now. After pounding on the door, she abandoned it and moved onto the next, hammering against the wooden slab.

After a long moment, she heard a muffled, "Just a minute."

Her heart minced the minutes as she waited. When the door finally opened, it gave only an inch or two. An older man with rumpled gray hair wore a blue terrycloth bathrobe. "Yes?"

"Anthony?" she asked.

The man's weary brown eyes narrowed with what appeared to be suspicion. "You know Anthony?"

"No, my friend"—she pointed back toward the car—"he does. You see, he needs help. He's hurt. And—"

"Get out of here. Now."

"But—" He was going to close the door! Panic arced through her. "I need help." Her voice cracked. "Please—"

"Call the police. Hospital is five blocks south." He stepped back, and the door closed.

"You don't understand!" She splayed a hand against the door. *How could she take Roc to a hospital? What would she say? He was attacked by a rabid young girl, a...vampire?* "Please, I need to speak to Anthony." She banged on the door. "Roc wants to see—"

The door jerked open again. "Look," the older man hissed through the crack, "Anthony disappeared. He's gone! And I was brought here to fill in for him. So go away. I can't help you."

Hope crumpled inside of her. She had no choice. She would have to take Roc somewhere, find a hospital somehow. That was his only hope. Otherwise, he might die. And if he died, then she might too. Her death mattered little. But not her baby. *Please, God, not Josef's baby!* But how would she get to the hospital?

When she stepped back off the step, she collided with something solid, and her heart jolted up into her throat.

"He disappeared?" Roc asked, standing behind her. He braced one arm against the brick wall, propping himself upright.

"Who are you?" the old man asked, his face pinched.

"A friend."

The old man's face blanched.

"This is the friend I told you about," Rachel said breathlessly, relieved to see him awake and standing, and yet afraid to be too hopeful. "He's looking for Anthony. We need your help. He's injured...bleeding—"

The door lurched closed. Roc lunged forward, shoving an arm past Rachel, and banged the door open, making the old man stumble back a few steps. Roc staggered inside, and Rachel followed him into the building, which she realized was a home.

"Where is he?" Roc asked. "Where's Anthony?"

The old man touched his forehead then belly, and each shoulder consecutively. His withered lips whispered something.

"He said Anthony disappeared," Rachel explained to Roc.

"When?"

The old man's eyes were wide. "What happened to your arm there?"

"When did Anthony disappear?" Roc repeated, his teeth clenched.

"T-two weeks ago."

"Who are you, then?"

"F-father Paul."

"You're his replacement?"

The man nodded.

"They didn't take long, did they?"

"A flock needs a shepherd, and this flock had been ignored by—"

At the look Roc shot Father Paul, the words died on his lips, which he flattened.

Roc walked farther into the house, leaving Rachel in the narrow hallway with the old man. His earlier anger having disappeared behind a frightened mask, he stood there trembling in his house shoes. He pulled a string of beads out of the pocket of his robe and mumbled words Rachel couldn't understand.

In a moment, Roc returned, his face flushed. "Where's his stuff? What'd you do with Anthony's stuff?"

Father Paul's throat convulsed. "I gave it to the p-poor. What was salvageable, that is. And…"

"And?" Roc stepped closer to the man, who was now shaking. Maybe the older man couldn't see what Rachel saw—that Roc was barely standing as he leaned forward, bracing a hand to steady himself on a table behind Father Paul.

"He had books…and things. An abomination."

"Where are they?"

Father Paul's chin lifted a notch, and he met Roc's gaze solidly, as if he had no regrets about his actions. "I burned them."

Roc's elbow buckled, but he caught himself.

"Anthony," Father Paul whispered, "was into witchcraft, and whatever happened to him…I suppose he opened himself to it. And if that is what you are into, young man, repent now. You can still be saved."

Roc grabbed the collar of the man's robe, clenched it in a fist, and leaned heavily against the old man's chest. The strength he'd managed at the beginning of this encounter seemed to be fading. Rachel reached out to help him, but he shrugged off her hand. "Anthony was worth more than you'll ever be. Don't ever say another word about him. Not one."

The older man swallowed hard. "I speak only the truth."

"You speak out of ignorance." Roc stumbled toward the door and grabbed the handle for support. "Rachel, let's go."

"We have to get you help." She wrapped an arm around his waist, and this time he allowed her assistance, leaning against her, hooking his good arm around her shoulders. He was breathing hard, his heat burning into her. Fear for his life mounted. "Where are we going?"

"To find a friend."

She opened the door, and the moist New Orleans heat smacked her in the face. "We have to go to the hospital."

"Later." He walked along beside her toward the car, his footsteps heavy and unsteady. "First, we'll find Brody. He will protect you. In case I can't."

CHAPTER TWENTY-SEVEN

ROC'S VISION SPUN. HIS limbs felt loose and disjointed. Swirls of lights and colors tangoed, spinning and colliding about him. Some looked like pieces of glass, flat like a mirror, as if they reflected light from some far-off source. Others appeared like serrated edges, sharp and jagged, the light piercing his retina. The lights gyrated and whirled around him, fading and glowing, going black then blazing to life again.

Voices assaulted his eardrums, darting in and out of a fog and storming through any barricades. Sometimes the voices sounded like his, other times like Rachel's, and yet another deeper one penetrated the confusion. Then a brick-red lava of pain flowed out of his shoulder, burning away the distorted sounds and leaving in its trail silence and the faint beat of his heart.

At one point, he realized he was lying down on his back, his left shoulder swollen to the size of a beach ball with air pumping into it then hissing out, in and out, in and out. The throbbing remained the one constant as the lights dimmed and faded and glowed and brightened.

But one thing he clung to: her voice. She spoke to him in quiet, soothing tones, velvety smooth as the rag she drew across his forehead. Sometimes she said encouraging words: "It's all right, Roc. You're going to be all right." Other times, she didn't speak to him at all: "Oh, Lord, help this man."

Then there was murmuring he couldn't decipher. It sounded as if she was speaking to someone else, not a prayer, but someone at a distance. Was it Brody? His father again? Had Anthony found them? Or Akiva?

Roc thrashed about, struggled to open his eyes, and she returned to his side, shushed him, and the cool rag once again drifted over his skin. He pried open his eyes, and through a haze, saw her astonishing blue eyes, now pinched with concern. He tried to speak, but his throat trapped any words.

"What is it?" she asked. "What do you need? Water?" She helped him sip through a straw, placing the plastic between his parched lips.

"Brody"—his voice croaked—"where is he?"

"In the other room."

"Get him."

She left, and while he waited, everything once again faded to black.

When light peeked through his eyelids, he forced them open. She placed her cool fingers against his brow, and hers puckered with concern.

"Brody," he managed. He had to talk to Brody. He had to understand what was happening, how to protect Rachel.

"Here. Drink this." Again, she positioned a straw against his lips, and he sucked down more ice-cold water.

"Where's Brody?" He searched the room, the bare walls, the open door behind Rachel.

"He's at work."

"My gun. Get it."

Her brow furrowed deeper. "Why?"

"If he comes…I have to be ready."

"It's okay." She touched the back of her fingers to his forehead. "We're safe here."

"Where's my stake?"

"Rest, Roc. Don't you worry about anything."

She didn't understand. She couldn't. She was too naïve, too ignorant of vampires and their ways.

She rearranged the blanket covering him. "Just rest. I'll be right back."

He watched her moving around him, shifting a bowl on a table beside the bed, folding a shirt, and taking the water glass to the other room. She was efficient and kind, her face solemn yet peaceful. Weights yanked down his eyelids and won the battle.

His dreams were of blood. He tossed and struggled against unseen forces, beings that surrounded him, crept up on him, attacked viciously from all sides. Again, he saw a young, innocent face, the skin smooth with a smattering of freckles, and then it transformed into a fierce predator.

His father came to him, shrouded in gray cloth and grizzled beard. Remy offered him a bottle, the taste of oblivion an arm's length away. Whiskey sloshed against the glass, and Roc could smell the potent scent, luring him more than the arms of a beautiful woman could. But then his father snatched the bottle away and guzzled it down himself.

———————

When Roc next awoke, sunlight streamed through vertical blinds covering a window. His shoulder ached but no longer throbbed, and his skin felt cool and damp, no longer hot and dry. Overhead, a ceiling fan circled and cast a cooling breeze over the room. He flung the sheet back with his good arm and sat on the side of the bed, planting his bare feet on the carpeted floor. His vision bobbed and weaved with the sudden change in position, and his insides shifted, his stomach lurched. Thankfully, it was empty, and nothing came up.

He remained still for a moment before attempting to stand. Someone had stripped him of his clothes, which were folded and lying on a dresser. He wore only his BVDs and a gauze bandage covering his shoulder.

One door in the room was closed, but another was ajar and revealed white floor tiles. Keen on a shower, he padded across the room and entered the small bathroom. There were no decorations, but a soap bar sat on the counter, and one was cradled in the shower, along with a bottle of gold shampoo. He rubbed his jaw, and stubble scraped his palm. In the mirror, he saw the white bandage covering his shoulder, stark against his tanned skin. His face looked like his skin had been bleached. But his eyes demanded close inspection.

They were dark as they'd always been, a dark brown, and he could see bits of red, amber, and green all mixed together. But no black. So the bite hadn't changed him. At least not yet.

He gave his shoulder a roll, testing the flexibility and hissed at the sharp pinching sensations. No use removing the bandage yet.

Flicking on the shower, he tested the water pouring out with his hand until it turned hot. He stood partly under the spray a good five minutes, trying not to get the bandage wet, but by the time he turned off the water, the bandaged edges had become damp and curled. He toweled off as best he could with one arm. He then put on his jeans but abandoned his shirt, which, although cleaned from all the blood, was ripped and torn.

Rachel's surprised gaze met his as he entered the living area. Her blue eyes assessed him, caused a strange effect on him again. He avoided them as he would a vampire's, and surveyed the room instead. The living room held a brown sofa and matching chair, along with assorted tables and a flat-screen television, all of which he recognized as Brody's den. He'd been there many times in the past. A quick scan told him no one else was in the apartment.

But he couldn't avoid her any longer. Rachel stared hard at him as if determined to keep her gaze on his. He must look a sight, probably frightening to this pregnant Amish woman.

Feeling awkward, he shoved a hand through his wet hair and tried to rearrange the strands into some semblance of order. He couldn't remember if he'd driven Rachel here or if he'd allowed her behind the wheel and simply given directions. He wasn't even sure what day it was, where he'd left his Mustang, or how much time had passed. A thousand questions assaulted him, and he tried to sort through them in order of priority.

"Good morning," she said before he could get his thoughts straight. "How are you feeling?"

He nodded, not entirely steady on his feet or settled in his stomach. "Better. Or so I think. You okay?"

She looked surprised by his question. "Of course."

The moment stretched between them, twisting into awkwardness. "And the baby?"

She smiled and touched the mound of her belly. "Kicking. Can I get you something? Toast or maybe coffee?"

He shook his head, and the more dire questions rushed forward: "Where's Brody?"

"I reckon at work or…" She shrugged. "He wasn't here when I awoke this morning."

His gaze shifted toward the sofa and the folded blanket he assumed she'd used in sleeping there. He nodded his agreement with her assessment. "He left you alone?"

"There is security," she said.

"What do you mean?"

She pointed toward the front door. Next to it a wide window looked out over the pool and its courtyard, but now the blinds were closed. "A police officer has been watching the apartment. I saw him yesterday and today."

"Good." So Brody was thinking smart, planning ahead. But what could Brody know of what danger they faced? No cop would understand or believe it. Still, relief washed away guilt over exposing Rachel to Akiva. At least she was safe for the moment.

He rubbed the back of his neck and took in the bachelor pad Rachel seemed determined to tame. The sink was filled with sudsy water, and a stack of folded rags rested on the counter, along with gray, wet ones. Part of the linoleum floor was wet.

"How long was I out?"

"Two days."

The answer surprised him and upped his worry. He glanced at the door. Light slanted through the blinds covering the window. "Have you been anywhere? Talked to anyone?"

"No."

"You've heard nothing from Akiva?"

"Did you think he'd call?" she asked.

He shook his head. "Nah, I just…" He smiled at her blunt question and his inability to answer. "He'll be looking for you. You know that, right?"

"For both of us." She wiped her hands on a towel she'd draped over her shoulder. Even though she was no longer wearing the traditional garb of an Amish woman, she looked decidedly Amish in her jeans, maternity top, and prayer *kapp*. "I am not afraid of him."

"You should be."

"The good Lord will do as He deems fitting."

"You prayed for me," he said, more to himself, yet his spoken words surprised and embarrassed him.

"Of course." Her serious blue eyes studied him. "Why wouldn't I?"

"I would think the question would be: Why would you?"

"Because you saved me." She stepped forward, and he noticed her bare feet, her toes pink and clean. With his own uncovered feet and torso, the moment felt far too intimate. But her focus seemed to be solely on his shoulder. "I should change the bandage. It has started to heal. Although I think you will have a terrible scar."

"It won't be the first." Clearing his suddenly clogged throat, he moved into the den. He glanced at the gauze covering his shoulder, focusing on the way the skin pinched when he attempted to move it. "Where did you get the tape and bandages?"

"Your friend...Brody got them for me. And he bought some food: eggs, bread, orange juice, and such. There was nothing much here to eat."

"He's a good guy. But definitely a bachelor." He'd pay Brody back somehow. Weariness settled into his bones, and he leaned his thigh against the sofa.

"You should sit down," she said, coming alongside him. "Here..." She readjusted a pillow, and with slight pressure on his good shoulder, she sat him on the sofa. She peered down at him, her hand propped on her hip. "You don't look so good, Roc. I will fix you some strong tea and toast." With a firm nod, she moved back to the kitchen.

He watched her go, noticing she moved easily in spite of the size of her belly. From the back, he couldn't tell she was pregnant at all, not with her slim hips and long legs. His awareness of her stunned him, and he pushed it away and focused on her fixing him food. He was, after all, hungry. On cue, his stomach rumbled.

From his vantage point, he could see her walk to the refrigerator and open it. The inside of the door gleamed with whiteness, as if it had been recently scrubbed. She pulled out eggs, a stick of butter, and a loaf of bread.

Roc dragged his gaze away from her, which seemed like dangerous territory, and spied a stack of magazines next to the laptop computer on the table. With his one good hand, he shuffled through them—*Maxim*, *Men's Journal*, *Maximum Fitness*, and *Smart Money*. A manila folder slipped out from between the magazines and fell open. It wasn't a police report but instead a small stack of printed papers, paper-clipped at the top. Articles, no…obituaries, which had apparently been downloaded from the Internet.

"How do you know him," Rachel asked from the kitchen, "your friend, Brody?"

"We were on the force together before—" He stopped himself, unwilling to discuss his past. "You can trust him, though."

"That is good. Your friend," Rachel said, distracting him, "doesn't like my cooking awful much."

Roc kept his gaze on the obits, flipping from one to the other. "He's a bachelor. He's used to eating out."

Pans clattered in the kitchen, and the refrigerator opened and closed again. "He seemed angry or even nervous. That's understandable, seeing how we barged in on him."

"Yeah?" Roc flipped through the pages, noting the obits were all races and ages. "He probably thought you were trying to get to him is all."

"Get to him? How's that?" She stood at the edge of the kitchen, a spatula in her hand.

"Don't you know the old saying, the way to a man's heart is through his stomach? He probably thought you were making a play for him."

She shook her head. "A play?"

"Ya know, coming on to him."

Suddenly, her cheeks flamed. She clutched the spatula like a weapon to ward off his thoughts. "Surely not! I am a married woman."

Roc raised an eyebrow but didn't argue against her statement. He reminded himself—to her, she was still married. "Who knows what he was thinking?" He sniffed and caught what smelled like scorched butter. "Is that my toast?"

"Oh!" She turned on her bare heel and raced for the stove. Clucking her tongue, she took a paper towel and wiped out the pan. She sliced another hunk off the stick and placed the butter in the pan, then cracked three eggs. Before the eggs were finished, the toaster popped up slices of browned bread.

Roc went back to the top of the stack of obits and noticed the most recent death was on top, and the dates went in order to the bottom. All of the deaths had occurred over the past three...four months. Was this some new case Brody was working on?

"I'm sure your friend will be relieved," Rachel said, walking toward him with a plate of fried eggs and stacked, buttered toast, "to learn you are recovering. He thought you were going to die."

Her statement splashed against him, and he closed the folder. He'd thought he might die too. And he wasn't exactly sure everything was all right now. But he was thankful the eggs and toast smelled good and he didn't have a hankering for raw, bloody meat. "And you didn't?"

She set the plate on the coffee table beside the laptop computer. "I was confident you were in the Lord's hands."

Setting the folder beside him on the sofa, he leaned toward his breakfast. "What did you tell Brody about what happened?"

She didn't answer at first, just looked at him like it was an odd question. "The truth."

Not Roc's first choice. "And what did Brody say to that?"

"He didn't say anything."

"He didn't say anything about your telling him I'd been attacked by a vampire? A little girl vampire?"

She held a napkin out to him as if he'd just said something normal. "Maybe he thought I was making it up."

Roc rubbed his forehead. Maybe he wasn't thinking clearly. Why would Brody put a security detail here to protect Rachel if he thought Roc was crazy or if he didn't believe her story? And yet, why would he believe? He forced himself to stand, ignoring the head rush, and walk toward the front door. "He didn't question you?"

She shook her head. "We were busy trying to get the bleeding to stop and get you comfortable."

Of course. Right. It made sense. And yet none of it sounded right. Roc knew Brody. He was a detective for NOPD, and any detective would ask a few questions. It would have been normal for Brody to have filled out a police report. Would Rachel lie to Roc about what she'd told Brody? He dismissed the thought. She was Amish, and they clung to the truth at all costs. So what was going on here? And here was the bigger question: If Brody thought his ex-partner was dying, then why hadn't he called an ambulance?

Roc peered through the peephole on the front door. It gave a wide-angle view of the stoop. Shifting sideways, he separated the blinds and peeked through them. He had a bird's-eye view of the swimming pool and courtyard, which had many empty lounge chairs. A cop stood guard down there. The guard looked up then, and their eyes met. But the face Roc saw was his father's.

He jerked back, and the blinds clattered into place. Forcing himself to breathe, Roc thought maybe he was going crazy. He ventured another look. The cop—or his father—was gone. Maybe the vampire bite distorted reality. Or maybe he was hallucinating. Or maybe he was plain crazy.

"Roc," Rachel said, "are you okay?"

"You sure Brody brought security here? He told you that?"

"I saw the policeman." She came over to him and took a look through the blinds. "He must be taking a break or went around the side of the building."

Roc went to the other bedroom door, the one he assumed was Brody's. He paused, not out of hesitation but wariness, and listened for any sounds from the other side. Nothing alerted him, but he reached for his gun—an automatic response. But it wasn't there. "What did you do with my gun?"

"Brody took it."

That made some sense. A basic precaution. And yet…

Her answer made him sweat. He gripped the handle on the door, pressing his injured arm against his belly, and twisted the knob slowly. Nothing jumped out at him. Nothing seemed out of the ordinary. He was probably being paranoid or schizophrenic or some other psychological term he didn't want to know. Still, he noticed the blinds were closed, the room dark.

He couldn't remember ever entering Brody's personal bedroom. Why would he have? He excused his intrusion now because he needed his weapon…and a shirt. Without his Glock, he was vulnerable. And that didn't set well with him.

"What about my wooden stake?"

"That too."

Emboldened by his defenselessness, he flicked on the light. A tan comforter covered the bed. The room was plain, everything in order and neat. Was that Rachel's doing?

He looked back at her. She stood at the doorway to the bedroom but did not enter. "Have you been in here?"

Her eyes widened with shock. "Of course not."

There wasn't anything much to see in the room, just a dresser with loose coins dotting the surface, a paperback novel by Dean Koontz, and a set of keys. He moved toward two doors. One revealed a bathroom similar to the one he'd utilized earlier, with the same green soap and shampoo, along with razor and shaving lotion on the edge of the sink. A towel hung from the plastic towel bar. He opened the mirrored cabinet next to the sink and found toothbrush and paste and an outdated prescription of pills for migraines.

Next he checked the walk-in closet. Only a few clothes hung on the metal rods. A row of shelves for shoes split the closet in half, but Brody didn't keep many spare shoes, just a pair of tennis shoes on the floor and a pair of black cowboy boots. Instead, he'd filled the narrow shelves with sunglasses. There must have been fifty pairs of shades stacked neatly in the shelves. Did Brody have a fetish? He'd never known his ex-partner to spend money so lavishly, but the brands—Ray-Ban, Maui Jim, Gucci—were easily top dollar. Above the metal bar for hangers was another shelf where Brody had stored a black suitcase the size of a carry-on. Roc reached for it with his good arm. It weighed more than he'd expected and came down hard. Trying to grab it with his other hand, he grunted, and the suitcase hit the carpeted floor with a dull thud.

"Roc?" Rachel called from the doorway. "Are you okay?"

One of those instinctive feelings came over him like a million spider legs crawling along his bare skin. He bent over the bag and fumbled with the zipper, which ran around the perimeter of the bag. When he lifted the lid, he simply stared at the contents while his blood congealed in his veins.

"Roc?" Rachel called again.

"Yeah, I'm okay." But he wasn't okay. They weren't okay. They not only had to leave but they should have already left.

CHAPTER TWENTY-EIGHT

Fly, envious Time, till thou run out thy race,
Call on the lazy leaden-stepping hours,
Whose speed is but the heavy Plummet's pace.

FOR THE FIRST TIME in two years, time became important
to Akiva.

He'd watched Brydon arrive at the police station. He'd
then waited most of the day. At some point, Brydon would
leave work and head home. And Akiva would follow.
Because Brydon was his best and only prospect for finding
Roc Girouard and Rachel.

He'd circled the city for two days, searching for the black
Mustang, but to no avail. Either Roc or Rachel was injured.
When he'd gone back to Acacia's body, he'd smelled the
blood—human blood—not the blood of a young vampire.
One was like walking through a peach orchard and inhaling
the ripe smells of those ready to be picked. The other was
like the smell after harvest when smashed peaches lay rotting
in the sun.

Akiva had walked through hospitals, listening to conversations, filtering through weeping and angst, trying to
locate Rachel. He'd traipsed through the airport, wharf and
cruise ships, as well as bus and train stations, where he'd
found another young runaway and taken enough time for

a snack. Keeping his appetite sated helped clear his head of any other urgency.

But he'd ended up back at the police station. Waiting.

Brydon had not contacted him yet. Was it because he had no news? Or was it because he was protecting Girouard?

Akiva clenched his teeth and tightened his grip on his gearshift. If he didn't find Rachel in the next day or two, he would head North. She would want to go home and hide among the Amish. But there was no safe place on earth for her. He would not be denied. Not now. Not ever. Her baby would earn him his ultimate freedom from this life.

Brydon emerged from the brick building with a tall, thin man. They were speaking in low, confidential tones that Akiva couldn't overhear from this distance. But he started his Jaguar's engine and waited. From the stance of the man walking with Brydon, the way he stood with his chin slightly elevated and sniffing the air, Akiva recognized he was a blood. The man stretched out mental tentacles, probing the air to seek out anyone who might be nearby, listening or following. Akiva shuttered his feelings and thoughts to protect his plans from scrutiny.

The two vamps gave each other a nod and parted company; the one returning to the police station and Brydon walking with a leisurely pace toward his Chevy truck. Sunlight gleamed off its dark exterior, the paint reflecting Brydon's image like a mirror. *What was this vamp hiding? Was he playing some kind of a game?* His superior attitude grated against Akiva. He had to know what was happening, what this blood was thinking. Brydon was young in his new life, and Akiva stretched weblike fingers to tap into his hidden thoughts. But the new vamp dipped his sunglasses downward and looked in Akiva's direction.

He'd been spotted. This Brydon was stronger than a typical new vamp. Or at least stronger than Akiva had been.

Brydon didn't hurry or rush in an effort to outrun Akiva, he simply climbed into the driver's seat and took off at a pace easily followed. He drove along busy streets, taking random turns, and even a brief ride on the freeway, until he pulled off and turned down several side streets. The rush of anticipation surged through him. Brydon must have made contact with Roc and Rachel. He was sure of it. And Brydon was leading Akiva right to them.

He spotted the black truck circling through the parking lot of an apartment complex, and Akiva followed. But then the truck did a quick maneuver and blocked the one-way entrance. A quick glance in the rearview mirror brought the sudden realization he'd been had. Behind him walked the other vamp Brydon had been speaking to earlier at the station. He must have trailed behind. And now Akiva was caught with no escape route. But he needed none.

He shoved the gearshift into park and leapt out of the driver's seat. Anger pumped through him. Without a glance behind him toward the other vamp, Akiva walked straight for Brydon, who had already disembarked from his vehicle.

"You didn't tell me," Akiva said in a low, menacing tone.

"Tell you what?" Brydon's shades reflected sunlight.

"That you were protecting your friend."

"I don't owe you any favors."

"Bloods stick together."

"Is that how you've lived the last two years, Akiva? I've heard about you."

With his whole body tense, ready to attack, Akiva managed to hold himself back. He wanted to kill this blood, to show this new vamp how inconsequential he was. He would have no guilt, no qualms in the least. And he would have leapt forward, if there hadn't been another vamp standing directly behind him. "Why are you risking so much for this vampire hunter? He has killed many of us. Girouard would kill you, if given half a chance."

"If he knew, yes, he would."

"So where are they? Where's Girouard and Rachel?"

"You can have the girl, but you will leave Roc alone. Do you understand?"

The concession irritated Akiva. He could almost taste the Cajun's blood. He'd love to do away with that vampire killer. After all, Roc Girouard had been on his tail for too long. But he had to cement his priorities. "Where is she?"

"Do I have your word?"

"Sure."

Brydon laughed. "That don't mean much from you, Akiva, does it? And I don't think threatening to kill you myself would prevent you from hurting Roc."

Keeping a cool façade, Akiva asked, "So what do you propose?"

"If you hurt Roc, I'll kill every member of your family."

Akiva laughed. "You don't know anything about my family."

"Don't I? I've been doing my research over the past couple of days. Where shall we start?" Brydon rubbed his jaw thoughtfully. "With your father? Jonas Fisher?" He held up a finger as if a better idea just occurred to him. "Or maybe your momma! Sally. Now that might be fun." But there was no humor in his tone or expression. "Or there's always your brother Levi…his new wife, Hannah…or even your little brother. What's his name? Samuel, is it? Maybe I won't kill him but make him just like his big ol' brother. Pennsylvania could use some more vamps. Whatcha think?"

A growl emanated from deep inside Akiva.

"That's what I thought. So take the girl...this Rachel. Do what you want with her. But leave Roc. Do we understand each other?"

"Fine." Akiva spat the word out between his tense lips. "Just take me to her."

This time, Brydon flashed his white teeth in a fierce smile. "My pleasure."

"'Hell is empty and all the devils are here.'"

Akiva grinned at himself for remembering the Shakespearean quotation, which seemed rather appropriate, considering the situation at hand.

"You think we are devils? Or them?" Brydon nodded toward the maroon apartment door.

"It probably depends on your point of view."

"But you think we are evil?"

Akiva's smile faded as he glanced at the new vampire. Did he hear doubt or confusion in Brydon's tone? Or defensiveness? He drew a breath and stated very clearly, "I do."

Brydon's features remained frozen, not a cringe or eyebrow lifted, not a flinch or delighted smile revealed. Like most vampires, he kept his thoughts to himself. If Brydon disagreed, then he might report it to Giovanni. But it wouldn't matter. It would be too late. "That's my apartment there. Two sixty-six."

"And Girouard and Rachel?"

"They were there when I left this morning."

Akiva cast his gaze over the grounds. Empty slatted chairs surrounded a glittering swimming pool in the center of the courtyard. A maze of sidewalks created a web as each led

toward a different building. In front of the three-story structure, a solitary figure strode, turning at a juncture and returning as if pacing in front of the building or guarding it. The
man wore dark clothing, some sort of a uniform, maybe a
policeman's uniform.

"Who's that?"

"He's been there on and off."

"Is he one of the guardians?"

Brydon shrugged. "Don't know what you mean."

Akiva almost laughed. Something this young vamp didn't
know! But instead of laughing with glee, he spoke quietly,
as if the man across the courtyard might overhear. "I haven't
seen them before in and around New Orleans. Doesn't mean
they aren't here, though. But I've seen them only when I
traveled to Pennsylvania. You will have to draw him away."

"Why me?"

Akiva snapped his head in Brydon's direction. "So I can
get in the apartment."

"You want in there, then you lure him away."

A low growl emanated from deep within Akiva's throat.
Obviously, he was going to have to handle everything himself.

CHAPTER TWENTY-NINE

Roc's heart thumped heavily, pushing his blood through his veins faster and faster. He stared at the contents in the suitcase, which lay scattered on the floor of Brody's closet. Snatching one of the wallets, he flipped it open. A cold, clammy sensation started at the top of his spine and worked its way down. He recognized the face in the driver's license as Delbert Reeves—age fifty-seven, black hair, brown eyes, organ donor—because the man's obit was in Brody's folder.

A grisly puzzle formed in Roc's mind. *It couldn't be.*

He tossed the wallet back into the suitcase and grabbed another, then another. Each one he opened held the owner's license, credit cards, pictures of family or friends, and cash. Each belonged to one of the deceased gathered in the folder.

A cold, hard knot formed in Roc's belly. There was no reason why Brody would have this stuff. No logical reason. And yet, one illogical, irrational, deadly reason emerged.

He slammed the lid of the suitcase closed and jumped to his feet. His vision swerved, and he paused for half a second, gripping a shirt hanging in the closet. Before he'd steadied himself, the shirt slid off the hanger, and Roc fell forward, stumbling out of the closet and slamming into the dresser. He held onto the shirt and dresser as if they would keep him afloat in the rocky sea of his wavering vision. Something

rolled around inside the wooden drawers. Once he'd steadied himself, he yanked open the top drawer, making it catch
and jerk awkwardly as if it was off its track. But the drawer
was empty. He tried the next and the next until he came to
the bottom drawer and found his stake. Its intricately carved
sides caused it to roll in a lopsided manner. Next to it, folded
inside a T-shirt, was his Glock. He scooped up both and
headed back to the living room.

Rachel was waiting for him, eyeing him cautiously.

"Get your stuff," he said, out of breath and out of time.
His shoulder throbbed, and the breakfast he'd eaten rebelled
in his gut.

"Stuff?" she asked.

He struggled to put on the shirt he'd pulled off a hanger
in Brody's closet. Rachel came to him, helped ease his arm
through the sleeve. "Any clothes…anything that's yours…"
His gaze dropped to her bare feet. "Shoes. Purse. Anything.
Get 'em. Now."

"I don't understand. What's going on?" She guided his shirt
into place, tugging the material up over his bandaged shoulder.

"We're leaving."

"But where…?" She looked up at him with those implor-
ing, trusting blue eyes. "Where are we going?"

He had no real answer for her. Coming here, he'd put her
life at risk. But he hadn't known. He hadn't even suspected.
What kind of a vampire hunter was he? Not recognizing what
Brody had become. He'd been a fool.

He snatched up his holster, shoved the Glock into place,
and then shoved his arm through the leather straps, which
scraped against his wound. He sucked in a breath.

"Let me," she offered. Carefully, as if she needed oven
mitts to handle it, she took the holster from him. He bit

down on a curse word as the thick, leather strap settled on his shoulder.

"That's good enough. Don't fasten it."

A jumble of plans and questions darted through his mind. *Where would they go now? And how would they get there?* He had to get Rachel someplace safe. And New Orleans was not safe. The logical choice was Pennsylvania. She could easily get lost in Amish country. "Have you called your folks?"

"They don't have a phone."

"Levi or Hannah, then?"

She shook her head.

Her family needed a warning they were coming. But how would he get her there? He couldn't drive. Not so far, anyway. And it would probably be better to ditch the Mustang, because Akiva and Brody knew his car. "Is there a neighbor who can get a message to them?"

"There's a Mennonite family nearby, the Detweilers."

"Good. Where's my cell phone?"

She pulled it and his wallet out of her front pocket. When he raised a brow in question, she said, "I thought I should keep them safe. Just in case we had to leave suddenly."

"We do." He looked into her stunning blue eyes and recognized common sense and quick thinking. For better or worse, they were in this together, and he was learning he could rely on her.

Taking the cell phone and pocketing his wallet, he dialed the phone number she gave him then handed the phone back to her. When her family's neighbor answered, she explained she needed to get a message to Levi for him to call them on Roc's cell phone.

While Rachel finished the call, Roc sat on the sofa and grabbed Brody's laptop. Ultimately, they needed to disappear for good. But for right now, they needed out of the area and fast. Faster than his Mustang could take them.

He had to get Rachel home. That was the only answer. So he did a quick search for flights out of New Orleans. But then a thought occurred to him.

"Do you have a driver's license?" he asked Rachel.

She shook her head.

"Then flying isn't an option."

That left two others: bus or train. But before he could make a decision, the door opened.

"Feeling better?" Brody asked. Sunlight spilled around him and made his features dark and sinister.

"A hundred percent," Roc lied, slowly closing the laptop.

"Good." Brody raised his shades to the top of his head, and solid black eyes met Roc's. Those eyes answered all of Roc's questions. "I brought you a visitor."

CHAPTER THIRTY

Levi forked the hay and pitched it into the bin for the cows. The sun bloomed, its rays spreading outward like petals, which soon began to wilt beneath the heat. He whisked off his flat-brimmed straw hat and swiped his forearm across his sweaty forehead. Bits of hay and dust stuck to his skin and itched.

It had been a long morning, and despite the warm, sunny weather, a cloud shifted across his heart. Hannah had woken early, and he'd found her praying and crying softly in their tiny kitchen. He'd tried to comfort her, but he knew firsthand no words could act as a balm to a wound in the heart.

When he'd lost his brother, Jacob, even scripture hadn't brought comfort. It shamed him to say so, but it was the honest truth. But he reminded himself: Hannah hadn't lost Rachel, not yet, anyway, and he prayed she wouldn't have to go through what he had.

But the not knowing…the wondering…the worrying… He understood that too. If something happened to Rachel, the regrets over not warning Rachel about Akiva would torment Hannah. Already, the guilt over hiding the truth about Josef's death clouded Hannah's eyes and her heart, which spilled over into every relationship.

Hannah tried to be upbeat around her mother and Katie, praying with them, sharing with them her confidence about Roc finding Rachel and bringing her home. But at night alone with Levi, her fears tumbled out, and her tears dampened his shoulder. He didn't mind the crying. It was understandable. But the helpless feeling gave Levi a restless frustration inside.

He heard the car motor and tires crunching the gravel before he actually saw the Detweilers' blue four-door stop in the drive. Ben and Linda had stopped twice in the last week to inquire about Rachel. Levi appreciated folks' interest and concern, yet as soon as the Detweilers left, Hannah's mamm would crumple into tears. Katie would join her, hugging her mamm, tears brimming in her own eyes, and Hannah would not be far behind. Daniel, Hannah's father, would head out to the barn and find some work to do. And Levi would be left without any recourse, without any answers.

With a weary sigh, Levi leaned the pitchfork against the fence railing and settled his hat in a respectable manner on his head. Ben Detweiler was a kindhearted Mennonite and a good neighbor to Daniel Schmidt. He had a small farm and worked in Lancaster at the local grocery store. His wife, Linda, stayed home with their four children.

Ben emerged from the car, and it appeared he was alone today. Levi hoped to head him off and answer his questions before any of the womenfolk saw him. But Ben must have seen Hannah's mamm, Marta, first off, for he gave a hearty wave in her direction and started toward the laundry line where Marta and Katie were stretching a sheet out to dry. Levi quickened his pace to catch up to Ben, but before he reached the laundry line, Ben was already conversing with Marta.

"Why, here comes Levi now," Marta said.

Ben turned to face Levi. He was almost Levi's height and wore plain brown slacks and a white, short-sleeve, button-down shirt. His brown hair had been clipped short, and his green eyes were friendly. "How do, Levi."

"Ben." Levi shook the man's hand. "Nice to see you."

"Mind if I have a word with you?" Ben asked, his tone serious and straight to the point.

Katie's gaze shifted back and forth rapidly.

Marta's brow collapsed beneath the weight of worry. "Is anything wrong, Ben?"

"Nah, just needed to speak to—"

"Sure." Relief washed over Levi. This way he could answer Ben's questions and keep the women from getting upset. Or so he hoped. "Come on out to the barn. You can say hey to Daniel while you're here."

Ben nodded to Marta and Katie. "Good to see you two. Linda says for me to tell you she's baking today and has a blackberry cobbler with your name on it."

Katie grinned, and Marta said, "*Danke*, Ben. You tell Linda to come on any time and stay long enough to help us enjoy her fine fixings."

"I'll do it." He turned toward Levi, and together they started the walk toward the barn. They were several steps away from the women when Ben spoke. "I had a telephone call today."

Levi glanced sideways, and his footsteps slowed.

Ben clapped his hand on Levi's back and angled him toward his car. "From Rachel."

Levi stopped walking, but his heart galloped ahead. "Is she...? Well, if she called, then I guess she—"

"She was all right when I spoke to her. She wanted you to call her as soon as possible. I took down the number."

"But"—he turned back toward Marta and Katie, who were busy hanging laundry on the line again—"shouldn't I tell—?"

"I think you should talk to Rachel first."

His heart took an uneven rhythm. "Did she say where she was? Did she say anything about...?" He couldn't hold on to all the questions popping up in his brain like weeds. "Did she mention Roc?"

Ben shook his head. "She didn't say much of nothing other than for you to call her and to keep it quiet."

Levi frowned. He wasn't much on keeping secrets anymore, but until he understood what was going on, a few more would do no harm.

"Wanna hop in my car, and I'll drive you over to my place?" Ben asked.

It began to sink in that Rachel had actually called. She was alive. She was okay. "You really talked to her?"

A smile creased Ben's face.

A reflection of his smile spread across Levi's own face. "This is good. Thank the Lord. This is very good news indeed."

CHAPTER THIRTY-ONE

THE WHISPERS ASSAULTED RACHEL as if they were a storm creeping over the horizon of her mind and darkening her thoughts.

Roc's friend, Brody, stood in the doorway, and she recognized those intense black eyes. The same as Akiva and Acacia. Brody locked gazes with her, and her world tilted precariously, as if she'd lost her footing and grip on reality.

What had Brody meant when he said he'd brought a visitor? Just as the thought flashed, another rumbled, and then another and another, until she was struck by a downpour of fear.

Rachel.

Was Akiva's voice in her head? More whispers whipped about her.

Then *BAM!* A sound exploded in the room. The concussion shook her eardrums. Rachel flinched and covered her ears instinctively, but it was a half second too late. Suddenly, her ears sounded muffled as if they'd been stuffed with cotton.

She glanced sideways at Roc. He pointed his gun toward Brody and said something, but she could see only his mouth move. Before she could scream for him to put the gun away, another *BAM* ricocheted around the room. This time, she wanted to cover her eyes. Bright red stain bloomed in the middle of Brody's chest. His expression fell from confidence to shock.

Then everything happened at once, like a tornado ripping through the apartment—crashing thunder, flashing lightning. Roc burst off the sofa, dumping the portable computer onto the floor, and lunged across the room. Brody slumped against the doorframe. Roc moved as though he had not been near death last night, like a lethal animal on attack. Jerking the leather contraption off his shoulder, he secured it around Brody, tugging him inside the apartment and slamming the door closed. The BANG of wood pulsed in her ears. Then he shoved the deadbolt lock into place.

Brody toppled over and crashed onto the floor. As if in slow motion, he rolled over, his arms splayed outward. In the meantime, Roc secured another part of the leather strap to the leg of a chair. But Brody didn't fight, not the way Acacia had. He blinked as if dazed and watched Roc.

"I'm sorry, Roc." His voice was raspy.

"Shut up." Roc pushed to his feet and stood over his friend, staring down at him, his chest heaving with each breath, his wounded arm hanging lax by his side.

"I won't fight you."

Roc turned away and went to the kitchen. "Rachel, get your stuff. We're leaving."

But she couldn't move. She was shaking so hard she thought she might fall to the floor.

Roc came back to the living area, a knife in hand. His face looked pale, his demeanor no-nonsense, his gaze shielded. But Rachel saw the tremor in his fingers. Before she could ask what he was doing, he bent toward Brody and jerked the gleaming blade across Brody's throat. The skin opened a gaping wound, and blood poured out. Rachel gasped, and her own heart faltered. Brody's eyelids fluttered before they closed.

Roc didn't speak to his friend, didn't comfort him, didn't wait. He stumbled to his feet, crossed toward Rachel, and grabbed her arm roughly. "Let's go."

"But…"

He still held the knife. "Now!"

And he whisked her toward the door. Her limbs stiffened and jerked crazily. Her stomach heaved. Suddenly, she was bent over, with Roc holding her forehead. She wasn't sure if she was ill from all the blood or from fear that Akiva might be outside the door.

Swiping a hand across her mouth, she glanced at Roc. "Where's the knife?"

"You okay?" he asked.

"The knife!" Her voice shook. Her chest constricted.

He pulled it out of his back pocket. Blood smeared the blade. She focused on it before drawing a breath and reaching for the door lock. With one more look at Roc, she asked, "You ready?"

"As much as I'll ever be." He gave a nod for her to open the door.

He stepped outside first, keeping her behind him. His muscles were tense, poised for fight or flight. When there was no threat, no one standing outside waiting for them, just the surrounding buildings and swimming pool below, he turned back.

And she saw in his features what the last few minutes had cost him. Roc shuddered violently as he stared at his friend on the floor, blood pooling around the too-still body. Rachel placed a hand on his and helped him close the door.

CHAPTER THIRTY-TWO

H E'D COMMITTED THE FORBIDDEN act. It branded him a traitor. An outcast. A predator. Now, they would be hunting him.

He had become what he'd been fighting. He'd killed his friend. It didn't matter if Brody was a vampire. He was also one of New Orleans's own. A cop.

Killing Brody was unthinkable. Unbelievable. Unforgivable.

But Roc couldn't stop for regret, to grieve Brody, or even to turn himself in.

Helping Rachel into the passenger seat of the Mustang, he glanced around the apartment parking lot. *Whom had Brody brought to visit him? Another cop? Or another vampire? Could it have been Akiva?* Whoever it had been, human or vampire, fled. Or was hiding. And Roc couldn't take the chance whoever might be lurking nearby, waiting for a chance to pounce. He had to get Rachel out of here.

Sliding into the driver's seat, Roc felt his body trembling and shaking in shock over the atrocity he'd committed. Now he would be a wanted man in New Orleans. Hell, everywhere. Chasing vampires was now the least of his worries. He would be chased by every police officer and law-enforcement agency.

What would he do? Continue to run? Hide? Or turn himself in? This was not a wrong he could right. He could never explain his reasons. *Who would understand or believe him?* He took no pride or pleasure in the death of Brody. The only solution was turning himself in. But before he could, before he could own up to what he'd done, before he could suffer the consequences, he had to get Rachel somewhere safe.

He tossed his cell phone in her lap and stuck the knife's handle in her hand. Her startled gaze met his. "If Akiva finds us," he said, "if he's here, we cannot hesitate. We must strike him first. If I can't, then you must. Do you understand?"

She swallowed hard then nodded.

He cranked the engine, shoved the gearshift into reverse, and avoided Rachel's gaze. He couldn't look into those blue eyes, so innocent and pure, and not see his own guilt. He'd never thought of himself as the bad guy. He'd always stood for what was right and good and tried his best even when he'd failed. But now, he detested himself.

Brody had been changed. *But when? When had it happened? While Roc was gone to Pennsylvania? Since he'd returned?* The obits Brody had collected were probably his victims, which went back three or four months. *Had guilt over what he had become made Brody hang on to his victims' wallets and personal possessions, and search out the obituaries? Had the same guilt kept Brody from fighting back against Roc? Had he allowed himself to be killed? Had he wanted to die? Had he planned it?*

Roc understood hating what he'd become and believing death held the only answer, the only hope, the only relief from the pain. But whereas Roc had struggled to change, to battle the thirst for alcohol, Brody had not really had an option. *How could a vampire fight what he was, the thirst burning inside him, a thirst that acted like acid?*

"Buckle up," he told Rachel as he swerved out of the parking space, shifting gears, and tore through the parking lot.

"Where are we going?" she asked, clutching the door.

"I don't know."

The cell phone rang, and Rachel's eyes widened. He grabbed it, checked the number, which was not local, and punched the button. "Yeah, Roc here."

"Roc, I am awful glad to speak to you. Is Rachel all right?"

Propping his elbow on the door frame, he leaned into his aching arm. "Yeah, Levi, she's fine."

At least for the moment.

A whispered "Thank the good Lord," came over the line.

"It's Levi?" Rachel asked, but Roc ignored her and kept his gaze on the road. "Is Hannah there? Can I—?"

Roc concentrated on what Levi was saying.

"And the baby?" Levi asked. "How is—?"

"Yes. They're both fine." Maybe this was divine providence. Maybe this answered all his troubling questions. He would take Rachel home. Levi would take care of her, keep her safe. She could be with her own people once more. She could be home when her baby arrived. And he would return to New Orleans and deal with the aftermath of Brody's death.

"Thank you, Roc," Levi said. "We cannot thank you enough."

Rachel plucked at his sleeve. "Ask Levi to tell Mamm and Dat I am well."

Roc nodded. "Look, Levi, we're in a fix. I need to get Rachel someplace safe. Now." He slammed on the brakes at a red light and then swerved out of the left lane and into the right. Sitting for any length of time was not safe. He glanced at the rearview mirror but saw nothing suspicious—only cars moving along in the regular flow of traffic. But vampires didn't need cars or usual methods of transportation. Akiva could just as easily appear in front of them. Or to the side. Or even above.

To Levi, he said, "I'm trying to figure out the best way to get her home." A long pause gave Roc time to give Rachel more instructions. "Keep an eye out for Akiva. Understand?"

She gave a quick nod, her hand clasping the knife more firmly, and she twisted her head to peer out the rear window then shifted again to peer out the side windows.

Then Roc recognized Levi's long pause as hesitation. Or maybe the phone had gone dead. "Levi? You there?"

"Yes, Roc, I am."

Something was wrong, then. "What is it?"

The Amish man cleared his throat as if paving the way for something difficult. "I'm not sure it's wise, your bringing Rachel here. Not if you're being followed. Or concerned you could be. If Akiva were to come back here…how would I keep my wife, Hannah, safe? And Rachel too? You know Akiva will come here, Roc, searching for her. It will not be safe."

Levi's questions punched Roc in the gut. Of course. He couldn't risk Hannah, either. But where could they go? "I understand, Levi. You're right. Rachel's my concern now." As he said the words, Roc felt the conviction forging in his chest. He wasn't sure why he was willing to take on the responsibility for a pregnant Amish woman. Maybe it was because she'd taken care of him. Maybe it was simply the right thing to do. It certainly wasn't the smartest or safest.

He shoved his hand through his hair then gripped the steering wheel again. "I'll leave a trail leading somewhere else. Don't worry about that, Levi. But always keep a watch. Okay? Call me on this number if you see anything suspicious…if you hear anything…"

"The Lord is good to us. May He protect us all."

Roc stared at the road, saw a red light up ahead, and cut in front of an oncoming car to turn left and avoid it.

"You will let us know you and Rachel are safe, will you not?"

"Yeah. Of course. Sorry I wasn't thinking earlier. I thought it would be easier to disappear in Amish country," he explained to Levi, thinking more out loud than anything else. And now New Orleans wasn't safe, either. Roc had no more allies here. If he stayed, he'd be arrested, and then he couldn't protect Rachel.

Struggling beneath the pain of his shoulder and watching the traffic, he tried to formulate some sort of a plan. Maybe Roberto could get them to South America.

"You have nothing to apologize for, Roc. You are a good man, a gift from the Lord to help us."

"Don't tell anyone you spoke to me, Levi. It will be better if you know nothing. Do you understand?"

"Yes. I understand." Levi paused then said, "You realize, Roc, that Promise is not the only Amish community."

Levi's statement made Roc bolt to attention. "Of course. Why didn't I think of that? Do you have a suggestion?"

"My folks live in Ohio. They moved there after Jacob…well, after everything started. You could take Rachel there and stay with them."

Roc glanced at Rachel. "You know where Levi's parents live in Ohio?"

"I know the name of it, *ja*."

"Okay," Roc said to Levi.

"Good," Levi said. "I will let them know you are coming. My father—" Levi paused again. "He knows about Jacob…and he can help you."

"Tell your father no one can know why we are coming. No one. It isn't safe."

"He won't tell a soul."

CHAPTER THIRTY-THREE

I'll follow thee
Like an avenging spirit I'll follow thee
Even unto death.

A SACRIFICIAL LAMB WAS what he needed.

Akiva fixated on the first "lamb" he could locate without regard to who it was or how difficult it would be to get her alone. A mental stopwatch ticked off the seconds, and he took a running start.

Using the oldest trick in the book, if there had been such a manual as "How to Sabotage a Stranger" or "Abduction 101" or "How to Lure Someone into Your Trap," he drew on his vast experience and whistled shrilly as he came around the corner of Brydon's building, hollering, "Here, Buddy! Where are you, Buddy?"

He looked everywhere but at the one person who was there, lying on her stomach on one of the slatted, poolside lounge chairs. One glance had told him all he needed to know: she had a deep tan the color of honey and long, wavy blond hair. A flowery tattoo sprouted just above the white bikini line on her left hip. He also knew what she was thinking…something about a missing clue, police tape, and murder weapon.

As Akiva rounded the corner, she closed the paperback

novel and sat upright, swinging her legs to the side of the chair. "Looking for something?"

He met her gaze, then. "My dog. You seen him? A big, goofy lab. Ran out the door and—" He gestured with his hand as if helpless. "Now I can't find him anywhere." Walking past her, he pretended to look behind bushes. He rounded the corner of another building then jogged back to the pool decking.

One more innocuous statement should do it. He bent over, bracing his hands on his knees, as if spent and out of options. "Haley…my girlfriend…is gonna kill me."

The woman smiled and placed her book on the ground beside a sweating plastic cup. "I'll help you. What's the dog's name?"

"Buddy." And then he hollered and whistled again.

When she stood and slid her feet into flip-flops, her legs looked even longer. "Buddy!" She walked around the pool. "Buddy!"

"Oh, great," he muttered not quite to himself.

"What's wrong?"

"I left the leash in my apartment."

"Want me to get it?"

He hesitated. "Would you mind? Buddy might not come to you."

"Sure. No problem. Where's your apartment?"

"Second floor. Two sixty-six." He nodded toward the building where Brydon lived, where he lay on the precipice of death. The timer in his head ticked away.

He glanced back at the clueless, helpless woman. "The leash is just inside the door."

She offered a smile meant to comfort. "I'll be right back." With an easy gait, she climbed the stairs. But a moment later, from the door to Brydon's apartment, she called down to Akiva, "The door's locked."

He tapped his forehead with the heel of his hand. "Sorry, forgot that." He jogged up the stairs. "Losing Buddy has me more upset than I would have thought."

"Of course. No problem." She waited for him, her gaze searching the pool area for a wayward dog.

"Was that a black tail?" Akiva asked suddenly, "between those two buildings?"

"Where?"

Behind her back, Akiva turned the knob in his powerful grip, and the door swung open. Brydon lay in a pool of his own blood, and Akiva gave a quick glance around to make sure no one else saw what he was about to do.

As the woman turned, her baby blues went wide at the sight of Brydon, and her glossed, picture-perfect mouth opened. But Akiva moved fast. He gave her a hard right punch to her belly, and the air went right out of her. Bent double, she gagged and sputtered. He hurled her into the apartment where she tripped over Brydon's outstretched legs and collided with the coffee table. She slumped onto the floor as Akiva stepped inside the apartment, confident no one could stop him.

"Oh, yes…'all the devils are here.'"

CHAPTER THIRTY-FOUR

THE TRAIN TOOK OFF just before midnight and chugged through the darkness. Rachel wished it would move at a faster clip to put more distance between her and the memory of what had happened.

Roc motioned for her to crawl into the smaller of the two beds in their sleeping compartment.

She hesitated. "I should see to your shoulder."

"It'll keep." His skin looked pasty beneath the stubble on his jaw, and dark patches circled his eyes, making them shadowy and haggard. His hair had long since fallen out of the rubber band he used to hold it back. To others, he must look unkempt and uncivilized, but to her, he was valiant. Because he had saved her life. Once again.

Reluctantly, she removed her prayer *kapp*, slipped off her tennis shoes, and climbed carefully into bed. Her ankles were swollen, and her lower back ached. But what did she have to complain about? Roc had a serious injury to his shoulder. He had been forced to kill his friend. And it was all her fault.

"You must be exhausted," she said.

He grunted in agreement before flopping onto the bed beside her and mumbling, "I won't hurt you."

"I didn't think you would."

His eyes were already closed. She laid her head on the soft pillow and listened to the rumbling of the train and

felt its rolling gait. He'd told her they were taking a train
north to Philadelphia, but then they would switch and head
west. Pittsburgh would get them closer. From there, they'd
make their way to the Amish community where Levi's folks
lived—Harmony Hollow.

Exhaustion seeped into her limbs. She imagined fields of
green, corn stalks growing, and fruit ripening. Her eyes shuttered closed, and her thoughts went blank.

When something jarred her, she abruptly awoke, blinked
against a pale light and saw Roc leaning one arm against
the sink.

She struggled to sit upright, the baby pressing on her bladder. "Are you all right?"

He grunted.

She shifted to the other side of the bed and set her feet
on the floor. The compartment on the train was the size of
a barn stall. Roc stood only a couple of feet away. His shirt
was untucked and open in the front. She caught a glimpse in
the mirror of his solid chest muscles and flat abdomen. She
pressed a hand against his forehead. His skin felt cool to the
touch, but a fever burned in his eyes.

"You okay? You don't look so good."

"Go back to bed, Rachel."

"Let me help you."

"There's nothing you can do."

Her heart ached for him. She had glimpsed the pain in his
eyes when he'd glanced one last time at his friend. She could
see the same pain now. "You're upset over your friend, *ja*?"

"Ya think?"

His sarcastic tone stung her, but she ignored it. "It's not
your fault, Roc. You had to do it. You could see he was
changed. He was different. Like Akiva. Like Acacia."

Roc faced her then, the tension in his face making his skin taut. "He didn't even fight back. He *wanted* me to kill him."

"You can't know that, Roc. Maybe you surprised him."

"He didn't fight back. *They* always fight back." He pointed toward his wounded shoulder. "Remember this?"

"Maybe," she said, "maybe Brody realized he was evil and didn't want to live that way."

Roc pushed away from the sink and stumbled back toward the bed. He sat on the edge and braced his elbows against his knees. His hands sought sanctuary in his hair. "It doesn't matter if he did or didn't. The fact is: I killed him. Maybe it's worse knowing he believed I would."

She came over to him, stood in front of him, wanting to reach out to him to offer comfort in some way, and yet knowing she should keep her distance. "Roc, I know there is nothing I can say, but—"

"You're right. There's nothing you can say. Go to bed. We'll be changing trains soon."

———

At the station, they left the train and made their way through a scant crowd to the next one, which departed an hour later. They picked up hot dogs and snacks to fill their hungry bellies and settled into the lounge, where they had upright seats. They hardly spoke a word. *What was there to say anyway?* But there were many questions Rachel wished to ask. *How long would they be in Ohio? Would she ever be able to go home again?* But Roc was in too much pain—both physically and emotionally—to bother with her questions. So she remained silent, following his lead and letting her thoughts race forward to what would be her future.

Levi's father, Jonas Fisher, had always seemed stern and

didn't speak much. But his mother, Sally, although quiet, was pleasant and a good cook. Rachel hoped she could be a help to Sally while she was staying in the woman's house. Levi had another brother, a younger one named Samuel. He would be about eighteen by now.

She wanted to ask Roc if she could call Mamm or even Hannah. It would feel so good to hear their voices. But Roc didn't want anyone to know their whereabouts, not only for their safety but for others, as well. She trusted him. *How could she not?* After all, he'd risked his life numerous times for her.

Out the big window, the landscape skidded past, blurring the colors and warping the shapes of trees and telephone poles. Occasionally, she glanced at Roc, who sat beside her, his hands folded across his stomach, his eyes closed. *Was he sleeping or simply shutting her out?*

Of course, he was still recovering from Acacia's attack. His shoulder injury must ache. She had patched it as best she could, but she suspected it might become infected. It would definitely leave an impressive scar. When they arrived at the Fisher home, she would ask Sally for some salve.

But the thought sent a streak of uncertainty through her. *Would Roc stay with them in Harmony Hollow? Or would he leave her?* Suddenly, the idea of being alone caused a cold knot of fear to form just under her left rib cage. The Fishers, of course, would be there. *But what could they do to help her?* She needed…wanted…Roc nearby. He would protect her. *Oh, Lord, help me not to feel afraid. Help me to be brave for whatever may come.*

"What's wrong?" His voice gave her a start, and the baby kicked in response.

"Nothing." She glanced at the other seats around them; some were empty, but a few held passengers who were reading books, fiddling with their cell phones, or flipping through newspapers. Morning sunlight poured through the wide windows. Some of the passengers had pulled the shades and slumped in their seats.

A young man slouched low in his seat. He had earphones over his head, and even from a few feet away, she could hear a steady beat. He somehow looked familiar, and she wasn't sure why until he glanced up and his crystal-blue gaze met hers. He had old eyes—not wrinkled with crow's feet, but ancient, steady, wise. And she'd seen him before, standing outside Brody's apartment. He was guarding her and Roc. The good Lord, she figured, must have sent him.

"You're about to twist that tie to your *kapp* into a knot." Roc placed his hand over hers. "You scared of"—his voice dipped lower—"you-know-who?"

"I know what he can do. *Ja?* But I'm not afraid anymore."

"What took away your fear?"

She pointed in the direction of the young man. "Him."

Roc arched an eyebrow and glanced in the direction she pointed. "Who?"

But the young man with the blue eyes was gone. His seat was empty. It should have startled her, but it didn't. And the young man's absence didn't alter her feeling of peace. She somehow knew he would be back if they needed him.

"Rachel," Roc said, "I'm here."

"Yes." He was. And she was grateful. She gave him an appreciative smile. "*Danke* for that…for all you've done for me, Roc. I am most grateful for your presence."

He remained silent, not responding to her thanks. He simply watched her, studied her like a farmer looking over his crops. "What then? Is it the baby? You feeling all right?"

She smoothed out the tie of her *kapp* and rested her hand

against her swollen belly. She hoped she would be home in time to give birth with her mamm beside her, helping her. *But what about Roc; would he wait with her?*

"What will happen when we reach Ohio?" she asked. "Will you stay? You're not well," she rushed on to say. "You need some rest."

"I will stay until I know the fear of any threat is over."

"When will that be?"

"After your baby arrives safely."

Disappointment mingled with relief. At least Roc would stay. But regret tightened her throat. "So we will be in Ohio till then?"

"Unless something else happens, yes."

She released the disappointment, and it slipped from her fingers. The important thing was for the baby to arrive safely. Then she would go home.

But a thought occurred to her: if they were going to stay in Ohio and hide out among the Amish, then Roc was going to have to change. He glanced at his worn jeans, cowboy boots, and wrinkled shirt, which was left untucked to hide the gun along the base of his spine. He wouldn't exactly blend in with the community. And questions would soon be asked.

"Then we're going to have to do something about your outfit."

His eyes widened, and he glanced at the green shirt he'd taken from Brody's closet. "What's wrong with how I'm dressed?"

"You don't look Amish."

"And you do?"

Her face burned as she glanced down at the maternity top Akiva had bought for her, and the slacks with the elastic waistband. "I will have to buy something suitable too. Or Sally may have something I can borrow."

His gaze shifted toward the window. After a moment, he spoke. "We should arrive to fit our story. Just in case anyone sees us. We don't want any questions asked."

She nodded her agreement. "And what is our story?"

"I've been working on that." His voice remained low, secretive, and gave her a slight tingle along her spine. "You're right. We need to look and act Amish...well, I do...You already are. You'll have to help me, as this is all new to me."

Again, she nodded. She didn't like lying. But these lies weren't simply to protect her baby or herself or even Roc. If questions were asked, if the vines of rumors grew unchecked, then it could be dangerous for the Fishers and the community at large. She didn't want to endanger anyone else. "I will do what I can."

"Good. And I've been thinking about this. We're going to have to say we're married." When her eyes widened, he rushed on. "Because that's the only way I'm going to be able to stay near you in order to protect you. It's not something I want, Rachel. But I have to be near you to keep watch. I'm too tired from this"—he tilted his head toward his wounded shoulder—"to hide in bushes or creep around the house in the dark right now. I'm sorry about that. I don't want to offend you or anything but—"

"Roc." She raised her fingers to stop his rush of rationalizations. She'd never heard him so talkative. "It's all right. I have no reason to question you or doubt your intentions. I understand...and I agree. It makes sense. I do not like to lie—"

"But—," he said for her.

"But," she said firmly, "I must think of it as we are protecting the Fisher family too. This is the best solution."

He waggled a finger at her. "You're smart."

The heat on her cheeks ratcheted up a notch. "I don't want to endanger others."

"We'll make sure they stay safe." His gaze locked with hers, and the certainty of his words, his commitment and promise sank deep within her.

"But—" He leaned close, his breath on her ear sending a rippling sensation down her spine. "You should take off your *kapp*…just for a while. So we don't draw attention *here*, either. I don't want us attracting *any* attention. If someone is trying to follow us, there can't be any trace, no memory lodged in someone's mind. And a woman wearing one of these"—he hooked a finger under her *kapp*'s tie—"catches folks' eyes and becomes memorable."

CHAPTER THIRTY-FIVE

THIS WOULD NEVER WORK.

Roc stared at his reflection in the small, dingy mirror outside the changing stall. It looked like someone had highjacked his body. Decked out in an austere black jacket, white shirt, black pants, and black work boots, he looked... ridiculous. This plain getup was fine for folks like Levi or any of the other Amish folks he'd met while in Pennsylvania, but for him...no way.

He never believed he belonged on the cover of *GQ Magazine* or anything. He'd always been a rebel, not a conformer. The only rebellious thing on him now was his beard, which was beginning to fill in but still looked scruffy. Since married Amish grew their beards long, he figured he could keep that unruly streak a while longer.

"This isn't going to work." He expressed his doubts to Rachel, who was now dressed in a plain, cornflower-blue dress with all the black accoutrements.

"It must." She spoke softly. "The Fishers' lives depend on it."

The new suspender rubbed against his shoulder wound, and he shrugged out of one coat sleeve and let the suspender dangle at his side. As he slid his arm back into the coat, he realized the problem with these pants—they needed suspenders. The loose sides of his plain trousers drooped. *Great.*

Where would he hide his Glock? He couldn't stuff it in the back of his pants, and he'd left the holster back in Brody's apartment. So for now, he slid the Glock in his coat pocket.

"Doing okay back there?" The store clerk walked toward them.

It wasn't much of a shop, more a catchall kind of place. When they had reached Peebles, Rachel had asked an Amish woman, who looked older than the hills, where they might buy some clothes. The elderly woman had directed them to this out-of-the-way, unassuming shop.

"Can I get you anything else?" the clerk asked.

Roc glanced at Rachel then told the clerk, "Yes." Then he thought better of his response and added, "*Ja.* A hat."

After being fitted with a wide-brimmed straw hat, Roc paid the shop owner.

"*Danke,*" Rachel said to the man. It was her subtle way of showing Roc how to behave. He watched her demeanor, the slight lowering of her chin, the demure look. *Did the men have to behave the same?* He tried to remember how Levi spoke and acted. Levi Fisher was a man—solid, strong, and yet humble all at the same time. Roc admired the younger man, and yet he didn't know if he could conduct himself in the same way. But he'd try. So he followed as Rachel walked toward the door and attempted to parrot her. "Yes...*ja,* right. *Danke.*"

He tried to pick up the rhythm of the speech and dialect, but it wouldn't be easy. His plan was to get to Jonas Fisher's place and stay in lock-down mode until the danger had passed.

Earlier, Roc had explained to the shopkeeper they had run away from home and eloped. They were coming back to apologize to their families, but they wanted to look respectable and plain as they did so. The man's gaze avoided Rachel's big belly, but he nodded and then had found what they needed.

Roc held the door for Rachel as she stepped outside. Both of them carried a small plastic bag with an extra change of clothes they'd purchased.

It was a sunny day with a cloudless sky, and the temperature was climbing its way up the thermostat. They'd taken train, bus, car, and bus again to get this far, purposefully taking a circuitous route. They were in Adams County, an hour or so away from Cincinnati, and not too far from the little community of Unity. Just beyond was Harmony, where Levi's folks lived.

This quaint town had a Main Street running through the center, where most of the businesses lined up respectfully. Mostly, cars traveled along the two-lane road, but occasionally he spotted a horse and buggy, the clip-clopping sound so reminiscent of Promise.

Most stores had hitching posts for the Amish buggies, which made Roc feel as if they'd time-warped back to the 1800s. The village was situated not too far off the Appalachian Highway, which placed them in a remote part of the country. A place Roc hoped Akiva would never be able to find.

"Now what?" Rachel asked, glancing around at the tall oaks and pines.

"While you were changing"—Roc guided her down the edge of the road, which didn't have a sidewalk—"I asked the shopkeeper if there was a driver we could hire to get us to Harmony." He'd remembered talking to Amish teens back in Promise, who had told him they couldn't own a car, but they could hire a driver without any ramifications or consequences from the *Ordnung*. He figured it was the best way to arrive at the Fishers'. "He told me of a fella who runs a nursery. A Mennonite. His son drives some of their Amish neighbors around."

She nodded. "But we need to take care of your beard."

"My beard?" Roc rubbed his jaw. "I thought a married Amish man grew a beard, and since we're supposed to be—"

"Yes, but"—she covered her upper lip with her forefinger—"not here."

"You're gonna make me shave my moustache?"

"Of course not," she said, her mouth curling at the corner.

He frowned. "All right, fine. We'll get a razor at the general store. You'll have to do it though, so it's authentic."

It wasn't a far walk to the general store and then the nursery, and his shoulder was feeling somewhat better as long as he didn't move it much. A sign for Serpent Mound grabbed his attention. Below the arrow, pointing cars in the direction of the tourist attraction, the sign read, "Ancient Native American Burial Mound." He figured he'd stay clear of that location. Cemeteries of any kind had never interested him, and since rescuing Rachel's sister in the Promise Cemetery he preferred to keep his distance.

It felt as if suddenly every eye in the village stared at him. The sun blazed downward like a spotlight, and Roc sweated as a couple of girls on bikes giggled at them. *What? Did he have his zipper undone? Oh, yeah, right. No zipper.*

A little boy pointed. Roc glowered back.

It was then that he realized they were all gawking at what they believed was an Amish couple walking along the sidewalk. Even in this area, with many Amish around, apparently they were still quite a novelty to the "English."

A woman in a car stared at them as she drove by, her car swerving out of her lane. Roc glared at the woman and opened his mouth to holler "Get a life!" when Rachel placed a restraining hand on his sleeve. It was a subtle touch, but it jolted him like a shock of electricity. He jerked his gaze toward her.

She gave a tiny shake of her head. "It's okay, Roc."

"No, it's not." His head swiveled back toward the woman in the car, but she was long gone. "What are they staring at, anyway? You'd think we were buck naked or something."

Rachel's cheeks brightened. "We're interesting to them."

"Like a zoo animal or what?"

"They're just curious."

"They're the freaks." He raised his voice and glanced around.

Her hand smoothed out the material of his sleeve as if she could soothe his flustered emotions. "It's all right. Just ignore them."

It wasn't that he was embarrassed or humiliated, but he felt protective of Rachel, realizing what all she and her family and friends had to put up with from these bozos. "So, you can do that? Just ignore them?"

As they slowed to a stop in front of the general store, she turned and looked right into his eyes. "We must."

———————

A few minutes later they had procured a ride from the Mennonite's son, along with a pair of scissors and razor. Roc sat on a metal stool behind a shed and refused to look at the hair falling around his feet as Rachel trimmed his hair into the bowl shape Amish men wore.

Finally, she gave his hair an approving nod and reached for the razor, examining it. "You sure you don't want to do it?"

He held a can of shaving cream in one hand and a snow-cone-looking pile of it in his other palm. "What if I shave the wrong part? Then I'll look wrong. Out of place."

She gave a grim nod. "All right."

Dipping her fingers into the mound of shaving cream, she dabbed it around his mouth. He ignored the sensation her touch provoked. It had been a long time since he'd been this close to a woman, but he stared straight at her swollen belly and reminded himself she belonged to someone else…if not in reality, then at least in her heart.

"There," she said, surprising him that she'd finished already. She wiped the excess shaving cream away with the corner of her apron.

He fingered the bare, smooth skin around his mouth. In an absurd way, he felt naked. Awkward and vulnerable in front of this woman, he avoided her gaze. His fingers followed the line of hair in a U-shaped beard, and he slapped his hat on his head. Then he rubbed his hand across his mouth and dared a glance at her. "So…what do you think?"

She was picking up the locks of his hair off the ground. "About what?"

"Am I…you know…Amish?"

She looked surprised by his question. "Of course not."

"I mean, do I look it? Well enough to pass for Amish?"

"Oh, well." Her gaze flicked over him. "Yes, you do."

"Good." He caught himself and then said it the way the Amish did: "*Goot.* I think. So the transformation is now complete."

"I believe something like that begins and ends in the heart."

"Yeah, well…" He avoided her penetrating gaze and rubbed his jaw and mouth again. "Do you have a mirror?"

She crossed her arms above her belly. "Are you that vain, Roc Girouard?"

"Just want to see how weird I look. In case I catch my own reflection sometime and shoot myself."

She giggled then hid her laugh behind the tips of her fingers.

His gaze sought hers for affirmation. If he had to look this strange, at least he wanted to be authentic. "So it's true? Looks real, huh?"

"Yes, you look Amish."

His lips twitched. "And why do the men do this?"

"It is a sign of a married man."

"But why?" Before she could answer, he said, "I know— the *Ordnung*."

He didn't understand why these people followed rules set out by some arbitrary group of people. But then again, didn't all societies? He followed rules and laws set forth by the government. Others followed the tenets of their religion, be they the Ten Commandments or fashion magazines. What was the difference?

"Why no mustaches, though?" he asked. "The Amish wives don't like mustaches?"

Her head tilted as if she didn't understand his question.

"You know, in case it tickles…when they kiss." He drew the word out, realizing his mistake in mentioning it.

Heat infused her face, and something stirred deep inside, a feeling he hadn't experienced in years. Why now? Why her? Rachel's eyes sparkled until she shaded them by looking at the ground. He cleared his throat, feeling awkward.

She spoke calmer than his heart rate. "It is considered vain to sport a mustache."

"Huh." He wasn't sure what to say or how to get out of this conversation. "All right then." He glanced down the pathway along the side of the nursery, searching for a distraction of some kind. But there wasn't much of one behind the shed under the shade tree, so he clapped his hands on his thighs and stood. "When is this guy supposed to be here to pick us up?"

"Should be soon." She shifted from foot to foot.

"Uh, here." He gestured toward the metal stool he'd been sitting on during her ministrations. "Take a load off." He realized then it had been a while since they'd last eaten at a bus station. "Are you hungry?"

"I'm all right." But her stomach rumbled.

He eyed her belly warily. He'd never been around pregnant women much, and it put him slightly on edge. "Was that the baby or you?"

"Me, I guess." She gave a soft chuckle. "Or maybe both."

"Come on then. Let's find something to eat."

CHAPTER THIRTY-SIX

*F*OOD, *GLORIOUS FOOD!*
The words of the old song floated through Akiva's mind as he finished off the last of his meal. It wasn't the taste of blood compelling him though, it was the powerful surge flowing through his own veins when he'd finished. It was intoxicating, invigorating, and more than addictive. He swiped his mouth on his sleeve, and pushed the remains of the body away, which flopped over into the dirt.

Slowly, Akiva turned toward his companion. The stocky male was lying on the ground in repose, his hands folded across his stomach, his eyes shuttered closed. But he wasn't sleeping. None of the bloods ever slept. It was something he missed from his old life. Because in sleep he could dream. He could conjure up people and places and anything he wanted. And for just a few hours, he could escape.

But no more.

He nudged the blood's foot. "I'm ready."

Brydon opened his eyes, and a dark, solemn gaze assessed him.

Akiva had garnered Brydon's trust when he'd saved him. Akiva had provided nourishment when Brydon had been too weak, too close to death to find what he had needed to recover.

Ever since, Brydon had remained quiet and aloof, as if something smoldered inside him like a coal of vengeance.

And Akiva had stoked it into a blaze, because he needed Brydon on his side to help him in the very near future. But he would never totally trust this blood, just as he'd never trust any of them.

"Where now?" Brydon asked.

Akiva sniffed the air. He'd followed the scent of Roc Girouard's blood for a while, but unfortunately, the smell had become too faint. Still, he sensed where they were going. "North."

He wasn't in a hurry. Plenty of time remained before Rachel's baby came. And he'd be there when it did.

CHAPTER THIRTY-SEVEN

THE APPALACHIAN HIGHWAY OPENED up a new world for Roc. He'd never known or imagined rolling hills quite like this, many expanding into lush green carpets and fields of corn, while others dipped and dropped into deep ravines or dried creek beds. Lancaster County, Pennsylvania, had been flat as a pancake, but this Amish world seemed hidden from the rest of civilization, set apart by the towering pines and maples. Whitewashed barns and houses dotted the landscape. Most had front porches and swings and laundry flapping on the lines. Some homes had a modern look to them, with cars and farm equipment in the drive, while others gave the appearance of weary trailers, exhausted from having traveled nowhere.

It had taken less than an hour to make the drive. On either side of the barely two-lane road, they'd passed farms where men worked in the fields. One Amish farmer sat on a metal contraption behind a team of honey-colored horses, a small child riding behind his father.

They eventually turned down Hidden Drive, a twisting, turning road, which ended up as one lane traversing a rickety bridge that must have been built at the turn of the nineteenth century. At a bend in the road, a large gray barn stood watch over the area. It looked as if it had been abandoned for some time.

The farther they went, the farther the road took them from modernization. They swooped and swerved around bends and turns, finally approaching the small community of Harmony Hollow. It didn't look like any community he'd ever known, just a smattering of houses, silos, and barns, more spread out than grouped together. Along the narrow road there was an occasional fruit stand, a saddle shop, general store (where they were told they could buy a newspaper and learn the local gossip), and bakery.

The curving road eventually led to a covered bridge, which looked like it was held together with spit and a prayer. They first had to pull to the side of the road and wait for a horse and buggy to travel through the tilted structure.

They survived to turn onto Secret Cove Road. Up ahead, a wooden sign read: Fisher Woodworking. They veered down the sloping gravel drive and through a white picket fence. It led to a whitewashed house surrounded by an assortment of summery flowers in all shades of yellows, blues, and pinks. Set apart from the house was a separate building with double-wide doors standing open, and Adirondack chairs spilling out into the expansive drive. Past the house, a paddock housed a chestnut horse, and a smaller pen kept a pig and a couple of piglets, which tumbled around in the grass together. A barn occupied the space behind the house, and beyond the laundry line, a garden grew corn and a wide assortment of other plants.

Rachel peered over the front seat through the windshield. "This is lovely."

"Let's hope it's enough of a secret," he said as he opened the back passenger door of the station wagon.

The wind stirred the leaves of the towering oaks and maples surrounding the homestead, sealing it off from the rest of the world. The dense forest border gave it a protective feel. Maybe this would be a good hideout.

A stern-looking Amish man walked toward him from what appeared to be a workshop, from which came the grating and hungry sounds of saws and sanders chewing into wood planks. Straightening the confounded black coat, which seemed to absorb every ray of sunlight and trapped the heat against his skin and reset his shoulder on fire, Roc slapped the new flat-brimmed straw hat on his head.

The Amish man's disgruntled, dyspeptic look gave Roc a bad feeling. *What had he gotten himself into this time?* Fighting vampires seemed infinitely easier than fitting into this out-of-date world, of which he knew nothing.

Roc leaned back into the car. The young teen sitting behind the wheel looked like he could have been Richie Cunningham's long lost brother. "Better stay behind the wheel..." Roc said to the teen who had driven them. Out of the corner of his eye, Roc measured the approaching Amish man's dirge pace. "I'll clap the top if all is clear for you to head on back. Otherwise..." He paused, for he wasn't at all sure this was going to work out.

"Rachel," Roc said, extending a hand to her. As she emerged from the backseat, he whispered, "Is this Jonas Fisher coming toward us?"

She nodded, her shoulder brushing his arm as she stood, and her fingers tightened on his hand.

"Is Levi's dad always this happy?"

Her mouth twitched with the start of a smile, and then she suppressed it.

Roc closed the car door behind her and turned to greet the older man. Every Amish man Roc had met over the past few months may have appeared stern or somber on the outside, but so far they'd also transmitted a tranquil manner, as if they were at peace with their choices, and a kindness toward others. Not the case with Jonas Fisher. Something about this man—maybe it was his metallic gray beard that seemed far older than his features required, or maybe it was the weariness in his wooden brown eyes—gave Roc a cold sensation in his gut.

Sticking his hand out toward Jonas Fisher, Roc greeted him. "Your son, Levi, sends his greetings, Mr. Fish—"

"Levi was wrong to send you here." Jonas Fisher's mouth was a straight, firm, uncompromising line. He ignored Roc's outstretched hand. "I won't have you here."

"But—" Rachel started, and Roc silenced her with a slight touch to her elbow.

"Mr. Fisher," Roc said for the two of them, "you of all people should know why I need a safe place for Rachel."

He didn't even glance in her direction. "I have my own family to think of. I won't get involved with—"

"Excuse me, sir, but I believe you're already involved. Now, we can stay here shootin' the breeze, or we can appeal to your neighbors down the road there."

The older man's eyes pinched at the corners. "You're not Amish."

"No one else has to know that."

"You open your mouth, and they'll know." The older man's gaze traveled over Roc. "You won't even have to open your mouth."

"Look, I'm here to protect Rachel till her baby gets here safely. Not preach or chat up the neighbors." If there were neighbors around. Because right now this place seemed very isolated.

Fisher stared at him, and beneath his thick, scraggly beard, a muscle tightened. "Rachel can stay in the house there." He tipped his head toward a white, clapboard, two-story house with a small front porch. A wire stretched outward from the porch toward the side building, and on the wire, clothes danced like skeletons in the breeze. "There's a spare room in the workshop for you."

The distance between house and workshop was far too wide, Roc couldn't take any chances. He had to keep Rachel safe, which required twenty-four-hour monitoring. "We're married."

The older man's eyes widened. "Levi didn't tell me that."

"Do you and Levi discuss everything?"

"He would have told me." He finally glanced at Rachel. "This is true?"

Her hand smoothed over the bump of her belly, and she hesitated a second too long.

"I'll not have anyone living in sin under my roof," Fisher said sternly.

Roc laughed. "You think we're gonna be doing *anything* with her in this condition?"

Fisher blanched at Roc's words.

"Jonas," Rachel said softly, "I wouldn't bring shame to your home or family."

"You didn't consider that when you went off with Jacob—" Abruptly, he stopped himself, and his features tightened.

"Jonas, please," Rachel pleaded.

The sun's rays slanted downward, and the heat soared beneath Roc's black coat. Sweat trickled down his spine.

Rachel stepped toward Jonas Fisher. "You've lost a son, and I've lost a husband." Her voice cracked. "I don't want to lose my baby too."

Fisher's lips compressed, and his gaze finally flickered

downward to Rachel's rounded stomach. He scuffed his work boot over the gravel drive as if he were teetering on the brink of sending them packing.

"Mr. Fisher," Roc began, "the fact is, if we don't stay, you are still in danger. Even in this remote place. While I'm here, I can protect your family too."

"Why do you say—?"

"Because Jacob could just as easily seek you out, along with your wife and youngest son. It's his family too."

The older man's mouth pulled sideways. "Sally don't know none of this. Neither does Samuel, my youngest. I'll not have them learning about it. Do you understand?"

"Of course," Rachel agreed before Roc could argue against it.

Roc reluctantly nodded, buttoning up his own lips in case he spoke out again. *Really, what did this old man think? That Jacob, now Akiva, might never come knockin' on his family's door? That his middle son was really buried in a lonely cemetery in Pennsylvania?*

For a long while, Fisher remained quiet, as if thinking over his options. Hammering came from the workshop, a pounding out of the seconds. Finally, Fisher shook his head. "This will never work," he stated plainly, and his gaze traveled over Roc. "Who would believe you were Amish?"

Contempt saturated the older man's words. Roc thought of telling the man he'd gone undercover many times as a panhandler, a pimp, a drug dealer, and even once as a teacher. But he didn't think any of those examples would impress this man.

"He doesn't have to leave the premises," Rachel interjected. "We'll stay here, keep quiet. No one except Sally and Samuel has to know."

"It'll be all over Harmony Hollow by sunset, probably already is. Sally has been looking forward to having company." Fisher's lips flattened against his teeth. "How long will you stay?"

Roc glanced at Rachel. "Till the baby comes."

"What if—?" Fisher glanced back toward the house, and when he turned back, he lowered his voice. "What if Jacob comes here?"

"I hope we led him away from here." Roc glanced down the sloping drive. "We didn't take a direct path from New Orleans. But if he comes, then I'll be ready for him. And I hope this nightmare will end."

Suddenly Fisher's face looked as if it had aged a decade, the creases around his eyes and along his brow deepening, his skin sagging with the weight of his secrets and fears.

Roc took the moment to press his point. "You can't hide here forever."

Fisher's chin snapped upward. "I'm not hiding."

Okay, mister, whatever you want to believe. "You and I want the same thing, Mr. Fisher: to keep all of you safe."

Fisher swallowed hard. After a few silent moments, he turned his gaze away from them and toward the two-story dwelling.

"Go on to the house, then. Sally will see to your needs."

Chapter Thirty-Eight

S ALLY FISHER WAS AS accommodating and kind as her husband was austere and contrary.

Roc couldn't blame Fisher for his attitude or fears. If the older man knew anything about what his son Jacob had become, then he would want to protect what was left of his family at all costs.

Still, Roc smiled at the pleasant woman, who bustled them into her kitchen and sat them at an old wooden table. Despite the warm weather, the kitchen felt cool in the shade of the trees, and a soft breeze blew through the open windows. Sally fussed over Rachel and her condition, and within a few minutes, she'd discovered they hadn't had a solid meal in a couple of days. She tsked as she pulled out dishes from the propane-powered refrigerator and fixed them hearty sandwiches of carved ham, along with potato salad, orange-and-carrot Jell-O salad, pickles she'd put up herself last week, and fresh strawberries sprinkled with sugar. Roc had never seen such a large offering for a simple midday meal, but he was grateful since he hadn't had his fill in days.

"For dessert, there's rhubarb pie," Sally said as she set glasses of iced tea and lemonade beside their heaping plates.

"Now this woman"—Roc got a solid grip on the sandwich with both hands and leaned toward it greedily—"knows the way to a man's heart."

Rachel stopped him with a soft clearing of her throat. "Shall we say grace?"

Roc pulled his teeth out of the home-baked bread and closed his mouth. "Oh, yeah." He set the sandwich back on the plate and watched Rachel for what to do next. "Okay."

She bowed her head. He followed suit. He checked clandestinely and saw her eyelids close, so he closed his too. Then he waited. No one said anything.

Were they expecting him to speak, to utter some sort of prayer, since he was the only man at the table? He tried to remember back to when he'd eaten with Hannah's family, but beyond the potato rolls, his mind was a big, blank canvas. Silence drummed on with a steady beat of guilt. *What should he say?*

His father had been more on the bottle than not, but occasionally Remy Girouard had tipped his head back and glared up at the ceiling, offering his own version of prayer, which Roc wasn't sure St. Peter would approve of: "Thanks anyway, God, but we got this ourselves." The only real prayers he remembered from childhood were things his mother uttered as she clutched her rosary beads and whispered *Hail Mary* and *Glory Be*.

The latter seemed better suited to these purposes, so as the silence stretched interminably, he spoke in his deepest, most solemn voice. "Glory be to the Father, and to the Son, and to the Holy Spirit." He rushed through as a child might in his race to remember all the words. "As it was in the beginning, is now, and ever shall be, world without end." Then as an afterthought, he added, "Bless this food." He opened his eyes then shut them tight again. "Amen."

Feeling a mixture of relief and pride, he reopened his eyes and raised his head. He couldn't help glancing in Rachel's direction for approval, but the look in her eyes was anything but pleasure.

It was Sally Fisher who finally broke the strained quiet. "Well, *danke*, Roc, that was a right nice prayer."

Heat surged up his neckline. So he focused on the food, grabbing it and stuffing a bite into his mouth. One thing he'd learned about the Amish: they appreciated when folks enjoyed their good cooking, and he grunted and munched and chewed in blessed silence.

When Sally rose from her chair to fetch him more tea, he dared a glance at Rachel again. He shrugged a silent question at her, wondering what he'd done wrong. She leaned toward him and whispered, "We often pray silently to the good Lord. Not always. But—"

He coughed, choking down the big bite of ham sandwich. Silent prayers. He could do that.

Sally turned as she poured tea into his glass. "You all right?"

He nodded and kept quiet. He figured silence was the safest thing he could do while they were staying at the Fishers'. Just keep quiet and keep a lookout.

"It is a long journey you two have made," Sally said after they'd finished dessert. "You must be mighty tired. Especially you, Rachel. If you want a rest, I can show you to your room."

"*Danke*, Sally."

"Mrs. Fisher," Roc began.

"Please, call me Sally. We don't hold to formalities here."

He nodded, beginning to feel the heaviness of the food filling his belly and his shoulder aching. "We appreciate your taking us in like this. Your husband was…" He floundered for the right words. "Well, Levi said…" He fumbled again.

Longing filled Sally's soft brown eyes. "How is Levi?"

Rachel set her fork on her plate. "He is good."

Sally smiled the type of smile only a mother has when speaking about her children. She started asking questions in Pennsylvania Dutch.

What was he supposed to do now? Pretend to understand or confess he didn't? He hoped she wouldn't ask him anything directly.

"He and Hannah are happy," Rachel said, speaking again in English so Roc could understand. She gave a nod toward him. "He doesn't speak Pennsylvania Dutch well yet. I'm teaching him."

Sally's eyes widened. "You married an *Englisher*?"

"He was. That's how he was raised. Now he's Amish."

"Oh, ach!" Sally's cheeks flamed red. "I am sorry for—"

"Don't worry about it," Roc said. "I'm just trying to learn your ways. So if I flub up, just let me know."

She gave him a solemn nod, as if taking a pledge. Slowly, her shoulders relaxed, and she glanced back at Rachel. "I am glad Levi is happy now. He loved Hannah a long time."

"No one really knew that." Rachel giggled. "Although I suspected."

"A mother always knows. He will make a good husband. I always thought…" Sally's voice trailed off, and she shifted her gaze toward her lap. She tapped her hand against the edge of the table and then looked up with an overbright smile. "I wish I could have been at the wedding."

An awkward silence filled the spaces between them. The shades over Sally's kitchen sink flapped with the breeze, which floated through the open window and brought the smell of cedar. There were a thousand questions he wanted to ask Sally Fisher or her husband, Jonas, but any answers would only satisfy curiosity, and few would help today's predicament.

"This was delicious, Mrs.…Sally." He wiped his mouth with the napkin.

"*Gut.*" She rose and took the dishes to the sink. Rachel scooted her chair back to rise, but Sally shook her head. "Rachel, you should rest."

"I can't not help while I'm here."

"Well, that's fine. Tomorrow, you can have chores, but today you rest."

Rachel rubbed the side of her belly, and Roc caught himself watching her, the curve of her fingers, her clean white nails, her strong yet soft-looking hands, the movement of material across the thickness of her waist and narrow hip. Then he jerked his gaze away only to find Sally watching him. The heavy material of his coat shrunk across the width of his shoulders.

"When is your baby due?" Sally asked Rachel as she scraped the plates.

"A few weeks yet." Rachel lifted her feet out in front of her, pointing her toes and then flexing her feet. "And I'll be glad for the baby to be here. My ankles have started to swell."

"Oh, *ja*, that will happen. I can make you a cup of tea."

Roc cleared his throat. "Think I'll go over to the wood shop and see if I can find something useful to do." He stood and walked toward the back door, feeling awkward. He'd scope out the property, get his bearings, scout out any vulnerable areas and any good watch points. "I'll, uh, be back later."

"I hadn't heard about Josef," Sally said to Rachel as he stepped out onto the porch, "...until Levi called to tell us you were coming here." Roc headed quickly across the yard, more than willing to let Rachel field those questions on her own.

CHAPTER THIRTY-NINE

RACHEL SAT AT SALLY and Jonas Fisher's kitchen table, keeping her gaze on her plate. The strain of silence stretched between them all as they passed around beef noodles, corn on the cob, green beans, creamed peas, bread, butter, and honey. Jonas had not said anything when he came in the door with his youngest son, Samuel. He'd simply shoved his straw hat onto the peg beside the door and sat down at the head of the table.

The boy, Samuel, was no longer really a boy but a man full grown. He reminded Rachel of Levi—tall, broad shouldered, with blond hair and startling blue eyes. His square, firm jaw had the slant of stubbornness. He ate like any other eighteen-year-old, piling the food on his plate and eating as if he didn't need to breathe between bites. Before the rest of the family, at their more leisurely pace, had finished, Samuel wiped his mouth on his sleeve and scooted back from the table.

"Whoa there, Samuel." His father slanted his gaze in his son's direction. "Are you in a hurry this evening?"

Without stopping, Samuel removed his plate from the table and set it on the counter. "I promised Rafe Peterson I'd help him out."

"With what?"

But Samuel only said, "He's waiting on me, Pop."

"Will you be late coming home?" Sally asked, her tone softer, less confrontational than her husband's.

Samuel plunked his straw hat on his head. "Don't wait up, Mamm."

As the young man whisked out the door, his father frowned and turned his attention back to buttering his corn. Nothing else was said, but Rachel understood the disquiet in the Fisher family. Many Amish families experienced the same when a child was in his running-around years. And as her own parents had experienced, some children caused more worry than others.

Jacob had definitely given his parents long, sleepless nights. Was Samuel as worrisome? Or was it because of their experience with Jacob and his sad end that they worried even more over their youngest?

After dinner, Rachel helped Sally with the dishes while Roc circled the premises. Before he came back inside, Rachel bid Sally and Jonas good night and headed to bed.

The upstairs bedroom was small and clean, efficient in its offerings: a double bed, dresser, and bedside table. The bathroom was only a few steps down the hall. Rachel went to the window to lower the shade but looked down on the quiet road, the blacktop glistening in the waning glow of the warm red sunlight.

From around the corner of the house came Roc, and she watched him walk beneath the shade of the soaring oaks. He moved slowly, steadily, cradling his wounded arm against his middle. She'd seen him wince several times throughout the day, but he'd never complained, never asked for help or sympathy, never offered excuses, not even when Jonas had told him he could muck the stalls tomorrow morning. Roc was a strong man, a proud one, and he made her feel safe, safer than she'd felt in months…maybe even years.

The sun had not yet set, and the red-and-orange rays doused the land with a friendly hospitality. She pulled the shade down over the window and changed into a white cotton nightgown. The material was soft on her skin, and she touched her belly. The baby shifted and moved beneath her hand.

She was just setting her prayer *kapp* on the bedside table and unfastening her hair when there was a light knock on the door. Her hands stilled, and she stared at the door. *Was it Sally? Or worse, Jonas?* Finally, she offered a tentative, "Yes?"

"Can I come in?" Roc's low and gravelly voice was anything but comforting.

Her stomach tipped sideways. "Of course."

The door opened, and Roc stepped inside, his work boots scuffing the hardwood flooring. He'd removed his hat downstairs. During dinner, he'd held himself in check, guarding his expression, but now she could see the exhaustion etched on his face. With his chin tucked down toward his chest, his dark gaze remained steadfast on her.

A cool shiver shimmied through her. "Is everything all right?"

"All locked up tight." The door latch clicked closed behind him.

She nodded and felt the weight of her hair cascading down one shoulder, as well as the headiness of their being alone together. Roc stood by the door, not moving farther into the plain bedroom, his gaze shifting sideways toward her dress, which hung on a peg in the wall. Soon his clothes would hang next to hers in the intimate way of husband and wife, side by side, and longing twisted deep inside her.

He cleared his throat. "Look, Rachel, I know this is awkward, but it's the best way for—"

"It's all right, Roc. Come in. You look so tired, as if you could topple right over."

The lines at the corners of his eyes pinched, but still he didn't move forward.

She felt the heat of her rounded belly against the top of her thighs. "I'm big and fat and pregnant, Roc, and I doubt you're panting with eagerness to get into bed with me. Am I right?"

He rubbed a hand over his wounded shoulder. "You have nothing to fear from me. I'll not disturb you."

Regret pinched her. She was no longer young and slim. Even though she was just over twenty years old, she felt a hundred years. It was a discomforting thought that she suddenly wanted Roc to look at her with desire, and she prayed for forgiveness.

Would she ever feel the soft, loving gaze of a man again? Maybe she shouldn't want that, but she did. She remembered Josef's look when he met her gaze across the kitchen table after he'd eaten the supper she'd fixed. *Would she ever feel a man's hunger and need? His weight atop her? The yearning, unfolding ache inside?* Heat surged up her neckline, and she straightened the material over her belly.

Roc moved across the room. He tugged off his boots and set his gun on the bed, which Rachel stared at, unsure if she should be appalled or grateful for its presence. Next to the gun went the heavy wooden stake, the tip stained dark, reminding her why Roc was here and what his weapons would do if given a chance. Even though the stake had been washed with water, nothing could remove the blood, just as nothing seemed to be able to remove her own sins.

She could hear the house settling, the creak of the stairs, Jonas Fisher's deep voice from down the hall, a toilet flushing.

She tried to avoid looking at Roc, but there wasn't much else to grab her attention. "I should look at your shoulder. The bandage needs replacing."

Padding barefoot across the room to the dresser, she retrieved the tape and bandages they'd bought at the pharmacy earlier. When she turned, Roc was standing beside the bed in only his pants, his torso bare. A white bandage covered part of his shoulder, and she focused on that patch to keep from staring at him, at his flat abdomen, the ripple of his muscles beneath taut skin, the shadow of dark hair trailing down below the waistband of his pants.

"Where do you want me?" he asked.

She blinked. Nerves jumbled together in her stomach like a tangled mess of yarn. "What?"

"Where do you want me to stand or…"

She gestured toward the bed. "You can sit."

He obeyed, and she took hesitant steps toward him. It was one thing to touch him when he was feverish and ill and even unconscious, but now…alone with him as he watched her, his breath brushing her forearm, he was so vital, so alive, so—

"Something wrong?" He twisted his head as if to peer at his own shoulder.

"No, it's…" She picked at the edge of the bandage and pulled part of it loose.

He sucked in a breath through his teeth.

"I'm sorry." Her fingers curled into her palm. She didn't want to hurt him.

"It's okay. Do it fast."

"Fast?"

"Just rip it."

"I don't know, Roc—"

"Just—"

She jerked the bandage off in one swift flick of the wrist. His eyes widened. His lips flattened against his teeth. But he said nothing.

He nodded his approval of her quick movement, but it was her turn to suck in a breath. Angry red-mottled skin surrounded the wound. An infection was taking hold. She went back to the dresser and retrieved the chickweed salve she'd borrowed from Sally earlier. She dabbed the wound with a coated finger and tried to ignore the way Roc's features tightened with discomfort. She worked as quickly as she could and then opened a new bandage and placed it over the wound.

Roc held his breath, trying to focus on the throbbing in his shoulder rather than the way Rachel smelled, her gentle touch, her nearness. It was insane. She was pregnant with another man's baby. She wore clothes that discouraged a man's thoughts going down the wrong trail. Her nightgown was buttoned up to her neck and brushed the tops of her toes, and covered everything in between. Still, his gaze shifted toward the material, which flowed over her breasts and molded to her legs as she walked. And he held himself in check, his body taut.

"Okay," she said, "all done."

He jumped off the bed, moving away from her as quickly as possible. As penance for his wayward thoughts and to get his mind back to fighting vampires, he slapped a hand against the bandage, and a stab of pain rocketed through him.

"Be careful, Roc."

"I'm good. Thanks."

She walked back to the other side of the bed and climbed in, tucking her feet beneath the sheet. The quilt made of dark blue, woodland green, and deep purple in a bold pattern had been worn thin by years of use.

Sweat prickled his forehead. "Is it hot in here?"

"Warm, I reckon."

He stared up at the ceiling: no vents, no fan, no air conditioning. "I'll open the window."

Taking his time, he lifted the shade, opening the window, and drew in huge gulps of warm night air. A moth flew into the room and circled the lantern on the bedside table. She turned the lever on the side of the lantern, and the light vanished. But moonlight filtered into the room, and he could make out her shadow, the stark white nightgown, and her pale features.

Moving toward the other side of the bed, he began to rethink this idea. Lying inches from an attractive woman, pregnant or not, was not going to help him sleep. But the barn or woodshop was too far away to protect her. Still, he knew his limitations.

He hesitated before sitting on the bed. "I'll make a place on the floor."

"Why?" Her voice came out of the darkness.

"Because..." He gestured with his hand toward the bed but couldn't seem to formulate the words he wanted to say. "You'll be more comfortable."

"Roc," she said calmly, "it's all right. If I trust you with my life and the life of my baby, then I can trust you with my tattered virtue."

Tattered? What did she mean by that? Still, the whole trust issue put a new spin on things, making guilt poke at him for even thinking indecent thoughts about her. "No need for you to be uncomfortable with me here. I can just sleep on the floor there and—"

"It would make me feel safer." Her voice quavered.

"Safer for me on the floor or...?"

"Here." She laid a hand on the quilt, her fingers curling to pluck at a thread.

He stuffed his baser needs. She was frightened, and why wouldn't she be? She'd been dragged halfway across the country, first by a maniac vampire, and then by Roc. He remembered the fear in her eyes when he'd killed Brody. All the blood. And what if Akiva had been on the other side of the door, waiting for them? She and her baby could easily have been killed. The only thing standing between her and death, then and now, was Roc.

"All right then," he said.

He stripped out of his pants, leaving on his BVDs, and flung back the sheet. Carefully, he lay beside her.

For a moment, it was only Rachel and Roc in the universe, their breath the only sound. He wondered if her heart hammered the way his did.

CHAPTER FORTY

H E SLEPT LIKE THE dead. But not at first.

When he crawled into bed, he was aware only of Rachel, her breathing, every slight movement. Then the sounds from outside crept into his awareness. In some nearby field, a cow bawled. Crickets chirped a persnickety response. Then bullfrogs complained. Some clicking sound went on and on as Roc tossed and turned and stared at the unending darkness. He'd assumed the country air would be quiet and peaceful, but it was louder than Bourbon Street on Saturday night.

Then, just as he grew deaf to all the insects and animals and his eyelids weighted downward and sleep was finally within grasp, a crowing made him jolt upright. He grabbed his Glock and blinked at the blackness encompassing him.

"Roc?" Rachel asked.

"What the hell was that?"

She shifted beneath the covers. "What—?"

The hoarse sound trumpeted again.

"That."

She laughed. "It's a rooster."

He groaned. "It's morning already?" Then he snatched his cell phone off the bedside table. "It's only two."

"Plenty of time for more sleep," Rachel murmured sleepily, rolling onto her side and growing still.

He lay back and stared at the ceiling, flinching each time

the rooster sounded his alarm. By three, he considered shooting the rooster. But by four, sleep washed over him and pulled him downward into a dark hole.

Until something…a sound, a feeling, the touch of cold sheets woke him. He sat upright, blinking at the light seeping around the window shades. Beside him, the bed was empty. Panic sliced through him. *Where was Rachel?*

He'd worried that he would embarrass himself in some way last night, but reality interfered and saved him—he was exhausted, too tired to do anything about his attraction to her. Not that he would, anyway. But then again, some reactions could not be controlled or ignored.

Sleep had finally crept up on him and knocked him out all night like a strong right hook, but now it was well into the morning. And he had to find her. It was his job to protect her. Sleeping so hard was not his way or in his job description.

He tripped getting out of bed; his foot tangled in the sheets. Stumbling, he bumped into the bedside table, wrenched his arm, and cursed. He froze and listened for some repercussion of his indecent language, like the roof caving in, a bolt of lightning out of the blue, or Jonas Fisher clearing his throat disapprovingly. But nothing happened. The house sounded empty and still. Too still.

Trying to hurry, he hobbled around as he pulled on his black pants, then his white shirt, his fingers fumbling as he buttoned and rebuttoned it. He was heading down the stairs, tucking his shirt in as he went, when he realized he'd forgotten his coat. And his Glock.

He returned to the bedroom, shoved the handgun in the back of his pants, the way he might jeans, and the weapon slid through the opening and down one leg. Gingerly, he pulled it free, thankful the safety was in place.

As he barreled down the stairs and into the kitchen, a soft-spoken voice startled him. He wasn't sure what Sally had said but assumed it was "good morning" or the Pennsylvania Dutch equivalent. He gave a courteous nod. "Morning. Have you seen—?"

"Did you sleep well?" She stood at the table, kneading a floury mound of dough.

Although in a hurry to find Rachel, he drew a gulp full of air and forcefully slowed his pace toward the back door. "Yes. I did."

"We thought you might need extra sleep with your shoulder injury. It's better, *ja*?"

He rubbed his shoulder and felt no pain the way he had last night. Maybe the chickweed salve had helped. "Yeah. It is. Thank you. *Danke*. Have you—?"

"Your breakfast is there beside the stove."

He saw a plate covered with tin foil. "And Rachel?"

"She's outside, hanging laundry on the line."

"I'll be back in a minute. Want to say good morning first."

Sally smiled in a shy way, as if she enjoyed the young husband's attentiveness toward his wife. If she only knew.

When she heard the back door open, Rachel snapped the sheet and clipped one wet end to the laundry wire. By the time she'd stretched out the sheet and was reaching to clip the other end, an arm bumped hers. She turned to look into Roc's gray eyes.

He was standing very close to her. "You shouldn't be doing heavy lifting."

"It's not so heavy." Her hands fumbled, and she dropped the sheet, but Roc caught it before it fell into the dirt. "And I'm not so weak."

When she moved to pick up the laundry basket, he scooped it up and tucked it under his arm. A warm breeze ruffled the sheet, and the cold, wet material rippled between them, giving her a reprieve from his serious gaze.

"I'm learning," he said, his voice like raw wool, "you're a lot tougher than I ever would have imagined."

Unsure what he meant, she watched him cautiously until a fly buzzed her ear, and she eased away from him.

He waved his hand, shooing the pesky fly, and followed her back along the laundry line. "That's a compliment."

Her heart hiccupped, and she tucked her chin downward as her cheeks warmed beneath his steady gaze. Shifting the subject, she asked, "How are you feeling today?"

"Good. Better."

She eyed his shoulder, which he seemed to be using more easily. "You shouldn't be lifting heavy things, either."

"I'm tougher than I look."

"I know that firsthand."

It was his turn to frown. "I'm not Superman or anything, Rachel. You know that, right?"

"Super man?" She shook her head as she clipped socks to the line. "I do not think this. I—"

"I can't make any promises, you know, about protecting you…your baby from Akiva."

"I am not asking for promises, Roc. My trust is in the Lord. He will take care of us. Or—" She stopped herself from saying "or not." Maybe the good Lord would see fit to punish her for her past deeds. Or maybe He would forgive. She would accept her fate whatever it might be. She simply prayed for the protection of her innocent, unborn baby. "But you are doing the Lord's work."

"That's one thing I've never been accused of."

"Accused?" She tilted her head to the side, confused by his words, which sometimes didn't make sense to her. "No, it is simply the truth."

CHAPTER FORTY-ONE

Giovanni tilted the glass and listened to the ice clink together. Using the swivel stick, he stirred the Bloody Mary and jiggled his foot as he waited. He hated waiting. It wasn't that he was in a hurry; there wasn't a time consideration at all. But he hated being inconvenienced. And *this* was an inconvenience.

Finally, the back door opened, and Lynn stepped out on the porch, his footsteps light as ever. He looked as if he weighed no more than a pocketful of air and moved like a wisp of a breeze. It had taken some training, but Lynn had become a fine servant. He swept toward Giovanni and gave his usual bow. "Orphelia has arrived."

"Send her in." Giovanni drank a deep gulp of the salty drink, licked the vodka-tainted blood off his upper lip, and set the glass on the arm of his chair. "And, Lynn, make sure we are undisturbed."

"Yes, of course." Lynn bowed again and disappeared through the doorway.

Slowly, Giovanni slid his hand down his thigh and prepared himself for this most unpleasant meeting. He'd been in charge of this district for almost a hundred years. When he had first experienced the change, he'd been thirty-five and an officer in the Mexican army. He much preferred New Orleans—its slower pace and lively nightlife—to how he'd lived in Mexico.

A moment later, Orphelia wrestled her overly large body through the narrow opening of the French door. Sweat dotted her forehead and made her dark skin glisten in the afternoon light. She mopped her face with a handkerchief and tucked it between her gallon-sized breasts.

"Good afternoon, Giovanni." She stepped hesitantly forward. "How can I help you this fine day?"

He didn't respond to her greeting or question, just watched her, her hands twitching with nerves, more sweat gathering above her upper lip. This kind of waiting he enjoyed. The anticipation.

She shifted before him from foot to foot. Her sarong-styled dress draped over her lumpy figure, and part of the hem dragged along the wooden planks. "I guess you heard the bad news."

He templed his fingers in front of his chest. "And what might that be?"

"About Acacia." Her eyes, black as midnight, dipped at the corners. "She was a good girl. Most of the time. Really, she was. But she could be so mischievous. And I reckon she done poked that little pug nose of hers into the wrong spot. That's the only thing I can figure. Because who would want to harm someone like her? She was as innocent as they come."

"Innocent? Are any of us innocent, Orphelia?"

"We are what we are. But—"

"Who did it?" He interrupted her. "Who killed her?"

"I…I don't know."

He tapped his index fingers together. "You've heard the rumors."

"No one can hold with rumors. Can they?"

"Then tell me the truth." He banged his hand on the arm of the chair. "Who did it?"

Orphelia flinched and edged back a step. "Some says Stephanos did. He may have wanted to. When he found Acacia in his room, watching him and that girl...well, he was none too happy. And I tore into Acacia. She shouldn't have been watching something like that. But he wouldn't have killed the girl. I don't believe that at all."

"I put you in charge of her, didn't I?"

Her thick neck convulsed with a swallow. "Yes, you did. And I did my best with her. I did. But—"

"You should want to know the killer as much as I do. You of all people know the plans I had for that girl."

She whisked the handkerchief from the front of her dress and swept it over her features. "I can find you another girl. Just as perty. You can pick her out. And I'll take care of everything, I will."

"Who did it?" His voice remained low and threatening.

"Could've been Akiva. He borrowed Acacia for a time... when he came here to see you."

Her insinuation pointed a fat finger at him. His gaze narrowed, and he leaned forward, pressing his lips against his index fingers. "That so? Why would Akiva do such a thing?"

"He don't understand our ways. He's a rebel for sure. Why, he is wild and unpredictable. It wouldn't surprise me one bit iffen—"

"He will pay. You can be sure of that. But first, there is another debt to be paid."

"That's right." Orphelia slid her damp palms along her hips. The white hankie fluttered in the breeze. "And you just pick out the girl...I'll bring you several to choose from. It won't be no problem—"

Giovanni moved as fast as lightning, rising from his chair. His glass tipped over and broke, blood and glass shooting outward. Before she could react, Giovanni grabbed Orphelia, wrapped an arm around her neck, and with a swift, hurling action, he ripped off her head.

Her body twisted around from the force then swayed as if in shock for a few seconds before her legs collapsed. Her body crumpled and flopped jerkily to the porch planks. Blood spurted and poured from the open neck. Holding out the head by her hair, Giovanni backed up to his chair and sat again. He held the head out and it dripped blood onto the floor.

The back door opened discreetly, and Lynn stepped out. He slid a fresh, clean glass with ice and vodka beneath the head and caught some of the blood. He exchanged Giovanni's glass for Orphelia's head. It would be strung up on a branch of one tree and Orphelia's body from another until the blood was drained from each and the job complete. It would then serve as a warning to other vamps not to cross Giovanni. Finally, the remains would all be burned until there was no more.

CHAPTER FORTY-TWO

WHAT WAS POP THINKING?

Samuel snapped his suspender in place, scratched his head, and walked toward the odd fellow who had moved into their upstairs bedroom. "Look here!"

Keeping an eye on this fellow, who didn't seem to know the first thing about livestock, was proving an annoyance. He knocked the shovel against the stall door. "You use this first."

Roc sneezed.

Samuel clapped a hand on the pole handle and shoved it toward Roc. "Not all manure clumps together."

"So I've noticed." Roc propped the pitchfork against the wall and rubbed his face with the front of his untucked shirt to rid it of sweat and bits of hay. He'd already removed his coat and rolled up his sleeves. Through the thin cloth of his shirt, Samuel noticed, it looked as if a bandage covered the man's shoulder.

Roc hesitated, the shovel swinging reluctantly in the air, and then he shoveled manure, wincing as he did so. But then, trying to reach beneath the horse without getting too close, he jabbed the shovel into the hay instead.

Samuel laughed but hid it beneath a cough. "You might find it easier if you took ol' Linda there out of the stall."

Roc leaned on the shovel handle. "That so?"

The mare snorted and stamped her foot. Roc jerked

upright, making Samuel laugh out loud this time. He walked into the stall then and took hold of Linda's halter. As he led the mare out, Roc gave them a wide space. But before they'd fully left, the mare lifted her tail and made another deposit on the hay-strewn floor.

"Thanks, stud." Roc grimaced.

Samuel chuckled. "Linda's a mare."

"Right."

Glancing downward, Samuel added, "Take the manure out to the garden. Mamm uses it for fertilizer."

Roc frowned. "Take it out how?"

Samuel looped the lead rope around a weathered board then patted the side of the mare's neck. "The wheelbarrow works well."

"Wheelbarrow," Roc repeated as if he didn't know what one was. "I'd thought of using that motorcycle I saw out back."

"Well, you'd have to get it working first."

"Is it yours?"

Samuel nodded. "Yeah. Paid good money for it but—"

"Maybe I can take a look at it."

Samuel paused, tilted his head, and studied Roc for a moment. "That would be appreciated."

"No problem. That is…if…"

"If what?"

"If you take the manure out to the garden. Deal?"

"It's your job."

"Your decision."

Samuel scratched his head. "How do I know you'll do more than look? That you actually know about fixing a motorcycle."

"Guess you'll just have to take a chance."

Shaking his head, Samuel went back to the feed storage and scooped out the oats for the horses. *Why had Pop allowed*

this man to come here? For the life of him, Samuel couldn't figure Pop out. Ever since Jacob had died back in Pennsylvania,
Pop had been a bit tetched in the head. Mamm said, "Give
him time." Samuel had tried, but he missed his brother. He
wished they could at least speak of him now and again. But
his brother's name had been shunned.

Samuel shooed a momma cat off its perch on the pile
of feed sacks, and hefted a fifty-pound bag onto his shoulder. He set it down against the barrel drums and pulled the
string to open one end. Pouring the contents into the empty
barrel, he wondered why Pop had allowed Rachel to come
here. Pop had never particularly cared for Rachel. She flirted
with the boys in the district. Pop had warned Jacob years ago
about taking her on his trek across America, but Jacob had
held firm.

Rachel had come home before Jacob had. Maybe that
was enough to cause Pop to forgive her. Or maybe Rachel's
father had written and asked for a favor. But Samuel didn't
think Pop kept in touch with anyone from the old district of
Promise. Even here in Ohio, Pop kept to himself. There had
been a time when Pop laughed, but those days were gone.

A clattering at the other end of the barn alerted Samuel.
He glanced over his shoulder but couldn't see around the
bend. With a sigh, he made his way back to the stranger who
seemed ill suited to the work and clothes of the Amish.

Linda, the sorrel mare, had pulled the lead rope loose.
Now, she had the stranger backed up against the wall and was
nuzzling his beard.

Samuel laughed as he approached. Hooking an arm around
the horse's neck, he turned her head. "Come on, ol' girl.
He's not your type." The warm mare's breath puffed against
his hand. He grabbed the halter and led her back toward

the stall. To Roc, he said, "You haven't been around horses much, have you?"

"Not much, no."

"Then I reckon you know cars or motorbikes. So it's a deal."

The strange man laughed and handed Samuel the shovel.

When Samuel left the stall, he noticed Roc's coat had fallen off the post where he'd placed it earlier, and reached to scoop it up. As he did, something clunked against the post.

"Whoa there!" Roc called and snatched his coat out of Samuel's hands. "Thanks. I…uh—" He hung his coat over his forearm and held it against his stomach. "I'll get the wheelbarrow for you."

CHAPTER FORTY-THREE

SUNLIGHT SCORCHED THE FLAT clouds, bleaching them to a lifeless white. Feeling depleted, Roc sympathized. He hadn't worked this hard in years, and anticipating the close of the day, he was thankful the Amish turned in early.

He had spent much of the day in the workshop, unloading a truck, which had delivered planks of wood. Jonas Fisher seemed to take perverse pleasure in handing out chores. At least with the chore he was headed to now, Roc would be alone for a few minutes.

He trudged toward the barn, head down, shoulder aching, and stopped at Samuel's motorbike. Kneeling at the engine, he checked the lines, valves, and—

"Ouch!" The high-pitched squeal gave Roc a jolt. It came from the barn.

It sounded like someone...Rachel maybe...was in distress. *Had something happened? Was she in labor? Or was it something more dire?*

He bolted toward the barn opening, running the thirty yards, and rushed inside. His eyes adjusted quickly to the dimmer light provided only by the sun's rays slanting through the doorway and cracks in the wood-plank walls. His heart pounded unevenly as he scanned the shadows.

"You stinker!" Rachel sat on the hay-strewn dirt floor.

Her voice tilted into laughter as she pulled a calico kitten off her lap, its claws clinging to her apron. She held the little creature up in the air and peered into its furry, whiskered face. "What do you think you're doing?"

The kitten mewed, and a gray one darted around from behind Rachel. She laughed, her eyes brightening. Then she saw Roc. The light in her eyes remained like a beacon. She tilted her head toward the kitten, nuzzling the furry critter against her cheek. "Aren't they cute?"

He was breathing heavily and slumped against a stall door. "Yeah."

Her brow puckered with concern. "Are you okay?"

He nodded, his heart rate subsiding to a steady rhythm. "I thought—" He shook his head. "I'll just—" He backed toward the doorway.

With a forefinger, she stroked the calico under its chin. "Come sit down for a minute."

"I need to...uh—" But he didn't know what he needed to do. He simply wasn't needed here.

"Oh, you can spare a minute. Or are you so eager to get back to helping Jonas?"

Certainly not. He'd regretted all morning saying to Jonas, "Sure, what can I do?" when asked if he'd like a chore or two to earn his keep. Of course, he thought he was earning his keep by protecting the Fisher family, but the Amish way of thinking, he'd learned, was definitely not his.

"I guess he can do without me for a minute," Roc said as he cautiously moved forward and sat a couple of feet away from Rachel, his legs folded. He clasped his hands in his lap, tapping his thumbs together. "I don't know much about carpentry work anyway."

She smiled as if understanding.

"Or horses. You like animals, I gather?" he ventured, not knowing what else to say or do.

She giggled at the kitten, which scrambled out of her grip. "Don't you?"

"I don't have anything against them. Never was around them much, though."

"Really? No cows in New Orleans?"

He eyed her curiously and decided, in spite of her serious expression, she was teasing him. "We get our milk at the grocery store."

"Eggs too, I suspect." Her eyes twinkled.

"Exactly." He focused on the kittens—calico, gray, and orange tabby—as they tussled and rolled over one another. One ran across his lap. "Like normal kids."

She grinned then, and the effect of her smile had him shifting uncertainly.

"What about a dog or cat? You never had one as a pet?"

"Couldn't afford it when I was growing up. Then was too busy, I guess." Although he remembered how Emma had wanted a puppy, and he'd avoided the subject…until it was too late. "Guess you grew up with a lot of these." He flicked the tail of an orange kitten as it darted past.

She rubbed the gray kitten's head against her cheek. She touched noses with the little pink one. "Every animal has a function."

"Cats? They're decoration…and they rule, right?"

"They eat barn rats and mice."

He smiled and looked at Rachel in a new way—she was tough in a practical way most other women were not. At least not any women he'd ever known.

She placed the squirming calico kitten into his arms. The kitten bolted, leaving a tiny red line across the back of his hand.

"Oh, I'm sorry." Rachel reached for his hand. "That's my fault."

"You're not the one with the claws." He wiped the back of his hands on his black trousers. "Did you come out here to play with the kittens or—?" He paused, not really knowing what to say.

"I wanted to smell home."

"Home?"

She smiled. "Hay and horses. Makes me think of home." Her gaze drifted. "What did your home smell like?"

"Booze." He said without thinking and regretted it when Rachel gave him a sorrowful glance. "And magnolia blossoms. My mother clipped them and placed them in a bowl on the table sometimes."

"That's nice."

But it had never covered the smell of booze nor the indefinable scent hovering in the New Orleans air like incense.

"Do you miss home?"

"Not so much." He avoided her gaze and searched for a new topic. The kitten returned and arched its back, rubbing the top against his knee. The long gray tail curled over his kneecap. "So now you want to be friends, eh? Just like a woman."

Rachel studied him. "You have difficulties with women?"

"Not all. Just seems typical."

Dipping her chin, Rachel stared at him. "Are you speaking of your wife?"

She couldn't have surprised him more if she'd punched him in the shoulder. Or hurt him worse.

He remained silent, not knowing how to answer her. He hadn't been thinking of Emma. Or had he? But maybe that's exactly how Emma was…loving him, making him believe and hope, and then carving out his heart and taking it with her when she died. Not that it was her fault.

"I'm sorry, Roc." Rachel interrupted his thoughts with her soft voice. "It isn't any of my concern."

"It's okay." He shrugged, batted away the calico kitten, and pushed against the floor to stand. But Rachel placed a hand on his arm.

"Did she hurt you so awful much?"

He met her inquiring gaze, his defenses squarely between them. "She died."

She withdrew her hand as if he'd slapped her.

"What'd you think? That she divorced me?"

"I...I didn't know. I'm sorry, Roc." She swallowed hard. Suddenly, she looked pale, her blue eyes filling with tears. "I know what it's like to lose someone you love."

He'd heard it said before: "I know how you feel." *But did anyone really?* Most of those who had declared such empathy had lost loved ones to cancer or a car wreck or a grandparent to old age. *But had anyone lost a loved one the way he'd lost Emma? Suddenly? Violently?* And yet, he'd seen Rachel's husband dead on the ground. So he held back his usual sharp retort and simply nodded his acceptance of her sympathy. She understood. And he understood her. Which made him nervous and in need of distance.

He jerked to his feet, unsteady for a moment in an awkward fashion. "I better get back to work."

She nodded and stretched out a hand to him. "Me too."

He hesitated before taking her hand then helped her to her feet, clasping one hand and bracing another beneath her elbow. Although burdened by her growing belly and the baby inside, she stood easily, light and graceful. She held on to his hand even when he would have released her.

"Thank you, Roc."

He took another step away. "For what?"

"For all you're doing to keep me and my baby safe."

He stared down at the floor. It's what he hoped some-one...Brody...would have done for Emma, if he'd been the one to die and she had lived. A hard lump formed in his throat. He walked out of the barn and glared at the fiery sun in the sky until it burned away watery emotions.

CHAPTER FORTY-FOUR

THE HEAVY FRAGRANCE SATURATED the night air. Akiva breathed it in deeply and fully, savoring the scent of blood. His outstretched limbs bobbled on the current keeping him aloft. For several minutes, he circled, each swoop smaller and lower than the last, as if he was sketching a funnel cloud in the twilight sky. Dark emotions swirled about him, the thoughts so deep and painful they could not be expressed through words, just pure emotion—anger darkening in the heat of hatred.

The house sat off the roadway, sheltered by a copse of trees. Just beyond was a shallow lake, the water level low this time of year. A dog barked at his sudden approach. A soft breeze ruffled the laundry left on the line. The isolated house appeared deserted, the windows dark, shades drawn.

He followed the scent toward the barn. *Were Roc and Rachel staying here with friends, or with strangers?* He had been following their faint scent for miles and was beginning to think he'd lost it, when he'd caught the strong smell in the air above the barn. A lantern glowed in the depths and lured unsuspecting moths and June bugs, which circled and buzzed. But the smell of blood drew him into the shadows.

He smiled to himself. Roc would not survive this night. And then Rachel would be his.

Altering his form, he never once slowed down but

continued the movement with rapid footsteps. He rounded a corner and came to an abrupt stop.

Tear-stained eyes widened at the sight of him. She was young, not more than fourteen or fifteen. She held a knife in her hand, the blade stained with her own blood. She'd drawn bloody lines across her forearm.

"Who are you?" she asked. "What do you want?"

Inside, he burned. He hadn't found them after all. He had been led astray by the wrong scent, the wretchedly wrong beating of a distressed heart. A heart that lured him off track.

Still, it wasn't a full loss. For he was famished. And he spoke in low tones: "'It was a low, dull, quick sound'—that which brought me here—'such a sound as a watch makes when enveloped in cotton. It is the beating of his'…or her"—Akiva smiled—"'hideous heart.'"

CHAPTER FORTY-FIVE

AFTER A WEEK, THEY'D settled into a routine. Roc made his usual rounds at twilight, the stars just beginning to poke holes in the grayness, the pale sky shimmering and the insects tuning up for the night's orchestrations. Roc walked the perimeter of the house and workshop where Jonas built rolltop desks, deck chairs, and bird houses of all shapes and sizes. The scent of pine, cedar, and sawdust hung heavily in the air, the fragrance tinted with the pungent odor of stain, paint, and sealer.

On this night, the Fisher family had already had their supper of chicken, corn on the cob slathered in butter, creamed peas, fresh-baked bread, and honey, and then the family scattered in their own directions. The women were cleaning the kitchen and planning to do some needlework. Jonas had settled into his chair in the family room to read *The Martyr's Mirror*, and Samuel had gone to spend time with friends.

From the guarded looks Jonas and Sally gave each other, Roc could tell they weren't pleased with their youngest son's outings, but they didn't say anything. Rachel had explained it was his *rumschpringa*—the time of his running-around years. Roc had learned about the time-honored tradition when he was in Promise, hanging out with rowdy teenagers, who'd provided him with lots of insights to the Amish. He remembered the young men he'd met there and shared a few beers with. They were basically good kids, and Roc suspected the same of Samuel. Kids were, after all, kids, and they needed freedom to make mistakes and learn and grow. But of course, he knew if he was ever a parent, he might feel differently. Not that he'd ever be a parent.

He'd wondered if Jonas and Sally kept quiet about their concerns because Rachel and he were visiting, but Rachel had assured him it was the Amish way. These parents turned a blind eye to their teenagers' doings, as long as they kept up with their chores and showed no disrespect. The teenagers, after all, had not yet made a pledge to God. "Sinners," she said, "sin. What else can you expect them to do?"

Roc would have preferred that philosophy utilized on him as a teen rather than his old man waking up from an alcoholic stupor and ragging on him for staying out and screwing around. But even that was drunken gibberish. What hounded Roc the most was the time when his father invoked his mother's memory. "It's a good thing she's gone." Remy would shake his head, his whole face drooping with disappointment. "Her heart would be broken."

"Yeah, well, what do you think she'd feel about you?" Roc had fired back, buying him a busted lip.

In the stillness of evening, as he walked the perimeter, Roc thought about his father. *Had Remy Girouard really visited him only a week ago? If so, what did it mean? Was his father dead? And why had Roc thought he'd seen Remy standing outside Brody's apartment, keeping guard?* It made no sense. And Roc had no answers.

Putting the past where it belonged, Roc veered toward the back of the workshop where the barn was situated, his footsteps more sure in the dark than when he'd first arrived in Ohio. A cooling breeze stirred the air, and the clouds bunched together. He'd grown more accustomed to the country sounds of horses and cows and chickens. But he wasn't going to become lax. Every sound kept him on alert and vigilant. He wasn't taking any chances that Akiva might be hanging out, lurking around, waiting for an opportunity.

Thankfully, he hadn't heard any whispers or seen any signs or even heard about any animals dying or folks disappearing. *But would Jonas Fisher tell him if there were?* Maybe he should visit the general store where stamps could be bought and gossip traded. For Roc knew Akiva would come if he could find them. And then all hell would break loose.

He stepped inside the barn and heard the stamp of a hoof and a whiffling snort. A kitten stretched out on a hay bale, its limbs askew and its eyes closed blissfully. The scent of hay and dung saturated the air. He wasn't a country boy and usually kept his distance from the horses, but still he walked between the stalls. Solemn brown eyes watched him. He gave a nod to each horse, which were all looking for a handout. He'd seen Rachel giving them carrots and apples, but he hadn't brought anything with him tonight. Maybe he should. Someday, they could be informers.

As he approached the last two stalls, he heard a shifting of hay. The last stall should have been empty. Maybe it was a kitten.

But then he heard whispering. Whispering so low he couldn't make out the words. Whispering, light and feminine. *Whispering*.

A jolt of fear shot through him. In less than a second, Roc whipped his Glock out of his pocket, fingering the leather strap he always carried. His stake was unfortunately in the bedroom.

Pointing his Glock toward the stall door, he kicked it

open. It crashed against the wall and snapped back. But the brief second provided a flash of bare skin and a shriek. Arms and limbs jerked and flexed and tried to cover up before the door slapped back into place.

Roc shifted the point of the gun toward the loft and backed away from the swinging stall door. With a wry grin and shake of his head, he waited in the walkway. Huffing accompanied whispers of "Let go. Get dressed!" Scrambling hands and feet scraped wood and kicked straw on the other side of the stall door. Finally, Roc shoved his weapon back in his coat pocket.

It had been a while since he'd broken up a romantic tryst. Back in New Orleans, he'd tapped on steamed windows and encouraged teens to find a safer place to do the deed. The boys were sometimes red-faced, sometimes not, but Roc always treated them like men and told them to treat their ladies right and get a room…and a condom.

The squeak of the wooden stall door gave him a heads-up, and he turned toward a very red-faced Samuel Fisher. From a distance, the tall, rail-thin teen had reminded Roc of Levi, but up close, the two were distinctly different. Samuel still had a smooth complexion. His eyes held a worldly knowledge but not wisdom. His shirt remained untucked from his trousers, and his suspenders hung down along his legs.

Samuel shoved a hand through his tousled mane of hair. "Uh, Roc, did you…uh need something?"

Funny how having seen folks in the altogether made it more difficult to find something to say to their face. "Nah, man." Roc attempted to fill the awkward silence without laughing at the absurdity of the situation. "Sorry about that. I heard…Well, it doesn't matter now."

"You're not gonna say—"

The stall door opened again, and a young woman emerged, looking as out of place in an Amish barn as Lady Gaga. Her long reddish-blond hair set off her pale skin and matched the occasional freckle. She wasn't classically beautiful but more striking, with cat-like green eyes, heavy-lidded still with desire, and a pouty and pink mouth. The skimpy top revealed the clear outline of her obvious curves and showed off her pierced belly button. Short shorts exposed every inch of her long legs.

It was easy to see what Samuel saw in this girl and what he wanted, but Roc wasn't so sure what this worldly gal saw in an Amish kid. Sure, he was a handsome kid, and maybe Samuel was showing her how things were done on the farm. Or maybe she liked corrupting innocent kids. Then again, maybe Samuel wasn't so innocent. Not that it was any of Roc's business.

"Andi," Samuel said, "this here's Roc."

She slipped an arm around Samuel's hips, her fingers hooking onto the waistband of his trousers.

Roc gave a nod. "Guess I'll head on back to the house. You'll lock up the barn when you're…uh…finished out here?"

"Sure."

Rubbing the back of his neck, as if he could erase the image burned into his brain, Roc turned away.

"Hey, Roc?" Samuel called. "What are you carrying that gun for?"

Roc hesitated. "Old habit."

"You hunt?" the girl asked.

"Occasionally."

"Samuel does too."

Roc's gaze shifted from the girl to the teenage boy, whose Adam's apple plunged and then rebounded. "Oh? What do you hunt?"

"Quail and deer. Pop likes venison in the winter."

"Maybe you boys can compare weapons some time." Andi grinned.

Roc rubbed his jaw, suppressing a reflective smile. She was a feisty one. "All right, then. G'night."

"So"—Samuel drew out the word in an effort to hold Roc in place—"does Pop know you're not Amish?"

Roc gave a flippant salute of forefinger to brow and walked away. "Does your father know what you do in his barn?"

CHAPTER FORTY-SIX

A KIVA WATCHED CLOSELY FOR his one chance. It came later in the week, once the moon had risen and given off watery light.

He'd lost Girouard's scent. So after he'd taken care of the cutter girl, he'd retreated to the only place he could think to look, the one place he couldn't imagine Girouard taking Rachel. Then again, maybe they had holed up in Promise simply because it was such an obvious spot.

Akiva heard the clip-clop of hooves approaching and stepped into the roadway until the yellow lantern light hit him squarely. The horse came to a halt and nickered. The driver leaned forward, peering into the darkness. Beneath his wide-brimmed straw hat, the man wore a typical Amish beard.

"What do you want, Jacob?" the driver asked.

"No 'good evening' for your own brother, Levi?" Akiva stepped solidly into the circle of lantern light, and the horse bobbed its head. "No 'how've you been?'"

The reins dangled from Levi's easy grip, but he didn't take the bait. Insects clicked a pulsing sound in the knee-high grass on the road's edges.

"You know what I want, Levi."

"Haven't you caused enough harm?"

Akiva laughed. "I haven't even begun."

When his laughter faded, Akiva squinted with effort as he pushed into Levi's mind.

Finally, my brethren, be strong in the Lord, and in the power of his might. Put on the whole armour of God, that ye may be able to stand against the wiles of the devil. For we wrestle not against flesh and blood—

A growl rumbled out of Akiva. He breathed heavily from the exertion. Levi had strengthened himself, fortified his mind with scripture, which acted like a thick wall impenetrable by Akiva.

"Is this really the way you want to live, Jacob?" Levi asked.

"Where are they?"

"'Finally, my brethren, be strong—'"

"I could kill you." Akiva fisted his hands.

Levi drew a calm breath. "You could. Yes."

"And Hannah."

"This is true. I doubt there is anything I could say or do to stop you."

"You always were the perfect martyr, Levi. Have you been reading that old garbage about our ancestors again?" Akiva clenched his teeth. "Now tell me: where are they?"

"Where they will be safe."

"Not for long."

Hatred swelled up inside him, and Akiva launched himself at Levi, transforming and taking flight, all in the blink of an eye. The horse startled and shied away.

But Levi didn't move, didn't flinch even. Akiva flew straight at Levi, but before he could reach him, several men suddenly appeared all around Levi, sitting beside and behind him. Their skin glowed brightly, and their eyes glinted like cut sapphires.

In terror, Akiva veered skyward, knocking the straw hat off Levi's head, and disappeared into the darkness.

CHAPTER FORTY-SEVEN

NIGHT HAD BECOME HIS friend.

Roc stayed outside later than usual, until the sun had made its final bow for the day, and the curtain of darkness had closed. A blanket of clouds hung heavily in the sky, making it look like gray flannel, and blocked any stars or moon, which he craved to light his path. Even the usual insect noise seemed quieter this evening. Or maybe Roc's focus was simply diverted.

The truth was: he was avoiding climbing those narrow stairs, shedding his clothes, and climbing into bed next to Rachel.

It had been a long time since he'd been with a woman— his wife—and he hadn't wanted a woman since Emma. Sure, he'd thought about a one-night stand here or there, even going to bars in New Orleans to pick up someone as needy as he. But he'd always found an excuse…her eyes were too close together, her boobs were too small, too big…it didn't matter the reason. The fact was: she, whoever *she* was, was not Emma.

He'd had his share of offers. Before he left the force, a few of the female officers made it clear they were available. But he didn't mix work and pleasure. And there were other excuses. It wasn't the right time. He was on duty. He was off duty. Even a wife of an officer came onto him. But he wasn't biting. So he'd ended up drunk, back alone in his own bed—even though sometimes he didn't know how he got there.

It was in those dark, lonely nights and days bleeding one into another when he began to understand his father. When his mother, Helen, had been alive, Remy hadn't been able to live up to her standards, and the guilt drove him to drink. And when she was gone, killed by a cancer that ate her from the inside out, Remy missed her, craved her scent, hungered for the taste of her, the feel of her soft skin, her warm body. At least that's how Roc imagined it. It was the closest he ever came to forgiving his father.

But tonight, loneliness crept over him. A croaking bullfrog sounded as if it was crying out and waiting for an answer. The night offered no comfort. Not here in Ohio, anyway. There were no distractions of movies or music or bars to detour his thoughts, his needs, his loneliness.

After finding Samuel and his girlfriend the other night, a raw need bore down on him, tightening his insides. He needed release. It was biological, normal. And yet when those feelings roused themselves inside him, and his thoughts focused on Rachel, as they did tonight, he felt anything but natural.

She was Amish. He was not. And never would be. She was fifteen-months pregnant, or so it seemed, and yet…she was beautiful, like a ripe peach ready for picking.

Steeling himself against any impropriety, he finally snuck into the house after everyone, even Samuel, had gone to bed. Every creak sounded as loud as the firing of a weapon and made his skin retract.

In the thick darkness, Roc scaled the stairs without the help of a kerosene lamp. He made his way along the stairwell then hallway and finally secluded himself in the bathroom—stripping, ripping off the shoulder bandage, and dousing himself with ice-cold shower water. He stood in the bathtub, surrounded by the white plastic curtain, for far too long before shutting off the water and toweling off.

The bedroom was dark when he entered, devoid of even moonlight slipping around the edge of the shades covering the window. Without the benefit of air conditioner or ceiling fan, the air felt hot and steamy. Roc edged forward, one step at a time, trying not to stub a toe. He hung his trousers on a peg, then with the towel wrapped around his hips, he took his side of the bed. The Glock went beneath a pillow. He checked his cell phone, but it still couldn't find a server. *Was there no service out in Sleepy Hollow or whatever this place was called? How would he ever get help if he needed it?*

Finally, he stretched out on top of the thin quilt. The chirping of insects outside and Rachel's soft breathing forced his mind to think of details…imperfections that would erect a firm barrier between them.

Of course, Rachel had no imperfections—her eyes were round and blue, her skin soft and supple, her mouth full and tempting. The imperfections were in him. Her deep, abiding faith pointed toward his deepest flaw. He'd seen firsthand what rock-solid faith could do to a woman. He remembered his mother whispering her prayers, clicking her rosary beads, planting concrete saints in the yard in hopes of driving away the demons threatening her family. But her desperation hadn't led to salvation. Her husband, a man without faith or hope, had never made life easier for her. And it felt as if Roc had now become that man too.

Rachel shifted, her foot jutting outward as she shifted and rolled onto her side, facing him. His breath caught in his chest. He watched her. In spite of the lack of light, his eyes had adjusted, and he could see her features, the soft contours, the slope of cheek, the squareness of jaw, fullness of lips, which parted slightly. She made a tiny noise in the back of her throat, and her brow furrowed. Again, she shifted, rolling over and facing away from him. Her hair streamed out behind her, and he resisted reaching out to smooth the long strands.

Slowly, he released the breath he'd been holding and focused on the noises outside the window. *Come on, rooster! Where are you when I need you?* But the rooster was silent.

Suddenly, the bed lurched, and Rachel bolted upright with a gasp on her lips.

"What is it?" His gaze jerked toward the window. *Had she heard whispering? Was it the baby?* "What's wrong?"

Her hand clenched the sheet, and she was panting.

He jumped out of bed and grabbed his cell phone. It was the baby. It had to be the baby. "Okay. Stay calm." But the cell phone was useless. "Don't worry. I'll get help."

But how? Would he have to run to find an ambulance or hospital?

"Roc," she gasped, breaking into his panicked thoughts. "It's my leg."

He blinked. "What?"

"My leg!" Her body contorted, pulling inward.

He rushed around the end of the bed to her side. Jerking back the covers, he ran his hands over her legs until he located the hard, knotted muscle in her calf. "Okay, just breathe." He kneaded the muscles. "Breathe deeply."

Slowly, after several minutes, the cramp loosened its grip, and Rachel relaxed. "Better?"

"Yes, thank you, Roc." She pulled away, tucking her leg beneath her. Then she sat very still.

"What's wrong?"

"Nothing. We should go back to sleep, I reckon."

Nodding, he stood and backed away. He reached back to rub his hands on his jeans, and suddenly realized he wore no jeans, not even trousers, or his towel. In the midst of the crisis of Rachel's crying out, he'd forgotten he was undressed. At least she couldn't see much in the darkness. He moved around the end of the bed, retreating back to his side, grabbed the towel off the floor, and wrapped it around his waist. Yet he hesitated before climbing into bed again.

"Roc?" Rachel's voice came soft and timid, floating out toward him like a feather wafting, whisking to and fro.

"Yes?"

"Is everything okay?"

"Yeah, sure. Why wouldn't it be?"

Silence answered him. Then he heard the bed squeak. He peered closer, leaning forward, and realized her shoulders were shaking.

"Rachel?" he ventured.

She didn't answer, but he heard her sniff.

"Are you crying?"

Still no answer, but her silence was answer enough.

"What's wrong? What did I do?" As he climbed into bed, edging closer to her, he saw her shaking her head, one hand cupped over her mouth. "What is it?" He reached behind her, his arm bending to accommodate the width of her shoulders, but hesitated. Yet when she made a snuffling sound, he pulled her toward him, sheltering her against his chest. Warm, wet tears spilled onto his bare skin. He smelled the soft, flowery scent of her hair, and he waited while she cried herself out. She finally gave muffled shudders as the last of the sobs wrenched free.

"I…I'm sorry." She pulled away, but he kept her close, his hand cupped around her shoulder.

Smoothing a hand along her silky, thick hair, he whispered, "It's all right." She remained pressed warmly against him for a couple more minutes before he asked, "Can you tell me about it?"

"It must be the baby." She sniffed and straightened her spine. "I'm more weepy now than ever before."

Hormonal surges, Emma had called the episodes she'd had occasionally. But she hadn't been expecting. And she hadn't lost her husband, either. "It's understandable. Don't worry about it."

Her shoulders shook again; then she held a hand out. "I'm sorry. Again. Really."

"Rachel," he said, "it's all right. Trust me—"

"But it's not all right. Is it? I shouldn't be doing this."

"What?"

"Living here. With you. This way." Her voice cracked. "In the Fishers' home!"

He turned her, bracketing her shoulders with his hands, and brought their faces close together. "Rachel, we're doing this to protect the Fishers, not to hurt or harm them. That's what you should remember."

She sniffed again, nodded.

"Do you want me to leave?"

She shook her head.

"Are you sure?"

She nodded.

"Okay, then." He lay down, adjusting the pillow beneath his head so he couldn't feel the Glock beneath it. "Let's go to sleep, Rachel."

It took her a minute before she finally settled back down beside him.

He focused on each breath, drawing it in, holding it a

few seconds longer, then releasing it slowly. When he finally fell mind-first into the black oblivion of sleep, he expected to dream about Emma, about losing himself inside her once again, and hopefully finding himself before it was too late.

He did dream of Emma, but in the dream her body was rounder, fuller, and moved against him. His hands roamed over the soft curves and sifted through long, silky hair. He tasted the sweetness of supple lips.

She called to him—"Roc. Roc!"

Her hand touched his chest, his stomach. Her touch sent him over the edge of reason and understanding and smack into pure instinct. He groped in the dark, palming a full breast, pulling a warm, shapely body against him, and tasting a soft, ripe mouth.

At first she was hesitant or reluctant, but then her lips became pliable, melting beneath him and then burning and devouring with her own desire. He couldn't get enough of her sweet taste. He wallowed in the sensations swirling around him, setting him on fire. He tugged and pulled at the barrier between his flesh and hers.

But then something thumped against his abdomen. Reality blasted away any illusions or distortions. His mind shrieked not to stop, but he became aware of his surroundings: sheets smelling of fresh-mown grass, the squeak of the antique bed's springs, the wooden headboard his hand fisted. And he opened his eyes.

Below him, blue eyes blinked in a soft, languid way. It wasn't Emma. It was Rachel.

Her mouth had a dewy, just-been-kissed look. His arms trembled as he braced his weight against the mattress. A shockwave of revelation rocked through him. One glance downward, and he glimpsed a cloud of white material, the swell of baby, a raised knee. He rolled off her in one swift motion, scooped the still-damp towel off the floor, and wrapped it around his bare hips.

Gray light slipped around the edges of the shade. He raked a hand through his hair and moved straight for his clothes hung on the peg by the door. He looped back for the Glock under his pillow.

Her hand stopped him, clasping his forearm.

"Roc."

It was then he realized he was breathing hard.

"You were dreaming." She'd already covered herself and was sitting upright in bed now, her hair tousled about her in a reminder of what they'd been about to do.

"Rachel—" *What could he say? How could he apologize?* He couldn't look at her. He'd promised her she'd be safe with him. "Look, I—"

"You were talking in your sleep." She patted the bed. "Sit down. Let's talk about this."

He stepped away. "What's there to talk about? It was wrong. I'm sorry." He couldn't tell her he'd been dreaming of her. "I thought you…I thought—It doesn't matter."

He stopped himself from saying anything else. It would only make it worse.

"I have bad dreams too." She shifted, sitting on her feet, and leaned toward him. "You can tell me about it."

"Go back to sleep, Rachel."

She looked away then. "I dream of Josef sometimes."

Her vulnerability pulled him back to her side. Carefully, he sat back on the edge of the bed. "Look, it's not your fault, Rachel. You're…we're both lonely. And this was my fault. Not yours."

"Roc—"

"Go back to sleep, Rachel. I won't bother you again."

"I blame myself." Her voice cracked.

"For this? Really, it's my fault. I'm f—" He stopped himself again.

"No"—she leaned back against the headboard—"for Josef."

Even though the light was dim, he read fear, pain, and regret in those blue eyes. "For Josef's death? Your fault? Why would you ever think that?"

"I sent him out that night. Otherwise he would have been home. Safe. And—"

Words sprang forward, but Roc held them back. Those words would only draw them closer together, and so he resisted. But her tears twisted his insides. Maybe if he confessed his regrets, his own sin, then she could release herself from her own guilt. "I blame myself for Emma. I couldn't save her…and I should have."

"You can't save everyone, Roc. Even me. If it's God's will for me to die, then you can't stop that."

"God's will? What does God's will have to do with this…with any of this?"

"It has everything to do with it."

"Then if it was God's will that Josef died, why blame yourself?"

"Because…" She released a breath. "I can't help it. I didn't say it was logical. I simply said that's how I feel. It's not logical that you should blame yourself either for your wife's death. But that's how it is. We shouldn't live by our feelings, though. We should temper our feelings with reality." She was silent for a moment, her hands clasped in her lap at the base of her belly. "You called her name…in your sleep."

It didn't surprise him. Again, he didn't know what to say, so he simply whispered, "I'm sorry."

"I know." She touched his arm. "I am too."

Silence pulsed between them for a long time. Rachel felt as if she just stripped in front of Roc and bared not only her body but her very soul, all the darkness, all the secrets. And yet there was still more he didn't know, he couldn't know.

She shivered, and he pulled the quilt up around her. She burrowed into the bedding as if she could cover her embarrassment as well as her sins.

"I dream about Emma," he said, his voice deep and resonating through her. He had strong, powerful arms, and they had swept away her loneliness for a moment as she'd clung to him. She'd wanted that feeling to continue. "That she's calling for me. That I'm racing to get to her. That she's just out of reach." His hand fisted as if he could hold onto his wife and their life together.

Rachel recognized that frustrating, painful feeling and couldn't restrain herself from placing an arm around his shoulders.

He stiffened. "Rachel, don't."

She studied his square jaw highlighted and softened by thick dark hair as his beard was filling out, the straight nose, the hard, glinting eyes fringed with long dark lashes. His muscles rippled underneath his tanned skin, and she smoothed her hand over his rounded shoulder in a gentle caress. "What are you afraid of, Roc?"

"What you should be."

"Everyone needs someone. I'm here for you. Just like you're here for me."

He raised an eyebrow. "This is acceptable in the Amish world?"

"There are things we cannot explain or defend or fight against. Like Akiva. These things don't exist in the Amish world." She slid a hand through the crook of his arm and clasped hands with him. "Come on." She tugged on him. "Lie down and go to sleep, Roc. I'll protect you from those dreams."

"Rachel, I can't." He got up from the bed, put distance between them. "I would ruin you."

How could he ruin her, she wondered, when she was already ruined. "Where are you going?"

"To the barn with the other animals."

And he left her alone.

CHAPTER FORTY-EIGHT

S HE REACHED OUT AND touched warm skin.

In the darkness, his arms came around her and banished the bad dream. Levi was there, as he'd always been—solid, warm, safe. Only in the last six or seven months had Hannah come to understand he had always been there for her, waiting patiently.

"You okay?" he asked, his voice husky from sleep.

Hannah nodded against his shoulder and snuggled closer.

"Another bad dream?"

"The whispers. And someone was tugging at me, pulling me down, and I couldn't breathe."

His hand rubbed along her back. "You're safe now. Meditate on this verse: 'For He shall give his angels charge over thee, to keep thee in all thy ways.'"

"Will they ever go away?"

"In time." His voice sounded solid. "I hope in time."

CHAPTER FORTY-NINE

CAREFUL TO HOLD ONTO the railing, Rachel came down the narrow wooden stairs. She felt sluggish, her ankles thick, her body ungainly, her spirit heavy. After the noon meal, she had taken a short nap and now planned to help Sally with some ironing or baking.

Sally looked up as she set the metal iron on the stove burner. "Feeling better?"

"*Ja.* I'm not usually so lazy."

"You're not lazy at all. Just expecting. Babies zap us of strength, before birth and after. When I was carrying Samuel, I waddled around like a duck, and every chance, I stuck my feet in a chair. It helped the swelling. And with Jacob—" Her lips pressed together, and she blinked rapidly as she wiped her hands on her black apron. "I'll brew you some tea."

Rachel took the older woman's advice and sat at the kitchen table, propping her feet on the bench where Roc and Samuel usually sat. She reached for a bowl of green beans and started snapping them.

"Jonas came back from the post office with the mail a few minutes ago." Sally handed Rachel an envelope. "And brought you a letter."

"For me?" Instantly, she recognized Hannah's handwriting, and her heart jolted with joy. She wanted to rip into the envelope and devour her sister's words, but she also sensed deep sorrow in Sally since she'd mentioned Jacob. The loss of a child, no matter the age or circumstances, left a jagged wound in a mother's heart. So for a few more minutes, she conversed with Sally about weeding the garden and the fresh tomatoes she'd brought inside earlier. She raved about Sally's ability to grow such fine vegetables. Finally, the other woman finished ironing the last shirt and headed outside to check the laundry.

With her heart racing, Rachel opened the letter and read as she sipped the lemon-balm tea.

Dear Rachel,

By now, you know the truth I tried to hide from you. It's not that I wanted to be cruel, I simply wanted to protect you. I am sorry. I thought I was doing right. If I had told you the truth about Jacob and Akiva and how Josef died, then maybe you wouldn't have gone with Akiva. Maybe then you would be safe at home now. I hope you can forgive me.

It has been very hot here of late. We are needing rain something awful. Mamm's garden lettuce has wilted, but the green beans are doing well.

Katie misses you, as do I. She has been cooking for Mamm, as it gets very hot in the afternoons, and I will say I think her blackberry cobbler is even better than Mamm's.

Sadie Detweiler is going to have another baby come spring. It looks like Amos Borntreger has finally won Rosalie's heart. We will see, come fall, if the Waglers start growing celery for a wedding feast.

Mamm is worried about you and the baby. She frets every day about not being near when your time comes. I asked Levi if I could travel to Ohio and stay with his folks so I could be

near you and help. Right now, he is not keen on the idea.
But if you are wanting that, I will ask him again.

Love,
Your devoted sister, Hannah

Carefully, Rachel refolded the letter and slid it back into
the envelope, her hands trembling. *The truth about how Josef
died? What did Hannah mean? And why did she think she now
knew? Did Roc know?* Her heart pounded, and tears swelled
up in her eyes. *What had happened that night?*

She became aware of the back door opening and closing.

"Everything all right with your family, I hope?" Sally
asked, her arms full of sheets.

"*Ja*, the family is well." Her throat tight with unshed tears,
Rachel rose and helped Sally fold the laundry, wrapping up
her own emotions and tying them up inside her heart.

CHAPTER FIFTY

ROC TURNED OFF THE whirring sander, and the quiet in the workshop startled him. Usually, hammering or the churning of the power saw kept the noise level high, but now in the sudden stillness, his ears thrummed. He'd learned the tools were powered by hydraulics through diesel generators. If there was a rule, he mused, there was always a way around it.

Roc was alone with skeletons of rockers, minicaskets, otherwise known as cedar chests, and a neighborhood of birdhouses for a retirement village of birds tired of the commute every year. At this time of the afternoon, he figured Jonas and Samuel had gone off to the barn to feed the horses.

He glanced out the back door, which looked out on the driveway used for the Fishers' buggy. Samuel's motorcycle was sitting in the shade of the barn on the back side of the building, not noticeable from the road. It was a ploy Fisher used, hoping his neighbors and fellow Amish would believe all was well and normal and plain at their home. But it was a façade, because there was something else abnormal about this family.

Roc suspected Jonas had run from Pennsylvania in his effort to forget the truth about his son Jacob. But he could run only for so long, because his troubles had followed him.

From the doorway, Roc saw the two men out by several

white boxes that sat near the back of their property and housed beehives. Jonas was wearing some sort of baggy covering, long gloves, and a helmet. Samuel was there too, and they were doing something with the bees, probably collecting more honey, which they sold in jars at a local bakery. Even though Roc had enjoyed honey on his biscuits each morning, he kept his distance from the hives.

A soft clearing of the throat alerted him to a visitor behind him. He turned toward a woman wearing shorts that showed off white, dimply skin and a tank top that revealed too much of everything—the rolls around her middle, her droopy breasts, and excess skin on her arms. With a last-ditch glance over his shoulder, wishing Jonas or Samuel were unoccupied, he strolled toward this woman, brushing sawdust off his sleeves and looking for all the world like a plain Amish man, and yet knowing he didn't come close. He hoped he could just point this woman in the right direction.

"*Guten morgan*," she chirped then laughed. "Oh that's morning not afternoon. Sorry. What is it you folks say in the afternoon?"

He blinked at the tourist, not quite knowing how to answer. "Hello works fine."

Disappointment made her cheeks sag momentarily. "Well, hello, then."

He nodded politely.

"I'm looking at these." She spoke in a distinctly loud and annoying tone, as if she thought he was hard of hearing or having a difficult time translating. She waved toward a wooden birdhouse that was anything but plain. It had an intricate roof with wood-chip shingles. The three-story complex could be a homestead for several generations of martins. "How much are these?"

To answer the woman's question, Roc nodded toward the sign on the wall.

Her jaw went slack. "That much? Good grief."

He simply waited, the way he'd seen Jonas do when customers came into the shop. Often they tried to bargain him down, but he knew what his woodwork was worth, and he didn't budge.

Finally, the woman shook her head, making her neck waggle like a turkey's wattle and shifted her focus. She meandered around, peering at the other woodwork: dressers, lazy Susans, which she spun, and grandfather clocks. She examined pieces as if she were an expert, even testing a rocker and moving it back and forth.

"So"—she clapped her palms against the rocker's armrests—"will you knock down the price?"

He shook his head, indicating no in any language or culture. Jonas had told him to stay clear of customers and neighbors, and not to talk, since he'd found it difficult to alter his New Orleans drawl to resemble the more clipped Pennsylvania Dutch accent. Since the Amish weren't talkative to strangers, he hadn't had too much difficulty so far.

"Are you—?" The woman stopped and glanced beyond his shoulder. Her hopeful expression flipped into a frown.

An Amish man stood in the doorway of the workshop. Roc had met a few neighbors who had come by to chat with Jonas, exchange a bit of news, or borrow a tool. By and large, Rachel and he had avoided church so far because last week was a "between Sunday" when the Fishers stayed home rather than traveling to one of their neighbors. Still, he hadn't met this neighbor.

"Well," the woman sighed, "I guess there's no arguing with you about it. You all stick together, don't you?" She pushed up from the rocking chair and waddled past quilt stands and turkey callers, past the Amish man, who stepped out of the doorway to accommodate her, then stepped back into the workshop. Roc bent, readjusting the rocker and hoping the Amish fellow would decide Jonas wasn't available and move on.

"Jonas here?"

Roc thought carefully about the best way to answer without revealing he wasn't truly Amish. Finally, he simply nodded.

The man said something in what Roc recognized as Pennsylvania Dutch. He had no idea what was said, but he took a steadying breath and tried to think of something else to say. Finally, he kept to the basics. "*Ja.*"

The man frowned.

Roc swallowed hard. *Now what?*

"Can I help you?" a female voice asked from behind the Amish man. At first sight of Rachel, Roc breathed easier.

"You Jonas's daughter-in-law? All the way from Pennsylvania, eh?"

She carried a tray with glasses of lemonade. "His son, Levi, is married to my sister. I'm Rachel."

"Aaron Weaver. And this here your husband?"

Her gaze shifted toward Roc. A smile touched the corner of her mouth. Or maybe it was his imagination. Finally, she said, "*Ja.* Would you care for some lemonade?"

Aaron shook his head and gave Roc a strange glance. "I was looking for Jonas."

"Honey." Roc pointed with his thumb over his shoulder toward the back door.

Rachel's blue eyes widened, and her cheeks flushed a rosy hue. Had she misunderstood him? Then she laughed, a delicate sound that acted like a potent drink to Roc. "Oh, yes, Jonas was planning on checking the hives today."

Aaron folded his arms over his chest. "I'll wait, then."

"Of course. You are welcome to some lemonade. If you don't mind, I came to borrow my husband for a moment."

Roc grinned out of relief and walked out of the workshop with Rachel. She led him away from both the house and workshop, and when they were far enough, she giggled like a schoolgirl. "Jonas won't be happy you were chatting with neighbors."

"Or customers." He nodded in answer to her silent question. "But it wasn't my fault. Wrong place, wrong time."

Their gazes met briefly, and Roc felt the stirrings of awareness. He wondered if he should apologize again for last night, but then she slipped her arm through his and led him away from the house and toward the barn. She was still smiling, still walking, still acting like all was normal and comfortable between them.

"Where are we going?"

"To town. Will you go with me?"

"How? On Samuel's motorcycle? It's fixed, but…"

Her footsteps slowed, and she looked shocked at his proposal. "We couldn't do that. We'll go in the buggy."

This time, he slowed and pulled back. "Rachel, I don't know—"

She kept moving toward the barn with a determined stride.

"—how to drive a buggy. Or even hitch it up. Can't—"

"I'll help," she said.

He planted his feet in the path, clasping her hand and forcing her to face him. "How are you going to do that? You're eight months—"

"Please, Roc." Her hand settled on his chest. At that very moment, he'd do most anything for this woman. Not a good place to be as her protector. "I need to go. If you won't take me, then I'll go alone."

"Well, that's not happening." He crossed his arms over his chest, feeling a slight pinch in his wounded shoulder, which was healing, thanks to her ministrations.

She met his gaze solidly, not backing down either.

"Okay," he agreed. "If the horse cooperates, we'll get it figured out."

Her smile gave him a disjointed feeling. She brushed a kiss against his cheek and then hurried on to the barn. "The horse could probably do it by himself."

"Good." Roc returned the smile. "Then I'll ask him."

CHAPTER FIFTY-ONE

AKIVA SET THE PACE, and Brydon matched it as they wove through the swarming tourists. They circled the building that paid tribute to the greatest of the greats in rock 'n' roll history, Akiva's gaze searching beyond teen groups and families on vacation, beyond the tourist buses. He searched out the individual, set apart, not belonging to a group or crowd or partnered with anyone.

Then he spotted a young man leaning against a concrete-slab building, his shoulders slumped indolently as he puffed on a cigarette, and his trousers hovered a centimeter from the tipping point where they would fall to his ankles. Akiva said to Brydon, "'Opposition is true friendship.'"

"Yeah?" Brydon's response sounded more like a grunt. "So what? Why'd you say that?"

"I didn't, actually. William Blake did." Akiva skirted a group waiting at a street light and jogged across the busy inter-section, Brydon at his heels. Gray clouds bumped against one another overhead, and thunder rumbled in the distance. "But I was contemplating your dilemma."

Brydon shifted his dark gaze toward him. "What's that?"

"You and this Girouard."

Brydon grunted again.

"You were friends, right?"

This time, Brydon remained silent and brooding.

"Weren't you?"

"What of it?"

"Well, he killed you." Akiva hooked a corner. "Or tried to. That don't bother you?"

Again, silence pulsed between them, and Akiva gave him space. He coughed into his hands. "Guess you're a better…well you know…than me."

Brydon's brow folded downward. "How's that?"

Akiva circled around the building again, slowing his pace as they approached the young man whose thin T-shirt was covered with skulls. "Mamm always said I had a bit of a vengeful streak. And if someone, especially a friend, done me the way Girouard slit through your throat—"

Brydon touched the neckline of his button-down shirt.

Akiva hid a smile. "Girouard didn't pause or have any regrets. Well, if it'd been me, I'd have already done away with him. But maybe you're the 'turn the other cheek' type."

"Don't know what I've done to give you that impression."

"Pardon me, then." Akiva moved past the young man, who paid no attention to them. He wore earbuds in his ears, and his head bobbed to a hip-hop beat, which would keep him from ever hearing Akiva's approach later on.

"You think I should—?" Brydon stopped himself. "Roc was a good friend. At one time, anyway." His brow furrowed with what Akiva figured were conflicting thoughts.

"Girouard didn't let friendship get in the way of what he believed he had to do."

"That's what makes a good cop." Brydon defended his friend.

"He isn't a cop anymore, is he?"

With flat lips, Brydon kept his thoughts inward. "So you think I should go after him, then, just because you say?"

"'The revenger of blood himself shall slay the murderer: when he meeteth him, he shall slay him.'"

"That your stance?"

"Actually, it's biblical."

Brydon laughed. "You quoting the Bible now?"

"There is wisdom to be found in the good book, wouldn't you say?"

"I don't know." Brydon shrugged. "Never had much need of it."

Akiva nodded. "Of course, that is why you are ignorant."

Brydon shot him a look. A flash of lightning pulsed out of the clouds. Akiva changed the subject. "You hungry now? Or would you rather wait till dark?"

CHAPTER FIFTY-TWO

THE TACK ROOM HELD the bridles and reins, and Rachel pointed out what was needed to hitch the horse to the buggy. Roc carried the equipment, noticing in the corner two rifles. Twenty-twos. He remembered Samuel saying he hunted deer and quail during season. But these might be handy for something else.

"Do you need help?" Rachel asked, backtracking to see what had delayed him.

"What are you in such a hurry for?"

"I'm not in a hurry."

But clearly she was. Roc followed her instructions and hitched the horse. He then helped Rachel into the open buggy.

He eyed her belly and wondered if it was a good idea for her to jounce all the way to town. "You sure you're okay to do this?"

She smiled. "Why wouldn't I be?"

He could think of a few reasons, but then he had a few reasons why he wasn't up for the task either.

She took the reins in what appeared to be very capable hands.

"Whoa, now." Roc put a hand on hers. "I'll take those."

She arched an eyebrow at him. "Have you ever done this?"

"No, but—"

"Well, I have." She held tight to the leather straps.

"You have?"

She made a face like it was the most natural thing in the world. "Any Amish woman can do this simple task."

"Really? Any Amish woman, huh?"

"*Ja.*"

"Then I should be able to handle one old nag." He winked at her.

Rachel batted his hand away from the reins and clicked her tongue. The horse trotted forward. Yellow and pink flowers led the way to the gate.

Roc frowned at the steep road ahead, which was shaded by birch trees. This hamlet was fairly secluded because of the hills, dales, ancient trees, and deep ravines. There might not be anyone to see now, but in a few minutes they'd be on a busier roadway, maybe even a highway, depending on how far Rachel wanted to go, and folks would stare at them as they passed. He wasn't the type to let a woman or anyone else drive as long as he was conscious, but he had no choice now.

"Won't it look odd if folks see you driving and me just sitting here?" *Like a doofus*, he thought but didn't say it. "Besides, this isn't what I would call safe."

"Who's looking? And besides"—she emphasized the word—"life is full of uncertainty and dangers."

"Like vampires," he mumbled.

Roc slumped in his seat. They were going fairly slow, and he began to relax. Until they came to the covered bridge.

"You might want to slow down."

"Why?"

"Someone might be coming on the other side. Only one car...or buggy can go through at a time."

"I'm watching."

His frown deepened. Roc's nerves began to jump and jangle. He wasn't a good backseat driver or even a passenger-seat driver, so to speak. A rumbling noise startled him, and he glanced behind them—a car was practically sitting on their bumper. "Whoa, now, you better pull over and let that car pass."

She shot him a disgruntled look. "There's not enough space to pull over. We're fine."

He clutched the side of the buggy with one hand. "This is not safe."

She reached over and patted his arm in a patronizing way that set his teeth on edge. "Don't worry," she said, "I can handle this."

The buggy crossed the rickety covered bridge, the sound rumbling and echoing around them as they traveled over the wooden boards. Roc held onto the buggy and braced himself in case the bridge gave way. But it managed to hold together.

Rachel pulled to the side and allowed the zippy little Z-4 to pass. The car sped up, taking the hill and disappearing around the bend. "They're in a hurry, no doubt."

Rachel kept her gaze on the road, her back straight, and her chin firm. The buggy's wheels rolled along, and the horses' hooves clopped on the asphalt. It would have been a soothing sound if they hadn't been on a roadway surrounded by trees, and basically alone. A great place for Akiva to attack.

His hands fisted, knuckles white until they turned one more time, pulled next to an unassuming building, and stopped at the hitching post. Rachel set the brake and smiled at him, which didn't do his nerves any better.

Three steps led up to the door, and he followed her inside. It looked like a store straight out of the 1800s. One side of the store held cards, stationery, pens and pencils, as well as slates and chalk. On the other side of the oversized room were shelves of books, magazines, and newspapers. A couple of Amish men stood next to the newspaper rack, with papers Roc had never heard of before but seemed to carry farming and Amish news. He avoided those men, not wanting to strike up a conversation, but their gazes followed him. Rachel made her way to the stationery and picked out a box of plain off-white paper with envelopes.

She walked back to him. "This will do nicely."

Roc stepped up to the check-out, which was an old table with an even older register. A young girl, maybe seventeen, nodded to Rachel and rang up their purchase.

"Do you carry stamps?" Rachel asked.

"*Ja.* How many? A sheet, book, or roll?"

"Just a sheet, *danke.*"

Then Roc was hanging on for his life as they turned back onto the roadway and made their way back to the Fishers'.

Soon they were back on a quiet road with shading oaks and hickories surrounding them, and the fields burgeoned with crops of corn and wheat. How little he saw of the land and scenery when he drove his Mustang. A sudden longing pained him. He doubted he would ever see his Mustang again. Because how could he ever go back to New Orleans? Except to be arrested. He'd have no need of his Mustang if he sat in jail.

He tapped the box of stationery on his thigh. "So what was the hurry for this?"

Rachel glanced sideways at him then back at the road. She was a confident buggy driver, which should have eased his concerns more. "No hurry, I guess."

"Who are you going to write?"

Her mouth stretched thin. "Hannah."

Her answer surprised him. "How come?"

"She wrote me." She released a soft breath. "She apologized

for not telling me the truth about Josef." She glanced at Roc, gauging his reaction, but he said nothing. "She believes I know what happened to my husband the night he died."

Still, he gave no response.

Her hands tightened on the reins, the skin stretching over her knuckles. "Do you know what happened to Josef?"

"Would it matter?"

"I'd ask you to tell me."

"Would knowing the details make you feel better or worse?"

"I don't know. But at least I'd know."

He placed a hand on hers then pulled back. "Rachel, I've had to tell wives their husbands died in a car crash. Or mothers that their daughters weren't coming home. Trust me when I say this: dead is dead. Knowing the details won't help."

Rachel swallowed hard and kept her gaze on the road. After a few minutes of listening to the clop, clop, clop of horse's hooves, she said, "Hannah wants to come here."

"Not a good idea."

"I know. Which is why I thought I should write her back."

"Good." He nodded.

Her mouth twisted. Roc wasn't sure if it was because she agreed or not. Maybe she was torn, wanting a connection with home and yet knowing how dangerous it could be for Hannah.

"Do you have brothers and sisters, Roc?" Rachel asked quietly.

"I have a sister." One thing Roc had learned about the Amish: family came first, right after God. He'd learned that's why they didn't adhere to cars, not because they were afraid of them or gasoline or anything else, but because they simply feared families would be separated by too many miles. For that argument, he could be a witness. "Deb…my sister," he continued, "married a while back and moved off. Went to Oklahoma."

"She doesn't come visit or write?"

He shook his head. "Nah. It was…no, she doesn't."

"And your folks?" She looked at him again, her eyes the blue of the sky and full of innocence; she could never understand what his life had been like as a child.

"What about them?"

"They're dead."

"Both?"

"My mother died when I was fourteen. And my dad… he's gone." He didn't actually know if Remy was dead or alive—there had never been word, never a funeral or grave. Remy had gone drinking and never come home. He'd taken to living on the streets. Roc had last heard about him before Katrina. He figured either the hurricane had killed him or the bottle had. He wasn't sure if he'd seen his father's ghost in Pennsylvania or if it had been a hallucination, but most probably, Remy was as he said—gone.

She eyed him again, her eyes softening. "I'm sorry."

"Yeah, well…" He looked out over the green fields, the corn stalks and thick, green leaves ruffling in the wind. Insects chirped and buzzed around them, and the clip-clop of hooves carried through the gulch, which led back to the covered bridge.

"Roc…" Her voice sounded hesitant. "What you're doing—protecting me and my baby—it's noble but dangerous."

He shrugged, keeping his gaze diverted toward the narrow roadway ahead.

"Well, what if something were to happen to you?"

"You mean if I die?"

She dragged her bottom lip between her straight white teeth. "Or get hurt again."

His shoulder muscle flexed in response, and he wondered

if she really cared what happened to him or if she worried she'd feel guilty if he died. She already carried a hefty dose of guilt over her husband's death. "It's the risk I'm willing to take."

"But—" She clamped her lips closed, and a muscle in her jaw flexed before she spoke again. "Who will take care of you? Who will…?"

"Weep? No one. And that's okay."

The clop of the horse's hooves ticked off the seconds of silence. "It's not okay. So if you don't mind, I want that someone to be me."

He met her solemn gaze. *What was she saying? Did she care? The way he was beginning to care for her?* The horse trotted on, but the fields faded into a haze. He was aware only of Rachel, the vulnerability in her eyes, the stillness of her hands, the rigidity of her spine. "You don't know what you're saying."

Her chin was firm with resolve. "Yes, I do."

"Well, then"—he stared at the horse's rump—"you're a fool."

CHAPTER FIFTY-THREE

IT WAS HOT, AND Andi was even hotter. She wore a swimsuit, two pieces, no bigger than rubber bands. It wrapped Samuel's mind and body tighter than he'd imagined possible.

She'd brought him all the way to Cincinnati to a friend of a friend's party. "Do you know whose house?" he'd asked her earlier in the day as he rode in front of her on his motorcycle.

"It doesn't matter." Her hands splayed across his chest. "Word got out about this party. And it's cool. Anyone can come. You'll see."

He wore the pair of jeans he'd bought months ago, letting her pick them out. She'd slipped into the dressing room at the store and slipped the jeans off his hips. She'd been working on removing the rest of his clothes when a salesperson had asked at the door, "How are those working for you?"

Andi had giggled and given his backside a squeeze. "Real nice."

Later she'd given him a T-shirt imprinted with "Virgin Islands" above his left breast. Across the back, it read: "What happens on the Beach Stays on the Beach." He suspected an ex-boyfriend had left it in her apartment, but to avoid the jealous haze that made his thoughts spiral into crazy thinking, he tried not to think about Andi with anyone else.

Now at the party, Samuel had never seen a house this big. Or a yard so massive with as many gadgets: swing sets, swimming pool, zip-line, Ping-Pong table, tennis court, sand volleyball, and those were just the things he recognized.

After a quick game of volleyball, where he'd given these *Englishers* a crash course in the way the Amish played volleyball, he'd dusted off his jeans and followed Andi to the pool, where she stripped out of a loose-fitting, zebra-print dress and revealed her black swim suit that would have shocked the girls back in the district and made them even more pious with jealousy.

Even though there were folks all around them, splashing, swimming, kissing in the whirlpool, Samuel paid attention only to Andi. He reached for her, his head a little muzzy from the "punch" she'd handed him in a plastic cup, and she spun out of his arms, laughing and casting him a come-and-get-me look.

He'd met her six months ago at the Lazy Cat bar. Not a story he ever wanted to tell his parents, who would be shocked out of their Amish shoes. He'd gone there last February on a dare Dan Ziller made on a Sunday night after the usual singing.

Samuel and Dan had been friends for years. Dan was two years older, like the older brother Samuel no longer had since Jacob had died and Levi still lived in Pennsylvania. Samuel wasn't allowed to speak about his brothers or say he missed them, or else his mother would weep and his father's face would harden like stone. But thinking of Levi and Jacob sent a jarring pain straight through his abdomen.

He and Dan had snuck off that long-ago night to drink a beer together in the Zillers' barn and talk about girls and booze and cars. Samuel was considering buying a car with the money he'd earned working for his father.

With the worldliness of a twenty-year-old, Dan suggested

he could buy a motorcycle for less than a car. "Come on. I'll show you some I've seen at the Lazy Cat."

Samuel's eyes went wide. "You've been there?"

"You haven't?"

"My folks would…"

"What?" Dan laughed and stood. "What are you afraid of?"

"I'm not afraid."

"Well, then…what are you waiting for?"

"How do you get in? You're not twenty-one."

Dan grinned. "It's not so hard. The bartender likes me."

Together they'd driven over to the bar, not ten minutes by Dan's Corvair. Samuel had felt conspicuous walking into the establishment, which had neon signs advertising shapely girls, beer, and whiskey. Inside, a cacophony of noise hit him all at once. Rock music blared from crackling speakers. Pool balls clanked and scattered. A group of guys laughed and groaned, depending on who was cheering for whom. Someone hollered, "Hey, Danny! Where've you been?"

Dan walked right up to the bar, smiling from ear to ear. The bartender, a tall, thin brunette, with the curliest, wildest hair Samuel had ever seen, slid a drink down the bar toward another patron then greeted Dan with, "What'll it be?"

"What beer you got on tap?"

Dan might as well have been speaking a foreign language as far as Samuel was concerned, but the woman rattled off a number of beers, and Dan requested, "Big Dog. And make it two. One for my pal here."

The bartender turned smiling brown eyes on him and grinned. She grabbed her loose hair and tied it up on top of her hair. Little curls spilled downward in tiny cascades. She had a long neck and several piercings in her ear. "Hey, there." She leaned one arm on the bar and jutted a shoulder forward. She wore a low-cut top revealing the soft mounds of her breasts, which Samuel couldn't stop looking at. "He's young, ain't he?"

"Not so young," Dan lied, "just right off the farm."

"Ah, sure. Well, welcome." She set the two glasses of beer in front of the boys. "Enjoy."

Dan picked up his beer and led Samuel to a booth. They sat there together, sipping their beers and talking about the bikes they'd seen outside. A smattering of folks sat at tables, some alone, others as couples. Then the door opened, and two girls stumbled inside. They leaned against each other, laughing and weaving as they headed straight to the bar. They ordered stronger drinks than beer, and when the short-haired one turned around, she spied Samuel and nudged her friend with her elbow. The redhead, with hair like a silk curtain down her back, swiveled around and took Samuel's breath.

He didn't remember much after that, other than Dan left with the short-haired girl, and the redhead—Andi—said she'd give Samuel a lift home. But they had detoured by her apartment instead. He learned she was nineteen and had been on her own since she was sixteen. She worked two jobs, as a fitness trainer during the day and then stocking shelves at the Acme store at night. Her one-bedroom apartment was sparse, without a television, which Samuel had hoped for. But it had a bed, where he'd surprised her with his knowledge of the birds and the bees, even though he'd technically been a virgin. Ever since, they'd been together.

Occasionally, she liked to tease him, playing like she might be interested in someone else. When she did, a thousand feelings welled up inside him, and he felt like he might explode. Tonight, her gaze slid toward a beefy guy in the pool who had a girl sitting on his shoulders as she tried to push another girl off another boy's shoulders. Their shrieks and splashing annoyed Samuel.

"So you know anyone here?" Samuel asked her as she wiggled out of his grasp again. "If not..." He could think of other things they could be doing.

"Maybe," she said, turning toward him. She kissed him once then twice, pushing her hands against his chest. "Now, be a good boy and stay here. I'll be right back."

Then she took a couple of running steps and dove into the pool's deep end. She swooped toward the bottom then burst through the water's surface. She swam toward the other side of the pool before pulling herself up out of the water, which sluiced down over her hard lines and sensuous curves. Her body made men's heads turn, and Samuel watched them now staring at her. He knew exactly what they were all thinking, because he was thinking the same thing. He wanted her. And he couldn't imagine ever not wanting her.

But then she walked up to a brawny older fellow who wore sunglasses, even though it was dark now. Was he blind? Or did he think he was something fancy? To Samuel, he looked stupid. But not to the other girls there. One brought him a plastic cup of punch then stood there awkwardly while the guy spoke to Andi, who also seemed to be fawning all over this guy.

A black liquid seeped out of Samuel's heart and wove its way through his body, turning him cold and then hot and drowning all rational thought. Violent notions replaced it, and his hands curled into fists. He felt numb and vibrant all at the same time.

He glared at Andi and the strange guy, who seemed interested in her, asking her questions. She would answer and then coyly glance over her shoulder at Samuel. *What should he do?*

Stalk over there and punch the guy? Storm out of the party and leave her? But if he did, then he might never see her again. And he couldn't not be around her. Maybe he should talk to another girl, do the same thing Andi was doing to him, see how she liked it. But he didn't want another girl. He wanted her.

The tinkling sound of her laughter carried across the pool. She once again looked over at him and then gestured for him to join her. He didn't need to be asked twice. Downing the rest of the alcoholic punch, he tossed the cup aside and walked around the pool.

"Samuel," Andi cooed as he approached. She hooked her arm through his and pressed her damp body against him. But he didn't glance down at her. Instead, he stared straight at the intruder. Suddenly his world wobbled, as if the spiked punch had gotten to him. Up close, Samuel could see tiny lines around the man's eyes and mouth, and a few gray hairs woven through his thick hair. "This"—she indicated the man—"is Brydon."

Samuel nodded and tried to keep his bearings.

"Brydon," she said, "didn't believe you were Amish."

Samuel gave his head a shake. "Is he an expert on Amish or something?"

Brydon laughed, a caustic sound. "No. I just knew someone once who was Amish."

CHAPTER FIFTY-FOUR

BRYDON FOLLOWED THE CURVING trail of the Serpent Mound then headed south a few miles before perching himself at the top of a silo. He stared out across the field toward the little whitewashed house. Another building was attached to its side, and folks came and went at regular intervals. Behind the house sat a small barn.

Occasionally Brydon stretched his wings and soared over the house, perching in the barn's loft. A cat, however, slumbered in a pile of hay with her kittens and was a distraction Brydon did not need. So he often kept watch from this distance.

Akiva had told him to monitor and report back to him. When he'd told Akiva he'd met a teenager named Samuel Fisher, Akiva's gaze had narrowed sharply. Tension rolled off him.

"What was he doing?"

"What most teens do."

The remark won him a darker scowl.

"Follow him."

"I already did."

"And?"

Brydon had described the home, workshop, and barn.

Akiva turned slightly away, pretending that he wasn't affected. But Brydon had detected a tremor in the other vamp's hand. "Anyone else there?"

"What looked like the teen's old man."

"Did you overhear any conversations?"

"Didn't bother." Actually he had, but he kept whatever information he gleaned to himself. It might give him an advantage at some point. "I knew who they were."

"How?"

"They were as you'd described them. You know them?"

Akiva jerked his chin. "Vaguely."

Akiva had raced out of Promise like a bat out of hell, feeling as if he was being chased by someone or something. Yet he knew that wasn't the case. Still, his encounter with Levi troubled him. Did Levi really not know where Rachel was? Or had he sent them somewhere he thought Akiva would never look...or want to look?

While he had traveled with Brydon, Akiva had described to him who he was now looking for, who Rachel might be staying with in Ohio. But he'd kept his connection to this family quiet, how he knew them, what they meant to him. Still, detectives weren't born but developed, and they didn't die easily. Obviously Brydon had done his homework. And he now knew this was Akiva's family. "And the woman... the teen's mother? Did you see her?"

Brydon sensed Akiva's keen interest, but he shrugged in response. "No. But she must be around."

"How do you know?"

"Dresses on the clothesline outside. Unless the teen is cross-dressing."

That bought him another black scowl.

Along their journey, Akiva had fed him hatred like treats. Before hooking up with Akiva, Brydon had hated himself, hated what he'd become. He'd welcomed Roc killing him, ending his torment and guilt. But Akiva explained it wasn't his fault he'd been changed. It wasn't his fault he had to feed on blood. Lions didn't feel guilty for eating an antelope. Polar bears didn't feel guilty for ripping into a seal. And Brydon shouldn't feel guilty, either. It was the law of nature: predators feed on prey.

Roc should understand these things, have sympathy for his ex-partner and respect for that relationship. Instead, Roc had not even hesitated before pulling the trigger, before tying Brydon down and slashing his throat. Roc was the killer. He had done the forbidden, killing a police officer and his own partner. Or at least he had tried to do so.

Akiva had saved Brydon, who should be grateful. He'd been given another chance. How many folks got so many chances?

Eventually, Akiva's arguments won over. Brydon became actually grateful for Akiva's quick action and decided he would pay back that debt by helping trap Roc and the pregnant woman, Rachel.

The secluded homestead, where Levi thought Akiva would never want to go, would actually work perfectly for Akiva and Brydon. Its isolation would make it easier to target Rachel and Roc…and anyone else who got in their way.

Now, he would watch and bide his time. And when the moment was right, they would strike.

CHAPTER FIFTY-FIVE

RACHEL SAT ALONE AT the kitchen table mid-morning the next day with the quiet of the house wrapping around her. Sally was picking vegetables in her little garden and had told Rachel to stay inside, as it was already too hot for her to be out. So Rachel took the few minutes alone to pull out the stationery. Now the point of her pen hovered over the paper as words flitted in and out of her brain.

After a few moments, pen touched paper.

Dear Hannah,

Thank you for your letter. I am well, as is Roc. The baby kicks me almost constantly. I believe he is eager to be born, and I hope it will not be much longer.

Sally and Jonas have been kind to us. Please tell Levi his mother has asked much about him and is happy he is married.

Her pen faltered as did her words. *What was she to say?* She told about the weather, the crops, the woodworking shop, but she couldn't manage to write she had forgiven Hannah. Her sister had done what she had thought was best, just as Rachel had done when she decided not to tell Hannah of her time with Jacob in New Orleans. It had been an effort to protect…but protect whom? Hannah? Or had Rachel simply been protecting herself?

Maybe if Rachel had been straightforward about their time together, then Hannah would have stopped grieving for Jacob sooner. But Rachel had not been able to confess her sins. Even now, they choked her.

And what of Hannah? Why hadn't she been truthful? About Josef…about Akiva? In many ways, Hannah's reluctance had spared Rachel more pain. And yet…if Hannah had warned her, maybe her life and her baby's wouldn't be in jeopardy.

So she simply finished the letter with:

It would be wonderful if you could be here, but you must not come. Please, Hannah, you must not even think of coming here. It is not safe.

Slowly, Rachel folded the stationery, sealed the envelope, and addressed it to Mrs. Hannah Fisher.

CHAPTER FIFTY-SIX

A FEW DAYS LATER, JONAS came in late for supper. His face was as dark as the clouds and lined with worry. Rachel knew something was very wrong.

"What is it?" Sally asked, pausing as she carried the rolls to the table.

He grunted and sat at the kitchen table. He spoke not a word through dinner and hardly ate any of the ham and mashed potatoes.

Rachel didn't feel like eating, either. She picked at her food and tried to gain Roc's attention, but he didn't seem to notice. He focused on his own plate, putting away enough for both him and Jonas combined.

Samuel gulped down his food but pushed away from the table earlier than the others. "I'll see you all later."

"No, Samuel," Jonas finally said, his voice solid.

The teenager tossed his head like a horse bucking the bridle and looked at his father, who never interfered with his son's running around. Sally sat very still, her gaze flickering between husband and son. The tension showed in her hand, where her forefinger and thumb pinched together.

"You'll stay home tonight," Jonas added.

Samuel hooked a hand on his suspender. "Why?"

"Because I said so."

"Pop, I can't. I made a promise—"

"It doesn't matter who or what you promised. You'll stay home. That's the end of it." Jonas hunched over his plate and cut into the ham.

The sound of an approaching car engine and tires on the gravel drive silenced any other protest Samuel might have made. Sally and Jonas turned toward the kitchen window.

"Probably a customer." Jonas tossed his napkin on the table and headed toward the back door.

"No, Jonas." Sally's eyes had gone wide with worry. "It's the *Englisch* police."

Jonas's gaze shifted toward Roc.

Was that an accusation? It jabbed a cold finger straight through her heart. Something had happened.

———

From the bedroom window, Roc kept an eye on the cop down below. It wasn't the local police but a sheriff's deputy. He stood beside the cruiser, talking to Jonas, with his hand on his gunbelt.

Roc's nerves cinched tight. If the New Orleans police had put out an APB, the cop might be here looking for him.

But what would Jonas Fisher do? Lie? The old man had lied to protect himself and his family. But would he lie to help Roc? A stranger? Not likely.

How would anyone know he was here? From a warrant? Maybe a picture had been posted in the post office when Jonas went to mail Rachel's letter to her sister. Or it could be worse. Isolated on this Amish homestead, Roc hadn't seen the news in the weeks since they'd left New Orleans. His picture and story could have been featured on *The Today Show*, CNN, or *America's Most Wanted*, or even some new reality TV show like *Cops Gone Bad* or *Hunting the Hunted*.

A plan formulated in his head. If Jonas gave him up, he'd have to run, taking Rachel with him in order to protect her. If he had to, he could take out this deputy. He'd shoot the cop, not fatally, just in a place to slow him down. Then he'd grab Rachel, and they'd take Samuel's motorcycle. They could be at a bus station in half an hour or at a train station in an hour. They'd change their clothes, cut Rachel's and his hair, shave his beard, and they'd—

A car door slammed. Roc snapped his attention back to the deputy outside.

Jonas stepped back from the deputy's cruiser and waited as the deputy backed slowly down the drive and left. Samuel walked up to his father and stood beside him, looking as if they were of one mind, and then the two men turned toward the woodshop.

Roc burst out of the bedroom and tore down the stairs. He barely saw Rachel or Sally standing in the kitchen as he ran past. "I'll go see what that was about."

Without waiting for a reply, he left the house and caught up with Jonas and Samuel. Jonas eyed Roc with a weary expression. "Go on back to the house, Samuel."

"Don't I have a right to know what's going on?"

"Do as I say. Now git on with you."

Samuel glared at his father, drew several heaving breaths, and stalked off.

Roc waited, watching the older man, who looked pale and shaken, the skin tight around his eyes and mouth. Finally, Jonas met Roc's questioning gaze. "It's happening again."

CHAPTER FIFTY-SEVEN

THE GAS-POWERED LIGHT BUZZED in the family room, pushing back the darkness creeping around the house. Thunder rumbled overhead, and rain slapped the windows. Rachel paced while Sally worked on a rag rug, her hands moving smoothly, not betraying the undercurrent of tension as she braided the threads. But Rachel twisted her fingers together, knotting them the way her stomach had.

What if Jonas had received word from her family? From Hannah or Levi? It had been more than a week since she had asked Samuel to mail Hannah's letter. *Why hadn't Mamm written to her?* A letter from Mamm would have eased her worries. Or made her loneliness worse, made her miss home more, made her fears loom larger. How she wished Mamm could be here with her now, to help her with the upcoming birth and to hold her hand through it. But she couldn't risk Mamm's life any more than she would put Hannah's in danger.

Finally, she could take no more of the waiting and worrying. "I need some fresh air."

Sally glanced up from her rug but did not say a word, her hands still moving.

Rachel stepped out on the back porch. The wood glistened from the rain, which had finally stopped. The shower had brought out the scents of soil, grass, and cedar. She glanced at the empty swing then at the barn, looking for Roc. Lantern light flickered in the double-wide doorway. Roc would ease her worries.

She found him bent over in the barn. At the sound of her footsteps, he straightened and turned. He held his gun in his hand and looked to be cleaning it. "What's happened?" she asked. "Why were the *Englisch* police here? Is everything all right?"

His look told her it was not, and her heart hammered.

"Where's Jonas?"

"He went to the woodshop."

"What did he say?"

"His neighbor, Jedidiah Zimmerman, lost a cow this week. Adam Kauffman lost a hog. And the police have been investigating a murder." At her startled look, he shook his head. "Not from New Orleans, a local murder. So Jonas had a bad feeling of déjà vu."

"Déjà—?"

He shoved a part of his gun, and it made a clicking sound. "Just means it sounded like something that had happened before, as in Promise, as with Jacob."

"He's here." Her heart stumbled, and her blood chilled. "Akiva."

"Sounds like it."

"But…what will we do?" Her hand touched her belly as her heart ramped up the pace. "Leave? Yes. We must leave. We're just putting the Fishers…and their neighbors…everyone in danger." Tears blurred her eyes. "But where can we go? Wherever we go…more folks will be in danger. Oh, Roc—"

"We'll be ready for them."

She blinked away the tears and stared at him. "We can't just sit here…and wait."

"We're not running. Not anymore, Rachel. This ends. Maybe tonight."

Her throat closed on the scream begging to escape.

He hooked a hand around her elbow and steered her back toward the barn opening. "Don't worry. I'm here." He flicked his gaze over the dark clouds. The rain had stopped, but the eaves of the barn still dripped. "And," he said, "I don't think anything will happen tonight. I think he's waiting."

"On what?"

His gaze settled on her belly.

The barn swayed in her vision, and she sagged. Roc held her against his side, tucked beneath the security of his arm, then sat her on a couple of stacked hay bales. "You okay? What do you need? Water?"

She shook her head. "Roc"—she sounded hoarse, and she clung to his arm—"we can't wait for that. We're risking everyone's lives."

"Don't you think I know that? But we have no choice. We're not running. Not anymore. Because no matter where we go, he will find us. Or we'll live the rest of our lives looking over our shoulders. That's no way to live."

"Can't we do something?" She drew her bottom lip between her teeth. "Maybe we could pretend the baby is coming, bring Akiva here. But how would he know? If we could lure him in, then we might be more prepared."

"You mean set a trap?"

"Yes, I guess." She squeezed his hand. "Is that possible?"

"I won't endanger you, Rachel."

"Roc, I'm already in danger. Let's do this now while we have some ability to swing things in our favor."

Through his eyes, she could see the wheels of his brain

clicking and churning, setting things in motion. "Yes, okay. It might work."

———

It was time to break the silence. He had imposed it on himself as a way to protect Rachel, but now continued silence put her in more danger. He needed help if he was to kill Akiva, and it was time to ask for it.

But Roc's cell phone didn't get service out here in the sticks. So the next morning, through the gathering fog that hovered over the damp ground, he walked the half mile to the Mennonite neighbor, Matt Larson.

Roc dialed the number from memory and waited impatiently while it rang. It was an old-fashioned phone, still attached to the wall by a spiraling yellow cord, so it tethered Roc to the kitchen. Larson's wife, Berta, an older woman with graying hair and a disapproving brow, bustled about, pretending to be busy in the spotless kitchen, but her ears seemed to be turning like giant satellite disks toward him.

After an interminable amount of time, the line clicked, and Roc heard a tentative "Hello?"

"Roberto?"

"Roc? Roc!" Surprise and relief brightened the priest's voice. "Where are you?"

Roc sidestepped the question. "Is everything okay?"

"As good as it can be. Where did you—?"

"I don't have long, but—" He glanced over his shoulder at Mrs. Larson, who had her back partially turned. He tried to word things innocuously. "Do you remember where Ferris ended?"

Silence was his answer before Roberto finally asked, "What's this about, Roc?"

Roc couldn't answer. Instead, he gave Roberto the name of a bus depot in Kentucky. "Someone will meet you."

Roc glanced over his shoulder again at Mrs. Larson, who was wiping an already clean counter, well aware that anything he said would be hitched to the Grapevine Express. "Can you do that?"

"When do you need me?"

"Yesterday."

"I'm leaving now." Roberto's voice held the same suppressed excitement Roc had heard many times when they'd been on the hunt.

Roc thanked the Larsons, insisted they take a twenty-dollar bill for their trouble and the long-distance call. He didn't want to be gone too long, but he was relieved he was finally doing something.

***

The sun rose steadily, a bright orb on the horizon, and made the light through the fog silvery as Roc took a brisk pace back to the Fishers'. The lonely stretch of fields and road magnified the sounds of the wind stirring corn stalks, insects chirping, and the crunch of his footsteps, playing on Roc's imagination and impatience to be back.

Then the growling of a motorcycle roared ahead of him. Roc stepped into the deep grass growing alongside the roadway. The rumble grew louder. Instead of zooming past, the motorcycle slowed until Samuel stopped in the middle of the road and stared at Roc.

"Samuel," Roc started, "I thought—"

"Are you ready to level with me, Roc?"

"About what?"

"About all that is going on. Why Pop allowed you and

Rachel to come stay with us, when you're obviously not Amish? Why the police are asking questions about dead animals and a missing *Englisher*?"

The motor thrummed between them as Roc weighed his options. Finally, he met the younger man's gaze squarely. This was a man of legal age, a man who had a right to know what was happening and what was coming.

"Let's get back to your folks." Roc didn't want to be gone any longer than necessary. "Then I'll tell you whatever you want to know."

CHAPTER FIFTY-EIGHT

WHILE SAMUEL STOWED THE motorcycle in the barn, Roc checked inside the house and made sure Rachel was safe. Restless and wide-eyed but otherwise fine, she was helping Sally with the wash.

He then took a loop around the house and made his way to the workshop. As he entered, he was surprised to see not Samuel, but Jonas.

"Where have you been?" Jonas asked, pausing in his sanding on an unfinished rocker.

"Checking around."

"You and Rachel need to go."

Roc stopped and faced the older man. Jonas had every right to ask Roc to leave. But it wouldn't save any of them. And it just might cost them their lives. "Go where?"

"That's your business. It would be better that way."

"Better for you, maybe. But…" He paused to give weight to his next words. "But maybe not. You've managed to outrun what happened to Jacob. But how far can you run? And for how long?"

"Forever if I have to."

"You gonna move your family again?"

"I'll do what it takes to keep them safe."

"And tell them what?"

"I don't have to tell them anything. I just have to say we're moving, and they will."

"Will they?" Roc asked. "Samuel isn't a boy anymore. He's—"

"I'm his father and—"

"He's a man, Jonas." Roc managed to keep his voice calm, even though Jonas's had grown louder with each exchange. "A man capable of thinking for himself and asking questions."

Fisher's features shifted from blustery anger to suspicion. His eyes narrowed. "What have you told him?"

"Nothing. Not yet, anyway."

The older man relaxed into defeated resignation. "I am only wanting to keep him good and safe."

"Of course you are. I understand." Even though Roc was dressed the same as Jonas the similarities ended there. "That's what I'm trying to do for Rachel. And you'd toss her out, just like that?"

Jonas leaned forward, the rocker creaking. Silvery sunlight slanted across his features, revealing deep angles and blanching his skin. "I'm not a bad man, but I'm not responsible for Rachel, either. Levi should not have talked me into letting you two come here. I am a simple man, trying to keep my family safe."

"At what cost?" Roc asked as he walked away.

Roc angled past the buzzing of the hives toward the barn, looking for Samuel. The kid had a right to know what had happened and what was about to happen. Maybe then Samuel could keep himself safe. Because whether Roc left or stayed, Jonas, Sally, and Samuel Fisher were in danger.

Samuel was waiting for him. The young man sat on a hay

bale, his forearms braced on his knees, his shoulders hunched. Beneath the wide brim of his hat, he glanced up at Roc as he entered the barn.

"So what is it you want to know?" Roc asked.

"I'll ask the questions."

Samuel's irritation surprised Roc, but he nodded his agreement and waited for the young man to formulate his thoughts.

Clasping his large, rough-looking hands together, man's hands from working in his father's carpentry shop, Samuel spoke carefully as if measuring each word. "I've heard the rumors."

Roc chose the cautious route, not giving away any information. "About?"

"Dead animals. A murder."

"All right. So what?"

"So what do you have to do with all that? You an undercover cop or something?"

"Or something."

"You after the person who's behind it?"

"Yes."

Samuel's face crunched into a frown of frustration. "Look, you can tell me. I'm not twelve. I'm a man."

"Yes, you are. So what do you think?"

Samuel blinked, as if taken back by Roc's question, which was a more polite way of saying "man up." Samuel's jaw flexed. "This all happened before, didn't it? It's what happened to my brother."

"Which brother?"

"Jacob. All right? Jacob!" Samuel lifted his voice to the rafters, and it came back to him, repeating his brother's name.

"Yes, it happened before. Back in Pennsylvania when your brother…and then six months ago again. That's when Rachel's husband died. And now here."

Samuel stood and began pacing forward and back. Eventually he stopped and stared out the barn opening. "Okay, so what are we going to do about it?"

It wasn't what Roc expected. "You're going to do what your father tells you. And tomorrow, when my friend gets here, you and your folks are going to pack up and leave. Until it's over."

Samuel shook his head. "I can stay and fight."

"With what? A pitchfork? No. You have to—"

"I'm strong. And I know how to shoot."

Roc couldn't help but smile. "You do?"

"Sure. Used to go deer hunting, remember?"

Roc had to admit it was tempting to have another pair of eyes, another weapon. But this wasn't deer hunting. Deer didn't shoot back. And they didn't bite. Roc wouldn't risk Samuel's life. The best place for Samuel and his folks was as far from here as possible.

"So why here?" Samuel asked. "Why our family? Does it have something to do with my father...Jacob?"

Roc wasn't ready to cross that line yet. He'd given Samuel enough of a warning. Trouble was on the way. But he wouldn't completely ignore Jonas Fisher's wishes either. Not yet. Not unless it had to be done.

Two days of phone calls and cryptic messages let Roc know Roberto was getting closer. Roc could use someone to spell him for sleep. He'd hardly slept the last two nights, propped in a chair beside the window. He'd kept watch while Rachel slept, her hand always against her belly, as if she was reassuring herself or her baby.

One night he'd dozed, his chin crashing forward, and he'd jerked awake, his hand going for the Glock.

"Roc," Rachel had whispered.

He'd given himself a shake. "What's wrong?"

"Nothing. Come to bed."

He sat up straighter, fought the urge to close his eyes. His muscles felt stiff and kinked with knots. "I'm fine."

"You'll be too tired to fight if there is ever a fight."

"There will be a fight, Rachel, and I promise I'll be ready."

She got out of bed and came to him, tugged on his arm. "You need rest. Let God and his angels protect us for the rest of the night."

He'd frowned, unable to put his faith in something unseen the way she could.

But now tonight, as he sat in the swing on the back porch while the women cleaned the kitchen, with the moon full and the sun not quite settled in its bed, the wind grew still. All was silent except for the occasional cricket chirping or bullfrog croaking. A firefly glowed nearby then extinguished. A bird flew from the barn toward the neighbor's silo. It seemed too calm.

With his stomach full from Sally Fisher's potato rolls, along with a juicy pot roast and all the trimmings, he felt his eyelids drooping. When he heard the creak of the back door, his eyes jolted open. Rachel stood in the doorway, frozen, as if caught.

"Where are you going?" he asked.

"Am I a prisoner?"

He frowned and pushed to his feet.

"I need to stretch my legs a bit." Her hand fluttered at the edge of her belly, as if she were indicating the baby was at fault.

"You feeling okay?"

"Just restless."

This waiting was killing him too. But tomorrow Roberto would be here, and they could put his plan into action. Then a sinking suspicion warned him of a different kind of trouble.

"Is it the baby?"

"We're both fine. Will you come with me or wait here until I return?"

He pushed up from the outdoor swing, another creation of Jonas's deft hands. The strain of waiting and watching was beginning to show in her eyes and the pinched corners of her mouth, but amazingly, she remained calm and steadfast.

"Where are you wanting to go?"

"Just down the road a bit."

"Rachel—"

"It's perfectly safe." She showed him a flashlight. "For when it gets dark."

"How do you know it's safe?"

"I don't. I just…it's as safe as we are here."

"We'd be out in the open." His gaze scanned the tops of the trees as well as the dips and rises in the land, which kept him from seeing too far in any direction. It created a haven and a hazard.

"Do you think that matters much to Akiva?" she asked.

A cough inside the house alerted them that they were not alone in their conversation. It might be nice to walk and be able to talk just between them. And maybe a few minutes' walk would help wake him up. Roc held out his arm to her, and she slipped her hand through the crook at the elbow. Together, they walked down the back steps and toward the narrow road adjacent to the Fishers' front yard.

For a few minutes, their footsteps were in sync, their strides matching, the crunch of Rachel's tennis shoes and Roc's work boots in rhythm. The sun slipped behind a hill, and shadows crept across the road. Roc flicked on the flash-light, placing the rounded light ahead of Rachel's footsteps.

How far they'd come in understanding, reading, and find-ing comfort in each other. He would lay down his life to protect this woman. Was it simply his honor and duty, or was it something more? He suspected his determination to see her safe was more than duty.

Of course, when he killed Akiva, he would have to take Rachel home. And then what?

And then nothing!

Ultimately, they were on different paths. When all was finished here, he'd take her home to Pennsylvania and leave her with her family. There was more he had to do...more vampires to hunt and kill. This job would never be over. *This* was his life now. And it was no life for a woman. Especially not for Rachel, who would have a baby.

He had come a long way in his grief to even consider opening his heart to someone other than Emma. And in its own way, it did please him. But even so, his journey from here on out would have to be a lonely one. And one day, it would end badly for him, the way Ferris's life had ended. A vampire would get the best of him. Death was his destiny. Not love.

Suddenly, Rachel's hand tightened on his arm, and her footsteps slowed.

"What is it?" He glanced around, but there wasn't much to see—shades of gray and black. The moon cast pale light over the fields and fencerows. A crop of corn rustled in the slight breeze, the leaves waving at them as they passed. There were no headlights or traffic lights out here, and so the dark was deep and absorbing

She looked at him, and he could see the moonlight

reflected in her eyes, which glinted with excitement. "Do you hear it?"

He listened, his ears straining, and he could make out a deep, rhythmic droning.

She quickened her pace. "Come on. It's a barn singing."

"What do you mean?"

She laughed and tugged on his arm. "You'll see."

He kept pace with her until they had a dark structure in sight. Outside the barn, several buggies stood idle, horses quietly grazing. Light flickered in the windows, gas lanterns he supposed. As they got closer, the droning became words, but words he couldn't understand. He supposed they were singing in German or Pennsylvania Dutch or whatever it was they spoke.

Rachel walked purposefully toward the barn, as if she had the intention of joining them, but he pulled her back.

"We can't go in there, Rachel."

"Why not?"

It took her only a moment before understanding glinted in her eyes. They did not belong. Or at least he didn't. And it would be difficult to hide his English ways in such close proximity to so many Amish.

Still several yards away from the barn, they stood together, listening, and his hand sought hers. "We can stay here and listen, if you'd like."

Tears welled up in her eyes, and she looked away from him, toward the light of the barn. He suspected she missed her home, her family. She missed the Amish ways, her district's activities, her friends, and most especially, her husband.

He understood, for he missed his own way of life. The New Orleans he'd grown up in. Being on the force. His friends. And most of all—

But everything had changed when Emma died. He'd never again fit into his group of friends. They were sympathetic, and yet they couldn't understand what he felt. Or he didn't believe they could. And now he was even more of an outcast. A wanted man. A killer.

There was no going home…no going back now.

For a long time, Rachel stood beside him, her eyes closed, her body swaying with the slow, rhythmic voices that ranged from bass to soprano. Her lips moved silently, as if she was singing along with them in her head.

"What are they saying?" he finally asked.

She blinked and kept her gaze on the barn. "It's an old hymn based on scripture from the book of Matthew. 'For the Son of man has come to save that which was lost. How think ye? If a man have an hundred sheep, and one of them be gone astray, doth he not leave the ninety and nine, and goeth into the mountains, and seeketh that which is gone astray? And if so be that he find it, verily I say unto you, he rejoiceth more of that sheep, than of the ninety and nine which went not astray.'"

Her voice broke at the end, and tears once again filled her eyes. He covered her hand upon his arm, trying to comfort her. She looked downward, and he couldn't tell if she was crying more, fighting the tears, or simply looking at their joined hands. He felt helpless to console her. But finally, she placed her other hand over his, until their hands made a tower on his arm. Then she looked up at him, and a tear toppled over and slid down her smooth cheek.

He didn't know what to say, what to do. "I'm sorry, Rachel."

"Don't you see? That song…that verse is about me. I am…was that lost sheep. And I came home. I thought I could make everything better, fix everything I had done wrong in New Orleans by living right. By doing the right thing. By marrying Josef." Then she shook her head. "But it only made things worse."

"You can't blame yourself for Josef's death."

"Of course I am to blame. And I had hoped the good Lord would forgive me. But I fear He has more punishment in store. I deserve it. But"—her voice broke—"I'm awful afraid He will allow my baby to die. And I cannot bear it. I cannot—"

He wasn't sure who moved first, whether she leaned toward him or if his arms went automatically around her. But he held her, and she buried her face against his chest.

He sheltered her against his body and whispered fiercely, "I'm not going to let that happen."

Maybe it pitted him against the Almighty. So be it. Was her God a god of vengeance seeking revenge on an innocent? Roc didn't know the answer, and he didn't much care. But he wanted to remove Rachel's guilt. And he wanted to protect her.

With a current of fear churning in their depths, her blue eyes sought his. "How can you stop it?"

"I will." He cupped his hands around her face. Her tears dampened his palms, and conviction gripped his soul. "It's not your fault, Rachel. You couldn't have done anything to warrant what happened to your husband."

"Then why do you blame yourself for your own wife's death?"

Her words scalded him, and he released her. Guilt was why he'd come here. At least originally. But now, his motivations had deepened. "Because I could have done something."

And he was the only one who could do something to save Rachel. And he would. *He would.*

"How?" she asked, not with a challenging attitude but one of innocence.

"I could have gotten there sooner…I could have—"

"No, Roc." She touched his face, her palm covering his jaw where he'd let his beard grow. "You couldn't have saved her. You can't be everywhere at all times. It's impossible."

"So I'm not allowed to blame myself, but you can?"

"Exactly." She gave him a sheepish smile. "If I hadn't married Josef in my sad effort to make things right, if I hadn't used him in an attempt to"—she shook her head—"then he'd still be alive."

"Rachel, really, I doubt you did anything that—"

"Oh, Roc…the things I have done…and seen…with Jacob."

"What did you see?" His instincts went on full alert. *What had they seen? What had they done together? Was there something she knew that might help them now?* He gave her shoulders a slight shake. "Tell me, Rachel. What did you see?"

"He…Jacob was fascinated with New Orleans, the culture, the debauchery. Eventually he took it even further, learning about voodoo and the occult. He said it was just for fun, and maybe it was at first. But it wasn't fun." Her eyes glazed as if she was seeing the events unfold again. "The things they did. Horrible things. And I was so afraid."

Her chin jerked upward. "I left him…Jacob, then. I took a bus and went home. I didn't think I'd ever feel clean again." She chafed at her arms, her eyes filling again. "Why won't you tell me what happened to Josef? How he died?"

"I told you, it won't make any difference—"

"What if someone told you your wife died but not how? How would you feel?"

He churned it over for a few minutes, and finally he said, "A vampire killed him. Drained him of blood. And then I killed her."

She blinked slowly then nodded. "Thank you." The words

were but a whisper. Her throat worked up and down and her features pinched in her valiant effort to stop the tears. But tears emerged and trailed down her pale cheeks. She looked up at the dark sky and wept. Her shoulders shook with the tremors of her sobs.

He pulled her against him, cradled her against his chest. She clung to him, wrapping her arms around his waist, and held onto him as if he could save her. If only that were true.

When she finally looked up at him with those tear-swollen eyes, he didn't think or question; he simply bent his head toward hers and kissed her damp lips. She tasted salty and sweet from the cinnamon-sugared baked apples they'd had at dinner, and he had the strangest feeling she was somehow saving him.

Stunned by the jarring need, he set her away from him. "I'm sorry. I shouldn't have…I'm no good. Not for you…not—"

She cupped his jaw, her thumb brushing his lips. "I think we're more alike than you want to acknowledge, Roc. I've done things I'm not proud of. Things I'm ashamed of. Things I wish I could erase. But I can't. I tried to forget what I saw in New Orleans, tried to hide within a quiet Amish life with Josef, but I think I was wrong to do so. God had a different plan for me, but I wasn't patient enough to wait. Maybe now he's given me…and you"—she dipped her chin and took a shuddering breath—"a second chance."

Roc's heart thumped heavily. He doubted God thought about him at all. He remembered going as a boy to a chapel of some kind with his mother. The ornate woodwork, the spires and vastness of the sanctuary, the Latin words spoken by the priest, the formality and tradition all making Roc feel small and insignificant. All these many years later, he still felt small and insignificant in the eyes of God.

He saw things simply too: black and white. Good and evil. He had one job—to protect Rachel and her baby. And he would do it with or without God's help. Even if it killed him. And it just might. But death—floating down the river of souls and getting lost in the depth of eternity—seemed easier than believing he could have saved someone and failed. He couldn't live with that guilt again.

Not because he loved Rachel. No, of course not, and she didn't love him, either. She was scared and clinging to the nearest lifesaver she could latch onto. But he wasn't one to scramble for safety. He preferred being adrift. Because loving someone, needing someone, depending on someone would be the ruin of him. Protecting Rachel now was simply his job.

"Look, Rachel, when this is all over, I'll take you home to Pennsylvania, to your family. Where you belong. But then I have another job. I have to hunt down more like Akiva. And I will. And you'll have a baby to raise. You have a life to live."

"But, Roc—"

"We're too different, Rachel. You have a faith I can't understand. It's just who you are. How you were raised. My mother said her prayers, clicked her beads, which helped squat. I can't take that leap."

She reached for him, but he took another step back.

"Let's get back to the house." His voice sounded gruff. He aimed the flashlight back the way they had come. "Tomorrow, this will end. And you will go home with your baby. Then I will be just a distant memory, like a fading nightmare."

CHAPTER FIFTY-NINE

WHEN THEY REACHED THE house, Rachel went upstairs to bed, her feet sounding heavier than usual. After watching for the lamplight in their room to flicker on around the edges of the shade, Roc sat on the swing and listened for any unusual sounds. He watched for anything that caught his eye. But mostly, he sat and tried not to think about Rachel.

The crunch of a footstep brought him to his feet, and he reached a hand inside his black coat.

"It's okay, Roc. It's me." Samuel came into view. He held out a brown bottle. Roc released his Glock and smoothed his hands down his thighs as he settled back into the swing. Then he took the proffered root beer with a nod of thanks. Samuel sat on the upper step, leaning his back against the porch railing.

Roc studied the bottle. "I haven't had root beer since I was a kid."

"It was that or lemonade." Samuel tipped his head back and took long swallows.

Roc shifted his gaze from the bottle to the young man, who seemed restless and frustrated like a caged animal. "Everything okay?"

Samuel rolled the bottle between the heels of his hands. His mouth flattened and cheeks dented. "My pop and I don't see things the same way sometimes."

Roc laughed, startling the young man. "That's probably true of every father and his eighteen-year-old son."

"You and your dad get along?"

Roc's good humor died. "Not when I was eighteen, and not now."

"How come?" Samuel asked.

Roc breathed deeply and released it. He questioned himself about what he should tell this young, impressionable teen, but he figured the truth was the best. "It's complicated, but suffice it to say I didn't like how he drank and pushed my momma around. And he didn't like it when I punched him back."

Samuel's eyes widened. "You—? Whoa." He dipped his head, his straw hat shielding his face, then he looked back at Roc. "That sucks."

With an exhausted chuckle, he nodded. "Sure does. Make your problems with your own pop seem not so bad?"

"Ah, you know, it is what it is. I don't know why he keeps insisting I stay home at night. Especially tonight."

"Something special going on?"

"Andi"—he shifted on the step—"she was expecting me tonight."

"You could explain to your dad—"

Samuel gave a humorless laugh. "How would I explain Andi to Pop?"

"Gotcha. Won't she forgive you for one night?"

"Maybe. Maybe not."

"I see."

Samuel gave a heavy sigh. "She could have any guy she wanted."

"But she wants you, right?"

The younger man shrugged. "For now."

"Might not be the kind worth keeping then, if you know what I'm saying." At Samuel's shocked look, Roc recanted. "I'm just saying, but I don't know. I'm not Oprah."

Samuel raised his eyebrows in question.

Roc let it go. "I don't know Andi. So…you love her, huh?"

"Love?" Samuel tasted the word like it was an unfamiliar piece of fruit, something exotic and strange on the tongue. He stared down at his hands circling the bottle, his thumbs pressing against each other. "Hadn't thought much about it."

Boys Samuel's age, Roc figured, weren't thinking. They were reacting, responding, igniting. Andi was like a fuse leading to an explosion. Or a drug addiction, and poor Samuel was suffering withdrawal tonight.

Young love didn't always involve the heart, often just other parts of the anatomy. Still, explaining that to an eighteen-year-old wasn't his place and probably wouldn't be well received anyway. So Roc remained silent and waited while Samuel wrestled with his thoughts and emotions.

"Sure, I love her. But it's complicated."

"Boy, I've heard that before." Roc leaned back in thought, questioning himself. Did he ache for Rachel only because she was pretty and happened to be sleeping in his bed? Was it just his love-starved anatomy talking? Or was it something deeper, some yearning from the heart?

Roc turned his gaze back to Samuel. "So is it the love-you-forever-let's-get-married kind?"

Samuel's eyes contracted a fraction. "Maybe."

"And so…you ready to bring her home to meet Mom and Pop?"

Samuel exhaled a harsh breath. "Yeah, right."

"Ah…that's the complicated part."

"Well, part of it." Samuel glanced over one shoulder and

then the other and leaned toward Roc. "Also, I'm not sure I'm going to join the church."

Roc mouthed an "oh." "Gotcha. Major complication."

He understood the boy's reluctance. The Amish way of life wasn't easy. In fact, in many ways it seemed they made things more difficult for themselves. And yet, sitting here on the porch in a swing, he could see the allure. It was a slower-paced life, simpler in many ways. Certainly simpler than chasing vampires.

"Would that mean you'd get shunned?"

"Nah. I haven't joined the church yet, so I wouldn't be shunned. But my folks would be disappointed for sure." Samuel looked down then added hastily, "It's not that I don't believe in God."

Roc nodded his understanding. "There are many ways to practice that belief."

His face lit up. "Exactly."

"So I'm guessing Andi isn't exactly wanting to become Amish."

"Can you see her in a bonnet?"

"Not really. But then"—he stretched out his arms—"I never thought I'd see myself in this getup, either."

Samuel laughed with him.

Then something alerted Roc. He cut Samuel off and set the bottle on the wooden plank at his feet.

"What is—?"

"Shh." Roc eased off the swing, careful not to make a sound. He pulled out his gun, pointing it upward toward the stars until he had something better to aim at. Carefully, he edged across the porch and down the steps, past Samuel. He peered into the darkness to the right and then left. A wavering light still glowed from the workshop. But he heard nothing and saw nothing. Maybe he was just being paranoid. Or maybe he was being watched.

He finally relaxed and shoved his Glock back into its hiding place beneath his coat. He didn't return to the swing but simply sat on the top step beside Samuel.

"So what's the full story, Roc? Some guy is hunting Rachel. Is that it?"

"Something like that."

"Somebody she met in New Orleans?"

Roc stared at Samuel, surprised. "How'd you know that?"

"I don't know much, but I know that's when a lot of our troubles started—when Jacob and Rachel went to New Orleans. And what you were telling me the other night about missing teens, dead folks, and animals? That's what happened to Jacob, isn't it?"

"What do you mean?"

"My brother was killed, wasn't he? I mean, Pop always said it was an accident in the workshop, but I don't think I ever believed that. Something happened, something that tore my family apart. So that's it, right? Jacob was killed by someone he met in New Orleans."

Roc weighed his options. Jonas Fisher didn't want his youngest son to know the truth. So Roc stuck as close to the truth as he dared. "That's pretty close…at least to what I know."

Samuel's gaze flickered downward. "I wish Pop had just told us the truth. This not knowing, not understanding, not being able to talk about it…makes it worse."

Roc nodded. "Tomorrow, I hope it will all end. My friend, Roberto, is coming to help me trap the killer."

Samuel's gaze met Roc's squarely. "What can I do?"

"First thing in the morning, go with your folks and get

out of Dodge. That's what your pop wants. And it's what you should do."

Samuel's pale brows furrowed into a frown. "Let me help."

"Your pop would shit a brick."

"Let him." Samuel leaned toward Roc, pushed his root beer into Roc's leg. "Let me help. I'm fully capable of making my own decisions."

Roc gauged the younger man for a minute. The Amish teens he'd met seemed more mature than English kids. Of course, they left school by fourteen and were ready to make lifelong decisions like marriage by the age of eighteen. Samuel might not agree with his father about religion, but he was a man with a mind of his own. If Jonas packed up his family and left, without letting Samuel have a say in his own destiny, he might lose another son. So Roc decided to give a little, if it would help. "All right then. You can pick up Roberto tomorrow morning. He'll be at a bus stop in Kentucky, I'll give you directions. Then bring him back here."

"Good. I'll do it."

"Fine. *Gut.*" Roc pronounced the word the Amish way, which garnered a smile from Samuel. "I'm grateful for the help. But after that, I want you off this property while I deal with this problem. Understand?"

Samuel's mouth twisted, but he finally nodded. "Deal."

They shook hands on it, and Samuel's grip held a firm resolve. Then he clapped Roc on the shoulder. Thankfully, not the injured one, because Samuel had quite a wallop. "So, now, tell me this. You and Rachel—"

"There is no me and Rachel." Roc gulped down the last of his root beer, wishing it was something stronger.

"What do you mean?"

"Come on, Samuel. Don't be naïve now."

"I'm not. I know you two aren't married. But I see how she looks at you…the way you look at her. And if that ain't love—"

"It isn't."

Samuel nudged Roc's arm with an elbow. "You don't look bad in that getup." He grinned. "You gonna become Amish for real? I could give you pointers."

Roc detected a teasing tone in Samuel's question, yet it jarred him anyway. "That's not a possibility."

"Probably right," Samuel agreed, his tone turning serious. "You know what would happen if Rachel married you, don't you?"

Roc chugged the rest of his root beer. It didn't matter, because it wasn't happening.

"She's been baptized, so she does have to marry someone Amish. If she married you, she would be shunned."

Roc leaned back. "Then make that reason nine hundred and fifty-two why we won't be getting married."

CHAPTER SIXTY

A DULL PAIN AWOKE Rachel.

She lay in bed a long while, assessing her lower back and breathing through the pain. After a minute or two, it eased. She probably shouldn't have gone walking so far yesterday. The baby stirred, and her belly tightened, her back aching. Any hope of more sleep slipped through her fingers.

Roc shifted in his sleep, and she listened to him breathing, the slow, rhythmic sound, deep and regular, gave her a sense of calm and peace. She hadn't heard him come to bed last night. He'd been running on little sleep, and had been sporting dark circles under his eyes for the last few days, so she didn't want to wake him.

She rose and greeted the day as quietly as she could. Moving about the room, she was careful not to cause a cramp in her calf and wake Roc. In the gray darkness, she dressed and tiptoed from the room.

By the time Sally came downstairs, Rachel already had biscuits rolled out and ready for the oven. Her palms had a dusting of flour, and she rinsed them in the sink.

"Aren't you the early bird?" Sally smiled. When Sally found humor or simply greeted another, her smiles brightened her face and lifted her features. But Rachel had also seen when Sally was quiet, her thoughts elsewhere, and her features sagged with the weight of worries and deep sorrow. Rachel's hand touched the side of her belly. What mother would ever stop mourning the loss of a child?

And her grief would be deepened if she came to know what Jacob had become. *Or did she know?* Sally had never mentioned or hinted at the possibility, and Rachel suspected Jonas had kept the truth from his wife. Just as Hannah had kept the truth from her. Both decisions were born of love, and yet was it best?

Sally touched Rachel's arm. "You feeling all right?"

"I couldn't sleep, so I thought I'd get started for the day."

Rachel touched her back. The pains had continued through the early morning hours. They didn't move across her belly, just focused in her lower back, which held a deep ache. But if she kept doing her chores or finding more to be done, she didn't notice the pain as much. So she kept going.

Roc suddenly came rushing down the stairs, looking as if he'd woken with a start and thrown on his brown pants and shirt. Part of his shirt was untucked, and he pulled on his coat hastily. Despite the slapdash appearance, his gaze was as intent as a hawk as he looked straight at Rachel. "How are you feeling?"

"Fine. Good." She wasn't about to burden him with her backache. It seemed insignificant. Roc had much more to think about than her little complaints. With the back of her wrist, she brushed away a lock of hair tickling her cheek. "And you?"

"I've got to go check on some things," he said as he headed for the back door.

Rachel watched him walk away, and stretched her arms above her head, easing out the kinks in her back. The pain seemed to be going away, and seemed as insignificant now as the cramp the other night in her leg. She would see the day through. Just as she and Roc would push through until they had trapped Akiva. Until then, neither of them needed any distractions.

CHAPTER SIXTY-ONE

ROC HAD ANTICIPATED HAVING to wake Samuel to go get Roberto, but the boy was already out of bed. Even though in many ways Samuel was a typical teenager, he was after all Amish and more accustomed to starting his chores in the gray light of this godless hour.

Roc walked the perimeter of the property first then made his way to the barn where Samuel was doing his daily chores.

"You remember what to do?" Roc asked, his voice low.

"Easy as pie."

"How would you know if pies are easy?"

"They're easy to eat." Samuel's grin widened, creasing his cheeks and the corners of his eyes. "You think picking up your friend is gonna be hard?"

"No. 'Course not." Roc was simply out of sorts. He was about a week shy of enough sleep, and he shouldn't have slept last night. He'd woken to some noise and found the bed empty, so not knowing where Rachel was he'd panicked. Even though he knew she was fine now, his nerves were still on edge.

He drew a steadying breath. "Shouldn't be difficult. Just pick up Roberto and bring him here."

"All right." Samuel dusted off his hands on the back of his pants and hooked his suspenders over his shoulders. "I'll finish feeding and head off."

"Good. Good." Roc stood there a moment, not knowing what to do or where to go. Then he turned back toward the barn's entrance but stopped. Facing Samuel again, he reached for the bucket. "Actually, don't worry about the feeding, I'll finish up. You go on."

"You don't mind?"

"Just go."

Samuel slapped his straw hat on his head. "You take care, Roc."

"You too, Samuel."

CHAPTER SIXTY-TWO

Samuel cranked his motorcycle and took off as the sun began its full assault, orange lines marching across the horizon. Wind rushed through his hair, pummeling his face, and he leaned into it. It gave him a sense of freedom he'd never had before he bought the motorcycle.

His eyes ached this morning, and the sun's rays made it worse. He hadn't slept well last night, tossing and turning, as he thought of Andi and what she might be doing. Imagined scenarios made his stomach churn—Andi out meeting other guys, guys hungering for her. He suddenly wished he had a cell phone like some of his friends had so he could call her, let her know why he hadn't arrived last night.

Then an idea came to him. Roc had sent him off early. He still had plenty of time left to get across the Ohio border and cross into Kentucky to pick up Roc's friend.

Smiling to himself, Samuel slowed down and took the next turn. Then he drove as straight and fast as his motorcycle would take him.

When he arrived, the parking lot of the apartment complex was quiet. A man carried a cup of coffee toward a car and climbed inside, flicking on his headlights. Samuel drove through the sleepy lot, finally parking next to Andi's red Echo.

Her car needed cleaning, and he promised himself he'd take care of it for her this week. Or he hoped she would let him.

The lump in his stomach grew larger and heavier as he walked up the steps to her apartment. *What would he do if someone else was with her? If she hadn't been alone and lonely all night like he had?* Samuel gnawed on the inside of his lip, glancing back at her car. Then with fierce determination, he fisted his hand and knocked against the door, hard enough to crack a knuckle.

He waited…listening, trying to hear inside the apartment. But he couldn't make out any sounds. All seemed quiet. Too quiet.

Of course, she was probably sleeping. Most days, Andi didn't have to be at work until 9:30. She thought he was nuts because he got up at four each morning to do chores for his dad. But what if she wasn't home? What if she'd gone out with someone? And what if she'd gone *home* with that someone?

The hard lump dropped sharply then bounced up to his throat. *Where was she?*

He pounded the door again, taking out his frustration and anger on the wood. This time, he heard something…a voice maybe…then the sound of an inside door opening. Finally, the chain rattled, and the knob turned.

The lump in his throat dissolved at the sight of Andi. Her auburn hair was in wild disarray, the curls spilling around her shoulders. She had raccoon eyes, her mascara smeared and smudged in all directions as it sometimes was after they went to bed eager and greedy. His gaze slipped lower to her fancy nightgown, which revealed more than it hid and highlighted areas that made his blood run hot. Then cold.

The lump in his throat congealed again into something hard and unyielding as it cut off his breath. Had she worn that red, lacy thing for someone else? Words lodged in his throat. Questions rose but couldn't escape. He froze, unable to step inside or walk away.

She blinked at him, her forehead puckering between her brows. "What is it, Sam?" Her voice had the gravelly, sleepy tone he loved. And maybe a hint of annoyance too. "Your watch not working?"

Definite annoyance. "Huh?"

"You were supposed to come by last night. You forget? Or did you get p.m. and a.m. mixed up?"

"I...I...something came up. I couldn't get away."

She leaned against the doorjamb, her arm straight, one foot crossed in front of the other. Her limbs were bare, and not much else was hidden from view. She didn't seem to care that anyone walking by in the parking lot could see her, although not many folks seemed to be awake this early.

"So, what do you want, Samuel?" Irritation sharpened her tone.

She hadn't told him to get lost, he realized. Although she might yet. And she hadn't said she was busy with someone else.

The lump shrunk slightly. He swallowed hard, his belly tense. Finally, he spoke from his heart. "I want you."

Her mouth curved to one side, and she pushed the door open wider. "Well, what are you waiting for?"

CHAPTER SIXTY-THREE

WITH EVERYTHING SET IN motion, and his nerves on edge, Roc couldn't imagine sitting down for breakfast. In the old days, on a stakeout, he would chow down on fast food, if he ate at all. But now there was much more at risk. Yet, in a practical sense, he knew he should eat.

Buttery biscuits came out of the oven and made his stomach rumble with suppressed need. Sally and Rachel waited a few minutes, busying themselves around the kitchen, until Jonas came in the back door. Slowly, he hung his hat beside the door and then settled in his place—a signal for everyone else to do so.

Before they bowed their heads in silent prayer, Jonas cleared his throat. "I don't know where Samuel got off to. I checked the barn and—"

"He's running an errand for me," Roc admitted.

Jonas narrowed his gaze. "What kind of errand?"

"Picking up a friend of mine at the bus station. They should be back soon."

"I can make more eggs," Sally volunteered.

Roc gave her a thankful nod and then met Jonas's stormy gaze. If Roc were ever to become a father, he would feel the same.

"He didn't take the buggy," Jonas said more to himself than Roc.

"Samuel took his motorcycle. That way he can get there and back quicker."

Jonas snatched a biscuit off the plate. "I don't like it."

Sally's mouth thinned, but she said nothing.

Jonas glanced in her direction and then at the biscuit in his hand. He set it on his plate as if it might shatter and then bowed his head. Both Sally and Rachel followed his lead. They prayed silently while Roc simply watched them, keeping an eye on the back door, the front one, and every window between.

The tension around the table absorbed the warm, enticing odors of the biscuits, eggs, and bacon, to the point where the only thing Roc could smell was sweat-induced fear. Jonas continuously wiped his brow with his napkin and finally gave up all pretense of eating. He pushed back from the table and stalked to the window, looking out, watching for Samuel's return. The clock seemed to be ticking ahead of itself, the time moving faster than normal.

"I'll be hitching the horse to the buggy. We don't have time to wait for Samuel." Jonas snatched his hat off the peg beside the door. He spoke these words to Roc then looked at his wife. "Be ready to go, Sally."

She nodded but said nothing.

Roc went to the door with Jonas, then to the barn. He tried to help with the horse but ended up standing awkwardly, not knowing what to say or do. He kept looking up at the rafters and outside as the sky turned from pink to blue, reminding him of the day's plan.

"When Samuel returns," Jonas said, "send him on to the Brennamans' farm. He knows where it is. Be firm with him. Make him do as I say. I want my son safe."

"I understand, Jonas," Roc replied. "I want the same thing."

CHAPTER SIXTY-FOUR

BRYDON WATCHED THE ACTIVITY from his usual perch. The sun's rays slanted across the green, budding, and ripening landscape, giving everything a shimmer of surrealism. Brydon settled his wings at the small of his back and moved back and forth from one foot to the other. He cocked his head sideways to better see what was going on around the little Amish house.

Earlier, the son, tall and sure of himself, had taken off on his motorcycle. Akiva had insisted the young man not be hurt in what was coming, which Brydon found unusual. It made him even more curious about the boy. After having watched the goings-on here for a while, Brydon knew it was odd for the kid to go off so early. Usually he used his bike only at night.

And now the old man and his wife were leaving in the buggy. The Amish man trotted the horse-drawn buggy around to the front of the house.

In a few minutes, Rachel and Roc would be alone. Finally.

Brydon hurriedly flew back to the motel, swooped down, and without a knock, entered the room.

"I think we should move now," Brydon stated.

Akiva was lying on a bed, a teenager sleeping next to him.

With his finger, he drew a pattern along her arm. She lay curled on her side and could have been dead, but there was no blood. Not yet.

Akiva's other hand held a book he was reading. Slowly, he closed the pages of Shakespeare's sonnets. "And what makes you think that?"

"There's movement. And early. Samuel Fisher left in a hurry. Jonas Fisher and his wife—"

"Sally." Akiva supplied the name. Brydon caught the look, understood that Akiva didn't want them hurt. But Brydon would do what must be done.

"They're all leaving. And Roc and Rachel are alone."

"For how long?"

"I don't know. But the girl, Rachel, is having pains."

Akiva tossed the book to the bed. "You're sure of this?"

"I read her mind."

Akiva was on his feet quickly, knocking the book to the floor, and the girl woke with a start. "Hey!"

"You're not mistaken?" Akiva's gaze sharpened.

Brydon never flinched. "No way."

The teen blinked, glancing down at herself, as if surprised to find herself still dressed. "What's going on? Who are you?"

Akiva strode toward the door, brushing past him.

Brydon fisted his hands on his hips. "What do you want me to do now?"

"Take care of her," Akiva tossed over his shoulder.

"But you promised me that Roc was mine."

"He will be soon enough. In the meantime, you need strength."

CHAPTER SIXTY-FIVE

SOMETHING SHOULD BE SAID. Just in case. In case Rachel never saw Jonas or Sally again. In case she never saw tomorrow.

It wasn't a possibility she wanted to think about, but it was as obvious as the sun that rose steadily in the blue sky. This could be their last day. They might die. Reality flashed as bold as the red and golden rays spraying across the blossoming sky.

Placing a hand at the small of her back to knead the ever-present ache, she came down the front steps. Jonas placed a small bag in the floor of the buggy and turned sharply at her approach.

"I want to thank you, Jonas." Her words came fast, not giving the older man time to speak. "It was kind of you to allow us to stay here with your family. I—"

"You don't have to say anything, Rachel."

"Yes, I do. And I will." She understood why Jonas didn't want to speak of these things, but she believed in facing things the way they were, not hiding them. "If you don't mind."

Jonas blinked at her firm statement, and his jaw went slack momentarily.

"I hope we did not place you and Sally and Samuel in any kind of danger. I do not know how this will turn out, but the good Lord is in control. Is He not?" It was a direct challenge to Jonas.

"Yes, of course."

"Then that is all we need to know."

Rachel faced Sally and held out her hands to the older woman. Sally clasped hands with her, and tears glimmered in her eyes. Rachel's throat closed. Sally didn't understand what had happened in Pennsylvania with her son Jacob, and she didn't understand what was about to happen here. She might never know the truth, but Rachel hoped to spare the woman who had been a friend to her for the past couple of weeks.

Suddenly, the older woman embraced Rachel and held her as close as she could around Rachel's belly. Rachel held onto the woman, wishing she could hug her own mother again.

"The Lord be with you," Sally said.

"And with you," Rachel whispered.

Jonas cleared his throat. He stood by the buggy, waiting on his wife.

Sally looked over her shoulder at him, nodded, and turned back to Rachel for one last word. "I will be back."

Roc came around the buggy as Jonas climbed inside and took the reins. He stood beside Rachel while they watched the Fishers leave. An assortment of emotions—fear, sadness, and relief—welled up inside her as she watched the buggy disappear down the drive. It was good that the older couple was safe. This was not their battle.

She reached over and took Roc's hand. She would fight this one with him. And if she died, then she would die because of her past sins. But she prayed her baby and Roc would live.

She squeezed his hand and looked up at him. He seemed distracted as he stared down the drive, his brows knit together with deep creases.

"What's the matter?" she asked.

"Samuel." Roc took a couple of steps toward the road and stopped. "He should have been back by now."

"Maybe Roberto's bus was late."

"Maybe." He squeezed her hand back reassuringly and turned to face her. "Go back in the house, Rachel. And gather your things."

"What do you mean?"

"I want you to leave too."

Her spine stiffened. "And go where?"

"Somewhere safe."

"Akiva would know."

"Would he?"

She nodded. "I heard the whispering this morning."

Roc glanced behind her as he reached inside his coat for his weapon, but he didn't pull it out. He simply kept a hand on it. "Why didn't you tell me?"

"It sounded like an insect buzzing inside my ear. Then it stopped, and I thought I could have imagined it. And I haven't heard it since."

He made a circle around her, walking first forward then backward, his gaze searching the house, workshop, and fields. "That's all the more reason for you to go."

"And how do you propose I get there?"

"When Samuel returns, you can go with him."

"I'm not going anywhere." She grabbed his arm. "If I did, Akiva would only follow."

Roc frowned, and she could see he believed she was right. "I'm going to walk around the house. If you hear the whispers again, call to me. If you see anything—"

"I will." She walked up the steps again and stopped. Her breath caught for a moment as something gripped her belly hard. The pain twisted into her back, and she leaned forward, holding onto the banister, the wood biting into her hand. When it finally released, she realized she was panting.

Roc bounded up the steps and peered into her face. "What's wrong?"

"Nothing. I'm fine." She tried to offer him a smile but feared she didn't succeed in reassuring him. Or herself. Worse, she feared what this actually meant. The dull ache had been easier to ignore. This pain, however, escalated, and panic shot through her. Suddenly she wished Sally were there, so she could ask the older woman's advice.

"You are not fine." Dread registered in Roc's eyes. "Was that a—?"

"Pregnant women have all sorts of weird pains."

"Pain? What kind of pain?"

She took the last step, but Roc stopped her with a hand on her arm. "It's nothing, Roc."

"Rachel," he said, his voice calmer than her heartbeat, "I'm a cop…or was…and I've seen women in labor. I've seen the look. And you've got it."

She scoffed. "Roc, really."

He quirked a brow, and suddenly her stomach grew hard again, a band tightening around her belly. When it released, she was holding Roc's hand, and he was saying, "Breathe."

But she couldn't for the fear swelling inside her, taking hold of her. Because her baby was coming. And there was no one to help. Sally had left. The buggy was gone. All she had was Roc and the fear that Akiva would soon arrive.

CHAPTER SIXTY-SIX

*D*ON'T PANIC.

But he was. This was bad. Bad timing. Bad everything. Roc led Rachel into the house. "Do you want to lie down?"

"No." She clung to his hand. "I feel better when I can walk around."

He read panic in her eyes, the same compressing his chest. "Okay. Then go about what you feel like doing, but rest. Tell me every time a pain comes." He checked his watch and went to the window, verifying it was locked. Not that a lock would keep out a vampire, but it was a start. And it gave him something to do besides panic.

He stared down the empty drive. *Where was Samuel?* If Samuel arrived soon, he could at least go get help. *But who could come? An Amish woman who was accustomed to delivering babies at home? Would he put that woman's life in jeopardy? What about an ambulance?* More lives at stake. *Which was worse? Would he risk Rachel's and her baby's?*

"Roc?" Rachel spoke in a strangled voice. She stood at an odd angle, slightly bent forward. Her facial muscles tensed as she stared at the floor.

He rushed to her side, took her hand again, which she squeezed hard. He whispered, "It's going to be all right. Hang on to me."

"But what about me?"

The strange voice came from his right, near the back door. A deep and otherworldly voice Roc instantly recognized.

Roc grabbed for his Glock and lunged, at the same time whipping the muzzle around and aiming at the dark figure. He squeezed the trigger as he hit the floor and kept firing. But the shadowy form folded in on itself and disappeared.

A slight breeze ruffled through the open back door. Roc rolled sideways and came to his feet in one bounding motion. "Rachel, are you—?"

He stopped abruptly at the sight of her. She stood, still slightly bent forward, but this time it was more of a defensive stance. She held Roc's stake in her hand, the tip pointed away from her. The look on her face was as fierce as any soldier, the way he imagined Joan of Arc met her enemies in battle.

"He's here." She spoke softly, as if Akiva might hear.

"Ya think?" Roc glanced back at the doorway, where his bullets had chewed the framing. "But where'd he go?"

"I don't know."

Glancing upward, searching the ceiling, he couldn't see any signs of the vampire. "If he wants to kill himself by using your baby, then why doesn't he just let me kill him now and be done with it?"

"He wants to exact as much revenge as he can." Rachel straightened and then released a held breath. "I need to sit down."

He nodded and walked toward the back door. But footsteps, heavy and running, made him aim for the opening. Roc held his breath. He wouldn't miss again. Not this time. The footsteps sounded louder as they raced toward the house. Roc braced a hand under his forearm to steady his gun.

Suddenly a reddened face appeared and then jerked out of sight again.

"Roc, hold your fire!"

Roc pointed the muzzle upward and released the trigger.

A few seconds later, a panting Roberto peeked around the door. He held a stake, raised for battle, and then a smile broke over his face. "Roc! Good to see you on guard."

"Next time," Roc said, breathing heavily, "give a shout out earlier."

"Then how would I launch a sneak attack?" Roberto lowered the stake. "What happened? I heard gunshots before."

Roc glanced over at Rachel to make sure she was all right. "Where's Samuel?"

"Not sure." The older man stepped through the doorway. "He was really late picking me up, but eventually did. But he didn't say much the whole way. And as soon as we got here, we heard the gunshots, and he took off. Scared him maybe."

"For the best then. Akiva's here. And Rachel's in labor."

Roberto shifted his gaze toward Rachel and gave her a nod. "At least we outnumber the vampire. Trust me, that's the only way you want to go into battle against one."

CHAPTER SIXTY-SEVEN

THIS WAS NOT HOW Rachel envisioned having her baby. She would have preferred her mamm in attendance, and fewer men around.

When the pains came, she clenched her teeth, stared at one point as hard as she could, and tried to breathe. Sometimes she squeezed a pillow, sometimes the arm of a chair, and when Roc was nearby, his hand.

Roberto kept vigil in a chair, much like the sturdy one Rachel sat in. His gaze traced the boundaries of the room, lingering at the windows, and he kept his hand wrapped around the hilt of a stake. Forming the last point of a triangle was Roc. Even though he sat in a recliner, he was tense and leaning forward, with his weapons at the ready.

How long, she wondered, could this go on? Soon, she would need more attention. Soon, the baby would come. She spent the time between pains praying the good Lord would have mercy upon them.

"Roc," she said, and he jerked to attention. "I'm worried about Samuel."

"Me too."

"Where could he be?"

"Maybe he went on to join his folks."

"What if he didn't? What if he's in the barn? And what if Akiva is—?"

"Rachel." Roc's tone was firm.

"Shouldn't you go to the barn and make sure?"

"No," Roberto said, "he should not."

The elderly man's tone startled Rachel. "But Samuel—"

"He could be dead." Roberto flung an arm wide. "There, I said what you've all been thinking. And if he is, then Roc wouldn't be much use to him other than to get himself killed the way—" Abruptly, the priest stopped. His eyes blazed with a fiery blue, and his cheeks flushed.

Roc shifted slightly. "He means the way Ferris died."

"Ferris?" she asked. "Who is Ferris?"

"My son," Roberto said, his voice soft once again.

"Your—?" Roc looked stunned. He shook his head as if he was trying to make sense of it. "I didn't know."

"Neither did Ferris." Roberto rubbed his palms against the tops of his thighs. After several minutes, he spoke again. "I was not always a priest, Roc. I fought vehemently against this evil, and at the same time, I loved deeply. Her name was Talia. She was beautiful. You understand, of course, the way a woman can touch a man's heart like nothing else." His gaze slid toward Rachel, and heat stung her cheeks. "But," he continued, "I could not stay and live a normal life with her. I had to protect her. You understand?"

Roberto touched the pads of his thumbs against each other, his long fingers folding together. "I told her God had a calling on my life. She believed I was to be a priest. She did not tell me she carried my child. I went off to fight my battles, spiritual and otherwise, battles she could not know of or understand. And when Ferris came to me a few months ago, he knew only that his mother had sent him to me, along with a sealed letter she told him only I could open. When I did, I read that her dying wish had been for her son to work alongside his father."

"I'm sorry, Roberto." Roc drove his fingers through his hair. "If I'd only known—"

"How could you know when Ferris did not even know?" The priest bowed his head, and his features sagged beneath the weight of despair. "He is with his mother now. He is safe once again." He turned his gaze toward Rachel then. "I am not a callous man. I know the pain of loss. It is not my intent for anyone else to die. But it would be foolhardy for Roc to leave you to help Samuel, who may no longer need our help."

Her throat was tight with raw emotions.

"That's the bottom line, Rachel," Roc said. "I'm not leaving you."

A creak upstairs ended the argument and forced her gaze toward the ceiling.

Roc stood slowly, took a step toward the stairs, but stopped. He looked over at Roberto.

"Could be a trick," the older man said.

"Could be nothing," Roc said. "It's an old house—"

Another creak interrupted him. In a slow blink of an eye, Roc gave a nod toward Roberto and then catapulted himself up the stairs.

Roberto stayed to protect Rachel. Fear gripped her. From upstairs she heard a huge banging, followed by a series of doors slamming open, along with the thud of footsteps down the upstairs hallway. Roberto crept to a standing position and moved slowly toward Rachel. She clenched the wooden armrests on the chair, her fingers curling over the edges.

Then something caught her gaze at the big window. A shadow. A movement. A blur. Two black eyes stared back at her. Then he was gone.

And Rachel screamed.

CHAPTER SIXTY-EIGHT

FROM WHAT ROC COULD tell, the rooms upstairs were vacant, the silence deafening, before a scream from downstairs shot through Roc and rattled him to the core.

Barreling back down the upstairs hallway, he felt as if it took half a century to cross the length of the house. He was aware of each second, footstep, heartbeat. When he reached the stair railing, he leapt down half a flight, took the mid-turn, crashing his shoulder into the wall, then threw himself down the last half of the stairs. He landed on his feet in a low crouch, his gun poised at the ready. His gaze sought Rachel first.

She was still sitting in the same chair, her whole body quivering, her features colorless. But Roberto stood battle ready.

"What is it? What happened?" Roc demanded.

"I don't know." Roberto's gaze darted about the room. "She just started screaming."

Roc looked back at Rachel. Was she having another labor pain? Or was it something else? Her gaze slid slowly toward the window, as if she expected something or someone to come crashing through the glass.

"Outside," she whispered. "I saw him."

"Akiva?"

She shook her head.

"Samuel?"

Another shake of the head. She licked her dry lips. "Your friend. The one you k…killed. Brody."

The shock plunged into his gut. How had Brody not died? Was he now seeking revenge too? If Brody was here, then the odds changed. "You're sure?"

She nodded, her eyes wide with fear and panic.

Then from outside came a blood-curdling cry. "Help me! Roc…help me!"

It was Samuel.

Roc lunged toward the door, but Roberto held him back. "They're toying with us."

Roc shook off the priest's hold, but he remained where he stood. "How can you be sure?"

"They don't want Samuel. Or me. Or even you. They want us out of the way. So they can get to Rachel. And her baby."

Roc stalked across the room, listening to more cries from Samuel. Was Akiva torturing the kid or faking Samuel's voice? He remembered when Ferris had died, how the cries had gone on and on. Yet from the remains Roc had seen, he doubted Ferris had lived long enough to utter much of a sound at all. Maybe Roberto was right. But Rachel's gaze pinned him, begging him to do something.

"Help me!" came the pitiful voice again.

"Akiva!" Roc bellowed, his voice shaking the foundation. He looked up at the ceiling and around the room at the different doorways. "Let's talk about this. Let's—"

The back door swung open, and a blast of warm air entered the living area. Roc stepped in front of Rachel.

A man walked into the house as if he owned the place. He was of medium build with dark hair. But those black eyes told Roc immediately what he was dealing with.

This vampire had a different look about him, one of authority and no compromising demeanor. He carried his head erect, his chin slightly lifted, and he glanced around the room with disdain.

Roc aimed his Glock, but the vampire waved his hand, and the gun went flying out of Roc's hand, clattering against the table, then the floor.

"Really," the vampire said, "please don't insult me with such barbarism." He walked into the room, giving each object and person a contemptuous glance before moving on.

"Who are you?" Roc asked.

"I am known as Giovanni. But who I am…that is not your concern."

Roc snatched the wooden stake out of Roberto's hand and raised it toward Giovanni. But the more experienced vampire lashed out with the back of his hand and smacked Roc fiercely, sending him soaring backward.

Roc slammed into the wall with a dull thud of body and limbs. He slid downward to the floor, where he collapsed into a heap, unmoving.

CHAPTER SIXTY-NINE

Pain slammed into Rachel all at once. Her belly tightened, and what felt like screws drove into her back. But her heart experienced the harshest, deadliest blow. A wailing seemed to go on and on, but no one else noticed. Was it Samuel? Or her own desperate cry?

Roberto lunged toward this new vampire, but Giovanni stopped Roberto with an outstretched hand. The confident vampire lifted his chin, tilted his head, and yet managed to glower at them all.

All Rachel could do was stare at Roc's still frame. Was he unconscious? Or dead? Raw emotions seized her throat, and her muscles constricted, making any screams or cries or even breathing impossible. All she could think was: *Not again. Please, God, not again.*

She'd lost a husband, and she had mourned him over the past few months. And yet, she had never felt like this for anyone. Not Jacob. Not Josef. Roc had become as solid as a boulder to her.

Was it simply because she owed him so much? Or because they understood each other? Because they shared so much? And now, if he were…if he had…how would he ever know or anyone understand how she felt? No one would know she had loved him. Not even Roc.

The fist in her belly began to relinquish its hold, and

she slid to the floor. She had not the strength to walk, so she crawled toward Roc. Hand, knee, hand, knee brought her closer to his side. But then a foot blocked her path. She looked up, tasting the saltiness of tears streaming down her face.

Giovanni glared down at her. "Where's Akiva?"

"I don't know." She shook her head. "Please—" She reached out toward Roc, but Giovanni knocked her hand away.

Something flashed in those dark eyes. "You're the one. The one Akiva was holding." His gaze flicked down toward her belly. "He wants your baby."

She placed a protective hand over her distended stomach. If only she could protect her baby.

"Please—" she repeated, looking toward Roc, knowing he needed someone to look after him. Roc would have scoffed at that. He wanted no help. He wanted to do everything on his own. But he needed her. Just like she needed him.

Giovanni knelt down beside her. His breath was cold on her cheek. "Do you know what Akiva wants to do? He wants to use your baby to commit the Forbidden Act." He drew a finger along the curve of her jaw, and a shiver of revulsion coursed through her. "Did you know that?"

She was crying hard now. "Please."

"Ah!" With a disgusted look, he jerked away from her. His fists tightened into hard balls. "I know he's here. He's a fool to think he can escape."

"You're out of your district," came a voice suddenly, resonating from overhead.

Giovanni laughed a deep, throaty laugh, but the caustic sound held no humor. "I can do whatever I please. I am stronger than you, Akiva."

"We'll see, won't we?"

"Yes, we'll see." Giovanni turned in a wide circle around the living room.

Roberto took the distraction as an opportunity. His gaze shifted toward the stake on the floor before he lunged. But Giovanni flicked the back of his wrist toward Roberto, who suddenly fell and rolled to the floor. The older man clasped his throat and gasped for air.

"What are you doing?" Rachel grabbed at Giovanni, snagging the hem of his jacket. "Stop it!"

Giovanni growled at her and pulled loose, circled around her, then focused his attention on her. Only her. He stalked toward her. "I'm going to kill this woman," he said low and menacing but not to her, "so she can't have that baby, and then I'm going to kill—"

A fluttering movement beyond the stairs appeared, shifted, and changed, growing larger as it rushed forward in a bluster of wind, accompanied by a low, deep, growing roar. Suddenly, the two vampires, Akiva and Giovanni, were grappling on the floor, and Rachel scrambled to get out of their way. Roberto was freed from whatever strangled him, and he, too, staggered to his feet, swaying slightly.

The two vampires rolled over each other, knocking into a rocking chair and breaking one of the legs. Giovanni flipped Akiva over his head then leapt to his feet, crouching low.

"'Hell is empty'"—Akiva grinned—"'and all the devils are here.'"

CHAPTER SEVENTY

H E WAS IN A womblike room, the walls pulsing around him. From far away, footsteps clunked, the sound growing louder as they neared. Then they stopped. Silence palpitated for several seconds before the voice came sharp, like the report of a gun: "Roc."

He heard his name, recognized it, and yet he could do nothing to respond. Roc's face was pressed against a hard, unforgiving, cold surface. His limbs felt weighted and unable to move.

"Roc!"

He blinked slowly. The room was dark, the floor shiny and polished, but he could not see the walls surrounding him. Maybe he wasn't in a room. It was as if he floated somewhere in the universe, and yet at the same time was confined to a tight-fitting enclosure, something like a casket.

"Roc," the voice said in a commanding tone, "what are you doing here?"

"Where is here?" he asked, pushing against the shiny floor and managing to sit upright. No pain restricted his motions. He felt only the cool air and hard floor beneath him. There was no smell, no other sounds, nothing. Even staring at the man standing in front of him—the polished shoes, a metal cane, the dark suit—gave him no feeling of surprise or shock.

Even when he recognized the man as Remy Girouard, his own father. "Am I dead?"

"Not yet. It's not your time. You have work to do."

"But I can't."

"You must have faith, Roc. You must believe."

"In what? In God?"

Those blue eyes softened but remained filled with an indescribable light. "Yes. But also in yourself, in His ability to work through you."

"I can't move." In defiance, he fisted his hand. "I don't know how or what to do."

"Rachel needs you, Roc. Go now. Do you hear me?"

The sound of her name gave him a jolt. Suddenly his heart thudded in his chest. He staggered to his feet, hands fisted, searching for the way out of this room, the way to Rachel's side. He ran a couple of steps in one direction, stopped, turned back, turned around.

"Go back, Roc."

"How?" He squeezed his eyes closed as he hunched over. "I don't know—"

"Yes, you do, Son."

Roc jerked upright and glared at the man. "Are you my father? Really, my father?"

Suddenly, those blue eyes blazed, and everything else about the man transformed, shattering and altering and blinding Roc momentarily with a flash of light. Then a creature taller than he, at least seven feet tall if not more so, stood before him. He held a burnished sword, tip down and hands fisted over the hilt. His skin glimmered like marble. Behind him, two wings unfurled.

"You see what you want to see. Now go, Roc, while you still have time."

Then the room ignited with a flash, and every feeble inch of his body throbbed in protest. His hand moved, and beneath it was the cool smoothness of a wooden floor.

Then he heard Akiva's voice, soaring and victorious.

CHAPTER SEVENTY-ONE

THE TWO VAMPIRES CIRCLED each other, testing each other, searching for a weakness. The minutes stretched outward. Even the room seemed to be holding its breath.

Then Akiva pounced. The force of his charge sent both of them stumbling, and they went headlong through the big window. Glass flew out across the porch and lawn, and the two vampires came down hard on the boards.

In that moment several things happened at once, and Rachel tried to make sense of it all and yet couldn't. Crouching over Roc, she wasn't sure any of this would ever make sense to her. Roberto grabbed a wooden stake off the floor and raced for the back door.

This was their one chance. While the vampires were occupied, maybe they could escape. She shook Roc's shoulder. But he didn't move. "Roc!" she tried again. This time he gave a heavy grown. "Roc, please!"

Struggling to push upward, he couldn't seem to raise his head. But when he looked at her, he looked right through her.

"Roc?" Relief stalled beneath a heavy dose of fear.

Like a quail rising into the air, Roc suddenly surged off the floor in a flurry of limbs and motion. Her heart jumped and clamored against her breastbone as she moved out of the way. He bounded across the living room toward the broken window, the glint of a blade flashing in his hand.

Rachel clamored to her feet, slower because of her bulk, and watched the fight from the window. The vampires had already broken the porch railing and were battling on the lawn. Without hesitation, Roc threw himself off the porch at the two snarling, snapping vampires and slammed the knife down between Giovanni's shoulders, jerking it out as he was thrown off and hurled to the ground.

The vampire reared backward with a howl of alarm and anger. He lashed out, but Roc scrambled out of the way. Akiva easily dodged the latest assault and took the advantage. But Roc sliced a nylon rope off the laundry line, hooked it around Giovanni's neck like a noose, and jerked him off his feet. Roc dragged the kicking, struggling, weakening vampire several feet and tied the rope to the porch railing.

Akiva staggered to his feet, breathing raggedly, his clothes torn. He stared down at Giovanni, this time circling the wounded vampire and laughed heartily, the deep sound filling up the air and sky. "You were wrong. You are the one who will not kill anymore. 'I'll follow thee!'" He raised an arm in a threatening manner. "'Like an avenging spirit; I'll follow thee.'" His lips pulled back from his white teeth. "'Even unto death!'"

"You're going to die, all right."

Akiva whirled toward the other male voice. "Brydon."

A shot rang out. Then another. And another.

Brydon's body flinched, and yet he did not stagger or fall. All eyes shifted toward Roc, but he no longer had a gun. Then to the old priest, who lay on the ground, a jagged rip across his chest. And finally to Akiva, who glanced down at his own white shirt. Three red spots bloomed across his chest. He hadn't felt the shots. He still felt no pain. But suddenly his legs weakened. He staggered back a step then another.

His vision wavered, but he finally caught sight of the weapon held by Samuel. His own brother.

Recognition lit the younger one's eyes. Samuel's face paled. His jaw went slack. He dropped the twenty-two. Akiva tried to walk forward to reach Samuel, but his footsteps went askew.

"Roc!" Rachel screamed. Her voice shattered and splintered the quiet into a thousand shards and disintegrated, grinding down into a pained silence.

Every eye turned, and it seemed as if time slowed. Akiva blinked rapidly, trying to focus, trying to remain standing. But it was Giovanni who rose to his feet, jerked on the material restraining him, which came loose. In his other hand, he held a jagged piece of glass about the size of a book. His arm cocked back to throw the glass as if it were a dagger. His glare bore into Rachel.

Akiva saw the look in Giovanni's eyes. And then, something inside Akiva shifted or opened, as if a buried part of himself rose out of darkness.

Without thinking, he hurled himself toward the porch to block Rachel. He never felt the cut. Sharp as a razor, the glass bit deep, slicing skin, muscle, arteries, and bone. The warmth of blood slid down his neck and the inside of his shirt. He landed hard on the ground, his body skidding several feet before coming to a halt.

He stared up at the blue sky. There were no clouds, just an ocean of blue, which wavered and undulated. The edges of his vision pinched inward, like gray clouds forming on all horizons. Forcefully, he shifted his gaze toward Roc, managed to hold onto him. Roc would finish him off. He knew it. At one time, he'd wanted to kill that man, but now he figured it didn't matter so much.

"I told you, Akiva," Giovanni bellowed, "I would destroy—" But his boast was cut off. His eyes widened, and his mouth twisted in a silent scream.

Roc had slammed a wooden stake into Giovanni's back. Before Giovanni could react, the glint of a blade flashed as Roc slit the older vampire's throat. Roc drove the stake in the ground and tied the rope still around Giovanni's neck to it. His limbs flailed, then twitched, and he grew still.

Tears sprang to Akiva's eyes, stung him with their potency. If only they could wipe away all he had done. So this is how it would end. "I didn't want this—"

Blood gurgled up, choking him, but he swallowed hard, gritted his teeth. "'Long since my heart has been breaking...'" He coughed, and blood spurted out of him, speckling his chin. "'Its pain is past...'" He tried to roll to the side but he couldn't seem to move. "'A time has been set...to its aching. Peace...comes at last.'"

"Roc?"

Akiva heard her voice, saw her reach for her protector. "Rachel."

"Jacob?" she called in return.

By the time she reached him, his vision was darkening. But he could make out the blue of her eyes, which blended with the sky. She reached out to touch him, but Roc pulled her back.

"Careful," Roc warned.

Rightfully so. He could not be trusted. Even now. Especially now when every fiber of his being cried out for survival. He resisted, restrained, digging his fingers into the ground. Samuel stood over him, his face blanched and stricken.

But she knelt beside him, her eyes filling with unshed tears. He'd caused too many tears.

"Tell…" Akiva gasped. "Han—"

"Hannah," she said for him.

He nodded. "'I loved with a love—'"

Above him, Roc Girouard held a blade. His time was short. It was better this way.

He'd meant revenge. He'd wanted to die. Now he would, without causing harm to someone else. It was better this way. Better. He deserved death. And worse.

He gazed up at the heavens. "Oh, God." He choked again, spluttering and spewing blood. He deserved it. He deserved hell. Or worse. But his lips formed almost involuntarily, although it must have been a cry from his heart—"Please…"

Out of the depths of his heart came the words of a song— *All the vain things that charm me most, I sacrifice them to His blood.*

Then the knife flashed in front of him, the blade catching the light. Those before him faded and folded into darkness.

His heart stilled. And Jacob died, as he should have died three years before.

CHAPTER SEVENTY-TWO

HIS HANDS WERE BLOODY.
The slippery body wobbled in his hands. Then the crying began in earnest.

The sound exploded in the room. As the baby's wail carried through the open window, Roc's throat closed with an assortment of emotions he hadn't expected. When he looked at Rachel, her eyes were full and overflowing with tears. Someone wrapped the baby in a blanket, and he placed the baby carefully in her arms then backed away.

"Roc," she said, her voice cracking, "thank you."

"You did all the work."

"My baby wouldn't be here except for you." He glanced out the window and saw gray smoke rising from the field where Roberto and Samuel had set a small bonfire to dispose of Giovanni and Akiva. Brydon had disappeared. There would be time later to go after him.

His gaze shifted sideways. He wanted to be finished with the task of hunting vampires, but he could never turn his back again, knowing innocents were at risk. He would have to go on and on and on, just like Roberto. Until one day, a vampire would get the best of him.

And he would never have a wife, never love someone… like Rachel, or have a family. It wouldn't be safe for them.

He wouldn't risk their lives. Again, his chest tightened as he looked down at Rachel cradling her baby.

"I'll leave you two—"

"Roc?" She held out a hand to him. He slipped his fingers between hers and clasped her hand, watched her cradle the baby boy in her arms. "You've done so much for me...for us, but I would ask one more favor."

"Anything." His throat squeezed tight with emotions he couldn't allow to release.

"Will you take me home to Pennsylvania?"

He nodded, focusing on the baby's fuzzy tufts of snowy white hair, the little frown as he squeezed his eyes closed, and the tiny little fists. "When you're ready to travel."

She smiled through her tears. "I have to say good-bye."

He understood what she meant. Saying good-bye to her might be the hardest thing he'd ever done. Burying Emma had been the most painful event in his life, but he'd had no choice. She was gone. But Rachel...this was his choice to walk away, to keep her safe. He'd always know where Rachel was. And one day, she'd marry some Amish man who would raise her baby as his own. But it would take every ounce of willpower not to stay with her, not to return to her, not to love her.

He gave a nod, patted her hand, and released his hold on her. He had no right. Walking out of the room to give her time alone with her baby, he whispered, "Not yet."

CHAPTER SEVENTY-THREE

"WILL YOU WAIT FOR me?" Rachel gazed at Roc with solemn blue eyes.

"Until you talk to your family and everything with them is all right." Roc didn't know all the rules of the Amish, but he was pretty sure they wouldn't be keen on the idea that she had gone off with a vampire, even if it wasn't of her own free will. Maybe it would be all right with them, and they would welcome her back with open arms. But he wouldn't leave her until he was convinced she'd be all right.

He had more doubts about himself at the moment. Even though it would be better for him to just leave her here in Promise with her family, the sooner the better for his heart, he would wait. Even if it killed him. And it just might.

In the bloody wake of Akiva's death and destruction, and after the birth of baby David, Roc had helped Roberto return to Philadelphia. Then, confident Rachel was safe, he had flown back to New Orleans, retrieved his Mustang, and driven to Ohio. That way, he could drive her home to Pennsylvania when she was ready.

But everyone, Sally Fisher especially, had insisted they wait until Rachel was strong enough and the baby at least a month old before they left—although Roc suspected Sally's insistence actually stemmed from her enjoyment of having a baby to care for. So he'd waited, trying to make himself scarce so as not to get any more attached to Rachel.

Samuel had been quiet after killing Jacob, and Roc hung out with the young man, hoping he could help him through whatever guilt he might be feeling. Together, they'd rebuilt the porch and swing, and refitted the window with new glass. But Samuel didn't want to discuss what had happened. Instead, he'd suggested Roc make a rocking chair for Rachel. The smile on her face and tears in her eyes when they gave it to her had made it worth every splinter he'd plucked out of his hands and fingers.

She hadn't allowed Roc to keep separate from her, though. In quiet moments when she'd rocked the baby, she'd called to Roc. "Look at this."

Little David pumped his fists and kicked his feet in the air. Together, they'd shared moments of tenderness and sweetness, which had brought healing to both of them.

Over the last few weeks, Rachel had changed Roc in ways he couldn't fully understand. Driving in the darkness together through New Orleans, wounded, fearful of her fate as well as hers, he'd learned of her calm resolve. Receiving her ministrations, he'd learned of her gentleness and determination. Watching her care for baby David, named for the shepherd boy in the Bible because he, too, had managed to slay a giant, he'd come to understand the depths of her heart that amazed him. She'd shown him how to hold her baby, laughed joyfully when David had smiled for the first time, and opened a place in his heart.

The day waned. He waited. As the heat of the afternoon punished him, the door to the Schmidt's home opened, and Rachel came out on the porch, still carrying her baby. He thought he saw her little sister, Katie, peering through the window, watching them. *What if they didn't want her back now? What if she was somehow tainted in their eyes?*

If so, he would take care of her. He wouldn't abandon her. Hope rose inside him like he'd never imagined—he loved her. He'd tried to deny it. He'd tried to avoid the truth. But he wanted her to be his, to protect her, to love her. And her baby.

His heart fluttered and battered his chest as he watched her walk toward him, her footsteps slow, her face somber. No, he was fooling himself. A life with Rachel was impossible. He must say good-bye to her. It was for her good. And for David's. Distance was the best way he could protect them from now on. But saying good-bye would rip him apart inside, and whatever healing she had brought to him would be destroyed.

As she drew close, he tried to read her expression but couldn't. "It didn't go well?"

"With my family?" Her lashes fluttered as if surprised by his statement. "No, they are delighted to have me back home safe and sound. Hannah and I have forgiven each other. All is well."

Hope sunk like a boulder deep into the ocean of his heart. He shoved his hands into his pockets. "Okay, then." He was no longer needed here. *Do it quick, Roc. Make a clean break. The faster the better.* "Well, you don't need me anymore. I'll be—"

She placed a hand on his arm. "Of course I need you."

"Don't make this harder than it has to be, Rachel. This is where you belong. And I—"

"I belong with you, Roc."

He shook his head. "You're Amish, and I can't ever be."

"I'm a woman. That's all. A woman in love with a man." Her lips parted, moist and hopeful. "You."

"What about your faith, Rachel? You're gonna walk away from all of that? Your family?"

"My faith won't change because I love you. I love God. I can do both. I want to serve Him. I've explained all of this to my family. Of course, they tried to talk me out of it. If I leave, they will have to shun me. But I understand. I know the cost, and I'm willing to pay it."

"But, Rach—"

"Roc, once I thought God had abandoned me and that He wanted to punish me for my past sins, but I learned He wanted to give me a purpose and set me on a new path." Her gaze was solid, unwavering, her tone quiet with resolve. "And He has. It's to help you. To be your helpmate."

Her words jarred him. "Help me how?"

She only looked at him with those luminous eyes. She wouldn't ask him. She wouldn't beg. She was simply offering herself, her heart, her love. "I told you I came back home from New Orleans and tried to live like I didn't know the evil out there existed. But I know now. I can't forget. And I can't do nothing. I must help you."

He remembered the cold feeling when he'd seen Giovanni aiming a jagged blade of glass right at her. How could he risk her life again? What if something happened to her? "Rachel, it's too dangerous."

"Roc, I believe God has called me to this. He will protect me."

His throat closed with a myriad of emotions. Could he have the same faith she did? He remembered the fierceness he'd seen in her eyes when she'd wielded his stake. She was stronger and braver than he'd ever imagined.

He didn't know how any of this would work. He had no concrete answers. But maybe *she* was his answer. Maybe he could have a tiny bit of her faith that God had brought them together to do some small amount of good. Just as God had provided Adam with Eve, He'd provided Rachel for him.

Not understanding, not quite believing what was happening, he grappled with hope, and it once more buoyed him. Roc wrapped an arm over her shoulders, sheltering Rachel and the baby.

Maybe he'd also learned from Rachel about faith, about putting trust in something that wasn't tangible. He could put his faith in their love...and maybe, in time, he'd come to understand more about her God. Because this, without a doubt, was his second chance.

Acknowledgments

This is one of my favorite parts of writing a book: getting to thank those who helped me on my journey, and there are always many! So many have encouraged me as I wrote this book, from readers and reviewers to booksellers and buddies. Thank you to each and every one who wrote encouraging words and asked when book two of this series would be out. I appreciate each and every one of you. And you know who you are! I have tried to thank you along the way.

Writing a book is always a journey, and there are many learning curves along the way. I have enjoyed the bunny trails and the highways I've traveled. Some of the lessons were difficult, some painful, and in the end all were a blessing.

A special thanks to Shelley Shepard Gray for a great visit and trip into Ohio Amish country. What a blessing your friendship has been. And what fun we've had!

I'd also like to thank those on my Sourcebooks team: y'all are spectacular!

Thanks also to my wonderful agent: Natasha, I'm blessed to know you and have you to offer advice and help.

My biggest thanks to my sweet and wonderful family, who not only pick up the slack when I'm getting close to deadline but also offer encouraging hugs and words and ask, "What happens next?" I love you!

ABOUT THE AUTHOR

Leanna Ellis is the author of the Plain Fear series. She is the winner of the National Readers' Choice Award, the Maggie Award, and Romance Writers of America's Golden Heart Award. She makes her home in Texas with her husband, two children, and a wide assortment of pets.